PENGUI

THE FI

SARATCHANDRA CHATTOPADHYAY (1876–1938) was born in Devanandapur, an obscure village of Bengal. His childhood and youth were spent in dire poverty as his father, Matilal Chattopadhyay, was an idler and dreamer and gave little security to his five children. Saratchandra received very little formal education but inherited something valuable from his father—his imagination and love of literature. He started writing in his early teens and two stories written then have survived—'Korel' and 'Kashinath'.

Saratchandra came to maturity at a time when the national movement was gaining momentum together with an awakening of social consciousness. Much of his writing bears the mark of the resultant turbulence of society. A prolific writer, he found the novel an apt medium for depicting this and, in his hands, it became a powerful weapon of social and political reform. Sensitive and daring, his novels captivated the hearts and minds of thousands of readers not only in Bengal but all over India.

Some of his best-known novels are *Palli Samaj* (1916), *Charitraheen* (1917), *Devdas* (1917), *Nishkriti* (1917), *Srikanta* in four parts (1917, 1918, 1927 and 1933), *Griha Daha* (1920) and *Sesher Parichay* published posthumously (1939).

The Final Question

SARATCHANDRA CHATTOPADHYAY

Translated by
Members of the Department of English
Jadavpur University

Edited by
ARUP RUDRA
and
SUKANTA CHAUDHURI

RAVI DAYAL Publisher

PENGUIN BOOKS

PENGUIN BOOKS

USA | Canada | UK | Ireland | Australia
New Zealand | India | South Africa | China

Penguin Books is part of the Penguin Random House group of companies
whose addresses can be found at global.penguinrandomhouse.com

Published by Penguin Random House India Pvt. Ltd
7th Floor, Infinity Tower C, DLF Cyber City,
Gurgaon 122 002, Haryana, India

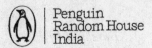

Penguin
Random House
India

First published by Ravi Dayal Publisher and Permanent Black 2001
Published by Penguin Books India and Ravi Dayal Publisher 2010

ISBN 9780143067788

Typeset in Perpetua by Gurutypograph Technology, Delhi

Printed at Repro Knowledgecast Limited, Thane

www.penguin.co.in

CONTENTS

Contents

Editors' Acknowledgements

THIS TRANSLATION IS THE COLLECTIVE EFFORT OF SEVERAL members of the Department of English, Jadavpur University. The first draft was prepared by Shirshendu Majumdar, Sipra Dasgupta (Mukherjee) and Sunish Deb. This was then worked over by the editors, who accept responsibility for all shortcomings. The project was conducted under the the the UGC Special Assistance (DSA) Programme of the Department.

We are grateful to Dr Amitava Das of the Department of Bengali and Professor Supriya Chaudhuri of the Department of English for contributing the Preface and Introduction respectively.

The Bengali text followed is that in the sixth edition published by Gurudas Chattopadhyay and Sons, Calcutta (no date).

Department of English   ARUP RUDRA
Jadavpur University, Calcutta   SUKANTA CHAUDHURI
October 2000

Preface

MORE THAN SIX DECADES AFTER HIS DEATH, SARATCHANDRA
Chattopadhyay or Chatterjee (1876–1938) remains the most
popular Bengali novelist ever, not excepting Rabindranath
Tagore (1861–1941). He was not a saint or sage, but the
most extraordinary of ordinary men. A recent biographer,
himself an eminent Indian writer, has described him as 'the
great wayward soul'.[1] In life he was sometimes a wanderer,
sometimes an ascetic; but his fiction takes domesticity as
its accustomed point of reference.

Saratchandra inherited his wanderlust from his father
Matilal. Matilal too was a poet and fiction writer, but his
dreams remained unrealized—owing to poverty, but also from
a wilful inconsistency of purpose. Much of Saratchandra's
childhood and youth were spent among relatives in Bihar; his
college education could not be completed for lack of money.
But he was an enthusiastic student of science, philosophy and
history, and more particularly of anthropology and sociology:
Herbert Spencer's *Descriptive Sociology* influenced him deeply.
He was also an avid reader of Dickens, Balzac and Bernard
Shaw. His vast personal library was destroyed in a fire in Yangon.

Saratchandra is a committed writer. This makes him more
overtly emotional than either Bankimchandra Chattopadhyay
(1838–94) with his classical, ethically attuned world view, or
Rabindranath with his unremitting engagement with artistic
form. Saratchandra's target readership lay among the middle

and lower middle classes. At a reception in the Calcutta Town Hall on his fifty-seventh birthday, he openly professed his

allegiance to those who have only given to the world but obtained nothing from it; those who are deprived, weak and oppressed; who are human beings, yet of whose tears humanity has taken no account; who, leading helpless stricken lives, have never discovered why they have everything, yet have no rights over what they have . . . Their pain has freed my utterance; they have sent me to tell humanity of the allegations laid at its door by human beings.

Saratchandra lacks detachment: this may have enhanced his popularity. The writer Pramatha Choudhuri (1868–1946) suggested two other reasons for that popularity:

First, his language . . . Saratchandra's language is simple, lucid and dynamic; it has a *flow*. His second virtue is that his novels do not imitate any English novel. The only ingredient of his narrative is what might happen, and does happen, in Bengali society.[2]

His social novels, like Dickens's, preserve the fading picture of a receding age. As Rabindranath said, 'He belongs entirely to his country and his age. That is no light matter.'[3]

Saratchandra's creativity flows out of a contradiction: he is full of tenderness and nostalgia for the very society that he castigates. He admits as much in his 1916 essay, *Samajdharmer Mulya* ('The Value of Social Order'). From 1903 to 1916, Saratchandra sought his living far away from Bengal, in Myanmar. His first novels and stories chiefly present an earlier phase of his experience, the rural Bengali life of the nineteenth century. In that milieu, life within the joint family was marked by an almost medieval obscurantism. The so-called Bengal Renaissance of the age was largely confined to the urban élite.

At a time when Calcutta was witnessing campaigns for widow remarriage, women's education and women's freedom, Saratchandra's village annals present Madhabi in *Bardidi* (*The Elder Sister*, 1913), the suffering child widow; Biraj in *Biraj Bou* (*Biraj the Wife*, 1914) with her tormented chastity and wifely devotion, even at the cost of her life; the young widow Rama in *Pallisamaj* (*Village Society*, 1916) with her frustrated love, in a community divided against itself; or Parbati in *Debdas* (1917), forced to marry the elderly, previously married Bhuban Choudhuri.

Yet in the midst of this, when Surendranath in *Bardidi* asks on his deathbed, 'Are you my elder sister?', Madhabi's reply frees her individuality from the confines of a socially determined identity: 'I am Madhabi.' In *Pallisamaj*, Rama cannot be united with Ramesh as she is a Hindu widow. 'Two great-souled people thus end up crippled and frustrated,' writes Saratchandra. 'If I can reach this message of pain to the closed doors of human hearts, I will have done enough.'[4] He shows the defeat of the individual spirit at the hands of a cruel society in many other works of this period: *Chandranath* (1916), *Arakshaniya* (*The Girl Who Must Be Married*, 1916), *Swami* (*The Husband*, 1918), or *Bamuner Meye* (*The Brahman's Daughter*, 1920).

In his later works, Saratchandra came to treat of certain new encounters between society and the individual. These explorations continued through the entire period between the two world wars. This was when he played his part as a dedicated fighter for independence. He joined Mahatma Gandhi's Non-Cooperation Movement; yet he also supported the armed struggle for self-rule, and had a warm friendship with Netaji Subhas Chandra Bose. His political novel *Pather Dabi* (*The Call of the Road*, 1926) was banned by the British government. He also exposed the economic exploitation of the colonial order in short stories like *Mahesh* (1922) and novels like *Dena-Paona* (*Owings and Borrowings*, 1923).

But his works strike the clearest note of modernity where he presents the individual's protest against the tyranny of society. Kiranmayi in *Charitrahin* (*The Rake*, 1917), Abhaya in *Shrikanta*, Part II (1918), or Achala in *Grihadaha* (*The Burning of the Home*, 1920) not only voice the social protest of the Hindu wife or widow but radically reassess the relationship between woman and man. *Shesh Prashna* (*The Final Question*, 1931) belongs here too.

The Final Question is not unexpected in the total context of Saratchandra's work. He had raised the same issues not only in the seminal essay *Narir Mulya* ('A Woman's Worth', 1923) but also in various novels and short stories. Over half a century earlier, Ibsen had placed Nora Helmer in an impasse without apparent solution. Saratchandra professed the same inconclusiveness in presenting similar problems: 'I have never, on any pretext, tried to foist my private opinion anywhere . . . My writings present problems but no solutions, questions to which no answer is to be found. I have always held that it is for the man of action to find solutions, not the man of letters.'[5]

Most of Saratchandra's novels and short stories are concerned with the state of women. Their sufferings make up the chief substance of his art. In the land-based economy of a quasi-feudal society, women counted as a species of animate landed property. They were akin to that destitute class 'who have only given to the world but obtained nothing from it'. Until the Hindu Succession Act of 1956, they had no effective right to property. Saratchandra, indeed, held that the ideal of chastity and the orthodox discipline of widowhood were concocted by a male-dominated order to retain its hold over women even after their menfolk's death. 'Single-hearted love and chastity are not quite the same thing: if this truth does not find place in literature, where will it survive?'[6] He therefore undertakes a virtual inner history of women's liberation through his narratives of 'fallen' women, widows, and even married women seeking an independent life in love. Abhaya in *Shrikanta* had taken a lover in spite of having a husband. She tells Shrikanta:

His [her husband's] wife, his children, his love—none of this is mine any more. Tell me, Shrikanta Babu: would my life have blossomed into fulfilment if I had stuck to him nonetheless, like a kept woman? Was it the greatest mission of my womanly birth to bear the pain of that frustration all my days? . . . Should I have denied the great love of my life simply to make a lifelong truth of a single night's wedding rites, that have become as false as a dream to husband and wife alike?

In his early work *Alo o Chhaya* (*Light and Shadow*, written by 1903 although published in 1917), the narrator had observed: 'Man and woman indeed, but not husband and wife. You may frown and say, "is it then illicit love?" I would say, "It is a deeply pure love." ' Moved by this 'pure love', Abhaya in *Shrikanta* could say of the offspring of her extramarital union: 'The children of our sinless love will be inferior to none in this world . . . They have been conceived in truth; truth will be their greatest resource.' Marital life, on the contrary, could harbour an insidious unchastity. Rabindranath has shown in *Jogajog* (*Relationships*, 1929) how Kumu's thwarted womanhood was trapped in a loveless, distasteful physical relationship with her husband.

Saratchandra had compiled the histories of nearly 500 'fallen' women under the title *Narir Itihas* (*The History of Women*). The manuscript was lost in the fire that destroyed his house in Yangon. But the task consolidated his conception of women: the essay 'A Woman's Worth' bears testimony to that. He admitted how men use women: 'The man does not face very many problems: there are many ploys open to him. Only the woman has no route of escape.'[7]

He also had the perspicacity to see that this helplessness and waste were linked to the woman's lack of economic independence. Gnanada in *Arakshaniya* illustrates this poignantly. When an aged aspirant to marriage comes to inspect her as a prospective bride, she decks herself with cheap powder and coconut oil before a cracked mirror in the stifling heat: no one comes to lend a hand. Her pathetic efforts induce even her infant nephew to lisp, 'Aunty has dressed up like a clown!' She was well aware that such a marriage would lead to imminent widowhood; yet she wanted to be free of the mutually burdensome dependence on her relatives.

Clearly, most of the questions in *The Final Question* were not raised there for the first time: they had evolved in course of Saratchandra's career. Sumitra in *Pather Dabi* had said, 'Woman must overcome the fascination of a futile married life.' Kamal in *The Final Question* wishes to grasp everything with reason and logic. Sumitra anticipates her stance: 'Something doesn't become true simply because many people have been saying it for a long time. That is simply a cheat.'

Kamal does not consider divorce to be dishonourable: she wants the relationship between man and woman to 'one day . . . become as free and natural as light and air'. She will live with Ajit but not marry him, because marriage would create a morgue, not a bedchamber.

Such matters were being widely debated in Europe as well. Bertrand Russell had raised the issue in his *Marriage and Morals* (1929): 'Love can only flourish as long as it is free and spontaneous; it tends to be killed by the thought that it is a duty.' Kamal too agrees that 'the history of the love between man and woman was the most authentic history of human civilization'. Simultaneously, she brings up questions of politics and patriotism: her debate with Rajen on the encounter of East and West reminds one of the debate between Sandip and Nikhilesh in Rabindranath's *Ghare-Baire (The Home and the World*, 1915).

But ultimately, it is the question of her womanhood that becomes for Kamal the final question. She seeks an answer beyond the bounds of male constructs and institutions. This gives a special import to the novel's location in the city of the Taj Mahal. For Kamal, the Taj is not a symbol of undying love: it is a monument to the artistic self-indulgence of the polygamous Shah Jahan, using the memory of Mumtaz Mahal as a mere pretext. The locale of the novel silently absorbs the substance of the fiction.

The Final Question created a sensation when it was published. A woman wrote to Saratchandra that if she had the money, she would print the book and distribute it free of cost like the Bible.[8] But clearly, such a response would not have been possible if the book had lacked intrinsic literary merit.

In another letter, Saratchandra wrote: 'In *The Final Question*, I have tried to indicate what truly modern literature should be like—to show that the *pivot* of literary hyper-modernity does not lie in the attitude, "We'll write thundering obscenities— of course we will".'[9]

This reaction compares interestingly with that of Rabindranath in the 1920s and 1930s, when, influenced by the continental writing of the time, Bengali literature was turning more and more to the depiction of poverty and a romanticized preoccupation with sex. In essay after essay, Rabindranath deplored such 'hyper-modern' literature, calling it 'the *curry powder* of reality', 'the arrogant flaunting of poverty', 'the unrestrained play of lust'. Saratchandra had protested against this attack in his essay *Sahityer Riti o Niti* ('Modes and Principles of Literature', 1927). He too had his differences with the 'hyper-moderns', but he wished to guide them towards a more constructive path rather than to suppress their movement altogether. Hence Tarashankar Bandyopadhyay (1898–1971), one of the leading exponents of the modern Bengali novel, could say, 'In the current of Bengal's literary life, Saratchandra marks the movement most proximate to ours.'[10]

It was his standpoint as a liberal humanist that made Saratchandra so receptive to new developments in his native literature. Yet the same standpoint made this annalist of Bengali life universal in reach and appeal. His works have been translated into virtually every Indian language, and many others as well. Romain Rolland, reading *Shrikanta* in translation, thought it worthy of the Nobel Prize.

AMITAVA DAS
(Translated by Sukanta Chaudhuri)

Introduction

^{IN A LETTER TO A FEMALE CORRESPONDENT}[1] WRITTEN AT LEAST
partly in response to the public outrage with which *Shesh
Prashna* (*The Final Question*, 1931) was received, Saratchandra
said that his purpose was not the reform of society; as a writer,
he wrote of human problems, but could offer no solutions to
them. One of the major difficulties that the reader of *The
Final Question* encounters is the curiously unresolved nature of
the novel, both in formal and in thematic terms. Far more
than even Tagore's *Ghare-Baire* (*The Home and the World*, 1916),
The Final Question uses the narrative strategy of the open ending
to posit a genuine uncertainty, not simply about the future, but
also about our understanding of the past. Yet this state of
uncertainty is reached through a process of strenuous dialectic,
so unremitting as to constitute a formidable test for the serious
reader of this novel.

What is most remarkable about this process is the extent
to which it both relies upon and goes beyond the novel's
techniques of realist representation, making our experience
of reading, in a deep sense, emancipatory. Early in the novel,
there is a conversation between Ashu Babu and Kamal about
the most splendid of Agra's historical monuments, the Taj
Mahal. Ashu Babu's admiration is expressive of a romantic, but
also conservative, idealism: the Taj is the poetry of love, an
emperor's grief and devotion embodied in pure white marble.
Kamal thinks this a profound misconception. Shah Jahan, she
points out, had other begums. Mumtaz's death was not the

xvii

sole event of importance in his life, only the immediate and accidental cause of this monument, which could equally have been inspired by religion or war. Is it not enough to think of the Taj as expressive of its creator's realm of joy? Ashu Babu is shocked by this answer: for him the Taj would lose its beauty if it were not associated with an ideal love. What we admire is the very idea of such love, not the splendour of its monument. Kamal disagrees again: a love so fixed and immutable is not worthy of our admiration. Human beings change; love too must change, must attach itself to new objects in order to live and grow. Manorama, who has disliked Kamal from the start and is angered by her indecorous assertion of these opinions in male company, insults Kamal by suggesting that her own attachments have not been permanent. But Kamal is not offended. Much later, almost at the end of the novel, she tells Ajit that she wants their love to be a room where a living person might lie, not a tomb for the dead.

The Final Question is set in Agra. The image of the Taj Mahal, both as symbol and in the reality of its historical presence, is a constant element in the novel's structure. But what it represents is open to the novel's chosen mode of questioning, just as the reminders of its presence are drawn into the structural pattern of repetition with difference. Kamal's conversation with Ashu Babu recalls Rabindranath Tagore's great poem on the emperor Shah Jahan (1914), a poem which also, in its structure of assertion, question and qualification, uses the dialogic mode of argument to make almost exactly the same point, though in the context of memory rather than devotion. Does the Taj speak to us of a never-forgotten love? Or has its creator moved away, on the path of oblivion that is also the road to freedom? At the end of the poem, it is the emperor who is absent, and therefore free; the poet, weighed down by memory, remains present before a monument whose meaning has become profoundly ambiguous. Saratchandra was undoubtedly drawing upon Rabindranath's poem, which would have been familiar to any cultivated reader. But Kamal's defence of change is not simply rehearsed; it is a necessary part of the novel's engagement with its setting, its willingness to confront the problems of history and open them up to further questioning.

History appears to be dead at the start of the novel, reduced to a customary knowledge about tombs and monuments, a habitual exercise of wonder at the fading splendours of Agra. The Bengalis resident here, we are told, have exhausted the resources of the city's past:

Epidemics of smallpox and the bubonic plague apart, they led profoundly peaceful lives. They had long since done the rounds of the Mughal forts and buildings; they knew by heart the complete list of all the large, small and middling, derelict and intact tombs of nobles and viziers. Even the world famous Taj Mahal had lost its novelty for them. They had wrung dry all customary ploys and stratagems to admire its beauty from both banks of the Yamuna: with a moist, languid gaze in the evening, with half-shut eyes in the moonlight, or staring vacantly through the darkness. They knew all the effusions of famous men, all about the poems and the men who wrote them, all about those who wanted to end their lives in rapture while standing in front of it. Their knowledge of history too was complete. Even their small children knew which begum used which apartment during childbirth; which Jat leader cooked his meal when and where—how ancient each charred smudge on the wall was; which bandit looted how many jewels and their estimated value. Nothing was unknown to any of them. (p. 1)

The deadness of this knowledge is momentarily stirred by fresh curiosity when Ashutosh Gupta and his daughter come to take up residence in the city. Social life acquires a new interest and urgency; the present, if not the past, compels and absorbs attention. Yet the narrator's amused, ironic account of the newcomers traces the possibility of their lapsing into precisely the same habitual indifference. When they undertake their late-afternoon excursion to the Taj, Ashu Babu is content to rest in the gardens below, secure in his reverence for ideal love; Manorama is anxious that Ajit, who has never seen the monument, should view it in the best light and from the most favourable angle. It is this entirely predictable social event that is interrupted by the meeting with Kamal and her husband Shibnath. The encounter not only postpones Ajit's intended raptures; it casts the whole substance of his experience into doubt, unsettling what these characters have assumed to be settled and known.

Kamal's function in the novel is that of disturbing known categories of belief and experience, and in formal and ideological terms she constitutes a major problem of representation. At times her presence in the realist fabric of the novel opens up an unbridgeable gap between the probable and the possible, reminding us of *The Final Question*'s own uncertain status between bildungsroman and dialectic novel. Like Rabindranath's Gora, whom she sometimes resembles in her passion for talk, Kamal is a deliberate attempt on the novelist's part to conflate East and West, a colonial hybrid more impure but less self-denying than Rabindranath's hero. Racially, she is the half-European product of a liaison between an English tea planter and a young Bengali widow (unlike Gora, who is an Irish child brought up by a Bengali family); but socially and psychologically, she appears untroubled by feelings of illegitimacy. She values the education she received from her father, whose saintliness and wisdom constitute one of the positive ideals she lives by; and though she tells Ajit that her first husband was an Assamese Christian, her own religion is in doubt. Yet in appearance, speech and social behaviour, she seems Bengali enough to gain entry to the society of the *prabasi* Bengalis of Agra. In personal life she presents an extraordinary blend of rigid self-restraint and an unabashedly hedonistic philosophy; her rationalism, absolute in many respects, is nonetheless qualified by Saratchandra's own concessions to public taste, social morality and realist representation.

Given the unlikelihood of all this within the nominal verisimilitude of the novel's bourgeois realism, it is easy to dismiss Kamal as an unsuccessful, even unworkable attempt on Saratchandra's part, late in his creative life, to construct a vehicle for his ideas about society, politics and women; and indeed Kamal's character is something of a project, a kind of blueprint for the future, not part of the novel's realist substance. Of all the characters in *The Final Question*, she is certainly the least interiorized, the least amenable to the reader's strenuous and ceaseless absorption of fiction into inner life. In the realist novel, it is this activity of the reader that opens places and persons to hermeneutic understanding, *verstehen* in the classic sense, though it may also prove a realist trap in its confusion of imagination with desire. Kamal stands resolutely, almost to the very end, outside the scope of this assimilation. Her opinions are accessible to reason; her actions form part of the formal logic of the plot. But we are prevented from knowing what she feels, perhaps because we know what she thinks. This relentless exteriorization of self, even where that self is most fractured by the contrary claims of reason, passion and history— as in Kamal's relations with Ajit and Rajen—makes her a character to be read against the grain of realism, just as she stands against the grain of social history. Her hybridity is not so much a matter of circumstance, the accidental outcome of unequal power relations in a colonial society, as a projective reading of the union of Western reason with Indian sensibility.

This is of importance in the understanding of Kamal's feminism, a crucial element in the novel's substance and differing in many respects from the liberal feminist ideology espoused in Saratchandra's other fiction. Much of Saratchandra's work concerns itself with the condition of women, whether in the rural settings of *Bardidi* (*The Elder Sister*, 1913) and *Pallisamaj* (*Village Society*, 1916) or among the more urban, displaced middle class of *Grihadaha* (*The Burning of the Home*, 1920). It is this concern, looking on the one hand towards contemporary campaigns for social and legal reform, and on the other towards the stubbornly local character of individual distress, that is the source of the characteristic pathos of his writing, as well as of its sharp edge of social satire. In the early novels at least, the treatment of suffering itself becomes a powerful instrument of censure; sentiment, here the sign of sympathetic identification, becomes a means through which public sensibility can be radically transformed. It would be a mistake to minimize, or to treat as *merely* sentimental the impact of such writing on the manners and mores of the Bengali middle class of the 1920s and 1930s. Nevertheless, in *The Final Question* Saratchandra consciously chooses a more intellectualized, in some respects more neutral and deliberative treatment of private lives and public identities. The feminism of the earlier works is inseparably linked to the moral function of sentiment, enlisting sympathy for women's suffering in an oppressive or cruel patriarchal order, and directing us towards a liberal advocacy of the right of choice while it enlarges our sense of the complexity, pain, and conflicting loyalties of women's inner lives. This advocacy of the right that women, no less than men, have to a personal good, is more open in the later writings, especially in the complicated patterns of freedom and responsibility traced in such works as *Charitrahin* (*The Rake*, 1917), or *Grihadaha* (1920). Yet it could be argued that liberal sympathy, produced by the imaginative ability to identify with the sufferings of a representative female character, is unthreatening to one's own sense of place in the established social order. This order can absorb without much disturbance to itself a certain idealization of women's suffering and sacrifice, as well as a reformist emphasis on the virtues of compassion, justice and even a restricted social freedom. Indeed, these become, as social historians have shown, an inseparable part of the ideology of nationalism and the construction of a Bengali personal identity from the late nineteenth-century onwards.

Unlike, say, *Ghare-Baire, Shesh Prashna* is an unfashionable point of reference in discussions of the narrative formation of female subjectivity in this period. Part of the reason for this may be the discomfort produced by Saratchandra's characterization of Kamal. It is important to realize how crucial this narrative formation was to national and social self-consciousness in the late nineteenth and early twentieth centuries in Bengal, especially as inflected by reformist social ideology.[2] Beginning with hortatory school primers for the education of young girls, and continuing through various kinds of writing aimed not simply at women, but at the men whose assumed responsibility it was to enlighten and educate them, we can trace a variety of efforts to construct models of female selfhood. Fiction might become the instrument for the invention of a new kind of woman, a woman who could both objectify the ideals of liberal education and bear, like Sucharita in Tagore's *Gora* (1909) and Bimala in *Ghare-Baire*, the burden of modernity, internalizing its problematic and offering a site for the uneasy resolution of a struggle between old and new which is almost entirely determined and directed by men. Women were urged to remake themselves in terms of these fictional projections while, at the same time, they were beginning to discover in their own efforts at fiction or autobiography the possibility of claiming a self through personal narrative. I am thinking here not only of the writings of early women novelists like Rabindranath's accomplished elder sister Swarnakumari Debi, Sharatkumari Chaudhurani, or Nirupama Debi (Saratchandra himself wrote a critique of the work of some female writers including Nirupama Debi[3]), but also of the emergent forms of autobiography or personal diary as attempted by Rassundari Debi, Kailashbasini Debi, Debi Saradasundari and Nistarini Debi[4]—or, for that matter, the actress Binodini Dasi whose autobiographical fragment *Amar Abhinetri Jiban* (*My Life as an Actress*) appeared in a journal edited by Saratchandra[5] in the 1920s. Saratchandra's own work, in the early twentieth century, had an important role to play in its idealization of female suffering and sacrifice, as well as its openly expressed indignation at women's dependence and deprivation in an unjust social order. *The Final Question* is clearly intended as Saratchandra's most considered and extended contribution to larger debates over the place of women, sexual morality and nationalist politics; but it is also a considerable departure from his earlier practice.

Instead of offering us a subject whose internalization of suffering is a means through which the reader can share in the process of self-realization, the painful growth and understanding of a personal identity, Saratchandra presents Kamal as a character whose identity is already formed, and who insists on subjecting the world and its inhabitants to an unsparing, rational critique of behaviour, belief and morality. The identity claimed for Kamal here is in a sense hypothetical; it is instrumental to the critique, which would be impossible without it. In his earlier novels, Saratchandra had used sentiment itself as a moral instrument; but *The Final Question*, remarkably, does not use sentiment in this way. This is an important departure, not simply in the treatment of the central figure of Kamal, but also in that of other women in the novel such as Manorama, Nilima or Bela (though Nilima may be a partial exception).

Freedom is the most important constituent of Kamal's feminist ideology, a freedom asserted in the most unpropitious, circumscribed social conditions. Her poverty and the necessarily restricted nature of her social interaction are never allowed to stand in the way of her insistent claim to the life of reason. It is in the exercise of this reason, not in social choice, that Kamal is free. The radicalism of *The Final Question* consists not only in the nature of the rational critique of tradition that she offers, but also, much more importantly, in that it is articulated by a woman. By the time Saratchandra came to attribute these opinions to Kamal, they had already become part of the discourse of reason in nineteenth- and early twentieth-century Bengal, a discourse shaped by the thought of the European Enlightenment and later influenced by the Positivism of Auguste Comte. What is remarkable about Saratchandra's choice of a vehicle for these ideas is his effort to conceptualize reform in the person of the new woman born of the unhappiness and inequality of the colonial encounter. Kamal's rationality, though it must inevitably sometimes appear to be the echo of a larger (and largely male) discourse, is also specifically the rationality of a female subject struggling to find her place in a changing world. It is a world in which—in real terms—the opinions of women are not of much moment; that they become so in this novel is also a gesture, on Saratchandra's part, towards the future.

Kamal can therefore refuse to idealize the widower Ashutosh Gupta (like the Taj Mahal, to which he is compared) as an embodiment of undying attachment to his dead wife, just as she can reprove Abinash's widowed sister-in-law Nilima for sacrificing herself to the 'duty' of caring for Abinash's household; she can accept the reality of Shibnath's abandonment of her, as well as the probable outcome of Manorama's elopement with him; she can freely choose to live with Ajit and not marry him. Moreover, she can defend these choices in lengthy conversations about marriage, religion, morality, the influence of Western ideas, the value of tradition, the nature of national identity, the lessons of history, the inevitability of progress. It is from the position defined through these conversations that she will criticize the unrewarding and often harsh asceticism of Haren's 'ashram', which imposes much physical hardship on its inmates, while she dissents from the backward-looking and obscurantist ideology of Hindu revivalism on which Satish seeks to found it.

In an important passage, late in the novel, Nilima speaks of the bitterness of being a woman in a society made and controlled by men. Her own situation as a childless widow, taught by convention to subdue her desires and satisfactions to those of others, makes her conscious of the falsity of a forced selflessness or self-sacrifice. Kamal had noted, almost on first acquaintance, the hollowness of Abinash's domestic idyll. This image of domesticity, like others in the novel, is now in disarray; directly or indirectly, Kamal's disruptive presence has forced a variety of individual rearrangements. But Nilima has nowhere to go; unlike Kamal, she lacks the confidence to choose her place. For her, she says, women's liberty or independence (the English word *emancipation* is also used later by Kamal) had remained empty terms until Kamal made her realize that liberty was a matter of self-knowledge:

I've now found out that liberty can be obtained neither by theoretical arguments, nor by pleading justice and morality, nor by staging a concerted quarrel with men at a meeting. It's something that no one can give to another—not something to be owed or paid as a due. Looking at Kamal, you can easily understand that it comes of its own accord—through one's own fulfilment, by the enlargement of one's own soul. (p. 274)

Kamal's own indifference to public opinion, her calm pursuit of a chosen mode of life, and the honesty with which she is shown to face the world make her a model of this inner freedom. It is a freedom conceived independently of social constraints, indeed of the restrictions of the real. It could not have been articulated had it not been disinvested of the burden of suffering, yet this results in a necessary falsification. For Saratchandra, a male writer struggling to conceptualize the new woman born of a colonial society in the process of self-modernization, it is a model which has to carry the discursive burden of Enlightenment reason, biological and evolutionary theory, Spencerian sociology and sexual ethics, as well as contemporary critiques of nationalism. It would be surprising if the model were able to bear this weight, and indeed there are moments when the strain is more than apparent.

Nilima sees Kamal's freedom as realizable in an ethic of engagement within the home, a commitment to meaningful domestic activity:

Not to work, not to know grief or sorrow or want or complaint, only to wander about everywhere—can this be the measure of a woman's freedom? God Himself has endless things to do, but who thinks He is in bondage? Don't I myself work hard in this household? (p. 275)

In the end it is the household that Nilima considers the site of a woman's work: her ideal is an image of fulfilled domesticity, in many respects more characteristic of her than of Kamal. She conceives of Kamal's freedom as a self-sufficiency within this space, a giving of the self which can still hold in reserve the power to withdraw the gift if attachment ends. It is impossible not to feel, even in the poignancy of this model of a free woman as projected by a childless young widow without a home, Saratchandra's own surrender to a deeply male fantasy of voluntary domestic devotion, not only free in itself, but free of compulsion, restraint and social determination.

Nilima describes Kamal, in her untroubled social interaction with men (she has just spent ten days unchaperoned in the house of an Anglo-Indian widower), as being like a fish in a river: 'She doesn't worry about her living, she has no guardian to control her, and no community of her own to frown on her. She's utterly free' (p. 273). This assessment makes Kamal's freedom a condition of her race: because she is situated both within Bengali society and outside it, one way for others in the novel to understand her is by seeing her as a stranger. Through the course of the novel, it is possible to trace the process whereby Kamal is estranged through this growing perception of her as a foreigner. The parallel with Tagore's *Gora* (1909), though not exact, is important. Initially regarded as Shibnath's wife, condemned for her low birth even if admired for her beauty and intelligence, Kamal steadily moves away from the social orbit in which she is first perceived. Isolated by Shibnath's abandonment of her, her movements are restricted by her poverty; at the same time, she forms intimate ties of affection with individuals whose final response to her is to note her difference from them. 'Kamal is Eastern to look at,' says Harendra resignedly, 'but her nature is Western . . . She has neither belief nor sympathy for anything in our tradition' (p. 304). Ashu Babu too is struck by this alterity: 'Life means something different to her—it has nothing in common with our view. She doesn't believe in destiny; past memories don't block her path . . . How young she is! Yet she seems already to have understood the true nature of her mind' (p. 271). That Kamal is constituted by Western knowledge, as by Western reason, is crucial to other people's perception of her. It is also one of the ways in which her freedom is understood—as a form of otherness, explained now by gender, now by culture, now by race. At the end of the novel, Ashu Babu says that he has learnt from her the truth that liberation comes not from imitation, but from knowledge. Kamal is free because that is her nature; for others to imitate that freedom might result in disaster. Yet it is, as Kamal puts it, her nature and her duty (p. 338) to initiate change in the world she inhabits, to destroy the past in order to create the future.

As a thinking subject, Kamal is articulated chiefly

through two lines of critique which run through this novel—
the critique of sexual morality and the critique of Hindu
nationalism. It is important to understand the positions
Saratchandra assigns to her in these debates, but to do so
adequately we need to understand the contexts of time and
place in which they are constructed. *The Final Question* is set,
not in the conflict-ridden, self-doubting climate of Bengal in
the first decades of the twentieth century, but amidst the
relocated (prabasi) community of Bengalis in Agra, hungry
for novelty and gossip, curious about one another's affairs, but
lacking the strict hierarchies of caste or social rank. It is
a community whose chief solace is visiting and news—even
where news is scanty and belated, as in the case of the Guptas,
father and daughter, whose arrival in the town constitutes the
novel's inaugural event. The narrative is well advanced before
we learn that the Guptas are Hindus, not Brahmos; that the
beautiful and educated Manorama is not single by choice, but
engaged to the engineer Ajit; that the wealthy Ashutosh
Gupta, with his deep reverence for Hindu ideals, is a barrister
educated in England. For the women in the novel—Kamal,
Manorama, Nilima, Bela, even the magistrate's wife Malini—
this society provides a relatively neutral, relatively unthreatening
space where personal and social identities can be articulated
without immediate danger to their existence. What is at issue,
for them as for the men, is not so much the question of
suffering as the question of happiness. Yet just outside this
space, on the margins of the fiction, there are women
whose existence is suffering in quite as fundamental a way
as for the heroines of Saratchandra's earlier fiction—Shibnath's
abandoned and ailing wife, whom he dismisses with cynical
rationality, and the widow of his partner, whom he has

cheated of her share in their business. These figures, mentioned early in the novel, exist almost as ghostly reminders of another world and another kind of fiction concerning women, a world of injustice and deprivation which has only been set aside, not superseded.

Kamal's fate is also to be an abandoned wife, but she accepts this with equanimity, recognizing the emptiness of the marital tie when attachment has ceased. Herself a widow, she has gone through some form of Shaivite marriage with Shibnath, clearly a euphemism for the absence of a legal bond.[6] Symbolically, she qualifies as a colonial subject of a peculiarly representative kind. She is the illegitimate daughter of an English tea planter and a Bengali widow of uncertain reputation. While she refers briefly at one point to the arrogance and contempt she has seen among the tea garden Europeans, she is deeply reverential towards her father, who is consistently described as noble and virtuous. This contrast may look back to Rabindranath's distinction between the *chhoto* and *boro ingraj* (small Englishman and great Englishman), but that was a distinction Tagore ultimately rejected as false.

It is perhaps more perturbing that the novel fails at any point to comment on the conditions of the tea plantations of Assam where Kamal spent her youth, conditions which could be described as near slavery. Wages were lower than anywhere else in India, and the law still required discharge certificates (mostly denied by magistrates on the grounds of non-fulfilment of contracts) for 'coolies' who wanted to go home. Saratchandra could scarcely have been unaware of the unrest created among the tea-garden labourers by the Non-Cooperation Movement in 1921, and of the mass exodus of upcountry labourers from Assam in the summer of that year, a trek which brought them to Chandpur in East Bengal in May, where they were brutally prevented from boarding a steamer by the Gorkha military police. This event led to strikes and hartals in the nearby towns and on the Assam-Bengal Railway as well as the steamer service. Domestic servants deserted their European masters: the local bar, schools and colleges were closed, and Chittaranjan Das rushed to Chandpur to direct the steamer strike at Goalando. Following this, cholera broke out in the refugee camp at Chandpur, and C.F. Andrews, who worked with volunteers from the Non-Cooperation Movement among the cholera-stricken refugees, spoke of the experience as a deeply humbling and moving one, calling up 'a deep feeling of charity' which united Bengal.[7] These events must be placed somewhat later than the presumed time of this novel, but they would have been part of the novelist's memory, especially because of the extraordinary public sentiment they aroused and the light they cast on the structures of colonial domination.

Yet Kamal's account of her origins fails to emphasize the vulnerability and sexual exploitation of women, as doubly colonized subjects, in these structures. In fact she never mentions her mother, who belongs if anything to that spectral company of destitute and dispossessed women mentioned at the start of the novel. Kamal's unproblematic acceptance of her paternal inheritance is something of a difficulty for us, especially when it is combined with the easy passage she secures, by virtue of her beauty and charm, into the heart of Bengali society. (It is true that there are some who condemn her, like Akshay, and some who dislike her, like Manorama, but they are in a minority.) We could respond by reading this situation, not in terms of realist representation, but allegorically, as Saratchandra may have intended. In that case we must take note of the paternalist bias of Kamal's theoretical convictions. Late in the novel (p. 291), we find her explicating the English word *emancipation* by telling Ashu Babu that in history it was the masters who freed the slaves: the strong must emancipate the weak, men must liberate women, fathers must set their daughters free. Implicitly, there is also the assumption that it is the English who must free India; that it is Western reason and Western morals, not a revival of Hindu values and ideals, that can release India from bondage.

In a midnight conversation with Ajit, Kamal says that she is not the kind of woman to attract men's lust (p. 232), and there is indeed something coolly intellectual about her personality. Nevertheless, one function she must perform in the novel is to serve as a model of sexual freedom. Saratchandra's enthusiastic reading of Herbert Spencer's *Descriptive Sociology* is attested by his extensive citation of this work in his seminal essay *Narir Mulya* ('A Woman's Worth', 1923), where, incidentally, he also cites John Stuart Mill's *The Subjection of Women*. His views on sexual morality, as evident in mature works like *Charitrahin*, *Shrikanta* Part II and *Grihadaha*, incorporate a liberal defence of the right to choose one's partner and to reject a meaningless legal bond. In Spencer he found a form of evolutionary ethics linked to the development of the 'higher sentiments' which would accompany the union of the sexes in more modern, industrialized societies: 'for sympathy, which is the root of altruism, is a chief element in these sentiments.'[8] The relationships between men and women will inevitably develop from the crude notion of women as property to the ideal of a companionate marriage: 'there will come a time when the union by affection will be held of primary moment and the union by law as of secondary moment;

whence reprobation of marital relations in which the union by affection has dissolved.'[9]

It is in the movement towards this state that, as Ashu Babu puts it, 'the history of pure love is the history of civilization' (p. 337). Kamal's idea of love, a love that does not require validation through the legal bond of marriage, is a notion which even Ajit has to struggle to understand. But it is this notion which informs her assertion of an independent sexual choice, and the articulation of this choice links *The Final Question* with novels like Rabindranath's *Jogajog* (*Relationships*) and *Ghare-Baire*, where the choice is shown to be constrained or corrupted. It also places Kamal in direct relation with the other women in the novel. Manorama, whose centrality in the novel decreases as Kamal's increases, chooses to elope with Shibnath——a tragically mistaken course of action, but she cannot be abandoned for 'following her heart', as Kamal tells her father. Bela, Ashu Babu's niece, has divorced her husband with her uncle's support, but she is explicitly condemned for living on her husband's money. Nilima, despite her admiration for Kamal, remains deeply committed to the Hindu ethic of fidelity and sacrifice. Yet she finds herself a drudge in Abinash's household and an embarrassment in Ashu Babu's: in the end she has no real choice at all. Despite her impoverished and marginal existence on the fringes of Agra society, Kamal's critical, often mocking exposure of sexual hypocrisy and traditional morality touches every character in the novel—— not least the brahmachari Harendra, whose willed celibacy is severely tested by Kamal's invitation to him to spend the night in her room.

Kamal's rational choice of happiness over self-sacrifice or duty is hedonism of a sort, and it is clear that Saratchandra is uncomfortable with some of the implications of this philosophy. He solves this problem by making Kamal, quite irrationally, extremely ascetic, in the manner of a Hindu widow of the most rigorous kind. It is true that Kamal explains her practice of eating the simplest food only once a day by her poverty, which has habituated her to abstinence; but there is no real reason why she should make this self-denial a matter of the strictest observance. In fact, apart from the curious interlude about the soap in Manorama's bathroom, Kamal is represented as avoiding even the meanest of self-indulgences. She goes on a long drive with Ajit, but she appears not to have sexual relations with anyone, she practically never eats or sleeps, and she works selflessly for the sick. Moreover, she demonstrates her womanhood in a tiresomely traditional way by insisting on cooking for Ajit or making him tea. It is impossible not to be conscious here of the symbolic value attached to the serving of food in Hindu society generally and Saratchandra's novels in particular.

If Kamal's presence in the novel disrupts the comfortable middle-class assumptions about sex, morality, marriage, domestic peace and filial obedience to which the other characters have grown accustomed, it is also destructive of the nationalist ideology preached by Satish and Harendra. The time is one of crisis in any case. If we date the events by the influenza epidemic described in the second half of the book, we should assume a rough date around 1918, immediately after the war. The influenza epidemic of that year killed more people all over the world than any epidemic before or since; it ranks with the Black Death in Europe and Asian outbreaks of plague as the most destructive in history. In India roughly 12,500,000 persons, or 4 per cent of the total population, are said to have been killed by influenza in the autumn of 1918; there was a less severe recurrence in the spring of 1919.

Historians in India have so far paid relatively little attention to the scale of this affliction, which far outweighed localized outbreaks of cholera or typhoid fever, and which combined with the economic distress of the post-war period to produce unparalleled misery. What is described at the beginning of Chapter 18 is almost certainly the autumn epidemic:

Within a few days, the appearance of this densely populated, prosperous town changed completely. Schools and colleges were closed, the shops in the markets shut down, and the river bank was almost desolate. The main roads were silent and deserted except for the timorous footsteps of Hindu and Muslim corpse bearers. Looking around, it seemed that not only the people but even the trees, houses and buildings had turned pale with fear.

As the town lay sunk in this state, many of the inhabitants, burning with anxiety, sorrow and bereavement, made up their differences. It did not require the effort of discussion or mediation— it just happened. Those who had still survived, those who had not yet been obliterated from the face of the earth, seemed by virtue of that to be close kin to each other. People who had not spoken for a long time now met on the street with moist eyes: one's brother, another's child or wife had died meanwhile. They no longer had the strength of mind to turn away their faces in hatred. Sometimes they exchanged words; sometimes not, only taking their leave silently, wishing each other well. (pp. 185–86)

Kamal's experience of death in the leather workers' slums affects her permanently; it teaches her to forgive Shibnath's conduct, and it shows her also the limits of her own endurance, which cannot compare with that of Rajen. She is more vulnerable at this time than at any other moment in the novel, more open to the access of sympathy, less censorious of others' mistakes. Her friendship with Rajen has also been educative in a quite new way; sparing of speech and argument, he shows himself to be stronger and more independent than she is. It is in this spiritually chastened mood, when the whole novel bears the horrific weight of the present calamity, that Kamal has her first extended conversation with Harendra (pp 187 ff.).

This conversation needs to be considered together with a later effort by Satish to persuade Kamal of the validity of his beliefs (pp 295 ff.). Given the dialogic mode generally adopted in *The Final Question* and specifically characterizing these encounters, it would be wrong to assume that Kamal's opinions are uncontestedly the author's. In the second conversation at least, the argument seems to be genuinely unresolved; despite the force and rationality of Kamal's position, her interlocutors can give only a qualified assent, and in much they are forced to disagree. The exchanges mark out an area of reasoned difference which more or less coincides with that traced in contemporary debates on nationalism and modernity in India. The struggle of the modern that we mark in Kamal's efforts to extend what Habermas might call the domain of public reason remains incomplete; in a sense it is overshadowed, at the very end of the novel, by the image of sacrifice provided through Rajen's death. As in so much contemporary discourse, the polarization of opposing arguments, the split between tradition and modernity, East and West, asceticism and materialism, produces a curiously schematic view of the conflict. This schematization is further reinforced by the divisions of race and gender which are allowed, in this fictional enactment, to structure the argument. For Saratchandra, the only means of reconciliation lies in sympathy: the sympathy of which Harendra is most intuitively capable, the love which Ashu Babu is readiest in offering. Whether this is enough is an open question.

Kamal's first conversation with Harendra is not in fact about the ideals of his brahmacharya ashram, but about her own relationship with Shibnath. It is important, in the total context of the novel, that Harendra who is 'immeasurably devoted to India's religious ideas and customs, her unique and distinguished civilization' (p. 195) should be so disgusted by what he sees as Kamal's immorality: 'He was repelled by the thought that Kamal's father was a European and her mother a harlot.' Unassimilable within ideologies of nationalism which equate the nation with the mother and idealize womanhood as the repository of the truest spiritual values, Kamal represents to Harendra the fallen, racially impure woman; the woman whose life embodies the other history of the nation, as prostitute and bastard. This revulsion is converted to respect in the course of this first exchange, but there is still, in the later conversation, the irreducible sense of Kamal's difference and otherness.

By the end of the nineteenth century, the ideology of social reform in Bengal, inspired by Western science and morality, had given way to a neo-Hindu revivalism asserting the need for introspection and a renewal of ancient tradition. Rabindranath, in his essay *Byadhi o Pratikar* ('Disease and Remedy', 1901), written 'in response to a work of social criticism by Ramendrasundar Trivedi, speaks of the hesitation and uncertainty of the present moment in contrast to the 'faith in modernity' of the past century. In that time, he suggests:

[Western] civilization seemed ready to honour all humanity irrespective of race and colour: such was the promise it held out. We were spellbound by this. We contrasted the large-heartedness of that civilization with the narrowness of our own, and applauded the culture of Europe.[10]

But this enchantment is already, for Rabindranath, a thing of the past. The inclusiveness of Western humanism was clearly a myth: science and reason were incapable, by themselves, of regenerating in a subject people the awareness of their own dignity and freedom. At the same time, Rabindranath criticizes, in his essays on nationalism as well as the seminal fiction of *Ghare-Baire*, the obscurantism and self-glorification implicit in the rhetoric of the nation, as well as its distortions of history:

for all our miseries and shortcomings, we hold responsible the historical surprises that burst upon us from outside. This is the reason why we think that our one task is to build a political miracle of freedom upon the quicksand of social slavery.[11]

In Saratchandra's fictional representation of the debate, it is impossible to miss the irony of the moment. Satish's identification of the Hindu ashram as the core of Indian greatness comes at a time when Harendra's ashram is in disarray. Despite Ajit's new-found enthusiasm and the money he is prepared to spend on setting up ashrams all over India, there is already a doubt at the heart of the enterprise. It is this doubt that Satish wants to set at rest by converting Kamal to his opinion. His failure to do so marks an irreparable rift in the ideology of the modern Indian state.

Satish's eulogy carries the weight not only of traditional belief, but of the historical context in which such belief could be nurtured: the culture of revolutionary terrorism in Bengal, bred in clubs and gymnasia for the training of young men in the service of the motherland.[12] It is no accident that Rajen is wanted by the police, though Harendra studiously avoids official interest in his ashram. The Indian ashram, says Satish, at its core feels a deep respect and commitment towards the heritage of India. Renunciation, celibacy and self-abnegation are not virtues of the weak and powerless. In these, in the past, the materials for nation-building were inherent. It's only by this path that the dying spirit of India can be revived. Through the rituals and observances of the ashram, we are trying to keep alive this faith and reverence. Through echoing hymns and the flames of holy fires, the ashram of an austere, spiritual India had once taken up the mission of working the genuine welfare of the nation. Is there anyone so foolish as to deny that the need for it is not lost? (p. 298)

The hypnotic rhetoric of this speech can only be undercut by mockery. Kamal's satirical comparison of the glories of ancient India to the dinosaur deliberately uses the discourse of evolutionary science to counter that of religious faith. This evolutionary critique takes into account not only the decay of the East, but also the inevitable failure of the West. Evil is not the real enemy of the good, asserts Kamal: the enemy of the good is the better. For Satish, freedom at the cost of sacrificing 'the wisdom and ancient doctrines of India' is not a victory for India but a triumph of the Western ethos and Western culture, equivalent to a death of the spirit. He notes the mistakes of history, the espousal of Western forms of knowledge by individuals in the previous century; but he contents himself with the lesson that 'our conscience revived by way of reaction. We recognized our error' (p. 303). Unexpectedly, even Ashu Babu agrees with him at a later point (p. 329): without endorsing Satish's intolerance and bigotry, he urges upon Kamal the need for an ascetic ideal of self-knowledge. Yet Kamal, who recognizes 'the pious, resolute Hindu heart burning like an unquenchable lamp in some secluded depth beneath the veneer of Western habits and manners', refuses to accept this ideal as purely Hindu, while she contests its claim to the highest moral ground. The good of a nation, for her, is the good of its people: 'If India lets herself be bound by Western knowledge, science and civilization, it might be a jolt to her pride, but not to her well-being' (p. 303).

The debate is not resolved, and the novel's structure suggests that its resolution is left open to history—a history that extends beyond the fictional dialectic within which these characters are placed. Because Kamal's future, and Ajit's, are made central to that history, we may feel that it is finally the argument of progress, the vision of the modern, that opens the novel out to the future. For those who are left behind, like Satish, Harendra, Akshay and Nilima, the departure of Ashu Babu as of Kamal herself, signalling the conclusion of the narrative plot, is a kind of closure, a mark of ending in lives that will continue, but which will seem less important, less touched by the urgency of the time. Yet the novel's close is marked by an event that contradicts this reading.

That event, the news of Rajen's sacrifice of his life to save the image of a Hindu deity from fire, can only be understood symbolically. Just as the heroism of the act consists in its significance for the believer, so too for us as readers, this is not an event in real time so much as a sign or token. The question—perhaps the final question—is: what kind of sign? Does Rajen's sacrifice validate—comfortingly for Satish and his friends—the ideology of sacrifice, the meaning of ritual, the faith of religion? The nature of the act may itself be taken as a corrective to the confusion of ritual with faith. What Rajen saves is the image of the deity in the temple's heart: everything else is burnt away by fire. The significance of his self-sacrifice lies in its identification of something at the core of religious faith that needs preserving. Stripped of ceremony and ritual observance, purged by fire, the living image of the god is seen as worthy of Rajen's instinctive devotion.

Yet the villagers who take out a procession to honour Rajen after his death have re-absorbed him into the fabric of their daily religious observances, blurring inevitably the distinction between the singularity of his act and the social practices that will naturalize it. The responses of Rajen's friends in Agra are also almost wholly conventional. This may be a concession to those likely to be offended by the radical content of Kamal's earlier critique of conventional idealization. Kamal's own uncharacteristic enthusiasm for Rajen's heroism is a means of reclaiming her for the nation. The incident and its aftermath offer a fiction of resolution, a means of closing the narrative plot while opening the plot of history. But in fact nothing is resolved. The incident retains in our minds the dramatic and unreal quality of nationalist myth, while inviting rational criticism. Is such a sacrifice either necessary or worthwhile? In a novel which chooses to ask questions rather than answer them, this last problem may prove the most intractable of all.

The Final Question is a novel that needs to be read today, in the context of current debates on nationalism and on women's freedom. More than half a century after Independence, we are faced with a crisis in the ideology of the nation-state: a crisis in which the historical and literary imagination must 'anxiously conjure up the spirits of the past' in order to understand the circumstances in which we find ourselves in the present.[13] The project of modernity which Saratchandra represents through Kamal in *The Final Question* is necessarily unfinished in the novel; to look back on it from the perspective of the present is to ask how well its premises have served us. For we know that reason and freedom, whether in public life or in private relationships, are not absolute values; they are constructed differently by different discursive imperatives. Kamal's own subject-position, the hybridity of her consciousness, her awareness of being a woman in a world largely determined by men, inflect her rationality and her power of choice. The struggle of the modern we witness through her is never free of its historical burden of debt, complicity and dependence. This is what makes Rajen's death, with its converse idealization of tradition and spirituality, symbolically so powerful.

Yet the very simplicity of this symbol, especially as read in present-day contexts of fundamentalist Hindu politics, is unsettling. As a character, Rajen is singular, even eccentric; so far as he possesses the capacity for personal attachment, he is attached to Kamal. His sacrifice is reductive of his personality in many respects while enhancing it in others. We would be doing an injustice to the insistently dialectical structure of the novel if we were to read Rajen's sacrifice as summative. Rather, it helps us to see, at the close of this narrative, the nature of the oppositions that Saratchandra has tried to represent in the nation's history. For us today, these oppositions are still valid, still unresolved. In our daily experience, we are called upon to negotiate the content of modernity (as Western liberal culture or as forms of political ideology) with religious belief or traditional ethics in complicated, unsatisfactory ways that may remind us of the unfinished conversations of this novel. At the same time, *The Final Question* may suggest to us, in its startlingly modern representations of a society struggling to come to terms with its own changes, the impossibility of a nationalism locked into a single, integrated mode of self-development.

Saratchandra is a supremely intelligent writer, never blind

to the problems he has created for himself and his readers. *The Final Question* is a book in which he takes unprecedented risks. In earlier novels he may be seen as risking a great deal for the sake of the unfree women at the centre of his plots; here, he places his whole narrative in danger in order to imagine a free woman. In trying to do this he draws upon himself the shadows of history, of politics, of social reality. No model of freedom can be valid without them; yet to some extent, as I have suggested, Saratchandra's conceptualization seeks to go beyond what is historically or socially probable. That he should attempt this is a gesture to the future: it is a way of speaking to us, as readers of his novel several decades after it was first printed.

SUPRIYA CHAUDHURI

Translators' Note

1. All English words present in the Bengali original have been retained in italics. They indicate the interlarding of Bengali speech with English words, a growing practice among educated Bengalis to the present day. The social and class message should not be missed, though the specific nuance might vary greatly from occasion to occasion.

2. A few Bengali terms of address need explanation.

'Babu' is added to the first name of an adult male, usually of the speaker's own or superior class, as a formal or respectful mode of address or allusion. It is roughly equivalent to the use of 'Mr' with the surname among Englishmen. The first name might be clipped for the purpose: thus Ashutosh Gupta becomes 'Ashu Babu'.

'Babu' can also be appended to words denoting real or assumed relationships. Thus Kamal calls Ashu Babu 'Kakababu' (roughly, 'respected uncle').

'Mashai' (Mahashay) is another way of addressing or referring to an adult male—sometimes formally, sometimes familiarly or jocularly. It is usually appended to the surname. Thus Nilima talks to or of Abinash Mukherjee as 'Mukherjee [Bengali Mukhujye] Mashai'.

Bengalis, like other Indians, commonly use familial terms for persons not related or even well known to them. Thus:

'Dada' (elder brother) and 'didi' (elder sister) are widely used of men and women of appropriate age. The words are sometimes curtailed to 'da' or 'di' and affixed to the first name of the person, which may also be curtailed for the purpose. Thus Harendra's younger friends and associates refer to him as Haren-da.

No clear distinction is made between siblings and cousins. 'Dada' and 'didi', like other terms for 'brother' and 'sister', can be used of siblings, cousins and indeed people with whom the speaker has no blood relationship and whom he or she may not even know very well.

'Ma' (mother) is used to address women of all ages, from a small child to an elderly person, with many shades of affection, respect or formality according to context. In most cases, even a rough translation is impossible, but the emotional implication is too important to miss. The term has been rendered in various ways. Where an elderly man like Ashu Babu uses it to address his daughter or some other young woman like Kamal, 'my dear' often appears to be a feasible equivalent.

1

AT VARIOUS TIMES AND FOR VARIOUS REASONS, MANY BENGALI families came westwards to settle in the town of Agra. Some had lived there for generations; others, recently arrived, were still at the lodging house stage. Epidemics of smallpox and bubonic plague apart, they led profoundly peaceful lives. They had done the rounds of the Mughal forts and buildings; they knew by heart the complete list of all the large, small and middling, derelict and intact tombs of nobles and viziers. Even the world famous Taj Mahal had lost its novelty for them. They had wrung dry all customary ploys and stratagems of admiring its beauty from both banks of the Yamuna: with a moist, languid gaze in the evening, with half-shut eyes in the moonlight, or staring vacantly through the darkness. They knew all the effusions of famous men, all about the poems and the men who wrote them, all about those who wanted to end their lives in rapture while standing in front of it. Their knowledge of history too was complete. Even their small children knew which begum used which apartment during childbirth; which Jat leader cooked his meal when and where— how ancient each charred smudge on the wall was; which bandit looted how many jewels and their estimated value. Nothing was unknown to any of them.

Then suddenly one day there was a flutter in the Bengali community, shattering this knowledge and serenity. Groups of travellers passed through Agra every day; there were occasional crowds, from American tourists to Vaishnavas returning from Vrindavan. Nobody took any interest in them; each day

passed like the rest. But around this time, a middle-aged Bengali
sahib with a charming, educated, grown-up daughter took a
large house at one end of the town, giving out that he had
come there to recoup his health. With him came a bearer, a
chef and a doorkeeper; housemaids, servants and a Brahman
cook.[1] His car, carriages and horses, chauffeur, coachman and
grooms filled up every corner of the vast house overnight, as
though through a magic spell.

The gentleman was called Ashutosh Gupta and his daughter
Manorama. They were obviously very rich. But the flutter
had less to do with their imagined wealth and property, or
even with the spreading fame of Manorama's education and
beauty, than with Ashu Babu's simple, unassuming, courteous
ways. Along with his daughter, he sought out and called on
everybody. He proclaimed his ill-health, described himself
as their guest, and indicated that he and his daughter could
scarcely survive in exile if everyone did not, of their own kind
natures, draw them into their fold. Manorama went into the
inner quarters of every home to make the acquaintance of
the womenfolk. On behalf of her ailing father, she also pleaded
that they should not be treated as outsiders, with more to the
same agreeable effect.

Everyone was pleased by this. From then on, Ashu Babu's
carriage and car would do the rounds of various houses, fetching
both men and women guests and taking them back.
Conversations, entertainments, music and repeated visits to
the local sights so cemented relations that it did not take more
than a week for everyone to forget that these people were
outsiders and immensely rich. However, nobody asked one
question openly—perhaps out of embarrassment, perhaps
because they felt it unnecessary. The question was whether

they were Hindus or Brahmos.[2] It did not really matter much outside Bengal. From their customs and practices it was clear that whichever sect they belonged to, like most well-educated upper-class Bengali families, they were not conservative about food and drink. Even if not everyone knew that they employed a Muslim chef,[3] everyone could tell that a person who had let his daughter remain unmarried so long as to give her a college education, had freed himself from many narrow prejudices, regardless of the sect he might belong to.

Abinash Mukherjee was a college teacher. His wife had died long ago, leaving a ten-year-old son; but he had not married again. Abinash taught at a college and spent his time with friends in various pleasurable ways. He was well off and led a peaceful, untroubled life. Nearly two years earlier his widowed sister-in-law had come to stay with him for a change of climate after an attack of malaria. The fever left, but the brother-in-law would not let her leave. She was now the mistress of the house, in charge of running the household and bringing up the boy. Friends joked about the relationship. Abinash would smile and say, 'Don't torture me with more embarrassment. It's my misfortune—I spared no pains. I think I would rather have been assailed by robbers searching for my rumoured wealth.'

Abinash had loved his wife deeply. One could see her photographs all over the house—of different sizes, in different poses. A large portrait adorned the bedroom—an oil painting, expensively framed. Every Wednesday morning Abinash would hang a garland over it. She had died on a Wednesday.

Abinash was a cheerful person. He was addicted to cards and dice, so that people gathered at his home on almost every holiday. One day, when the local offices and the college were closed for some festival, the community of professors arrived at his home after lunch. Two sat over a chessboard on the broad mattress spread across the floor; two others squatted beside them to watch the game. The rest were noisily discussing the disproportion between the merits and salaries of deputy magistrates and local judges, and airing their *righteous indignation* and contempt for the government.

Just then a large car pulled up at the front door. The next moment, everybody rose to welcome Ashu Babu and his daughter. The *righteous indignation* melted away, the game too was temporarily suspended, and Abinash said with deference, 'It's my good fortune that you have stepped into my house. But I shan't be able to receive you properly at this unexpected hour.' He offered Manorama a chair.

Ashu Babu, meanwhile, lowered his huge body into the nearest armchair and, filling the room with sudden uproarious laughter, said: 'Do you think Ashu Gupta cares about proper times? Even my youngest uncle can't malign me so, Abinash Babu.'

Manorama said with a gentle smile, 'What are you saying, Father?'

'All right, let's not talk about my uncle,' Ashu Babu replied. 'My daughter objects. But even my daughter's father couldn't have chosen a better example.' With this he almost brought the roof down by laughing loudly at his own joke. He then went on: 'But what can I do, gentlemen? I'm crippled with gout, otherwise you'd have had to hire a servant to clean the dust I'd bring into the house with constant visits. But today I can't stay long. I have to leave immediately.'

Everybody stared at him, puzzled by his haste. 'I have an appeal to make,' said Ashu Babu. 'I have even dragged my daughter along to extract your consent. Tomorrow is another holiday. We're having a musical evening. You must all come with your families. There'll be a bit of food after the soirée.'

'Mani,' he asked his daughter, 'go into the house[4] and get the necessary permission. Don't take too long. And there's something more, *my young friends*. For us men, if not for the ladies, there will be two different bills of fare[5]—that is, if you have no *prejudice*. I hope you get my meaning.'

Everybody understood and declared in unison that they had no *prejudice* about food.

'I expected nothing else,' said Ashu Babu happily. Then he said to his daughter, 'Mani, don't forget to ask the ladies how they feel about the food. It'll be late evening by the time we've called at every house and found out what they want. So get your errand over quickly, my dear.'

Manorama was on her way in when Abinash said, 'My house has been empty for a long time. There's my sister-in-law, but she's a widow. She loves music greatly. So you can take it that she's coming; but as to eating . . .'

Ashu Babu said, 'Don't worry, Abinash Babu. There'll be suitable arrangements for her. My Mani will be there, you see. She touches neither fish nor meat, garlic nor onion.'[6]

Abinash was surprised. 'She doesn't eat fish or meat?' he asked.

'She used to eat everything,' Ashu Babu replied, 'but Babaji[7] doesn't like it. He's something of an ascetic.'

A flush rose to Manorama's face immediately. Interrupting her father, she said, 'What nonsense, Father!'

The father was nonplussed. The natural softness of his daughter's voice could not hide the bitterness within.

The conversation languished after this. Though Ashu Babu kept up the flow for the few more minutes that they tarried,

Manorama seemed somewhat abstracted. When they left, an unwelcome gloom settled on the company.

Nobody said anything explicitly, but everyone wondered where the 'Babaji' had suddenly come from. Everybody knew that Ashu Babu had no son, that Manorama was his only daughter; she was still unmarried—at least she bore no sign of a married woman.[8] Of course no one had asked openly about the matter, but no one had had any doubt about it. What then?

Yet whoever this ascetic Babaji was, or wherever he was, he must be a redoubtable person. Not by injunctions but by simple reluctance, he had made the only educated daughter of a prosperous and luxury-loving man give up fish and meat, onion and garlic!

And what was there to be ashamed of or to hide in all this? The father had recoiled in hesitation, the daughter had sat blushing and speechless. The whole thing seemed to everybody like an unpleasant mystery. Suddenly, the even, limpid flow of their growing relationship with this family was disturbed.

IT WAS THOUGHT THAT ASHU BABU WOULD NOT EXCLUDE ANYONE in the town from his soirée. But in fact only distinguished Bengalis were invited. The professors arrived in a group; the women had been brought earlier in the car.

The soirée was to take place in a fairly spacious room in the house, laid out with a large, expensive carpet. Squatting on the carpet, two local musicians were tuning their instruments. A number of children stood in a circle around them. The master of the house was busy somewhere inside. On hearing that the guests had arrived, he came running out breathlessly. Raising his arms theatrically, he exclaimed, 'Welcome, gentlemen! *Most welcome!*'

Pointing to the musicians and winking at his guests, he said in a low voice, 'Don't be apprehensive! I haven't invited you to listen to their caterwauling! You'll bless me before you leave for the songs you'll hear today.'

Everybody was pleased to hear this. The ever-cheerful Abinash Babu said, beaming, 'How can that be, Ashu Babu? I know everybody in this wretched place. Where did you find such a jewel?'

'I've discovered him, gentlemen, I've discovered him. It's not that you people don't know him at all—it's only that you've forgotten about him. Come, let me show you.' With this, he practically pushed the guests forward and, drawing aside the curtains of the sitting room, entered it.

A man of somewhat dark complexion, but otherwise

exceedingly handsome, sat there. He was tall and straight, and faultlessly built. His nose, eyes, eyebrows, forehead, even the curve of his lips, seemed more perfect than imagination could conceive. His good looks were actually quite startling. He must have been close on thirty-two but appeared younger at first sight. Settled on a sofa, he was conversing with Manorama. He straightened himself, smiled a little, and said, 'Do come in.'

Manorama stood up and greeted the guests, but they were too startled to return her greeting. Abinash Babu was the oldest member of the gathering, and also the most exalted by virtue of academic rank. He spoke first. 'When did you come back to Agra, Shibnath Babu? You're a fine one: none of us knew of your return.'

Shibnath said, 'Didn't you? Strange!' Then he smilingly added: 'I didn't think you would wait so anxiously for my return.'

At this Abinash Babu attempted to smile, but the faces of his companions grew stern with anger. Whatever the reason, it was obvious that these people were not happy with this handsome, talented man. The hostility behind the sarcastic words of the one and the stern faces of the others was so bitter, harsh and obvious that not only Manorama and her father but even the ever-cheerful Abinash were embarrassed.

But the matter did not proceed further, and ended there for the time being.

The ustads could be heard warming up in the adjacent room. The next moment the steward came and announced deferentially that everything was ready: they could start as soon as the guests had settled themselves.

The music was of the usual classical variety offered by professionals: humdrum, devoid of any speciality. But soon Shibnath began to sing to the small audience, and his songs were truly remarkable. His voice was incomparable, and, moreover, exceptionally well trained. His unostentatious, disciplined style, the limpid flow of the melody, the singular nuances of feeling upon his face, the involved, abstracted look—all these were concentrated in an instant to a focal point. At the end of this exercise in pure melody and rhythm, it seemed to everyone that Saraswati had poured all her blessings upon this devotee of hers.

Everybody remained speechless for some time. Only old Amir Khan remarked slowly in Hindustani: 'Never heard anything like it!'

Manorama had been trained in music since her childhood. She was a tolerably good singer, and had listened to much music in her brief life. She never knew, however, that there was such music as Shibnath's in the world. She did not know that the rhythmical play of music could produce such an aching sensation in the heart. Her eyes filled with tears and, in order to hide them, she turned her face and left the room silently.

Abinash said, 'It's not easy to persuade Shibnath to sing, but we have heard him earlier. That didn't compare with his performance today. He seems to have *improved infinitely* within a year.'

Akshay taught history. He was known among his friends as a severely plain-spoken and upright man. Though he had a weakness for music, he was otherwise thoroughly puritanical. Precisely because of this, he was not only concerned about his own character but also extremely alert about the purity of others. He was assailed by fears that the unexpected return of Shibnath might again vitiate the atmosphere of the town. He was particularly anxious because women were present. The possibility that they too might be attracted by Shibnath's singing and appearance greatly worried him. He said, 'I remember hearing Madhu Babu sing. You might find this music sweet, but it has no life.'

Everybody kept silent because, first, none of them had heard the unknown Madhu Babu sing, and secondly, no one except Akshay knew precisely how music might or might not have life. The ecstatic Ashu Babu was ready to defend Shibnath's performance, but Abinash stopped him with a look.

They went on discussing the music, each one expatiating on the sort of music he had heard earlier. As they talked, evening began turning to night. It was conveyed from within the house that the women had finished their dinner and were being taken home. An old sub-judge left on the pretext of the advancing night; a dyspeptic magistrate joined him after having a glass of water and a paan. Only the professors stayed back. Soon they too were called to dinner. Places had been set on the open veranda upstairs, with cushions on the floor. Ashu Babu joined them. Manorama's duties towards the women guests being over, she too came to look after things.

However hungry Shibnath might have been, he did not wish to eat; he wanted to return home immediately. But Manorama would not let him go. She persuaded him to sit with the rest. The arrangements befitted a rich man's house.

Ashu Babu described in detail how he had met Shibnath on the train from Tundla and how a few days' acquaintance had deepened into intimate friendship. He described this in great detail and, bubbling with self-congratulation, exclaimed: 'But the greatest credit should go to my ear. From a little faint humming I knew for certain that he was a worthy man, a rare talent.' Calling his daughter as witness, he added: 'Well, Mani, didn't I tell you that Shibnath Babu was a great man?

My dear, didn't I say that it's a matter of good fortune to know people like him?'

Yes Father, you said so,' replied the daughter, her face beaming with joy. 'You said it as soon as we got off the train.'

'But look here, Ashu Babu . . .'

The speaker was Akshay. Everybody grew wary. Abinash anxiously tried to stop him. 'Let it go. Let's not discuss such things today.'

Shutting his eyes to avoid embarrassment, Akshay shook his head a number of times and said, 'No, Abinash Babu, we mustn't hush things up. I feel it my duty to expose everything about Shibnath Babu. That man . . .'

'What are you doing, Akshay? Don't we have a sense of duty too? We'll take it up some other day.' Abinash nudged him to stop but did not succeed. The nudge moved Akshay's body but not his strength of purpose. He said, 'I don't suffer from misguided diffidence. I can't allow any indulgence towards corruption.'

The impatient Harendra broke in: 'Do you think we want to indulge corruption? But everything has its place and time.'

Akshay said, 'If he hadn't chosen to return to this town, if he hadn't sought intimacy with a respectable family, and especially if an unmarried lady like Manorama had not been involved, then . . .'

Ashu Babu became restive with anxiety. Manorama paled with an unknown apprehension.

'*It is too much*,' said Harendra.

Akshay protested loudly: '*No, it is not.*'

Abinash exclaimed, 'Now, now, what are you doing?'

Akshay paid no heed. He said, 'He too was once a professor in Agra. He should have told Ashu Babu how he lost his job.'

Harendra said, 'Why, he gave it up himself, to start trading in stone.'

'That's a lie!' retorted Akshay.

Shibnath was eating silently, as if he had nothing to do with this heated argument. He now looked up and said very casually, 'It certainly is a lie because had I not resigned my job on my own, I would have had to do it at others' behest—that is to say, at yours. And that's exactly what happened.'

Ashu Babu was very surprised and asked, 'Why?'

Shibnath said, 'Because I drink.'

Akshay protested, 'No, not on charges of drinking but on charges of being drunk.'

Shibnath said, 'Whoever drinks gets drunk sometime or other. Anyone who doesn't, either lies or drinks water.' He laughed.

An enraged Akshay sternly said, 'You may laugh shamelessly, but we can't forgive such an offence.'

'I never slandered you by saying you could,' Shibnath replied. 'I quite agree that all of you laboriously exercised your free will to make me resign my job of my free will.'

Akshay said, 'Then we expect that you will readily confess another truth. You may not be aware that I know a good deal about you.'

Shibnath shook his head and said, 'No, I'm not. But one thing I do know, that your curiosity about others is boundless. So too is your perseverance in gathering information. Please tell me, what should I confess?'

Akshay said, 'Your wife is still alive, but you've deserted her and married again. Isn't this true?'

Ashu Babu suddenly became angry. 'What's all this nonsense, Akshay Babu? Can such a thing ever be?'

Shibnath interrupted. 'But that's exactly what has happened, Ashu Babu. I have deserted her and married again.'

'What are you saying? What really happened?'

Shibnath said, 'Nothing much. My wife is a chronic invalid. She's nearing thirty—that's quite old enough for a woman. Moreover, she seems to have grown really old, with her teeth falling out and her hair turning grey from a long illness. That's why I had to leave her and marry again.'

Ashu Babu looked at him, dazed. 'What! Just for this? She hasn't offended in any other way?'

Shibnath said, 'No. What's gained by making false accusations, Ashu Babu?'

Enraged by this unsullied truthfulness, Abinash said, 'What gain indeed, Ashu Babu! You scoundrel, let your gain and loss go to hell. Why don't you lie for once and say that you deserted her because she committed some grave offence? One more lie won't add to your sins.'

Shibnath remained unruffled. He only said, 'But I can't tell such a lie.'

Harendra instantly flared up. 'Don't you have something called a conscience, Shibnath Babu?'

Shibnath was not annoyed even by this. He calmly said, 'That sort of conscience means nothing. I don't support being chained by a false conscience and crippling oneself. The aim of life is not continual suffering.'

Intensely hurt, Ashu Babu said, 'But think of your wife's misery. Her illness is a matter of grief, and to fall sick is not an offence, Shibnath Babu. Without any fault on her part . . .'

'Why should I suffer all my life for no fault of mine? I don't believe in passing one's misery on to another.'

Ashu Babu did not argue further. He sighed deeply and kept silent.

Harendra asked, 'Where did this second marriage take place?'

'In our village.'

'Her people gave away their daughter in marriage, knowing that you had a wife? Perhaps she'd lost her parents.'

Shibnath said, 'No. She's the widowed daughter of our maidservant.'

'The daughter of your maidservant? Excellent! What's her caste?'

'I don't know exactly. They may be weavers.'[1]

Akshay hadn't spoken for a long time. Now he asked, 'I suppose this person is totally illiterate?'

Shibnath said, 'I wasn't tempted to marry her for her education. I married her for her looks. She has no dearth of that.'

At this remark Manorama tried to get up and leave, but her feet seemed as heavy as stone. Everyone was curious and tense, and no one noticed her. Had they done so, they would have been alarmed.

Harendra said, 'Then this was a civil marriage?'

Shibnath shook his head and said, 'No, it was a Shaivite marriage.'[2]

'Thereby leaving the doors of deception open on all sides,' said Abinash. 'Isn't that so, Shibnath?'

Shibnath said with a smile, 'You say this out of anger, Abinash Babu. The previous marriage, which was solemnized in the presence of my father, was perfectly valid but full of loopholes. One must have the ability to spot the loopholes.'

Abinash couldn't reply. His face turned red with anger.

Ashu Babu sat silently with downcast eyes, thinking: 'What

a disaster! What a disaster!' Nobody spoke for two or three minutes. An air of stifling gloom and bickering had filled the room: a gust of wind from outside was absolutely necessary. Abinash suddenly said from some such feeling, 'Let's drop this. Shibnath, are you still in the stone business?'

'Yes.'

'Didn't you have to look after the minor children of your dead friend? Is their mother alive? How are they doing for money? Not too well, I suppose?'

'No, they're very poor.'

Abinash said, 'What a pity he died so suddenly. We thought he'd left some money. He was a true friend to you.'

Shibnath nodded and replied, 'Yes, since our earliest schooldays.'

Abinash said, 'That's why he did so much to help you once.' Then, pausing a while, he went on: 'Whatever it be, Shibnath, since you yourself must now look after the whole business, why didn't you demand a share? By way of salary, as it were . . .'

Shibnath interrupted him to say, 'What share? The business is entirely mine.'

The professors were amazed. 'How did the stone business suddenly become yours, Shibnath Babu?' asked Akshay.

Shibnath gravely replied, 'It's most certainly mine.'

Akshay said, 'Never. All of us know it belonged to Jogin Babu.'

Shibnath said, 'If you knew it, why didn't you go and bear witness in court? Did you ever hear of any document that said so?'

Abinash gave a start. 'I never heard anything. But did the matter reach the courts?'

'Oh yes,' said Shibnath, 'Jogin's brother-in-law appealed in court. The verdict was in my favour.'

Abinash sighed and said, 'That's fine. So finally you didn't have to pay anything to the widow and her children.'

'No,' said Shibnath. 'No. Khalim, these kebabs are excellent. Could you bring some more?'

Ashu Babu sat in a daze. Looking up suddenly, he said, 'You're not doing justice to the food, gentlemen.'

Everyone's appetite had disappeared. As Manorama was leaving silently, Shibnath called to her and said, 'How's this? You're leaving before we've finished!'

Manorama did not reply, or even turn around. Her entire body shrank in disgust.

3

A WEEK HAD PASSED SINCE THESE INCIDENTS. IT HAD BEEN WET and cloudy for the last two days, but now, after a few showers, the rain stopped at midday, though the clouds remained: it could start raining again any moment. Manorama, ready to go out, came into her father's room. Ashu Babu, draped in a thick quilted shawl, was resting in his armchair, book in hand. His daughter was surprised and said, 'What's this, Father, aren't you ready yet? We're supposed to visit the tomb of Etwari Khan today.'

'True enough, my dear, but this gout . . .'

'Then let me send the car back. Perhaps we could go tomorrow.'

Her father stopped her and said, 'No, you'll get a headache if you don't go out. Why don't you take the air for a while? I'll browse through this magazine in the meantime. There's a good story in it.'

'All right, I'll go. But I shan't be long. Tell me the story when I return.' She went out alone.

Returning within the hour, Manorama entered her father's room and asked: 'How did you like the story, Father? Have you finished it? Who's written it?' As soon as she had spoken, she was taken aback to see that her father was not alone. Shibnath sat in front of him.

Shibnath stood up, did namaskar and said, 'How far did you go?'

Manorama did not reply to the greeting. She turned

17

her back to him and addressed her father: 'Have you finished reading it, Father? How did you like it?'

Ashu Babu only answered: 'No.'

The daughter said, 'Then let me take it. I'll return it as soon as I've finished.' She went away with the magazine, but sat silently in her room. She did not change her clothes or wash her face. She did not even open the magazine to find out what the story was about or who had written it and how well.

What she thought as she sat there remains uncertain. Seeing the servant pass, she asked him, 'Has the man in my father's room gone away?'

'Yes,' he replied.

'When did he leave?'

'Before it began to rain.'

Manorama drew aside the window curtains and saw that he was right. It had started raining lightly. She looked up and saw that the clouds on the western horizon were growing thicker. There might be a heavy shower at night. As she entered her father's room, magazine in hand, she found him sitting silently. She placed the magazine slowly on the arm of his chair and said, 'Father, you know I don't like all this.' She sat down on a chair beside her father. Ashu Babu looked up and asked, 'What don't you like, my dear?'

Manorama said, 'You quite understand what I mean. I know how to appreciate a talented man, but isn't it too much to indulge an unprincipled debauchee and drunkard like Shibnath?'

Ashu Babu seemed to grow pale with shame and diffidence. A large number of books were piled on a table in a corner of the room. Manorama had not yet arranged them properly for want of time. Looking in that direction, he could only say, 'There he is . . .'

Turning her head nervously, Manorama saw Shibnath standing at the table, hunting for a book. The servant had misinformed her. She felt like sinking into the earth with embarrassment.

Shibnath came and stood before her. She could not look at him. He said, 'I couldn't find the book, Ashu Babu. Goodbye for now.'

Ashu Babu could not say anything either. He only blurted out, 'But it's raining outside.'

'Let it,' said Shibnath, 'it isn't much.' He was about to leave, but suddenly stopped. Addressing Manorama, he said, 'What I've accidentally heard is both fortunate and unfortunate. You needn't feel embarrassed about it. I often have to hear such things. I know that, though your words were about me, they weren't meant for me to hear. You'd never be so unkind.'

He paused and continued: 'But I have another grievance. The other day Akshay Babu and the other professors hinted that I had some design in trying to get intimate with this family. Of course, everybody's sense of right and wrong is not the same. Equally, whatever you see from outside is not the whole truth. However that may be, I neither had any sinister intent in entering your circle at that time, nor do I have any now.' Turning to Ashu Babu, he added: 'You like hearing me sing. I don't live far away. If ever you wish to, do drop in. It will be a pleasure.'

He did another namaskar and went out. Neither father nor daughter could say anything in reply. Many questions jostled in Ashu Babu's mind, but he kept silent. It was pouring heavily outside; yet he could not say, 'Shibnath Babu, wait here for a while.'

The servant laid out the tea things. Manorama asked, 'Shall I make some tea for you, Father?'

'Not for me,' replied Ashu Babu. 'Shibnath had asked for a little tea.'

Manorama signalled to the servant to take the tea away. In spite of his rheumatism, Ashu Babu rose from his chair and started walking about the room. Suddenly he stopped before the window, looked intently for a while and said, 'Isn't that Shibnath standing under the tree? He couldn't go after all. He's getting drenched.' The next moment he said, 'There's a woman with him. She wears her sari Bengali-fashion. The poor girl seems to be even more drenched than him.' He called for his servant and said, 'Jadu, go and see who those people are, getting wet under the tree near our gate. Is it the same gentleman who left just now? But no, wait a moment . . .'

He stopped in mid-sentence, suddenly struck by a terrible doubt. Could that woman be Shibnath's new wife?

'Let him call Shibnath Babu in,' said Manorama. She rose and stood beside her father at the open window. She said, 'If I knew that he'd asked for tea, I wouldn't have let him go.'

Ashu Babu slowly replied to his daughter: 'No doubt, Mani. But I'm afraid the woman is probably that wife of his. He didn't have the nerve to bring her in with him. She's been waiting somewhere outside all this time.'

As she heard this, Manorama too was certain that this was the woman. She hesitated for a moment, debating whether it was permissible to invite her into the house under any circumstances. However, looking at her father's face, she made up her mind. Calling the servant, she ordered, 'Jadu, bring both of them in. If Shibnath Babu wants to know who's invited them, tell him I have.'

The servant went away. Ashu Babu anxiously said, 'Mani, was this the right thing to do?'

'Why, Father?'

'Whatever Shibnath may be,' said Ashu Babu, 'he is, after all, an educated gentleman—it's different with him. But should we set up acquaintance with that woman because of her connection with Shibnath? We may not care much about her caste, but after all there is a difference. One can't be friends with maids and servants.'

'There's no question of making friends, Father', said Manorama. 'Even a traveller off the road can be given shelter for a few hours in times of danger. That's all we're doing.'

Ashu Babu was in two minds. He shook his head a few times and said slowly, 'It's not that. I'm worried as to how you should behave with the woman when she comes.'

Manorama said, 'Don't you have confidence in me, Father?'

Ashu Babu smiled drily and said, 'Of course I do, but I don't understand this business. You know how to treat people of your own class—few women know better. Your treatment of the maids and servants is faultless. It's just that I have an affection for Shibnath and admire his talents. By an unlucky accident, he has suffered much humiliation today. I don't want to hurt him further after inviting him back into the house.'

Manorama realized this was a complaint against her. 'As you please, Father,' she said.

'It's not so simple,' Ashu Babu said with a smile. 'I'm not sure what ought to be done. The only thing I know is that Shibnath shouldn't feel hurt in our house.'

Manorama was going to say something, but suddenly gave a start and said, 'They are here.'

Ashu Babu came out of the room agitatedly. 'Now there, Shibnath Babu, you're completely soaked!'

'Yes,' replied Shibnath, 'it suddenly started pouring. But she's much wetter than I am.' He pointed to the woman with him. But he did not identify her clearly, nor could they ask directly who she was.

She was indeed thoroughly soaked. Her clothes sagged with water, and water was dripping down her shoulders from her thick black hair. Father and daughter both gazed at the new arrival, speechless with utter amazement. Ashu Babu was not a poet, but it struck him immediately that it was such feminine beauty that poets of the past had compared with the dew-washed lotus, and that there could be no better comparison. The answer that Shibnath had given in disgust at Akshay's battery of questions that day—that he had married her not for her education but for her beauty—had not then been grasped for the truth it was. Now Ashu Babu silently recalled Shibnath's words again and again. He felt, in fact, that even if their relationship was indecent and immoral, even if they lacked the sanctity of the husband–wife relationship, an immortal truth of creation had blossomed in these two mortal forms of man and woman in this mortal world. More amazingly still, in a nation which had no special procedure for choosing beauty, a nation where one had to shut one's own eyes and rely on another's, how had they come to know of each other through the darkness?

It did not take more than a second for him to get over his stupor. He anxiously said, 'Shibnath Babu, get out of your wet clothes. Jadu, take this gentleman to my *bathroom*.'

Shibnath went away with the servant. Manorama was now in trouble. The girl was almost her own age; she too needed to change out of wet clothes. In view of her origins as recounted by Shibnath the other day, Manorama was not sure how to address her. However great her beauty might be, she was an uneducated, uncultured, low-born maid's daughter. Manorama hesitated to address her by the familiar *tumi* before her father; equally, she was revolted by the thought of respectfully calling her *apni* and taking her to her own room.

The woman herself soon solved the problem. She looked at Manorama and said, 'I too am completely wet. I must have a sari.'

'I'll get one.' Saying this, Manorama took her inside the house and told the maid to show her to the bathroom and give her whatever she needed. The young woman scrutinized Manorama repeatedly from head to toe and said, 'Tell her to give me a fresh sari from the wash.'

'So she will,' replied Manorama.

'Is there some soap in the bathroom?' the woman asked the maid.

'Yes,' answered the maid.

'I don't use soap already used by someone else.'

The maid was startled by the stranger's remarks. She replied, 'There's a box of new soap in the bathroom. But didn't you hear it's my mistress's bathroom? What's wrong with using her soap?'

The woman pursed her lips and said, 'No, I can't do that. I'm squeamish. Besides, you can pick up diseases from soap used by just anybody.'

Manorama flushed with anger, but only for a moment. The next instant, her eyes shone with a frank smile. It seemed as if a cloud had lifted from her mind. Smiling, she asked, 'From whom did you pick up all this?'

'From whom?' countered the woman. 'I know all this on my own.'

'Really?' said Manorama. 'Then teach this maid of ours a few of these useful things. She's quite ignorant.' As she said this, she laughed again. The maid also laughed. She said, 'Well, mistress, first wash yourself with soap and get ready, then I'll learn many fine things from you. Who is she, madam?'

If Manorama had not turned away to conceal her own smile, she would have seen traces of fun and subdued ridicule on the face of this unknown, uneducated woman.

MANORAMA WAS NOT ONLY ASHU BABU'S DAUGHTER; SHE WAS his friend, companion and adviser all rolled into one. Thus she often could not maintain the deferential distance that Bengali society enjoins on a child to protect paternal dignity. They often discussed matters that would jar on many fathers' ears, but not on theirs. Ashu Babu's love for his daughter was unbounded; she was one of the reasons why, after his wife's death, he could not think of a second marriage. Whenever the question arose among his friends, he would shelter behind the pretext of his huge bulk and crippling gout, saying ruefully, 'Why ruin yet another girl? I know what anguish Mani's mother carried to heaven with her. That should be enough for Ashu Vaidya.'[1]

Whenever Manorama heard this, she would protest strongly and say, 'Father, I can't bear these words of yours. When people come here and see the Taj Mahal, they think of so many things. But I think only of you and Mother. How can you say that Mother suffered anguish?'

Ashu Babu would answer, 'At that time you were just ten or twelve. Only I know who garlanded whom, Mani[2]—only I know!' His eyes would grow moist as he spoke.

In Agra he mixed freely with everybody, but had become more intimate with Abinash Babu than anyone else. Abinash was a man of patience and self-control. There was a natural tranquillity and contentment in him that easily drew everyone's respect. However, he impressed Ashu Babu for another reason as well. Like him, Abinash too had not married a second time;

and as proof of his devotion to his wife, he had hung portraits of her around his house. Ashu Babu used to tell him, 'Abinash Babu, people praise us for what they think is our self-control, as though we were performing a very difficult task. I wonder how the question comes up at all. People who marry twice do so because they want to. I don't accuse them or belittle them; I only feel I can't do it. I only know that it's not only difficult but impossible for me to accept another woman as my wife in place of Mani's mother. Do other people know this? No, they don't. Isn't it so, Abinash Babu? Ask your own heart whether I'm right or not.'

Abinash would smile and say, 'But as for me, I simply couldn't manage to get anyone. I live by teaching. I have no time and I'm getting old. Who's going to offer me his daughter?'

Ashu Babu would gladly agree. 'Quite so, Abinash Babu, quite so. I too have told everyone that I weigh three and a half maunds.[3] I'm crippled with gout, and no one knows when my heart might fail. Who'll offer me his daughter? But I also know that many men would do so; only the person to accept her is dead—dead, Abinash Babu, Ashu Vaidya is dead!' And the doors, windows, and the very panes and shutters would shake with his uproarious laughter.

Every afternoon, when Ashu Babu went out to take the air, he would get down from his car at Abinash's house and say, 'Mani, I want to stay out of this cold evening breeze. Why don't you pick me up on your way home?'

Manorama would smile and say, 'It isn't cold, Father. On the contrary, there's quite a warm breeze.'

The father would parry, 'That isn't very good for me either. A warm breeze is also harmful for an old person. You go on your own. We two old men will have a chat meanwhile.'

Manorama would smile again and say, 'Chat as much as you like, but let me remind you that neither of you is old.' With this, she would depart.

On days when the gout left Ashu Babu completely immobile, Abinash had to visit him. Ashu Babu would send his car, or a messenger, or else an invitation to tea. Abinash could not possibly avoid such importunities. When they were together, Shibnath would often figure in their conversation, among many other matters. Ashu Babu could not forget the time when Shibnath was invited to his house and everybody drove him out after humiliating him. Shibnath was a scholar, a man of parts; he was full of youth, health and beauty. Were all these nothing? Why then did God bestow such profuse gifts on him? Was it to banish him from human society? He had been a drunkard; so what? Many people get drunk. Ashu Babu himself had indulged in such things when he was young. Had anyone cast him out for that? Being strongly inclined to forgive (though not to entertain) human errors and lapses, Ashu Babu often argued the matter over with himself as he did with Abinash. True, he did not now dare invite Shibnath openly to his house, but his heart still yearned for Shibnath's company. However, he had no satisfactory answer to one question from Abinash: how could Shibnath abandon an ailing wife and take up with another woman?

Ashu Babu would diffidently say, 'I too wonder how a person like Shibnath could do such a thing. But you know, Abinash Babu, perhaps there's some mystery behind it— perhaps. You can't explain everything to everybody, nor should you.'

Abinash would say, 'But he himself admitted before everybody that his wife was innocent.'

Worsted, Ashu Babu would nod and say, 'He did indeed.'

Abinash would go on: 'And what do you have to say about his cheating his deceased friend's wife, of taking over the business as his own?'

This mortified Ashu Babu. He felt as though he himself had committed the offence. Slowly, like a criminal, he would add: 'But you know, Abinash Babu, there might be some mystery all the same. How did the court come to judge in his favour? Did they investigate nothing?'

'Don't talk about the courts of the English, Ashu Babu,' Abinash would say. 'You are yourself a landlord—when did the weak win over the strong here?'

'No, no, that's not true,' Ashu Babu would say. 'That's not true. Of course, I can't say you're wrong either. You know, however . . .'

If Manorama suddenly came in, she would smile and say, 'Everyone knows, Father, that you're convinced Abinash Babu's arguments are not wrong.' Ashu Babu would then fall silent.

It seemed that Manorama was the person most averse to Shibnath. She said little, but the father stood more in fear of his daughter than of anyone else.

For two days after Shibnath and his wife got drenched and sought shelter in his house, Ashu Babu was kept in bed by a severe attack of gout. Abinash too, pressed by other duties, could not keep him company. When he finally came, Ashu Babu at once forgot his gout and, drawing himself up in his armchair, said, 'Dear Abinash Babu, we have had the pleasure of meeting Shibnath's wife! The girl is an exact image of the goddess Lakshmi. I never saw such beauty. I felt God had brought them together for some purpose.'

'Really?'

'Of course. If you sat them down next to each other, you

wouldn't be able to turn your gaze from them. I assure you Abinash Babu, you simply couldn't turn your eyes away.'

'Perhaps not,' said Abinash smiling, 'but once you start praising somebody, Ashu Babu, you don't know where to stop.'

Ashu Babu stared at him for a while and said, 'I admit I have such a fault. I might have crossed the limit in this case too, but that's impossible. Whatever I say about them will remain to the left of the dividing line; it'll never cross over to the right-hand side.'

Abinash might not have believed him entirely, but he let go the banter. 'Then Shibnath wasn't boasting for nothing that day. But how did you get introduced?'

'It was just fate,' said Ashu Babu. 'Shibnath had some business with me. His wife was with him, but he didn't have the courage to bring her in. He kept her waiting outside under a tree. But when fate is contrary, human wiles don't work; even the impossible becomes possible. That's what really happened.' He described in detail that day's rain and storm, adding, 'But our Mani wasn't happy about it. She is of the same age, perhaps a bit older, but Mani said Shibnath had told the truth the other day. The woman is really the child of an uneducated maidservant. Manorama has no doubt that she doesn't belong to our polite society.'

Abinash was curious. 'How could she know that?'

Ashu Babu said, 'The woman asked for a clean sari to change into, and said that she hated using someone else's soap.'

Abinash did not see what there was in her request that lay beyond the norms of polite society.

Ashu Babu agreed with him. He said, 'I don't understand even now what's unbecoming about it. Mani said it was not her words but her manner of speaking: you couldn't tell unless you heard it. Besides, you can't deceive a woman's eyes and ears. Even our maid had no difficulty in figuring out that the woman belonged to her own class and not her employer's. It seems a classic case of someone who has suddenly risen from a very lowly state.'

Abinash remained silent for a while and said, 'That's very sad, but how did you get to know her? Did she speak to you?'

'Of course,' replied Ashu Babu. 'She changed out of her wet clothes and came straight to my room. She wasn't shy at all. How easily she asked about my health, my diet, my treatment and whether I liked this place. Rather, it was Shibnath who was stiff; she showed no signs of diffidence in either words or manner.'

'Perhaps Manorama wasn't present at the time?' asked Abinash.

'No. I can't tell you what a dislike of them she's developed. After they went away I asked, "Mani, why didn't you even come to say goodbye?" She replied, "Father, I can obey everything else you say, but I can neither welcome maids and servants nor bid them goodbye, not even in my own house." What more could I say after that?'

Abinash himself did not know what to say. He only responded mildly: 'It's hard to say, Ashu Babu. But it seems to me Manorama may be right. It isn't desirable that women from our families should be acquainted with women of this sort.' Ashu Babu remained silent.

'That may have been why Shibnath was hesitant,' continued Abinash. 'He knows everything. He was afraid that his wife might say something ugly or untoward.'

Ashu Babu smiled and said, 'Perhaps.'

'It must have been so,' said Abinash.

Ashu Babu did not protest. He only said, 'That girl is a perfect image of Lakshmi.' He gave a little sigh and lay back in his armchair.

Abinash was silent for a few moments. He then asked, 'Are you displeased with what I said?'

Ashu Babu did not sit up. He said slowly from the same half-reclining position: 'It's not a matter of displeasure, Abinash Babu; but I do feel a little hurt. That's why I was so anxious to see you. How sweet were the girl's words—not to speak of her beauty.'

Abinash replied smilingly, 'I've neither seen her beauty nor heard her speak, Ashu Babu.'

'If you ever have the chance,' said Ashu Babu, 'you'll admit our injustice in abandoning them. Whether anybody else feels it or not, I'm certain you will. As they were going away, the girl told me, "You like listening to my husband sing, so why don't you invite him over sometimes? You needn't take any notice of me. I don't wish to come between the two of you."'

Abinash was somewhat surprised and said, 'These are not the words of an uneducated woman, Ashu Babu. It sounds as though whatever we may do to her, she wants her husband to be accepted in polite society.'

'In fact,' said Ashu Babu, 'it appears from her words that she knows everything. Shibnath didn't hide from her the fact that we had driven him away after insulting him. Shibnath is not a very reticent person.'

Abinash agreed. 'That's his nature. But surely he's concealed one thing. Whoever this girl may be, he hasn't really married her.'

Ashu Babu said, 'Shibnath says that the girl is his wife; the girl says that he is her husband.'

'Let them say so,' said Abinash, 'but it can't be true. Akshay Babu will certainly expose the mystery some day.'

'I don't doubt you,' said Ashu Babu. 'Akshay Babu is a formidable man. But isn't there a truth in their mutually declared acceptance? Does the truth lie only in exposing some hidden mystery before the world? Abinash Babu, you are not Akshay. I didn't expect this from you.'

Abinash Babu was abashed, but nonetheless continued, 'We must think of society. At least for its well-being . . .'

Before he could finish, Manorama pushed the door open and came in. She did a namaskar to Abinash Babu and said, 'Father, I'm going out. I suppose you won't be able to?'

'No, my dear; but do go yourself.'

Abinash stood up and said, 'I have an errand. Couldn't you drop me near the market, Manorama?'

'Of course I could—do come.'

Before he left, Abinash said he had to go to Delhi the next day on urgent business. He was unlikely to return before a week.

ABINASH RETURNED FROM DELHI AFTER SOME TEN DAYS. HIS ten-year-old son Jagat handed him a short letter. It bore a single sentence: 'Do come in the evening—Ashu Vaidya.'

Jagat's mother's widowed sister looked through the curtains, her face like a rose in bloom. 'Was Ashu Vaidya sitting with his eyes glued to the road,' she asked, 'to send you this urgent summons the moment you arrived?'

Abinash said, 'Perhaps there's some pressing need.'

'Don't speak of need. Do they want to swallow you up, Mukherjee Mashai?'

Abinash sometimes affectionately addressed his sister-in-law as his 'younger wife', sometimes by her name, Nilima. Smiling, he said, 'Dear Younger-Wife, strangers certainly feel a little tempted when they find heavenly fruits lying uncared for under the tree.'

Nilima smiled. 'Then they need to be told it's not ambrosial fruit, but rotten inside.'

Abinash said, 'You can tell them, but they won't believe you—rather they'll be still more tempted. They won't stop reaching out for it.'

Nilima said, 'That won't be much use, Mukherjee Mashai. I'll put up a strong fence to keep them away.' She suppressed her laughter and vanished behind the curtain.

When Abinash reached Ashu Babu's house it was still daylight. The master of the house welcomed him very warmly and then, feigning anger, said, 'You're very impious—staying away for ten days, leaving your friend behind in an alien place. Meanwhile I'm in ten kinds of states.'

Startled, Abinash said, 'As many as ten? Begin with the first.'

'I'll tell you. First of all, my two legs have not only grown strong, but even started travelling upstairs and downstairs at great speed.'

'How worrying. Tell me the second.'

'The second is that today, in order to celebrate some festival, the Hindustani womenfolk have assembled on the banks of the Yamuna, and a flock of scholars such as Akshay and Haren have just proceeded there with detached indifference.'

'Very good. Tell me the third.'

'Ashu Vaidya is awaiting Abinash with heart aflutter, agog to see him, praying that he should not demur.'

Abinash smiled and said, 'He grants your prayer. Now for the fourth.'

'This is a little more serious,' said Ashu Babu. 'Having returned from England to India, Babaji first went to Varanasi, and has thence arrived in Agra the day before yesterday. His car's giving some trouble; Babaji is engaged in setting it right himself. His work is almost over, and he will turn up in a moment. We want to go together to see the Taj at moonrise today.'

The smiling face of Abinash turned serious. He asked, 'Who is this Babaji, Ashu Babu? Is he the person about whom you were going to speak one day, but suddenly stopped?'

'Yes,' Ashu Babu replied, 'but today I don't mind telling you. Ajitkumar is my would-be son-in-law, my Mani's future husband. Their love is a wonder of the world. The young man is a gem.'

Abinash remained silent. Ashu Babu continued, 'We don't

belong to the Brahmo sect. We are Hindus. All our rites are performed according to Hindu custom. They were supposed to get married at the proper time, that is four years ago. The marriage should have taken place then, but it didn't. The way they came to know each other is also strange. It won't be an exaggeration to call it predestined—but let that be.'

Abinash still remained silent. Ashu Babu went on: 'The turmeric ceremony[1] of Mani's marriage was over when my youngest uncle arrived from Varanasi by the night train. After the death of my father, he was the head of our family. He had no children—he had been staying in Varanasi with his wife for a long time. Unshakeably given to astrology, he declared that this marriage could not be solemnized just then. He and other experts had calculated that if it were, Mani would be widowed in three years and three months' time.

'There was a furore. This would overturn all the arrangements. But I knew my uncle well: I realized he would not budge. Ajit too is from a very rich family; he had no living relatives besides a widowed aunt. She was outraged. In sorrow and indignation, Ajit left for England on the plea of studying engineering. Everyone thought the marriage had been scuttled for good.'

Deeply interested now, Abinash said, 'Then?'

Ashu Babu continued, 'We were all disappointed, but Mani herself was not. She told me, "Father, what's so dreadful about this that you've given up eating and sleeping? Is three years such a long time?"

'I knew how badly hurt she was. I said, "My dear, may your words come true; but in such matters even three days' delay is dangerous, not to speak of three years."

'She smiled and said, "You have nothing to worry about, Father. I know him well."

'Ajit had always been a pious, ascetic sort of person, with unwavering faith in God. Before he went away he left a small note for Mani. During these four years he didn't write a second letter. But even if he didn't, my daughter knew everything in her heart. Ever since, she has led the life of a *brahmacharini*[2] without lapsing for a day. Yet you can't make that out when you see her, Abinash Babu.'

In a reverential voice, Abinash said, 'It's truly impossible to tell. My blessings for their happiness.'

Ashu Babu bowed his head, as if on behalf of his daughter, and said, 'A Brahman's blessings shall not be in vain. The first thing Ajit has done is to go to my uncle. He has given his consent. Otherwise he probably wouldn't have come here.'

They fell silent for a while; then Ashu Babu went on, 'When I didn't hear of Ajit for two years after he left for England, it's not that I didn't look around for another groom. But one day Mani came to know of it and stopped me, saying, "Don't make such attempts, Father. You may not have given me away publicly in marriage, but you have already done so at heart." I said, "Such things happen in many cases, my dear." My daughter's eyes seemed to fill with tears. She said, "No, they don't. Perhaps there's a little talk of a possible match, but nothing more. No, Father—pray that I may be able to bear whatever God has designed for me. Don't order me to do anything else." Tears began rolling down both our eyes. Wiping my tears, I said to her, "I have committed a mistake, my little mother. Pardon this foolish old son of yours."'

His voice choked suddenly with the rush of old memories. Abinash himself couldn't say anything for a long time. Then he softly said, 'Ashu Babu, we make so many mistakes in life, and entertain so many wrong ideas!'

Ashu Babu did not quite catch the point. He asked, 'About what?'

'So many of us think that once women are educated they start behaving like memsahibs, and that the sweet, ancient customs of the Hindus find no place in their hearts. What a mistaken notion!'

Ashu Babu shook his head and said, 'Of course we make all kinds of mistakes; but Abinash Babu, the fact is that neither education nor ignorance matters. The main thing is to receive what is necessary. Everything rests on this. Otherwise you shift one man's offences on to another's shoulders, and then you have problems. Hello, Ajit! Where's Mani?'

A handsome, robust youth of about thirty entered the room. His clothes were stained with grease. He said, 'Mani was helping me all this time. Her clothes too are dirty, so she's gone to change. The car's been repaired, and I've told the chauffeur to bring it round to the front.'

Ashu Babu said, 'Ajit, this is my close friend Abinash Mukherjee. He's a professor in the local college. He's a Brahman: touch his feet.'

The young man bowed to the ground and touched Abinash's feet. Then he rose and said to Ashu Babu, 'It won't take Manorama more than five minutes to come, so please get ready quickly. If we're late, we won't have time to see everything. They say one can't see enough of the Taj Mahal.'

Ashu Babu said, 'It really is endlessly attractive, my boy. But we're ready. It's you that's late: you haven't changed yet.'

After a quick glance at his clothes, the young man said, 'I don't need to change; this will do.'

'With these stains?'

The youth said, 'It doesn't matter. This is our profession. Stained clothes are no shame for us.'

Ashu Babu was very happy to hear this. Abinash too was charmed with the youth's modest simplicity.

Manorama appeared. Looking at her now, Abinash was startled. He had not seen her for a few days, during which time there had been an unexpected, happy change in her life. After what he had heard from her father, he had expected to find something ineffable in Manorama's face, something that he had never seen in his life. But nothing of that sort happened. Her clothes were utterly simple. Her inner delight did not show itself anywhere; no calm radiance born of deep content manifested itself on her face. Rather, a veil of fatigue dimmed her eyes. Abinash felt that either Ashu Babu had misunderstood his daughter out of paternal affection, or else what had once been true had now grown false.

Soon they all left in the large car. Along the river bank, the crowds of women in search of piety and men in search of beauty had thinned. Even so, throughout the long and pleasant road they saw men and women in all kinds of colourful attire, lit up by the setting sun. As they reached the gates of the Taj Mahal, the short late-autumn day was about to end.

Akshay's group had seen everything to be seen on the bank of the Yamuna, and reassembled already without bothering to look around. They had seen the Taj so many times as to have got bored with it. So instead of climbing up to it, they sat in a corner of the garden below. Seeing Ashu Babu and the others arrive, they welcomed them clamorously. Stretching out his gout-ridden bulk on the grass and heaving a long sigh of relaxation, Ashu Babu said, 'Ah! What a relief. Let those who wish take as much pleasure as they like from seeing

Mumtaz's grave. Ashu Vaidya salutes Her Highness from here. He can't do more.'

Manorama said with disappointment, 'That can't be, Father. We can't leave you alone.'

'Don't worry, little mother,' said Ashu Babu, 'no one will steal this old father of yours.'

Abinash said, 'No, there's no fear of such a thing. How can someone lift him without chains and pulleys?'

Manorama quipped, 'Don't make digs at my father; your evil eye has made him a lot thinner since he came here.'

Abinash said, 'If that's so, we must admit we're to blame: he might have been no less a spectacle than the Taj.'

Everyone burst into laughter. Manorama said, 'No, Father, you must come with us. Half the beauty of the place will be lost if we don't see it through your eyes. Whatever somebody else might tell us, nobody really knows more about these things than you.'

Only Abinash knew what this meant. He was himself about to make the request, when everyone's eyes turned to an unexpected sight. Coming round the eastern end of the Taj, Shibnath and his wife appeared before them. Shibnath tried to take a different route, pretending not to have noticed them, but his wife drew his attention and happily exclaimed, 'Look, Ashu Babu and his daughter have come too!'

Ashu Babu called out to them. 'When did you come, Shibnath Babu? Do come here.'

Shibnath and his wife moved over to them. Ashu Babu introduced Shibnath's wife to the company. Then turning to her he said, 'I still don't know your name.

The young woman said, 'My name is Kamal. But don't address me formally as apni, Ashu Babu.'

Ashu Babu said, 'Nor should I, Kamal. These are my friends; your husband knows them too. Please sit down.'

Kamal pointed to Ajit and said, 'But you haven't introduced him.'

Ashu Babu said, 'Of course I will. He's very close to me. His name is Ajitkumar Ray. He returned from England a few days ago and has come to see us. Kamal, is this the first time you've seen the Taj?'

The girl nodded and said, 'Yes.'

'Then you're very lucky. Ajit is luckier still because he hasn't yet seen this wonderful object at all. He'll see it now. But it's getting dark and we mustn't delay any longer, Ajit.'

Manorama said, 'But Father, you're the one who's causing the delay. Please get up.'

'It's not easy for me to get up, my dear. It needs some preparation.'

'Then do make your preparations, Father.'

'Yes, yes. Well Kamal, how did you like it?'

Kamal said, 'It's really something to wonder at.'

Manorama did not speak to her. Her attitude did not even show that she knew her. She urged her father on, saying, 'It's getting dark, Father. Now get up.'

'Yes, yes,' said Ashu Babu, without making the slightest effort to rise.

Kamal smiled a little and looked at Manorama. She said, 'He's not well, and it would be a strain for him to climb up and down. Why don't you go around while we sit here talking?'

Manorama did not respond to this suggestion, but only went on at her father stubbornly: 'That won't do, Father. You must get up now.'

But hardly anyone was inclined to get up. In comparison to the living beauty of this unknown woman, the inarticulate marble building seemed to have faded on the instant.

Abinash awoke from his trance. He said, 'He must go. Manorama is convinced that unless seen through the eyes of her father, half the charm of the Taj will be lost.'

Kamal raised two innocent eyes and asked, 'Why?' She turned to Ashu Babu. 'Are you an expert on the subject and know all about it?'

Manorama was surprised. This did not sound like the words of an illiterate maid's daughter.

Ashu Babu was delighted and said, 'I know nothing at all. I'm not at all an expert—I don't know the rudiments of aesthetics, nor do I view it from that angle, Kamal. I think of the emperor Shah Jahan. I think how his limitless grief is bound up with every block of stone. I see his unwavering love for his wife, made immortal in this poetry of stone.'

Kamal looked at him and said unaffectedly, 'I've heard that he had many other begums. The emperor loved Mumtaz as he loved so many others—perhaps a little more, but you can't call it unwavering, Ashu Babu. He didn't have that kind of devotion.'

Everybody was startled by this alarming, unorthodox remark. Neither Ashu Babu nor the others could find an immediate reply. Kamal said, 'The emperor was contemplative and poetical. With his power, wealth and patience, he built this immense and beautiful object. Mumtaz was only the accidental cause. He could have built such an edifice around any other occasion. It might have been inspired by religion, or even built to celebrate a conquest costing millions of lives. This is not the gift of single-minded devotion, only of the emperor's very own realm of delight. Let that be enough for us.'

Ashu Babu seemed hurt. He repeatedly shook his head, saying, 'No, that's not enough, Kamal, not enough. If what you say were true, if the emperor didn't have a single-minded devotion, then this massive memorial has no meaning. Whatever great beauty he may have created, it would find no place in people's hearts.'

'If there were no place, it would show the people's folly. I don't say that devotion has no value, but it doesn't deserve the value people have attached to it through the ages. It's neither healthy nor pleasing to hold with a kind of fixed, inert numbness of the mind that your feelings towards someone you once loved can never change.'

Manorama's wonder knew no bounds. It was hard to dismiss this woman as a maid's daughter, but she was upset that a young woman like her had made these remarks before so many men. She had not spoken all this time; but she could restrain herself no longer. In a stern but subdued voice she said, 'I realize this attitude may seem very natural, to you at any rate, but others may find it neither pleasing nor decent.'

Ashu Babu was extremely distressed and said, 'No, no, my dear!'

Kamal was not offended. She smiled a little and said, 'People can't bear it when old, deep-rooted customs are suddenly attacked. You have rightly said that this attitude comes naturally to me. My body and mind are full of youth, there's life in my mind. The day I find it can't change even when necessary, I'll know it's finished—it's dead.'

As she raised her face on saying this, it seemed to her that Ajit's eyes were flashing fire. Who knows whether Manorama noticed this, but in the middle of the conversation she burst out, 'Father, the day's about to end. Let me take Ajit Babu around as much as I can.'

Ajit came to his senses and said, 'Yes, let's go.'

Ashu Babu was pleased and said, 'Good idea. We'll be sitting here. But come back quickly. Perhaps we'll come again a little earlier tomorrow.'

6

WHEN AJIT AND MANORAMA CAME BACK AFTER SEEING THE TAJ, the sun had set but there was still some light. Everyone sat in a close circle, and their arguments grew more and more heated. They had forgotten about the Taj, about returning home, even about Ajit and Manorama. Akshay was fuming silently: he looked as though he had shouted himself hoarse and was recouping. Ashu Babu was listening intently, stretching his lower body outside the circle and devising a way of resting his torso on his arms. Abinash was leaning forward and looking sharply at Kamal. Clearly the question-and-answer session was now confined to these two.

They looked up at the newly arrived pair. Some nodded briefly, others did not even find time for that. Kamal and Shibnath too looked up towards them. Strangely enough, while the former's eyes were burning like flame, the latter's looked tired and dim. He seemed neither to see nor to hear anything. Although in company, Shibnath seemed to have wandered far away.

Ashu Babu only said, 'Do sit down.' But he paid no heed where they sat or whether they sat at all.

Abinash seemed to be trying to pick up the broken thread of Akshay's argument. He said, 'Let's forget about the emperor Shah Jahan for the moment. I admit there are good reasons to ponder about him—it's a complex matter. But when the issue is as clear as this white marble, as limpid as water, as simple and transparent as sunlight, like the life of our own Ashu Babu—well, we all know about it. He wanted for nothing; his friends and relatives spared no effort—yet he couldn't conceive of bringing somebody in to supplant his dead wife. It was beyond his imagination. Just think how great an ideal this is for the love of man and woman! How high and noble!'

Kamal was about to say something; but she turned round on feeling a soft touch at her back. 'Let's drop this discussion now,' said Shibnath.

'Why?' asked Kamal.

By way of answer, Shibnath only said, 'Oh, just like that,' and fell silent. Nobody paid much attention to his words; no one could tell what remained unsaid behind his listless, unmindful eyes, and no one cared to find out.

Kamal said, 'Oh—just like that? Perhaps you're in a hurry to go home? But you're carrying your home with you.' And she smiled.

Ashu Babu was embarrassed. Harendra and Akshay smiled wryly, and Manorama turned her face away; but Shibnath, to whom the words were addressed, showed no change on his marvellously attractive face. He seemed to be made of stone, incapable of either seeing or hearing.

Abinash was growing impatient. He said, 'Answer my question.'

Kamal replied, 'But my husband has told me not to. Should I disobey him?' She began to laugh. Abinash too could not but laugh. He said, 'It wouldn't be an offence in this case. So many of us are asking you. Please reply.'

Kamal said, 'I've seen Ashu Babu on two occasions only, but I've already come to love him in my heart.' She pointed at Shibnath and went on, 'Now I can see why he told me not to speak.'

Ashu Babu himself interrupted and said, 'But you have no

reason to hesitate on my score. This old man is harmless, Kamal. You have judged him quite well within a short time. Soon you will realize that there's no greater mistake on earth than to be afraid of him. Please speak frankly: I really enjoy listening to such things.'

Kamal said, 'But that's precisely why he asked me not to speak. And that's why, in reply to Abinash Babu's question, I hesitate to say that in matters of love between man and woman, I hold his principle to be neither great nor ideal.'

Akshay spoke. There was a sting in his words. 'Quite possibly the two of you don't believe in such principles. But could you tell us what you believe in?'

Kamal looked at him, but did not really seem to be answering him. She said, 'Ashu Babu had once loved his wife, but she is no more. There's nothing to give her, nor anything to get from her. She can neither be pleased nor hurt. She isn't there any longer. The object of love has disappeared; all that remains is the memory that he had once loved her. The person is no more, only the remembrance is left. I don't understand what great ideal can lie in nurturing that remembrance day and night, in holding the past as a fixed truth outvying the present.'

Ashu Babu was again hurt by Kamal's words. He replied, 'But Kamal, this memory is the only resource left to the widows of our country. The husband passes away, but his memory upholds the sanctity of widowhood. Don't you accept this?'

'No,' said Kamal. 'A grand name doesn't of itself make a thing great. You should rather say that this is the injunction laid down for widows in this country. People have been cheating them by giving falsehood the glory of a truth. That I won't deny.'

Abinash said, 'Even if that be so, if people have been cheating them, shouldn't we grant the honour of sanctity to the *brahmacharya*[1] of widows—well, no, let's not talk of brahmacharya—but at least to the ascetic lifestyle that accompanies it till death?'

Kamal smiled and said, 'Abinash Babu, this too shows your fascination with grand words. The word "self-control", dignified over a long period of time, has been so puffed up that it can be used indiscriminately. As soon as it is uttered, people bow their heads in reverence. They're afraid to admit that it's nothing more than a hollow phrase; but I'm not afraid. I'm not that kind of person. I don't accept something just because many people have repeated it for a long time. I can't accept a self-sustaining view of sanctity, holding that widows spend their days nursing their husbands' memories in their bosoms, unless it's proved true to me.'

Abinash looked dazed and was speechless for a while, but eventually spoke: 'What are you saying?'

Akshay joined in. 'Perhaps you don't even accept that two and two make four, unless it is proved?'

Kamal was not offended, nor did she reply. She merely smiled.

Another person was not offended either, and that was Ashu Babu, although he had been most affected by what Kamal had said.

Akshay spoke again. 'These ugly notions of yours don't agree with those of respectable society. They are not current here.'

Smiling as before, Kamal replied, 'Yes, they certainly aren't current in respectable society. I know that.'

Everyone was silent for some time. Ashu Babu gently said, 'Kamal, let me ask you one thing more. I'm not talking about purity and impurity. I'm thinking of those who, because of their nature, can't do otherwise—myself, for example. I can't even imagine putting someone else in place of Mani's dead mother.'

Kamal said, 'The fact is that you've grown old, Ashu Babu.'

Ashu Babu said, 'I admit I'm old today, but I wasn't when she died. I couldn't think of it even then.'

Kamal said, 'You were old even then—not in body but in mind. Some people are born with aged minds. Under the admonitions of their aged minds, their feeble, distorted youth bows its head in shame forever. The aged mind gleefully says, "Ah! This is good! No worries! No excitement! This is bliss, this is the ultimate truth of human life!" What a glut of superlatives! What cheers and applause for the aged mind! Its ears are filled with the drumbeats of fame; it doesn't realize that this isn't the sound of victory. It's a requiem for the life of pleasure that it has sacrificed.'

Everybody felt the need for a strong reply: their ears smarted at the unabashed paean to frenzied youth from a woman's lips. Yet no one could find anything to say in reply.

Then Ashu Babu softly said, 'What do you mean by an aged mind, Kamal? Let's see whether it applies to me.'

Kamal replied, 'By an aged mind I mean a mind that cannot look ahead, that is tired and palsied, that gives up all hope of the future and lives on its past as if it has nothing to do, nothing to demand. The present to it is extinct, unnecessary, absent, meaningless; the past is everything. The past is its delight, its grief—its capital to invest. It wants to bank it and live all its life on the interest. Now compare this with your own state, Ashu Babu.'

Ashu Babu smiled and said, 'I'll do that sometime.'

Ajit had sat silent through this long argument, only gazing steadily at Kamal. Suddenly something happened to him. He could not control himself any more, and blurted out, 'I want to ask you something. Look, *Mrs* . . .'

Kamal looked straight at him and said, 'Why *Mrs*? Why not simply "Kamal"?'

Ajit blushed. 'No, no, how can that be? It seems somewhat . . .'

'No "somewhat" about it,' said Kamal. 'My parents gave me the name for people to call me by. I don't take offence if they do.' She suddenly looked at Manorama and said, 'You're Manorama. If I called you by that name, would you be offended?'

Manorama nodded and said, 'Yes, I would.'

Nobody had expected this reply from her. Ashu Babu wilted with embarrassment.

Only Kamal was not embarrassed. She said, 'A name is nothing in itself. It's only a word by which one person addresses another. But many people can't break old habits; they want to embellish this word in various ways. Don't you see how kings add a number of meaningless words before and after their names before they let people utter them? Otherwise it hurts their dignity.'

She suddenly laughed and, pointing to Shibnath, said, 'He, for example, can never say "Kamal". He calls me "Shibani".[2] Ajit Babu, I'd rather you called me "Shibani" than "*Mrs* Shibnath". It's a short word, and everyone will understand it. At least I will.'

Yet for some reason Ajit couldn't speak even after such clear orders. His question remained suspended on his lips.

The light had faded by now; hazy moonlight was spreading across the misty late-autumn sky. Drawing her father's attention to it, Manorama said, 'Father, it's getting chilly. Please get up now.'

'Yes, my dear,' said Ashu Babu.

Abinash said, 'Shibani's a pretty name. Shibnath is a man of talent: he has chosen a lovely name and matched it marvellously with his own.'

Ashu Babu was elated. He said, 'It's not Shibnath that has done this, my dear Abinash—it's He up there.' He looked at the sky and said, 'That ancient matchmaker seems to have forgone food and sleep to match them in all respects. May they live long.'

Akshay suddenly sat up, shook his head two or three times, dilated his small eyes to their utmost extent and said, 'Well, can I ask you a question?'

'What is it?' asked Kamal.

Akshay said, 'I'm asking you this as you have no inhibitions. Though the name Shibani is a fine one, are you really married to Shibnath Babu?' Ashu Babu's face darkened. He said, 'What's all this, Akshay Babu?'

Abinash said, 'Have you gone mad?'

Harendra said, '*Brute!*'

Akshay said, 'You know I don't suffer from false delicacy.'

'Neither false nor true,' said Harendra. 'But we do.'

Kamal, however, began to laugh as if it were all a great joke. 'Why are you losing your temper, Harendra Babu?' she said. 'Akshay Babu, here's my answer. It's not that there was no marriage ceremony. We went through something like a rite. Those who came to see it laughed and said it was no marriage at all, only a cheat. When I asked my husband he said we'd been married in the Shaivite manner. I said that was better in a way. Why should I worry if I were married to Shiva in the Shaivite way?'

Abinash was sorry to hear this. He said, 'But you see, the Shaivite rite of marriage is no longer accepted in our society.

If he were ever to deny the marriage, you'd have nothing to prove that it took place, Kamal.'

Kamal looked at Shibnath and said, 'Well—would you do such a thing?'

Shibnath made no reply. He sat looking grave and thoughtful. Kamal jokingly beat her head and said, 'A curse on my luck! If he were to deny it, would I ever go to seek justice from others? Shouldn't I first find some rope to hang myself with?'

'You might,' said Abinash. 'But isn't it a sin to take your own life?'

'Nonsense,' said Kamal. 'But it won't happen that way. Even my Creator won't imagine that I could ever commit suicide.'

'Spoken like a true human being, Kamal!' applauded Ashu Babu.

Kamal addressed him plaintively: 'See how wrong Abinash Babu is.' Then, pointing to Shibnath, 'Could it be that he'd deny it and I'd force him by the neck to admit it? That the truth would sink out of sight and I would tie him down by a ritual I don't myself believe in? Would I do such a thing?' Her eyes seemed to blaze as she spoke these words.

Ashu Babu gently said, 'Shibani, we all admit that truth is a great thing in life, but ceremony isn't false either.'

Kamal retorted, 'I don't say it's false. But in the same way, life is true and so is the body. Does the body remain true when there is no more life?'

Manorama pulled her father by the arm and said, 'Father, it'll turn chilly. You must get up now.'

'Yes, my dear.'

Shibnath stood up suddenly and said, 'It's getting late, Shibani. Let's go.'

Kamal rose immediately. She did a namaskar and said, 'It appears that we met only to argue. Please don't be offended.'

Shibnath smiled at last and said, 'You only argued, Shibani. You didn't learn anything.'

Kamal replied in a surprised tone, 'No. But I don't recall that there was anything to learn.'

'You wouldn't,' said Shibnath. 'It remained hidden. If you can, try learning to have some respect for Ashu Babu's mind, which you find so old and decrepit. There's nothing greater that you could learn.'

'What are you saying?' said Kamal, amazed.

Shibnath did not reply. He bid everybody goodbye and said, 'Come, let's go.'

Ashu Babu heaved a sigh and only said, 'Strange!'

7

IT WAS INDEED STRANGE. WAS THERE ANY OTHER WAY OF PUTTING the matter? In fact, their sudden exit was like drawing the curtain halfway through a fascinating play—leaving who knows what marvels hidden behind the screen. This was the very thought that rocked every mind. They all felt that they had come only for this. The moon rose in the sky. The white-marbled Taj looked like a phantom palace in the dewy moonlight of late autumn. But no one looked at it.

Manorama said, 'If you don't get up now you really will catch cold, Father.'

Abinash said, 'It's getting cold. Let's go.'

Everybody stood up. Ashu Babu's large car was waiting at the gate, but the driver of Akshay and Harendra's tonga was nowhere in sight. Perhaps he had left with another passenger, lured by a higher fare. So everybody squeezed into the car.

They were silent for some time. Abinash was the first to speak. He said, 'Shibnath lied to us. Kamal can't be the daughter of a maidservant. Impossible!' He looked at Manorama as he spoke.

The same doubt had repeatedly arisen in Manorama's mind, but she remained silent. Akshay said, 'Why should he lie? What he said doesn't show his own wife in a good light, Abinash Babu!'

'That's what I can't understand,' said Abinash.

Akshay said, 'You're all surprised, but I'm not. She was simply echoing what Shibnath says. What she says is full of *bravado* but devoid of matter. I can tell the false from the true. It's not so easy to deceive me.'

'Goodness!' exclaimed Harendra. 'Deceive you! Challenge your *monopoly?*'

Throwing him an angry glance Akshay retorted, 'I can confidently say there isn't a quarter paisa's worth of respectable *culture* in her. Such words from a woman are not just *immoral* but obscene.'

Abinash protested. 'Maybe what she said doesn't sound decorous coming from a woman, but one can't call it obscene, Akshay.'

Akshay said stiffly, 'It's all the same, Abinash Babu. Didn't you see that marriage is a matter of jest to her? When everybody told her it was no marriage but a farce, she only smiled and said, "Is that so?" Didn't you *notice* her *absolute indifference?* Is it either fitting or possible for a well-bred woman?'

What Akshay said was true, so everybody remained silent. Ashu Babu had not said anything till now. He had heard everything, but was sunk in his own thoughts. The sudden silence broke his meditation. He said slowly, 'Perhaps it's not marriage but the form of marriage in which Kamal has so little faith. Any ritual will do for her. She told her husband, "They say that our marriage is a cheat." Her husband replied, "We were married in the Shaivite way." Kamal was delighted and said, "What can be better than to marry Shiva in the Shaivite way?" How sweet her words seemed to me, Abinash Babu!'

Abinash's mind was also tuned to the same pitch. He said, 'And think of her gazing at Shibnath's face and asking smilingly, "Well, my dear, would you ever do such a thing? Are you going to deceive me?" So many words passed after that, Ashu Babu, but that strain is still ringing in my ears.'

Ashu Babu smiled and nodded by way of reply. Abinash then said, 'And what about the name Shibani? Is it any less sweet, Ashu Babu?'

Akshay could not bear all this any more. He said, 'You really amaze me, Ashu Babu. Everything about them is honey-sweet. As soon as you added a "ni" to the name of Shibnath, honey started dripping from it; wasn't that so?'

Harendra said, 'It's not a question of adding "ni", Akshay Babu. If I called your wife "Akshayni", would that ooze honey-drops?'

Everyone broke out in laughter at this. Even Manorama looked out of the car to hide her smile.

Akshay was furious. He roared, 'Haren Babu, *don't you go too far*. Let me tell you straight that I consider even the hint of a comparison between a lady and a woman like this highly insulting.'

Harendra remained silent. It was not in his nature to bandy words, nor his practice to prove himself by labouring his point. He would say something abruptly and then sink into so deep a silence that even a thousand jibes would not make him talk. That is exactly what happened now. Akshay diverted his attack from Shibani to Harendra for the rest of the journey. When the car pulled up at Ashu Babu's gate, he was still deploring in great dudgeon how Harendra had made an ugly, uncivil sneer at a lady, and how Shibnath's wife-by-Shaivite-rite had no whiff of culture in her speech or conduct, which showed her despicable lack of education and refinement.

Abinash and the others got down. The car went on to deliver Harendra and Akshay to their homes. 'I'm worried that the two of them might start fighting on the way,' said Ashu Babu.

'You needn't be afraid,' said Abinash. 'This is an everyday affair. It doesn't affect their friendship.'

As they sat sipping tea in his room, Ashu Babu said in a subdued voice, 'Akshay Babu's nature seems to be very hard.' He was incapable of uttering a harsher word. Then suddenly turning to his daughter, he asked, 'Well, my dear, have you changed your earlier notion about Kamal?'

'What notion are you talking of, Father?'

'I mean . . . I mean . . .'

'But why should you bother about my notions, Father?'

He did not say anything more. He knew that Manorama was very averse to this woman. This hurt him, but to discuss the matter further would be both unpleasant and futile.

Suddenly Abinash spoke out. 'There's one thing that perhaps escaped you: I mean Shibnath's last words. If all that Kamal said was an echo of someone else's words, Shibnath wouldn't have had to tell her to learn to respect you, Ashu Babu.' He himself looked at Ashu Babu reverentially and went on, 'Really, how many people around us are worthy of respect? I can pardon many of his misdeeds only for this—that from such a brief encounter, Shibnath could grasp such a great truth.'

Ashu Babu grew restive as he heard this. His huge bulk seemed to shrink with embarrassment. Manorama, her eyes brimming with gratitude, looked up at the speaker and said, 'That's the real difference between him and his wife, Abinash Babu. Now I know that the other day, under pretence of asking for a sari and a piece of soap, she was actually mocking me. I couldn't see through her playacting. But Father, all her wiles and mockery amount to nothing if she hasn't seen how superior you are to everybody else.'

Ashu Babu was upset. 'What nonsense you talk,' he said.

'There's no hyperbole in this, Ashu Babu,' said Abinash. This is what Shibnath was trying to tell his wife as they left. He didn't say much today, but from that one remark of his, I can tell that there's a lot of difference between the two.'

Ashu Babu said, 'If there is, it's Shibnath's fault, not Kamal's.'

Manorama blurted out, 'I don't know with what eyes you look at her. But can one ever forgive someone who shows so little respect for a man like you?'

Looking at his daughter's face, Ashu Babu replied, 'There wasn't the slightest hint of disrespect to me in her conduct.'

'But there wasn't any respect either.'

Ashu Babu said, 'That was not to be expected—on the contrary, if she had shown anything of that sort, she would have been acting a lie. What seems to you my exceptional strength is to her merely a lack of strength. She told me that you can love a weak man by force of affection. But by not forcing herself to accord me a value she didn't see in me, she neither belittled me nor demeaned herself. She acted rightly: there's nothing to feel hurt about, Mani.'

Ajit had seemed inattentive till now, but he looked up at this. He knew nothing, nor had he had the opportunity to know anything. To him everything was vague, and Ashu Babu's words did not make matters any clearer. Nonetheless, he seemed to wake up within.

Manorama kept silent but Abinash Babu spoke excitedly. 'Are you suggesting that self-sacrifice has no value?'

Ashu Babu smilingly said, 'That's not a fitting question from a professor. Be that as it may, it has no value for her.'

'Then self-restraint has no value either?'

'No, not to her. Meaningless self-restraint is fruitless self-denial. And to air one's superiority on that account is to deceive not only oneself but the whole world. As I listened to Kamal it seemed to me that this is what she wanted to say.' He remained silent for a while and again said, 'I wonder where she got the idea from. But when you suddenly hear it, it surprises you.'

'Surprises you!' said Manorama. 'Doesn't it make you burn from top to toe? Father, won't you ever assert yourself? Will you always agree with what anyone might say?'

Ashu Babu said, 'No, my dear, I haven't agreed. But if you try to pass judgement with malice and hostility, you deceive not only your opponent but yourself. Kamal didn't say quite what we're putting into her mouth. Perhaps what she wanted to say is that the premises we have imbibed as the truth through our blood, from long custom, only make up one side of the question. There is another side as well. Does it help if we shut our eyes and shake our heads, Mani?'

Manorama said, 'Father, hasn't there been anyone in India all this time to show us the other side of the question?'

Her father smiled a little. He said, 'These are angry words, my dear. You know that neither in our country nor anywhere else have our forebears provided the answer to the final question: in that case, creation would have come to a halt. There would be no point in its continuance.'

He noticed that Ajit was looking at him fixedly. He said, 'I suppose you're wondering what this is all about. Isn't that so?'

As Ajit nodded, Ashu Babu recounted the whole sequence of events and said, 'Akshay has lit such a holy fire that no one can see anything by its light——their eyes simply smart from the smoke. But the funny thing is that though our charge was against Shibnath, we have punished Kamal. He was a professor here. He lost his job for drinking, abandoned his sick wife and brought Kamal to his home. He declared that they had married according to Shaivite rites; Akshay Babu made enquiries and found it was all a fraud. Shibnath was asked if the bride came from a respectable family; he replied that she was the daughter of a maidservant in their house. We asked whether she was educated; Shibnath answered that he had married her not for her education but for her looks. Just hear that! I don't find any fault with her, Ajit, and yet we have cast her out from our company. Our repugnance has landed chiefly upon her head. This is how society dispenses justice!'

Manorama said, 'Do you mean to draw her into our society, Father?'

Ashu Babu said, 'What would it avail if I did? There are men like Akshay Babu in our society; they are the stronger party.'

The daughter said, 'Had you been alone you would have called her back, wouldn't you?'

The father evaded the question by replying, 'Does everyone come when you call?'

Ajit said, 'What amazes me is that it's with you that she disagrees most, yet it's your affection she has most attracted.'

Abinash said, 'There's a reason for it, Ajit Babu. We know nothing about Kamal, we only know her revolutionary opinions and her worse traits. Hence her words scare and anger us. We think we are about to lose everything.' Then pointing at Ashu Babu, he continued: 'No shadow of suspicion, no touch of fear can fall on his sinless body and unstained mind. It doesn't matter to Mahadeva[1] whether he drinks venom or nectar; it'll remain in his throat and not reach his stomach. Whether it's gods or demons who surround him, he remains indifferent and undisturbed—he's happy as long as he's not crippled with gout. But we . . .'

Before he could finish, Ashu Babu raised both his hands and stopped him. 'Not a word more, Abinash Babu, I beg of you. I spent a whole decade in Britain. I don't even remember everything that I did there. If Akshay comes to learn of it, I'm lost. He'll fish out even the most arcane details, and then what shall I do?'

An amazed Abinash said, 'Did you really go abroad?'

Ashu Babu said, 'Yes, I've committed that sin.'

Manorama said, 'All of Father's *education* since his childhood was in Europe. He's a barrister, and he holds a doctorate.'

'Indeed!' Abinash said.

Ashu Babu continued in the same vein: 'Don't be afraid, Professor, I've forgotten everything I learnt. I've long been a vagrant, wandering with my daughter from place to place, setting up school here and there. As you were saying, my mind has been washed absolutely blank and innocent: there's no mark left anywhere. But however that may be, don't let Akshay Babu know of this.'

Abinash smiled and said, 'Are you so afraid of Akshay?'

Ashu Babu admitted to it at once. 'Yes. It's hard enough to live with my gout; now if his curiosity is roused, I'll be quite dead.'

Manorama laughed at this even though she was angry. 'Now, Father, this is very wrong of you.'

Her father said, 'I don't care. Everybody has the right to self-defence.'

Everyone began to laugh. Manorama asked, 'Well, Father, don't you think people like Akshay Babu are needed in human society?'

Ashu Babu said, 'That word "need" is the source of all the trouble in the world. Let's solve that problem first, then perhaps we can find a proper answer to your question. But that will never happen; the debate has dragged on through all time to no end.'

Manorama was vexed and said, 'You dodge every answer in that way, Father. You don't say anything clearly. I think this is very wrong of you.'

Ashu Babu smilingly said, 'Your father isn't wise enough to give clear answers—that's your misfortune. What's the use of being angry with me?'

Ajit stood up abruptly, saying, 'I have a headache. I'd like to go out for a walk.'

A flustered Ashu Babu said, 'One can't blame your head, but what about the cold and darkness?'

An expanse of soft moonlight had spread over the carpet through an open window. Ajit pointed to this and said, 'It's a little cold perhaps, but not so dark. Let me go out for a while.'

'But don't go on foot.'

'No, I'll take the car.'

'Put up the hood and see that you don't catch cold.'

Ajit agreed.

Ashu Babu said, 'You might also take Abinash Babu home. But don't be too late.'

'All right,' said Ajit, and went out with Abinash Babu.

A smile flickered on Ashu Babu's lips. He said, 'The boy has not yet got over the habit of driving around in a car. He's gone out even in this cold.'

8

ABOUT A FORTNIGHT LATER, AS EVENING WAS CLOSING IN, AJIT
left Ashu Babu and Manorama at Abinash Babu's house and
drove on alone. This had become his usual practice. He drove
along the road which led from the north of the town,
passed the college and then turned westward. On a lonely
stretch, he suddenly heard his name called out in a woman's
shrill voice. He was startled, and stopped his car to find that
it was Kamal, Shibnath's wife.

She was waving and calling to him from a shabby garden
outside an old, dilapidated two-storeyed house fronting the
road. As the car stopped, she drew near and said, 'I saw you
the other day too. I called so many times but you didn't hear
me. Why do you drive so fast? It stops one's breath to watch
you. Aren't you afraid?'

Ajit got down from the car and said, 'Why are you
alone? Where's Shibnath Babu?'

Kamal said, 'He's not at home. But you too are alone.
There was no one with you the other day either.'

'No,' said Ajit. 'Ashu Babu hasn't been well for the last
few days, so they didn't go out. Today I've left them at
Abinash Babu's house and come out for a drive. I simply can't
stay indoors in the evening.'

Kamal said, 'It's the same with me. But I can't say so—
poor people have many things to do.' She looked at Ajit's
face and suddenly asked, 'Will you take me with you? Just
for a little drive?'

Ajit was embarrassed. He didn't even have the chauffeur with him today, and Shibnath Babu, he had been told, was not at home. Yet he felt it awkward to refuse. He hesitated for a moment and said, 'Don't you have any companions here?'

Kamal replied, 'What a thing to ask! Where should I find companions? Just take a look at this place. It's almost outside the town, called Shahganj or something like that. There must be a leather factory nearby—my neighbours are all leather workers. They go to the factory and come back, drink and clamour all through the night. This is the kind of place I live in.'

Ajit asked, 'Aren't there any decent middle-class people here?'

Kamal said, 'I don't think so. And what good would it be if there were? Would they let me step into their homes? In that case, I could even have gone to your place if I felt very lonely.' As she said this, she climbed into the car through the open door and continued, 'Let's go! I haven't had a car ride for a long time. You must take me for a long drive.'

Ajit did not know what to do. He said diffidently, 'If we go too far, it may get very late. Shibnath Babu might take it amiss if he doesn't find you at home when he returns.'

Kamal said, 'No, there's no chance of his taking it amiss.'

Ajit said, 'Then instead of sitting beside the chauffeur, why don't you sit at the back?'

Kamal said, 'But you're the chauffeur. How can we chat if I don't sit near you? How can I travel tongue-tied at the back? Get in, don't let's delay.'

Ajit got in and started the car. The road was pretty but lonely. Occasionally they passed one or two people, but no more. The already speeding car sped faster. Kamal said, 'You like to drive fast, don't you?'

'Yes,' said Ajit.

'Aren't you afraid?'

'No, I'm used to it.'

'Habit is everything.' After a moment's silence Kamal continued, 'But I'm not used to it; yet I'm liking it. It must be my nature, mustn't it?'

'Maybe,' said Ajit.

'Certainly,' said Kamal. 'Yet there's danger in it—both for those who ride and those who get run over. Isn't it so?'

Ajit said, 'Why should they get run over?'

Kamal said, 'What's wrong with getting run over? There's joy in speed, whether it's a car or whether it's life. But cowards can't enjoy it. They move slowly and carefully. They think it enough to have saved the trouble of walking. They are happy in outwitting distance, never realizing that they're fooling themselves. Isn't it so, Ajit Babu?'

Ajit couldn't understand what she said. 'What do you mean?' he asked.

Kamal looked at his face and smiled a little. After a few moments she said, 'There's no meaning to it. It's just something I said.' He concluded that she did not want to make her meaning clearer.

It was getting darker. Ajit wanted to return. Kamal said, 'So early? Let's go a little further.'

Ajit said, 'We've come a long way. As it is we'll be late getting back.'

'What does it matter?'

'Shibnath Babu may not like it.'

'Let him not,' Kamal replied.

Ajit was surprised, but keeping his surprise to himself, he said, 'I have to take Ashu Babu home. We shouldn't be late.'

Kamal said in reply, 'There's plenty of transport in Agra. They can easily make their way back. Let's go a little further.' Thus, as if forcibly, Kamal pushed him further and further ahead. The lonely road became utterly desolate. Darkness thickened. There was absolute silence in the fields stretching to the horizon on every side. Finally, at one point, Ajit slowed down and anxiously said, 'No more! Let's go back now.'

'All right,' said Kamal.

On the way back she slowly said, 'I was thinking what priceless treasures of life people waste by trying to compromise with untruth. How diffident you felt about taking me out alone! If I had stepped back in fear, I would have missed this pleasure.'

Ajit said, 'But you can't be sure of something till you've reached the end. When you return, you may be fated to find sorrow instead of joy.'

Kamal said, 'What a long, breathless ride I've had today on this dark, lonely road, sitting alone beside you! I can't tell you how much I enjoyed it.'

Ajit realized that Kamal had paid no attention to his words. It was as though she was talking to herself. Perhaps there was really nothing to be ashamed of, yet he shrank within himself at first. Nobody seemed to know anything about this girl beyond hostile speculations and scandalous rumour—much of it probably baseless, and whatever was true so overcast by the distorting shadow of untruth that there was no way of detecting it. Those who might have tested the evidence chose not to do so, as though it were a joke.

Ajit's silence brought Kamal to her senses. She said, 'Oh yes, weren't you saying that on my return I might find not joy but sorrow? Of course I might.'

'And then?' said Ajit.

Kamal said, 'That wouldn't prove that I didn't relish the pleasure I got this evening.'

This made Ajit laugh. 'It doesn't prove that, but it does prove that you're a fair logician. It's hard to outwit you.'

'You mean I'm what they call a logic-chopper?'

Ajit said, 'No, not that. But what ends in sorrow, though it began in joy, can't be said to be truly joyful. Wouldn't you agree?'

Kamal said, 'No, I wouldn't. I believe in accepting as true whatever I get whenever I get it, so that the fire of sorrow may not dry up the dew of past happiness. However small it is, however little its value in the world, I hope I shall never deny that happiness. May the joy of one day not be shamed by the grief of another.' She fell silent for a while, then added: 'Ajit Babu, in this world neither joy nor sorrow is true in itself. Truth lies only in fleeting moments of joy and sorrow, in the rhythm of their motion. You can truly make them yours only through your judgement and your heart. Don't you think so?'

Ajit could not reply to this question, but even in that darkness he sensed the other's eager eyes looking at him expectantly. She wanted to hear something definite.

'Well, why don't you answer?'

'I didn't understand you very clearly.'

'Didn't you?'

'No.'

There was a suppressed sigh. Then Kamal slowly said, 'That means it's not yet time for you to understand it clearly. If ever the time comes, remember me. Will you?'

'Yes,' said Ajit.

The car stopped before the neglected garden. Ajit got

down and opened the door for her. Then he said, looking at the house, 'There isn't a flicker of light anywhere; perhaps everybody has gone to bed.'

'Perhaps,' said Kamal as she got out.

'There! You see how inconsiderate you've been,' said Ajit. 'You didn't leave any message. Who knows how worried Shibnath Babu might be.'

'Yes,' said Kamal. 'He's worried himself to sleep.'

Ajit asked, 'How will you enter in the dark? There's a lantern in my car. Shall I light it and come with you?'

Kamal gratefully said, 'That would be a great help, Ajit Babu. Please come. Let me give you a cup of tea.'

Ajit said imploringly, 'I'll obey all your commands, but don't command me to have tea so late at night. Let me just reach you home.'

The front door opened at a touch. A Hindustani maid lay sleeping on the veranda inside. She woke up at the noise of human entry. It was a two-storeyed house with two small rooms on the upper floor. A hurricane lantern was burning dimly below the very narrow staircase. Picking it up, Kamal invited Ajit upstairs. In an agony of embarrassment he replied, 'No, I must go. It's really very late.'

Kamal obdurately said, 'That won't do. You must come.' Seeing Ajit still hesitant, she said, 'You're thinking that if you came in, it would embarrass Shibnath Babu; but why don't you realize that if you didn't come in, it would embarrass me much more? Please come in. I won't be able to sleep tonight if I churlishly let you go away from here.'

Ajit went upstairs into the room and saw that it had practically no furniture: only a cheap armchair, a small table, a stool, three trunks and, in a corner, an old iron bed on which bedclothes and pillows were piled so untidily as to suggest they were seldom used. The room was empty. Shibnath Babu was not there.

Ajit was surprised but also relieved. He asked, 'Why, isn't he back yet?'

'No,' said Kamal.

'Perhaps he's singing to his heart's content at our place tonight.'

'How do you know?'

'He didn't go there yesterday or the day before. If he went today, Ashu Babu might have insisted that he make up for his absence.'

'He goes there every day,' said Kamal. 'Why didn't he do so the last two days?'

Ajit said, 'You should know that better than us. Perhaps you didn't let him go. He doesn't look as though he would willingly keep away from us.'

Kamal stared at his face for a few seconds, then suddenly started laughing. She said, 'Who knows whether he goes there just to sing? Really, it's unfair to hold back a man against his wishes, isn't it?'

'Certainly,' said Ajit.

Kamal said, 'It's only possible because he's so very good. Now, would you like being held captive in this way?'

'Never,' said Ajit. 'Besides, there's no one to hold me captive.'

Kamal said smilingly, nodding her head a few times: 'That's the problem. One never knows who might be lurking somewhere to take one captive. Just see, I've been holding you captive this evening; but you haven't noticed it at all. Never mind, there's no point arguing about everything. But it's getting late as we talk. Let me go into the other room and make some tea for you.'

'And shall I sit silently by myself? That won't do.'

'No need,' said Kamal. She took him into the next room and, spreading out a new mat for him, said, 'Do sit down. But what a strange world this is, Ajit Babu. The other day when I liked this mat and bought it, I'd thought I would ask somebody else to sit on it and tell him——well, things meant for one person can't be said to another. Still, I've asked you to sit on it. Yet how little time has passed in between!'

It was difficult to make out what she meant: maybe something very simple, maybe very recondite. Yet it made Ajit blush. He tried to say something, hesitated, but nevertheless spoke. 'Why then didn't you let him sit?'

Kamal said, 'This is where men make a mistake. They think everything lies in their power; but there's someone somewhere who upsets plans, no one knows how. Should I put plenty of sugar in your tea?'

'Yes, please,' said Ajit. 'I drink tea because I like the milk and sugar. Otherwise I have no special fondness for it.'

'Nor have I,' replied Kamal. 'I don't understand why people drink it. Yet I was born in a place where tea is grown.'

'Was it Assam?'

'Not just Assam, but actually on a tea garden.'

'And yet you don't like tea?'

'Not in the least. I drink it out of politeness when it's offered.'

Cup in hand, Ajit looked around and said, 'Is this your kitchen?'

'Yes.'

'You do your own cooking? It appears you haven't had time to cook today.'

Kamal said, 'No.'

Ajit grew hesitant. Kamal looked at him, smiled and said, 'Now you'll ask what I'm going to eat today. I'll reply that I don't eat anything in the evening. I eat only once a day.'

'Only once?'

'Yes,' said Kamal. 'But next it ought to occur to you— what will Shibnath Babu eat on his return? You've seen how much he eats—and not just once a day. So? In reply I'll say that he always has dinner with you. Why should he worry? That's true, you'll say, but he doesn't go there every day. I'll hear you and think, what's the use of discussing all this with an outsider? But even that won't stop you. So at last I'll have to say, "Ajit Babu, you needn't worry. He doesn't come here any more. Perhaps he has lost his infatuation with the Shibani of his Shaivite marriage."'

Ajit genuinely failed to grasp what she meant. He stared at her face in deep astonishment and asked, 'What do you mean? Are you saying this out of anger?'

Kamal said, 'No, I'm not angry. Perhaps I don't have the right to be angry any more. I thought he'd gone to Jaipur to buy stones. It's from you that I've gathered he hasn't left Agra yet. Come, let's go and sit in the other room.'

Moving there, Kamal continued: 'Look at our bedroom. This is all that it ever contained: everything has remained just the same. But if you'd seen what it looked like earlier, I wouldn't have had to tell you that I'm not angry. But really, it's very late, Ajit Babu. You shouldn't stay here any longer.'

Ajit rose and said, 'Yes, I'd better be going.'

Kamal stood up at once. Ajit said, 'If you allow me, I shall come again tomorrow.'

'Yes, do come,' said Kamal, following him downstairs.

Ajit hesitated for a few moments and then said, 'If you don't mind, may I ask a question before I go? How long has Shibnath Babu not been here?'

'For quite some time.' She smiled. In the dim light of the lantern, Ajit could clearly see that this was a different sort of smile. It bore no resemblance to the earlier ones.

9

IT WAS THE DEAD OF NIGHT WHEN AJIT RETURNED HOME. THE streets were silent, the shops were closed; there was no sign of anybody anywhere. He took out his pocket watch and saw that it had stopped at eight because he had not wound it. Perhaps it was one o'clock, or two—he couldn't guess exactly. He was sure that anxiety at Ashu Babu's house must have reached a great pitch. They might not have had their dinner yet, let alone gone to bed. He could not imagine what he would say. He could not tell them the truth. It was futile to argue why he could not, but it was so. It was easier to lie. But he was not in the habit of lying; otherwise, having gone out alone for a drive, he could easily have concocted a story to explain the delay.

The gate was open. The gateman saluted him and said that the chauffeur was out looking for him. Parking the car in the coach-house, Ajit entered Ashu Babu's sitting room to find he had still not gone to bed, but was waiting up by himself in spite of his illness. He sat up anxiously and exclaimed, 'There you are! I've kept saying there must have been an accident. I've warned you over and over not to go out alone! Now see for yourself how an old man's warning comes true. I hope you've learnt a lesson.'

An abashed Ajit forced a smile and said, 'I really am sorry about causing all of you so much worry.'

'Put off your sorrow till tomorrow. Look at the clock: it's already two. Have something to eat and go to bed. I'll hear you tomorrow. Jadu! Jadu! Has that rascal also gone to look for you?'

'It really isn't fair to make him do so. Where will he look for me in this big town?'

Ashu Babu said, 'You tell me it's unfair. But you don't know how worried we've been. Shibnath finished singing at about eleven o'clock and since then—but where's Mani? I haven't seen her either since then.'

Ajit said, 'Perhaps she's gone to bed.'

'Gone to bed! How can that be? She hasn't yet had her supper.' Suddenly something flickered in his mind. 'Did you see the coachman in the stable?'

'Why, no.'

'Here's a bother!' A new anxiety made Ashu Babu sit up once again. 'Just as I thought. She too must have gone out in the carriage to look for you. How very wrong of her! And she said nothing to me in case I should stop her—just stole out. Who knows when she'll return? I'm afraid this is going to be a sleepless night.'

'Let me check if the carriage is there.' Ajit hurried out of the room. He found the carriage parked in the coach-house; the horse was placidly eating grass and pawing the ground from time to time. He was relieved of one anxiety. At the northern end of the ground-floor balcony there were a few casuarina and palm trees that had somehow survived neglect. Manorama's bedroom was just above them. Before returning to Ashu Babu, Ajit thought he would pass that way to see whether there was a light in her room. As he approached, he heard human voices from among the bushes. They were very familiar voices, discussing the tune of a particular song. There was nothing objectionable about their talk, nothing requiring concealment under the dark shadow of a tree. For a few seconds a sudden numbness froze Ajit's feet. It was only for a brief moment. The conversation continued; he went away as silently as he had come. Neither of the couple could know that there had been a witness to this nocturnal tête-à-tête.

'Any news?' Ashu Babu asked eagerly.

'The carriage is in the coach-house and so is the horse. Mani hasn't gone out.'

'What a relief, my boy!' said Ashu Babu. 'It's very late. Perhaps Mani felt tired and went to bed. Poor girl! I think she's gone without food tonight. Go, my boy, have something to eat and get to bed.'

Ajit said, 'I won't have anything so late. But please get some sleep yourself.'

'All right. But won't you eat anything at all? Just a little bit?'

'No, nothing. Please don't wait any longer. Please go to bed.'

Having sent the ailing man off, Ajit went to his room and stood before the open window. He was sure that after ending the discussion about music, Manorama would pass that way to see her father.

Mani came, but half an hour later. First she went to her father's study and found the room dark. Perhaps Jadu had been awake and at hand after all; he had not answered his master's call, but had put out the light after the latter left. Manorama waited there for a moment. As she turned, she saw Ajit standing silently before his open window. His room too was dark, but a faint beam of light from the portico fell on his window.

'Who's there?'

'I'm Ajit.'

'Oh! When did you come? I think Father has gone to bed.' She tried to be silent after this, but the arrested flow of her words would not be halted. 'See what you've done. Everyone in the house was dying of worry that something had gone wrong. This is why Father keeps telling you not to go out alone.'

Ajit did not respond to these questions and remarks. Manorama said, 'But I'm sure he hasn't been able to sleep. He must be lying awake. Let me go and tell him you've returned.'

'There's no need,' said Ajit. 'He went to bed only after he saw me return.'

'Went to bed after seeing you! Then why didn't you call me?'

'He thought you'd gone to bed.'

'To bed! How could I? I haven't yet had dinner.'

'Then have it and go to bed. The night's almost over.'

'Won't you eat anything?'

'No,' said Ajit, and moved away from the window.

'Fine! Not a very nice thing to say!' She could utter nothing more than this. But there was no answer from Ajit. Manorama stood still, alone, outside. Though she had no equal in coaxing, storming or obdurately pressing her point, a strange reticence now sealed her lips. Ajit had returned home when the night was almost over; everyone in the house had been in endless suspense. And after such a grave offence, this man had humiliated her utterly; yet not a word of protest passed her lips. Not only did her tongue remain silent, her whole body was numb for a while. No one returned to the window, no one cared to see whether she was there or not. In that dead of night, Manorama stood there silently; then, after a long while, she slowly went away.

In the morning Ashu Babu learnt from the servant that neither Ajit nor Manorama had eaten the previous night. Over morning tea he asked Ajit with deep concern, 'You must have had a bad accident yesterday, wasn't it so?'

'No,' said Ajit.

'Then you must have run out of fuel.'

'No, there was enough fuel.'

'Then why were you so late?'

Ajit only replied, 'For no particular reason.'

Manorama did not drink tea herself. She made tea for her father and offered Ajit a cup along with his breakfast. She neither asked anything, nor did she raise her face to look at him. The father marked this change of mood in both of them. As Ajit finished his breakfast and went for his bath, he found his daughter alone and said to her with concern, 'No, my dear, this is wrong of you. However close Ajit may be to us, he is after all a guest in this house. He must be treated properly.'

'I never said he shouldn't, Father.'

'No, no, you didn't, but even a slight show of annoyance in our behaviour would be offensive.'

'I agree,' said Manorama. 'But who told you that I behaved badly?'

Ashu Babu could not answer this. He had heard nothing, he had seen nothing, the whole thing rested on speculation. Yet he wasn't pleased, because one could argue in this way without freeing a father's mind of misgivings. After some time he slowly said, 'Ajit didn't want to eat anything so late at night. I too went to bed; you were already in bed. Who knows, we might have appeared to neglect him. He's not in good spirits today.'

Manorama said, 'If someone wishes to spend the whole

night away from the house, should we too spend a sleepless night for him? Is that the host's duty towards his guest, Father?'

Ashu Babu smiled. Pointing at himself, he said, 'If by "host" is meant this poor crippled patient, then, my dear, his duty is to go to bed by eight, or else it's disrespect to a much more estimable guest—the gout. But if someone else is meant by "host" then I'm nobody to lay down that person's duty. Today I remembered an incident long past. Your mother was alive then. I had gone to Guptipara to fish, but couldn't return that day. A matter of only one night—yet somebody sat up not only one night, but three whole nights beside the window. It didn't occur to me then to ask who had taught her such dutiful ways, but when I meet her next time I won't forget to ask.' He turned his face away for a while to hide his eyes from his daughter.

This was not a new story. He had recounted the incident to his daughter many times, yet it never grew stale. Whenever he recalled it, it was in a new garb.

The maid came and stood at the door. Manorama got up and said, 'Father, I'll soon be back after settling today's meals.' She hurried out, relieved that the discussion had not proceeded any further.

Ashu Babu enquired about Ajit several times during the day. Once he gathered that he was reading; another time, that he was in his room writing letters. At lunch he virtually did not speak, and went away as soon as he had finished. Compared to his behaviour on other days, this was as rude as it was surprising.

Ashu Babu was immensely agitated. 'What's the matter, Mani?' he asked.

All day Manorama had been avoiding her father. Now,

too, without looking anywhere in particular, she said, 'I don't know, Father.'

For a while Ashu Babu was absorbed in his own thoughts.

Then, as if talking to himself, he said, 'I sat up till he returned. I told him to eat something, but as it was so late he decided not to. Perhaps it wasn't right of you to have gone to bed, but what's so terribly wrong about it either? What can be more surprising than his taking such a trifle so seriously?'

Manorama kept quiet. So did Ashu Babu for a while; then, conquering his diffidence, he said, 'You could have asked him the reason, couldn't you?'

'What's there to ask, Father?'

There were many things to ask, but it was difficult to ask them—particularly for Mani. He knew this, yet he said, 'But he's obviously angry. Perhaps he thinks you're neglecting him. We can't let him have such a wrong notion.'

Manorama said, 'If he's developed unjust notions about me, that's his fault. How can one person make up for another's faults?'

The father could not reply to this. He had brought up his daughter in such a way that he could not tell her to do anything that would hurt her self-respect. After she went away, his mind was in turmoil over this point and he felt depressed. He told himself over and over that such wrangles were common, that this misunderstanding was only momentary. He repeated this conclusion repeatedly to himself, but that did not give him any peace. He knew Ajit well. Not only was he well trained in all respects; he had evinced such a frank and sincere personality that today's wilful apathy did not fit in with that image at all. In spite of being the cause of everyone's boundless anxiety, he had shown anger instead of being ashamed. This appeared so improbable that it was hard to explain.

In the afternoon a tonga entered the gate. Ashu Babu saw it and learnt on enquiry that it had come for Ajit. He sent for Ajit, and when he turned up, forced a smile and asked, 'Why this tonga, Ajit?'

'I'm going out.'

'But why not in the car? What's happened to it—a breakdown again?'

'No, but you might need it.'

'Even if I need to go out, there's the horse carriage.' He remained silent for a moment and said, 'Ajit, my son, tell me the truth. Has there been any unpleasantness about your using the car?'

'Not that I know of, said Ajit.' 'But there's going to be a soirée at your house again today, and you'll surely need the car to bring your guests and take them home. The carriage won't be enough.'

Being worried about so many things since the morning, Ashu Babu had forgotten all about this. Now he remembered that after last evening's soirée, he had invited his friends today as well: they would arrive soon after dark. It also occurred to him that Manorama had planned to offer them dinner. But he smiled to himself: the unease caused by this apparent strife had driven the matter out of his own mind, and now that he remembered it, he did not like the idea. He could therefore guess how vexing it must be for his daughter. So he said, 'No, Ajit. We'll have to cancel the programme.'

'Why?'

'Why? You may ask Mani.' He shouted for the servant and asked him to call Mani. Then, with a brief smile, he said, 'Now that you're so angry, who'll want to listen to music? Mani? Let's leave all that for another day. Take the car and go out for a while. But you mustn't be late in returning. And remember, you mustn't go alone. That wretched chauffeur is getting lazy.'

Thus, having solved a grave problem to his satisfaction so unexpectedly, he stretched out luxuriously in his armchair and heaved a deep sigh of pleasure, saying: 'You going out in a hired tonga! What an idea!'

Manorama stepped into the room and bridled on seeing Ajit. Ashu Babu felt her presence and sat up straight. Then brightening his face with a tender, amused smile, he said, 'Well, I hope you remember about today's programme, my dear. Or have you forgotten it completely?'

'What is it, Father?'

'We've invited everyone here today. After the music, you're arranging dinner. Don't you remember?'

Manorama nodded and said, 'Of course I remember. I've sent the car to fetch them.'

'Sent the car to fetch them! But what about the dinner?'

Mani said, 'It's all arranged, Father. There won't be any lapse anywhere.'

'Good,' he said, and leaned back again. Someone seemed to have dyed his face over with ink.

Manorama went away. Ajit too was about to leave, but Ashu Babu signalled him to wait and sat quietly for a long time. Then, sitting up, he said, 'Ajit, I'm embarrassed at having to apologize on my daughter's behalf. But her mother's dead. If she were here, I wouldn't have to say this.'

Ajit remained silent. Ashu Babu said, 'Her mother would have found out why you are angry with her, but she isn't here any more. Can't you tell me the reason?'

His tone was so defenceless that anyone would have been distressed. But Ajit kept silent.

'Haven't you had a word with her?' Ashu Babu said.

'I did,' said Ajit.

Ashu Babu grew eager. 'You had? When? Has Mani told you that it was only an accident that she fell asleep last night?'

Ajit remained still for some time. Perhaps he was thinking out his reply. Then slowly he said, 'To stay awake till so late to no purpose is neither easy nor reasonable. If she had fallen asleep, there would have been nothing wrong. But she hadn't fallen asleep. I met her some time after you had gone to bed.'

'What happened then?'

'I shan't tell you anything more,' said Ajit, and left. From outside the door he announced: 'I may go away from here tomorrow or the day after.'

Ashu Babu did not understand what was happening. He only realized that some terrible mishap had taken place.

He heard the tonga leave with Ajit. After a few minutes the car returned with the guests in great clamour. He heard that too, but he did not move: he went on sitting motionlessly like a statue. When everything was ready, the servant came and announced that his master was not feeling well; he had gone to bed.

The music that evening was spiritless. The dinner lacked excitement. It struck everyone repeatedly that one member of the house had gone out on the pretext of getting some fresh air; and another, who with his huge bulk and pleasant smile used to shine so brightly in the assembly, had left his special place empty that evening.

10

IN THE MEANTIME AJIT'S TONGA STOPPED BEFORE KAMAL'S house. Kamal was waiting on the narrow roadside balcony. As soon as her eyes met Ajit's, she did a namaskar. Pointing to the tonga she said, 'Send him away, or he'll keep pressing you to return.'

They met at the foot of the staircase. 'You sent it away, but can I get another to return in?' said Ajit.

'No, but it's only a short walk. You can go on foot.'

'On foot!'

'Why? Are you scared? Then I myself will escort you back. Come.' She took him to the kitchen and spread out the same mat he had sat on the previous day. Then she said, 'Just take a look at all these dishes I've cooked through the day. If you hadn't come, I would have given them all away to the leather workers in a huff.'

Ajit said, 'You seem to have a very bad temper. But if you had given away the food to the cobblers you would have put it to better use.'

'What do you mean?' Kamal looked at Ajit for a while and then said, 'You mean that you lack nothing and will waste much of this food—but that they're very poor and would have had a square meal. So the proper use of the food would have been to feed such people. Isn't that so?'

'Quite so,' said Ajit with a nod.

'That is the virtuous man's way of judging good and bad, the godly logic of holy men. They want to record this as the most worthwhile sort of expenditure in the account book of the next world. But they don't understand that this is false. How should they know that only wrongful extravagance can give the utmost joy?'

'Do you then think there's no joy in one's sense of duty?' said Ajit in astonishment.

'No, not a bit,' said Kamal. 'The joy in doing one's duty is deceptive and is simply another name for sorrow. One is forced to accept it by the rule of reason. That's a kind of bondage. Otherwise how could I draw joy from wasted love when I invited you to sit on a mat I had meant for Shibnath? Then again, you see that I have gone without food the whole day, yet cooked plenty of things only because you would come and dine. Don't you see where the joy lies in this dereliction of duty? You won't understand my point now, Ajit Babu; it's no use my trying to explain. But if the time comes when you grasp such perverse ideas independently, please remember me. Let's stop for now; come and have your dinner.' She put before him plates piled with a variety of food.

Ajit was silent for a long time, then said: 'It's true that I haven't followed your last remarks, but I feel it's possible to understand them. I might do so if you explained them.'

'Who'll explain them, Ajit Babu? I? Why need I?' She smiled and pushed the rest of the dishes towards him.

Ajit began to concentrate on the food. 'Perhaps you don't know that I didn't eat last night,' he said.

'I didn't know, but I was afraid you might not have, after returning so late. And so it proved. You suffered because of me.'

'But today I'm making up with interest,' he said, and at once remembered that Kamal had gone without food all day. He felt ashamed. 'But I'm being as selfish as a brute.

You haven't eaten all day, but I simply didn't remember that and have started eating.'

Kamal smilingly replied, 'But this is more important than my food. That's why I made you sit down quickly to your dinner.' After a pause she said again, 'Besides, I don't eat all this meat and fish.'

'But what will you have then?'

'See there.' She pointed to something covered with an enamelled bowl. 'That's my dinner—rice, dal and boiled potatoes. That's my royal dish.'

Ajit's curiosity was not dispelled, but he hesitated to ask anything more in case she alluded to her poverty. He changed the subject and said, 'The first time I saw you, you aroused an inexpressible wonder in me.'

Kamal laughed at this. She said, 'That's because of my looks. And even there I lost to Akshay Babu. I couldn't overwhelm him.'

Ajit was abashed, yet he smiled and said, 'Perhaps not. He is a diamond from the Golconda mines. You can't even make a scratch on him. But I was very surprised when I heard you. Sometimes you suddenly lose your patience and grow angry. It seems you don't want to admit the truth; that it's your nature to block its path.'

Perhaps Kamal was offended. 'Maybe,' she said, 'but there was something there of greater wonder than myself—of a different kind. Huge bulk matched with great tranquillity— the Himalaya of patience. No vapour from any steam reaches there. I wish I was his daughter.'

These words touched Ajit deeply. He revered Ashu Babu like a god. But he said, 'How would two such opposite natures meet at a point?'

Kamal said, 'I don't know. I'm just saying what I would have liked. I wish I too were his daughter like Mani.' She paused for a while and added, 'My own father was no less a person. He too was so gentle, so serene.'

Ajit had heard from everyone that Kamal was the daughter of a low-caste maidservant. Now hearing her own account of her father's qualities, he became curious about the mystery of her birth. He could not ask any questions, lest his enquiries hurt her. But his heart filled with compassion and charity.

Dinner was over. Kamal asked Ajit to get up, but he refused and said, 'I'll get up only after you've finished.'

'Why should you put yourself out, Ajit Babu? Please get up. Why don't you go and wash your hands, and then come and sit here while I eat.'

'No, that's impossible. I'm not going to budge an inch from this place till you've finished.'

'What an odd man you are!' With a smile, Kamal uncovered her plate and started eating. She had not exaggerated at all. It was nothing but a plate of rice, dal and boiled potatoes, dry and almost colourless. He did not know what she normally ate on other days. But today, set against such sumptuous fare, her deliberate self-denial almost brought tears to his eyes. The previous day he had heard that she ate only once a day; today he saw what her meal was really like. So whatever she might say by way of logic and debate, when it actually came to the pleasures of life, her rigorous self-restraint overwhelmed Ajit and transformed her in his enraptured eyes into an image of grace and reverence. He felt endless scorn for those who had humiliated her through deprivation, disrespect and neglect. As he watched Kamal eat, he could no more hold back his feelings. He said with great ardour, 'Those who think themselves superior to you and turn you away with insults, those who backbite you for nothing, are not worthy to touch your feet. If anyone deserves the place of a goddess in this world of ours, it is you.'

Kamal raised her face in genuine amazement and asked, 'Why?'

'I don't know why, but I can take my oath on it.'

Kamal's wonder was not dispelled, but she kept quiet.

Ajit said, 'Will you forgive me if I ask you a question?'

'What is it?'

'Have you taken to such self-denial only after that wicked Shibnath insulted and robbed you?'

Kamal said, 'No. I took to this after my first husband died. So I don't find it difficult.'

It was as if someone had poured ink over Ajit's face. He was dumbfounded for a few moments, then composed himself and asked slowly, 'Have you been married before?'

'Yes,' replied Kamal. 'My husband was a Christian from Assam. After his death my father also died suddenly, falling off a horse. An uncle of Shibnath's was then the head clerk of the tea garden. He didn't have a wife, and he gave shelter to my mother. I too was taken into his household. Having gone through so much distress, I've got used to having one meal a day. You may call it self-denial, but it keeps me fit in both mind and body.'

Ajit sighed and said, 'I've heard that you belong to the weaver caste.'

Kamal said, 'People say so. But my mother used to say that her father was a kaviraj,[1] of the same caste as you. It means my mother's father was not a weaver but a Vaidya.' She smiled a little and added, 'Whatever be his caste, it's no use resenting or deploring it.'

'Quite right,' said Ajit.

Kamal went on, 'My mother had beauty but no discrimination. There was some scandal after her marriage. So her husband fled with her to a tea garden in Assam. But he didn't live long: he died of a fever within a few months. About three years later, I was born to the burra sahib of the garden.'

Hearing this account of her birth and parentage, Ajit's heart, which a moment ago had been bursting with love and veneration, shrank to a dot from abhorrence and mortification. What struck him most was that she did not feel the slightest shame in narrating this disgraceful account of herself and her mother. How unabashedly she could say that her mother had beauty but no discrimination! The infamy, which should have made her sink into the ground, seemed to her nothing more than an aberration of taste.

Kamal went on: 'But my father was a saintly man. In morals, erudition and honesty, I have seldom seen a man like him, Ajit Babu. For nineteen years of my life, I was brought up under his personal care.'

A flicker of doubt arose in Ajit's mind that she might be joking. But what kind of joke could this be? 'Are you telling the truth?' he asked her.

Kamal was a little surprised and said, 'I never tell a lie, Ajit Babu.' For a moment, the memory of her father lit up her face with a serene glow. She said, 'My father taught me time and again that never in my life should I resort to false thought, false conceit and false words.'

Yet Ajit was reluctant to believe all this. He said, 'If you were brought up by an Englishman, you must have learnt English.'

In reply she only smiled and said, 'I've finished my dinner. Let's go to the other room.'

'No, I should be going.'

'Won't you stay any longer? You can't leave so soon today.'

'I must, I have no time.'

Kamal looked up and marked a severe sternness on his face. Perhaps she could even guess the reason. Looking fixedly at him for a few moments, she said, 'Well, you may go.'

Ajit could not find anything to say after this. At last he said, 'Will you stay on in Agra?'

'Why do you ask?'

'Suppose Shibnath Babu doesn't come back to you. You don't have any claim on him.'

'No, I don't.' After a moment's silence she went on: 'As you've said, he goes to your place almost every day. Couldn't you discreetly find out what his plans are and tell me?'

'What good would that do?'

'Well, this month's rent has already been paid. I could leave the house tomorrow or the day after.'

'Where will you go?'

Kamal did not answer but remained silent.

'I presume you have no money.'

She made no reply to this either.

Ajit too was silent for a while and then said, 'I have brought some money for you. Will you take it?'

'No.'

'Why not? I know quite well that you have no money. Whatever you might have had, you have spent on me today.' There was still no answer. He said once more, 'Doesn't one take help from a friend in a time of need?'

'But you're not my friend.'

'Even if I'm not, doesn't one borrow from those who are not friends? And pay it back too? At least you could do that.'

Kamal shook her head. 'I've already told you that I never tell a lie.'

Her words were soft, but sharp as arrowheads. Ajit realized that she would not do otherwise. Looking at her, he noticed that the ornaments she was wearing on the first day they met were missing today. Perhaps she had used them to pay for her rent and upkeep in the interim. Suddenly his heart wept in agony. He asked, 'Have you really made up your mind to go away?'

'What else can I do?'

He did not know; and as he did not know, he continued to suffer the ache in his heart. He tried one last time. 'Isn't there anyone in this world whom you could ask for help at a time like this?'

Kamal thought for a while and said, 'Yes, there is somebody. I can go only to him and beg for help like a daughter. But it's getting late for you. Shall I escort you?'

Ajit grew flustered and said, 'No, no, there's no need for that. I can go alone.'

'Goodbye, then.' With this she went into her room.

Ajit stood stunned for a couple of minutes. Then he silently stole away.

11

IT WAS AFTERNOON, AND VERY COLD. THE WINDOWS OF ASHU Babu's parlour had been shut all day. He was reading something intently, stretching his legs along the arms of his chaise-longue. A shadow from the door fell on the pages of his paper. He thought that his servant had got up from his afternoon nap. He said, 'I hope you haven't woken up from too brief a nap, my man. That might give you a headache. If it's not too much trouble would you please cover the feet of your humble servant with that wrap?'

A quilted wrap lay on the carpet. The silent entrant picked it up and wrapped it round his feet, tucking it carefully all the way down.

Ashu Babu said, 'That's enough, you needn't exert yourself so much. Now give me a cheroot and recline yourself again— there's still some time. But tomorrow you'll get what's coming to you'—meaning thereby, 'You'll lose your job tomorrow.' There was no response, because the servant was used to such remarks from his master. It was as useless to protest as it was unnecessary to worry.

Ashu Babu stretched out his hand to receive the cheroot and, at the sound of a match being struck, raised his face from the paper. He was dumbstruck for a while, then said, 'I knew these couldn't be Jedo's[1] hands. Nobody in his line of descent could cover the feet so expertly.'

Kamal said, 'But my fingers are getting burnt meanwhile.'

Ashu Babu hastily took the burning matchstick and threw

it away. Holding her hand in his own, he drew her close and said, 'Why haven't I seen you for so long, my dear mother?'

This was the first time he had addressed her as 'mother'. But as soon as he asked the question, he realized it was meaningless.

Kamal was about to draw up a chair at some distance, but he stopped her and said, 'Not there, my dear; come and sit near me.' He drew her very close to him and said, 'Why at this unexpected hour, Kamal?'

Kamal said, 'I felt an immense wish to see you, that's why.'

In reply Ashu Babu only said, 'That's good.' He couldn't say anything more. Like everybody else, he too knew that Kamal had no friends here, that no one liked her, that she did not have entry to anybody's house. The girl led a very lonely life. Yet he could not say, 'Kamal, come and see me whenever you like. It may be different with others, but with me you have no reason to feel shy.' Perhaps because he did not know what to say, he remained silent and abstracted for two or three minutes. The papers slipped and fell from his hand; Kamal bent down, picked them up and said, 'You're reading and perhaps I've interrupted you by intruding like this.'

Ashu Babu said, 'No, I've finished reading. It doesn't matter if I don't read the rest, and I don't really want to.' Then, pausing a little, he said, 'Besides, I'll be alone after you leave. I'd rather you talked to me and I listened.'

Kamal said, 'I would be happy to talk to you all day. But others wouldn't take it kindly.'

In spite of the smile on her lips, Ashu Babu was hurt. He said, 'You're not wrong, Kamal, but none of those who would take offence is present here. The new magistrate here is a Bengali. His wife is Mani's friend; they were at college together.

She came to join her husband two days ago. Mani has gone to pay her a visit. It might be quite late before she returns.'

Beaming, Kamal said, 'You said many people would take offence. Manorama is one of them. Who are the others?'

Ashu Babu said, 'Everybody. There's no lack of such people here. I used to think Ajit didn't hate you, but now I see that his hatred is the greatest; it seems to exceed Akshay Babu's.'

Seeing that Kamal was listening quietly, Ashu Babu went on: 'He wasn't like this when he came here, but he seems to have changed over the last few days. I find this so with Abinash as well. They all seem to be conspiring against you.'

Now Kamal smiled. She said, 'That's like a thunderbolt striking shoots of grass. But why should there be a conspiracy against a humble, ostracized woman like me? I don't call on anyone.'

Ashu Babu said, 'It's true that you don't. Nobody knows where you live, but that doesn't mean you're insignificant. That's why they can neither ignore you nor forgive you. They have no peace or contentment unless they discuss you and hurt you.' Suddenly, holding up the papers in his hand, he asked, 'Do you know what these are? They're Akshay Babu's work. If they hadn't been written in English, I would have read them out to you. There are no names mentioned, but from beginning to end he speaks of you and attacks you. The inaugural meeting of the Women's Welfare Society is supposed to be held at the magistrate's house tomorrow. This is the opening address.' Hurling the papers away, he continued: 'It's not simply an essay. At times there are characters who have been made to speak in the form of fiction. No one would oppose the fundamental principles laid out here—there could be no conceivable reason to oppose them. But that's not the point.

The writer's real pleasure seems to lie in hurting a particular individual at every step. I don't share Akshay's idea of pleasure, Kamal. Hence I can't praise his writing.'

Kamal said, 'But I'm not going to listen to him. What's the point of attacking me?'

Ashu Babu said, 'There's no point. Perhaps that's why they've given it to me to read. Something is better than nothing, I suppose. They want to heal their rancour at an old man's cost.' He drew Kamal's hand to his side once more.

Kamal did not understand what this touch meant, but she felt a deep turmoil within her. She said, 'They've spotted your weakness, but they haven't come to know the real man.'

'Have you yourself been able to do so, my dear?'

'Perhaps better than they have.'

Ashu Babu did not reply to this. He remained silent for quite a long time and then said softly, 'Everyone thinks that this old man must be the happiest being on earth. He has a lot of money, a lot of property . . .'

'But that's not untrue.'

'No, it isn't. I have enough wealth and property. But how much does wealth mean to a man?'

'A great deal, Ashu Babu', said Kamal with a smile.

Ashu Babu turned to look at her. Then he said, 'If you don't mind, may I say something?'

'Yes.'

'I am old, and you are my daughter's age. It's odd to hear you call me by my name. If you don't object, why don't you call me your uncle—"Kakababu"?'[2]

Kamal's astonishment was boundless. Ashu Babu went on, 'As they say, "A blind uncle is better than no uncle." I'm not blind, but I'm lame—crippled with gout. If Ashu Vaidya were put on sale, no one would pay a dud coin for him.' He wagged his thumb in jest and said, 'Let them not; but someone whose father is dead shouldn't be so fastidious. It's better for her to have a lame uncle.'

As he got no response, he went on, 'If anyone taunts you, tell him this is good enough for you. Tell him that to the poor, tin is as good as gold.'

Sitting behind his chair, Kamal could not reply, but raised her eyes to the ceiling to hold back her tears. The two had nothing whatsoever in common: not only through lack of kinship but through their immense differences in education, custom, habits, wealth and social standing. Kamal's eyes filled with unaccustomed tears at this subterfuge of binding her to him by a form of address when there was no real kinship.

'Well, my dear?,' asked Ashu Babu. 'Would you be able to address me as Kakababu?'

Holding back her tears, Kamal only said, 'No.'

'No! Why not?'

Kamal did not reply but changed the subject. She said, Where's Ajit Babu?'

Ashu Babu was silent for a while. He then said, 'Who knows, maybe he's at home.' After another silence, he added softly, 'For the last few days he hasn't been coming to me very often. He may be leaving this place soon.'

'Where will he go?'

Ashu Babu made an effort to smile and said, 'My dear, do you think people tell everything to an old man like me? They don't. Perhaps they don't feel the need.' Then pausing a little, he said, 'Perhaps you've heard that he's been engaged to Mani for a long time. They suddenly seem to have fallen out over something. They hardly talk to each other.'

Kamal was silent. Ashu Babu sighed and said, 'It's all the Almighty's wish. One's absorbed in music, and the other's trying to give his old habits a new lease of life. That's what's going on.'

Kamal could not remain silent any longer. She eagerly asked 'What are his old habits?'

Ashu Babu said, 'It's a long story. Once he put on saffron robes and became an ascetic; now he's fallen in love with Manorama. He's gone to prison for his country; he's qualified as an engineer from England. Returning home, he'd intended to marry and set up house, but now his intention seems to have changed somewhat. He was once a vegetarian, then he began eating meat and fish, but he has given that up again over the last two days. Jadu says, "The babu practises yoga for an hour every day in his room, plugging his nostrils to stop breathing."'

'He practises yoga?'

'Yes, the servant says that on his way back he'll do penance at Varanasi for having gone on a sea voyage.'[3]

Kamal asked in utter amazement: 'Penance for his sea voyage! Ajit Babu'll do such a thing?'

Ashu Babu nodded and said, 'He might. His talent flows in all directions.'

Kamal broke into laughter. She was about to say something when a shadow fell across the door, and the servant who had supplied his master with such varied information appeared in person to announce the cruel news that Abinash, Akshay, Harendra, Ajit and their band were about to arrive. At this not only Kamal but even Ashu Babu, whose habit it was to welcome all friends jubilantly, turned pale.

When the visitors presently entered the room, they were astonished. It was beyond their imagination that they could meet this woman here in such a situation. Harendra raised his hands in a namaskar to Kamal and said, 'How are you? I haven't seen you for a long time.' Abinash, attempting a smile, turned his head once to the left and once to the right in a meaningless gesture. And Akshay, the man of direct methods, stood stiff as a plank for a while; then, scattering contempt and irritation from his eyes, he pulled up a chair and sat down. 'Did you go through my *article?*' he asked Ashu Babu. As he said this, he noticed that his writing was lying on the floor. He was going to pick it up when Harendra said, 'Let it stay there, Akshay Babu. The servant will throw it away when he sweeps the room.'

Akshay pushed his hand aside and picked up the sheets.

'Yes, I've read it,' said Ashu Babu, sitting up. He noticed that Ajit, sitting on a sofa across the room, had already started browsing through that day's newspaper. Abinash was relieved to have found something to talk about. He said, 'I too have read through Akshay Babu's paper carefully, Ashu Babu. Most of it is correct and valuable. If the social system is to be reformed, it should be guided along well-known and well-established lines. I admit we've gained a good many things through contact with Europe, and that we've come to recognize many of our failings; but our reforms should follow our own course. It's no use imitating others. If out of greed or infatuation we corrupt all that is distinctive in Indian women, we shall fail in all respects. Isn't that what you are saying, Akshay Babu?'

All this was very well, and it was all drawn from Akshay Babu's article. Akshay kept silent out of modesty; but in an unspeakable glow of self-congratulation, he half shut his eyes and nodded his head a number of times.

Ashu Babu frankly admitted the point. 'There can be no

argument about it at all, Akshay Babu. Many great men have been saying so for a long time, and perhaps no Indian would oppose it.'

Akshay Babu said, 'There's no way you can oppose it. Besides, I have other things to say which I haven't put into the article, but tomorrow I'll speak of them during the lecture at the Women's Welfare Society.'

Ashu Babu turned his head and looked at Kamal. He said, 'You haven't been invited to the Society, so you won't be there. I too am down with the gout. It doesn't matter whether I go or not, but it's all about the well-being of your kind. Well, Kamal, I take it you have no objection to these proposals?'

At some other time Kamal might have kept her silence in a situation like this. But on the one hand she was depressed; on the other, these men were united in an unmanly bond. This made her heart blaze in proud opposition. But controlling herself to the utmost, she raised her face and smilingly asked, 'Which proposal, Ashu Babu? The imitation of the West or the Indian practice?'

Ashu Babu said, 'Suppose I am talking of both.'

Kamal said, 'Imitation, when only outward copying, is a cheat. In such a case, even if it matches the outward shape, it falls short in the essence. But if outward and inward merge into one, there's nothing to be ashamed of.'

Ashu Babu shook his head and said, 'But of course there is, Kamal, of course there is. By total imitation we lose what is distinctive to us. That means losing oneself completely. If this is not a matter of sorrow and shame, what is?'

Kamal said, 'What's wrong with losing one's distinctiveness, Ashu Babu? There's a difference between the characteristics of India and those of Europe. But in no country do men live for the sake of their national characteristics; the characteristics are valued for the sake of men. The real question is whether such characteristics are beneficial at present. Everything else is only blind infatuation.'

Ashu Babu was aggrieved and said, 'Only blind infatuation? Nothing more?'

'No, nothing more,' answered Kamal. 'What's the use of casting everybody in the mould of some national characteristic simply because it has been that way for a long time? No human characteristic is greater than mankind itself. When we forget that, the characteristic disappears and we lose the human being too. Here lies the real shame, Ashu Babu.'

Ashu Babu seemed stupefied. He said, 'But that would lead to total chaos. We wouldn't be identified as Indians any more. Such things have happened in history.'

Looking at his embarrassed, indignant face, Kamal smiled and said, 'We may not be identifiable as the descendants of sages and holy men, but we shall be identified as human beings. And he whom you call God will also recognize us. He won't make any mistake.'

Akshay hardened his face in scorn and said, 'Is God only ours, not yours?'

Kamal replied, 'No.'

Akshay said, 'That's only an echo of Shibnath's words, something you've learnt by rote.'

Harendra said, '*Brute!*'

'Look here, Harendra Babu—'

'I have. *Beast!*'

Ashu Babu seemed suddenly to wake from a dream. He said, 'Look, Kamal, I don't speak of others, but the uniqueness of India is not a matter of words. It would be impossible to measure its loss. So much faith, aspiration, myth, history, poetry, fable, art—such priceless wealth survives even today under shelter of this uniqueness. Nothing of this would survive in such an event.'

Kamal said, 'Why should you worry about their survival? What is not perishable will not perish. They will return in new forms with fresh charm and fresh value to meet human needs. That will be their true identity. But why should it be preserved just because it's continued a long time?'

Akshay said, 'You don't have the wit to understand that.'

Harendra said, 'I object to your discourtesy, Akshay Babu.'

Ashu Babu said, 'Kamal, I don't say that your reasoning has no truth in it; but what you so contemptuously dismiss has much truth in it as well. For various reasons, you are sore with our social laws and customs. But don't forget one thing, Kamal, that we have had to suffer many external attacks, yet we exist today because we have always sought shelter in truth. Many nations, on the other hand, have perished completely.'

Kamal said, 'Why should that be deplored? Why should they need to occupy their places forever?'

Ashu Babu said, 'That's a different matter, Kamal.'

'So what?' said Kamal. 'My father told me that a branch of the Aryans had settled in Europe. They no longer exist, but those who exist in their place are mightier. If something similar had happened in this country, we too would not simply have mourned our ancestors, nor passed our days priding ourselves on our antique uniqueness. You were talking of past troubles, but how do we know that there are no greater troubles awaiting us, or that we have outlived all dangers? And if that happens, what power will protect us?'

Ashu Babu did not reply to this, but Akshay grew excited.

He said, 'Then too we shall survive by the strength of our everlasting ideals, the ideals that have lived on unwaveringly in our hearts through the ages—the ideals that lie behind our sacrifice, our piety, our devotion, the ideals inherent in the inviolate chastity of our womankind. This will keep us alive. The Hindu never dies.'

Ajit threw away his newspaper and looked at him wide-eyed for a while. Kamal too was speechless for a moment. She felt that this was the man who had attacked her gratuitously in his article, and that he would read it arrogantly before so many women in the cause of women's well-being. She knew his final remark was directed at her. She flushed with irrepressible anger, but once again she controlled herself and said in a normal tone, 'I don't wish to talk to you, Akshay Babu. It hurts my self-respect.' Then turning to Ashu Babu, she said, 'I wanted to tell you that an ideal is not eternal simply because it has existed for a long time. Nor is there any shame if it undergoes change, not even if a race thereby loses its uniqueness. Let me give you an example. Hospitality is a great ideal in our country. Many poems, many fables, many moral stories have been composed about it. To satisfy his guest, the magnanimous Karna slaughtered his own son. Countless people have shed tears over the story, but today it seems not only ugly but horrific. The virtuous wife had carried her leprous husband to the brothel: this ideal of chastity was once held incomparable, but today it only breeds contempt in people's minds. The ideal of your own life, the self-denial that causes reverence and astonishment among men, may one day become a matter of pity. People will ridicule this excessive, fruitless self-mortification.'

The ruthlessness of the attack turned Ashu Babu's face

pale with affliction for a moment. He said, 'Kamal, why do you see it as mortification? It's happiness to me. It's an age-old treasure that I've inherited.'

Kamal replied, 'Let it be ages old. An ideal is not valued by counting the years. Thousands of years of a rigid, inert society might be washed away by the torrent of ten future years. Those ten years will be of much greater worth, Ashu Babu.'

Ajit suddenly stood up straight like a released bowstring and said, 'These gentlemen might be amazed by your aggressiveness, but I'm not surprised. I know the source of this alien spirit, this deep hatred for all our benevolent ideals. But come, gentlemen, we don't have time to waste— it's five o'clock.'

Everyone silently followed Ajit out. No one said goodbye to her or even spared her a glance. Having lost out on reason, the male company asserted their triumph in this way and thereby preserved their manliness. When they had left, Ashu Babu mildly said, 'Kamal, it's me you have hurt the most today, yet it's me who has loved you today with all my heart. You seem no less worthy than my daughter Mani.'

Kamal said, 'You think so because you are truly large-hearted, Kakababu. You're not a fake like these men. But I too am getting late—I must go.' She came close, bowed low and touched his feet.

As a rule, she did not touch anyone's feet. Ashu Babu felt embarrassed at this unprecedented gesture. He made the sign of blessing and asked, 'When are you coming next, my dear?'

'Perhaps I won't come again, Kakababu,' she said as she left the room. With his eyes fixed in her direction, Ashu Babu sat on silently.

12

THE NEW MAGISTRATE'S WIFE WAS CALLED MALINI. IT WAS ON
her initiative and at her residence that the Women's Welfare
Society was being founded. The opening session had been
arranged on some scale, but it did not go off well—indeed, it
ended in disorder. Although the affair was chiefly for women,
men were not excluded. In fact, on this occasion they were
specially invited. Abinash had been put in overall charge.
Akshay was known as a thoughtful writer, and he had himself
taken responsibility for whatever needed writing. Hence,
following his advice, no one except Shibnath was left out.
Abinash's sister-in-law Nilima went from door to door,
irrespective of rich and poor, to invite all the Bengali women
in town. Only Ashu Babu did not wish to go. But the severity
of his gout could not protect him today—Malini herself
went and brought him over. Akshay was ready, papers in hand,
and after a few formal protestations of modesty he stood up
straight and stiff and began to read his paper.

It soon became clear that the paper was as tasteless as
it was long. As is customary, he referred to Sita and Savitri
of yore and sneered at the loss of their ideals among modern
women. He felt no scruples about denigrating the 'so-called'
education of women in the house of a modern, cultured
lady. Akshay was proud of his boldness in pronouncing harsh
truths. Hence whatever truth the discourse might have
contained, it did not lack harshness. And to explain the term
'so-called', the example he implicitly drew on was Kamal.

Akshay utterly humiliated this absent girl in his discourse. Towards the end of his speech, he was forced to confess with deep regret that a woman of this very nature was living in the town and enjoying the continual indulgence of respectable society—a woman who knew that her marital relationship was illicit and yet, far from being ashamed, only laughed scornfully—a woman for whom the marriage ceremony was a meaningless rite and the unwavering devotion of husband and wife a mere failing of the heart. In conclusion, Akshay also declared that though for himself he had no doubt about the proper appellation and dwelling place for that educated woman who, despite being a woman, rejected the highest ideals of womanhood, he could not express them out of delicacy. He apologized to everyone for this shortcoming.

None of the women, except Manorama, had seen Kamal. But there was very little about her beauty and her ill-repute that had not been carried to them through their menfolk. It had even reached the ears of Malini, the president of the newly formed Women's Welfare Society. Thus there was immense curiosity about the matter among women on both sides of the purdah. The enthusiasm to judge taste and morality, and the acuteness of the questions raised, would no doubt have led to a lively discussion of personalities, had not the writer's intimate friend Harendra sternly opposed it. He stood up straight and said, 'Akshay Babu, I utterly protest against this piece of writing: not only because it is irrelevant, but also because to criticize a woman in her absence is in *beastly* taste, and any uncalled-for reference to her character, uncivil and mean. The Women's Welfare Society should condemn the writer of this paper.'

Pandemonium broke out at once. Akshay lost his senses

and turned abusive, while the reticent Harendra replied only with an occasional '*Beast*' or '*Brute*'.

Malini was a newcomer to the place. She felt beleaguered by the sudden violent eruption. In that heated atmosphere, no one refrained from expressing his personal opinion. Only Ashu Babu was silent. He had sat with bowed head since the paper reading began, and did not look up till the meeting was over. Another person did not participate greatly in the debate: that was Abinash, so accustomed to such wrangles between Harendra and Akshay.

Malini knew, of course, that the Society did not aim at assessing individual characters, and that such discussions brought welfare to neither man nor woman. She felt extremely upset on realizing that this paper even sneered at Ashu Babu. When the meeting was over, she quietly left her seat and, sitting down beside that elderly gentleman, said in a shy, low, apologetic tone, 'I'm sorry to have disturbed your peace of mind for nothing, Ashu Babu.'

Ashu Babu attempted a smile and said, 'At home, too, I would have been alone. At least this helped to pass the time.'

'That would have been better than this,' replied Malini. She paused a little and continued, 'My husband isn't at home today. Manorama will have dinner here and then return.'

'Good. I shall send the car for her after I reach home. But what about the other ladies?'

'They too shall have dinner here.'

Ashu Babu was about to board the car with Abinash and Ajit when Harendra and Akshay appeared and asked for a lift. Ashu Babu agreed, but he remained silent all the way, repeatedly recalling that, while alluding to Kamal today, Akshay had made improper insinuations about him in front of the ladies.

The car reached home. An unknown gentleman was waiting in the portico. He was dressed like a Bombayite. He approached and greeted Ashu Babu in English.

'What is it?'

In reply he handed him a piece of paper and said, 'A letter.'

Ashu Babu passed the letter to Ajit. Ajit read it by the car headlights and said, 'It's from Kamal.'

'From Kamal? What does she say?'

'She simply writes that the bearer of this letter will tell you everything.'

As Ashu Babu looked enquiringly at the man, he said, 'She didn't want anybody else to read this letter. You're her relative—she owes me some money.'

Before he could end, Ashu Babu suddenly turned furious and said, 'I'm not her relative. In fact, she's nothing to me. Why should I pay you on her behalf?'

From inside the car, Akshay remarked, '*Just like her!*'

Everybody heard him. The gentleman with the letter said in embarrassment, 'You don't have to pay, she'll pay. If you'd only agree to stand surety for a few days . . .'

Ashu Babu got angrier still. He said, 'There's no call on me to stand surety. She has a husband. Tell him about this loan.'

The gentleman was amazed. He said, 'I didn't know she had a husband.'

'You will if you enquire. *Good night.* Come on, Ajit, let's have no more delay.' He went upstairs with Ajit, and leaning from the balcony, reminded the driver again that he must not be late in reaching the magistrate's bungalow. Ajit was going straightaway to his own room, but Ashu Babu called him into the sitting room and said, 'Sit down. Did you enjoy the fun?'

Ajit understood what he meant. Indeed, Ashu Babu's unnecessary and uncharacteristic harshness a moment ago, so contrary to his natural generosity, his love of peace and his habitual patience, had not failed to perturb everybody present except Akshay. Once, without knowing anything about her, Ajit's heart had filled with reverent wonder for this mysterious young woman. But ever since the day Kamal had so readily laid bare her past before this unknown man in her lonely room at night, his disgust and hatred for her seemed to have no bounds. So Ajit was not sorry about the sneers the principled Akshay had hurled at her at the Women's Welfare Society in the guise of moral counsel for women. He seemed to have hoped for something like that. But however sharp the barbs of Akshay's barbarity, Ashu Babu's act just now seemed tantamount to boxing Kamal's ears—not because it was unexpected but because it was unmanly.

Ajit did not approve of Kamal. He found nothing unfair in the violent criticism of her opinions and social attitudes. Within his own self, a deep repugnance for this woman was steadily growing. He felt it was not wrong to cast out someone clearly unfit for respectable society. But what was this? In Ashu Babu's turning down the plea of a wretched, debt-ridden woman for a trifling sum of money in her hour of distress, he sensed a deep dishonour for the male race and felt mortified. He recalled their conversation that night, the details of her past life in the tea garden, as she served him with utmost care: her mother's story and her own, the account of her birth in the English manager's house. It was all as strange as it was tasteless. What was the need for such a confessional? What harm would have come had she concealed all this? But perhaps Kamal had not remembered the simple calculations of worldly good sense. Even if she had thought of it, she had ignored it.

And the most astonishing thing was her indomitable patience. She had learnt fortuitously from him that Shibnath had not gone anywhere but was lying low in the town. She had remained silent, without any sign of distress or complaint. She had not protested to anyone against such false conduct. She was carrying out to the last word what she had uttered smilingly in jest on the river bank before the empress Mumtaz's memorial that day.

Ashu Babu himself had seemed distracted for a while. Now he suddenly became alert and, repeating his former question, said, 'Did you see the fun, Ajit? I'm certain this is a trick of that man Shibnath.'

'Perhaps,' said Ajit. 'We can't tell without knowing.'

'That's true,' said Ashu Babu. 'But it's my belief that this is Shibnath's cunning. He knows me to be rich.'

'Everybody knows that,' rejoined Ajit. 'So does Kamal herself.'

Ashu Babu said, 'Then she's even more to blame. It's wrong of her to hide things from her husband.' Ajit remained silent. Ashu Babu went on: 'Do you realize how wrong it is for a wife to borrow money without her husband's knowledge or against his wish? One can't possibly encourage such a thing.'

'She didn't ask for money,' said Ajit. 'She only requested you to stand surety.'

'It's all the same,' said Ashu Babu. He fell silent for a while, then continued: 'And why deceive that person by passing me off as a relative? I'm not really her relative.'

Ajit said, 'Perhaps she truly looks on you as a relative. I don't think it's her nature to deceive anyone.'

'No, no, I didn't mean quite that, Ajit.' Ashu Babu seemed

to be justifying his words to himself. Since he had refused the gentleman on the spur of the moment, he was feeling deeply miserable. He said, 'If she really considers me a relative, and she really needed a few hundred rupees, she could herself have come to get it. Why need she send an outsider in front of all those people? Whatever you might say, the girl has no sense.'

The servant came and announced that dinner was ready. Ajit was about to rise when Ashu Babu said, 'Did you *mark* the man, Ajit? What a sinister face—he's a *moneylender* after all. He might go back and concoct all manner of tales.'

Ajit smiled and said, 'He won't need to concoct anything, Ashu Babu. It'll be quite enough if he tells the truth.'

As Ajit was about to leave, Ashu Babu grew truly distressed and said, 'This Akshay is a perfect nuisance. He passes the limits of tolerance. Well, why don't you do something, Ajit? Call Jadu and open that drawer. You might at least send whatever might be there—six or seven hundred rupees—for the time being. The chauffeur ought to know their house: he has driven Shibnath home at times.' And he himself began to shout for the servant.

Ajit stopped him and said, 'Whatever has happened has happened. Let's not do anything tonight. We can think about it tomorrow morning.'

'You don't understand, Ajit,' protested Ashu Babu. 'She wouldn't have sent the man over at night if there hadn't been urgent need.'

Ajit stood still for some time. At last he said, 'The chauffeur is not at home. We don't know when he'll return with Manorama. Meanwhile Kamal will have heard everything. After that it won't be advisable to send the money, Ashu Babu. She might not accept it from you.'

'But this is just your guess, Ajit.'

'Yes, what else can it be?'

'But in this unfamiliar place, she might have all the more need of money.'

'Perhaps, but it might not be greater than her self-respect.'

'That too is just your guess,' said Ashu Babu.

Ajit did not reply immediately. He remained silent for some time with downcast face, and then said, 'No, it's more than a guess. It's my conviction.' Having said this, he slowly walked out of the room.

Ashu Babu did not call him back. He looked after him, eyes dilated with grief. He knew quite well that such a conviction about Kamal was neither impossible nor unjustified. In helpless remorse, he felt something clawing at his heart.

13

AFTER RETURNING FROM THE WOMEN'S WELFARE SOCIETY, Nilima began to entreat Abinash. 'Mukherjee Mashai, I want to see Kamal once. I want very much to invite her to dinner.'

Abinash was surprised and said, 'You're a brave woman, Younger-Wife. You not only want to get acquainted with her, but actually to invite her!'

'Why, is she a tiger or a bear? What's there to be afraid of?'

Abinash said, 'You don't find tigers or bears in these parts, or else I could have invited them at your command— but not her. If Akshay comes to know of it, he won't spare me. He'll drive me out of the land.'

Nilima said, 'I'm not afraid of Akshay Babu.'

Abinash said, 'There's no harm if you aren't. It would serve his purpose as long as I am.'

Nilima stubbornly said, 'No, that can't be. If you don't go, I'll go myself to invite her.'

'But I don't know their house.'

'Thakurpo[1] knows it,' said Nilima. 'I'll take him with me. He's not a coward like you.' She reflected for some time and said, 'From what you tell me, it's Shibnath Babu's fault. I don't want to invite him. I want to see Kamal and talk to her. If she agrees to come, the magistrate's wife has said she'll come too. Do you understand?'

Abinash understood everything but could not consent openly. Yet he did not have the courage to oppose her either. He held Nilima not only in affection and respect but also in awe.

Next morning Nilima summoned Harendra and said,

'Thakurpo, you must do me a favour. You are a bachelor, you don't have a wife at home to box your ears in the name of propriety. You share your home with a horde of orphan students—you have nothing to be afraid of.'

Harendra said, 'We'll talk about fears later on, but what do I have to do?'

Nilima said, 'I want to see Kamal, talk to her, bring her home and feed her. You know their house. You must take me there to invite her. Tell me what time would suit you.'

Harendra said, 'Whenever you command. But what about the master of the house, my Sejda?[2] What does he wish?' He pointed to Abinash across the balcony. He was sitting in his armchair reading the *Pioneer*.[3] He heard everything but made no response.

Nilima said, 'Let him do what he wishes. I'm not interested. I'm his sister-in-law, not his sister-in-law's sister that he should wield his club over me as lord and master. I shall feed anyone I like. The magistrate's wife has said that she too will come if I ask her. If he doesn't like it, he can go somewhere else at the time.'

Without taking his eyes off the paper, Abinash said, 'But it won't be prudent, Harendra. I hope you remember yesterday's incident. Even an unflappable person like Ashu Babu has to be cautious.'

Harendra did not reply; and afraid that the shameful business of the money should crop up and reach Nilima's ears, he quickly buried the subject and said, 'Why don't you do something else, Boudi?[4] Why not invite her to my place? You'll be the mistress of ceremonies. At least there will be the advent of Lakshmi[5] for a day in the house of this unprosperous wretch. The boys too will be happy to taste a few good things.'

With a touch of resentment in her voice, Nilima said, 'All right, let's do that. I'll be safe from digs and insinuations later on.'

Abinash sat up and said, 'That would be a scandal of the worst kind, because there would be no reason left to justify inviting her to the exclusion of Shibnath. It would sound better to say that the women want to get to know each other.'

This was reasonable enough. So it was decided that after college, Harendra would take Nilima in a carriage to invite Kamal.

Harendra came in the afternoon to say that there was no need to go. Kamal had already been asked to dinner the following day and agreed to come.

Nilima was excited. Harendra went on: 'While I was returning from your house, I suddenly met her on the way. There was a porter with her, carrying a big box on his head. I asked, "What's that? Where are you going?" She said, "I've got something to do." Then I told her about you and said, "Sister-in-law has invited you home tomorrow evening. Only among women. You have to go." She remained silent for a while and then said, "All right." I said, "She wanted to come with me and invite you in a befitting way, but need she any more?" She smiled a little and said, "No." I asked "Can you come by yourself or should I come to escort you?" On hearing this she began laughing again. She said, "I can go on my own. I know Abinash Babu's house."'

Nilima tenderly said, 'The girl is very good in this way, very modest.'

Abinash overheard everything from the next room, where he was changing his clothes. He called out, 'And what about the box on the porter's head? You didn't tell us its history, brother.'

Harendra answered, 'I didn't ask about it.'

'It would have been better had you done so. She was probably going to sell or pawn it.'

Harendra said, 'Quite possibly. If she comes to you to pawn it, ask her about its history.' He was about to leave on this note, but suddenly paused at the door and called out, 'Boudi, you heard Akshay's paper at the Women's Welfare Society, didn't you? We call that man a *brute*. But if the poor fellow had a little more flair for hypocrisy, he could easily have passed for an honest man in society. What do you say, Sejda? Isn't it so?'

Abinash roared from the next room, 'Oh yes, you ever-genial Lord Shri Gouranga![6] There's no doubt about it. Go and teach your friend the art.'

'I'll try. But goodbye, Boudi. I'll be here on time tomorrow.' And so he left.

Nilima spared no effort in making the arrangements. Manorama had been vehemently hostile to Kamal from the very beginning; it being known that she would not come in any event, no one from Ashu Babu's family had been invited. Malini had been asked but could not come, having suddenly fallen ill.

Kamal arrived punctually, not in any vehicle but alone on foot. The mistress of the house welcomed her very cordially. Abinash was standing there. He had not seen Kamal for quite some time. Today he was surprised by her appearance and her dress, which bore clear signs of poverty. He said in surprise, 'Why did you walk all the way here at night, Kamal?'

Kamal said, 'The reason is very simple, Abinash Babu, and not at all hard to understand.'

Abinash was embarrassed. To hide his embarrassment, he said, 'No, no, don't talk like that. It wasn't a safe thing to do. Oh, Younger-Wife, this is Kamal. Her other name is

Shibani. This is the lady you were so anxious to meet. Do come in and sit down. I hope you're ready with your arrangements? Then there's no point in holding back dinner—after all she must return home in good time.'

Most of his advice and enquiries were redundant. They neither required answers nor sought them.

Harendra arrived and greeted Kamal. He said, 'I'm sorry I wasn't here to welcome the guest, Boudi. Akshay had come over and it took me some time to get rid of him with sweet talk.' He began to laugh.

On going into the house, Kamal looked at the plethora of food and was silent for a moment. Then she said, 'You've cooked all this for me, but I don't eat this sort of food.' Seeing everybody grow anxious, she explained, 'I eat only the kind of food that widows take.'

Nilima was surprised to hear this. 'How strange! What misery has befallen you that you should eat widow's food?'

'That's a fair question,' said Kamal. 'It's not that I have no cause for grief, but at least my sense of loss is less because I don't eat these things. Please don't mind.'

One could not but mind. Nilima was vexed and said, 'If you don't eat anything, all this will go waste.' Kamal smiled. 'What has been done has already been done. You can't undo it. Why should I myself go to waste by eating this?'

Nilima made a last pitiful attempt, saying, 'Just for today, for a single day, can't you break your vow?'

Kamal shook her head and said, 'No.'

Only one smiling word: when first heard, it sounded like nothing at all. Harendra alone realized how irrevocable it was. That is why as soon as the mistress of the house began repeating her request, he interrupted her, saying, 'Let it be, Boudi; no more of this. Your preparations won't be wasted. The boys at my place will come and gobble it up clean. But don't press her any more. Rather, try to give her what she would like.'

Nilima angrily said, 'I will. But you don't need to console me, brother. Please stop. This is not grass that you can bring your flock of sheep to graze on. I'd rather throw all this away than let them have it.'

Harendra smiled and said, 'What makes you so angry with them?'

Nilima retorted, 'All your misery is because of them. Your father left behind a lot of money. You earn quite a bit yourself. If you had a wife, your house would have been full of children by now. Things wouldn't have taken this wretched turn. But you're a bachelor like the god Kartik, and you're bringing up your flock in the same way. I'll never feed those boys—I give you my word! I'd rather let all this be wasted.'

Kamal did not understand any of this; she looked on in puzzlement. Harendra was embarrassed and said, 'She has this old grudge against me, and this is my punishment.' Then he explained the matter briefly: 'I have a few orphan boys who stay with me and go to school or college. All her rancour is towards them.'

Kamal was amazed and said, 'Is that so? Why, I never heard of this.'

Harendra said, 'There's nothing to hear. But they are all good, well-disposed boys, and I love them.'

Nilima said in a fury, 'Yes, they have vowed that when they grow up they will save the country. In other words, like their guru, they too will become brahmacharis and set out to conquer the world, I suppose.'

'Will you pay them a visit, just once?' asked Harendra. 'You'd like meeting them.'

Kamal agreed immediately and said, 'I can come tomorrow—if you fetch me.'

Harendra said, 'No, not tomorrow but some other day. Rajen and Satish of our ashram have gone on a visit to Varanasi; I'll bring you to the ashram after they return. I'm sure you'll be pleased to meet them too.'

Abinash had just entered. When he heard this, he opened his eyes wide and said, 'Has your den of young wretches now become an ashram? What a hypocrite you are, Haren!'

Nilima was offended. She exclaimed, 'This is unfair of you, Mukherjee Mashai. Thakurpo hasn't asked you for money for his ashram; why should you accuse him of being a hypocrite? It isn't hypocrisy to bring up other people's children at your expense. Rather, those who say it is should be called hypocrites.'

Harendra smiled and said, 'Boudi, you abused them yourself just now as being a flock of sheep. Does Sejda get this reward for echoing your own words?'

Nilima answered, 'I said so in anger. But how in shame can he say so? Let him first be clear in his own mind what hypocrisy means; then let him teach others.'

Kamal said, 'Do all your boys go to school or college?'

'Yes, ostensibly that's what they do,' Harendra replied.

Abinash said, 'And why don't you tell her frankly what goes on behind the scenes—all those exercises in suspending and regulating the breath, and all the rest of it?'

Everyone laughed at this. Nilima told Kamal imploringly, 'Don't judge Mukherjee Mashai by his mood today. Sometimes he's much calmer, or I'd have had to run away long ago to save my life.' She began to laugh.

A little heat had been gathering for some time, but it was dispelled by this soothing jest. The Brahman cook came to announce that Kamal's food was ready. So everybody got up, suspending the discussion for the time being.

After the meal, nearly two hours later, when everybody had again gathered in the sitting room, Kamal took up the thread of their earlier conversation. 'The boys may not practise regulating their breath to purge their souls, but they must be doing things other than learning from their textbooks— what are those?'

Harendra said, 'They do. They spare no effort to grow up as true human beings for the future. But I'll explain everything the day you honour us with your visit. Not today.'

Abinash was vastly irritated that such excessive respect was being paid to the young woman, but he remained quiet.

Nilima said, 'Why not tell her today, Thakurpo? You may not reveal your ways of training them, but what's the harm in telling her that you are teaching them brahmacharya according to the ancient Indian ideal, in your own way? You once hinted at such a thing to me.'

Harendra politely said, 'I don't say you're wrong, Boudi.' As he spoke, he recalled the argument they had had the other day. Looking at Kamal, he asked, 'I suppose you don't have any sympathy for me either?'

Kamal said, 'Haren Babu, I can't tell you unless I know exactly what you are about. But it's not reasonable to suppose that bringing up boys in the ancient mould necessarily means following the true model of humanity.'

'But that's what our Indian ideal is!' said Harendra.

Kamal said, 'Tell me who has decided that the Indian ideal is the ultimate ideal for all ages.'

Abinash had not spoken so far. He controlled his anger and said, 'It may not be the ultimate ideal, Kamal, but it's the ideal of our ancestors. Indians have always aimed at it—it's the only path for them to follow. I don't know about Haren's ashram, but if he has adopted this path, my blessings on him.'

Kamal looked at him silently for a while and said, 'I don't know why people make this mistake. They seem to recognize no Indians other than themselves. We have many other communities as well. Why should they adopt this ideal?'

Abinash was enraged and retorted, 'To hell with them. This argument means nothing to me. It's enough for me if I can see our own ideal clearly.'

Kamal slowly said, 'You're saying this out of extreme anger, Abinash Babu. I don't think you're so bigoted as a rule.' After pausing a little, she continued, 'But who knows—perhaps all males think like this. The other day the same topic came up with Ajit Babu. His face blanched with pain at the thought that India's lasting uniqueness, her distinctive identity, was being impaired. He had once been a staunch nationalist—perhaps he still is in his heart of hearts. To him, this possibility is simply another name for the end of the world.' And she sighed deeply.

Abinash seemed about to say something, but Kamal took no notice and went on: 'But I wonder what there is to worry about. Why must I cling to the customs and practices of a particular country forever, just because I happened to be born there? What does it matter if its distinctiveness is lost? Need we be so attached to it? What's the harm if everyone on earth shares the same thoughts and feelings, if they stand under a single banner of laws and regulations? What if we can't be recognized as Indians any more? Where's the harm in that?

No one can object if we declare ourselves to be citizens of the world. Is that any less glorious?'

Abinash could not think of an answer immediately. He said, 'Kamal, you don't understand what you're saying. This would spell disaster for mankind.'

Kamal replied, 'It won't, Abinash Babu. It'll only destroy the conceit of the blind.'

Abinash said, 'These are all Shibnath's words.'

Kamal responded, 'I didn't know that—does he say such things?'

Abinash now forgot himself. His face darkened with a sneer as he said, 'You know it very well. You have learnt his words by heart, and you say you don't know whose they are!'

Kamal did not reply to this gross discourtesy. Nilima did. She said, 'I don't care who said it, Mukherjee Mashai. As a teacher you can shut your students up by scolding them, but you can't solve a problem that way. There's nothing to be ashamed of if you can't answer a question, but it's shameful to break the rules of decent behaviour. Thakurpo, please call for a carriage. You must see her home. You're a brahmachari, so I have no fears about letting you go with her.' She looked askance at Abinash and ended, 'Seeing how amiable Mukherjee Mashai is starting to look! It wouldn't be wise to wait any longer.'

Abinash said sombrely, 'Well, why don't you sit and talk? I'm going to bed.' He rose and left.

The servant had gone to call a carriage. Harendra said to Kamal, 'You really must visit my ashram one day. If I come to fetch you, you mustn't stop me.'

Kamal said smilingly, 'Why invite me to an ashram of brahmacharis? Wouldn't it be better if I didn't go?'

'No, that can't be. You needn't be afraid of us because we're brahmacharis. We're very simple people. We neither wear saffron clothes nor have matted hair and bark loincloths. We live among ordinary people—you can't tell us apart from them.'

'But that isn't good either. To hide among the ordinary in spite of being extraordinary is also a kind of wrongdoing. Perhaps this is what Abinash Babu calls hypocrisy. Saffron and matted hair and bark loincloths are far better. They make it easy to identify such people and harder to be deceived by them.'

Harendra said, 'One can't beat you in argument—one has to call a retreat. But really, don't you appreciate our institution? Whether or not we are successful, our ideal is a noble one.'

Kamal said, 'I don't agree with that, Haren Babu. Like all kinds of abstinence, sexual abstinence also contains truth; but it's a truth of a lesser order. Presented sanctimoniously as life's chief truth, it turns into a sort of incontinence which carries its own punishment. Spirituality grows weak through the arrogance of self-mortification. But all right, I shall come to your ashram.'

Harendra said, 'You must come—I won't stop pestering you until you pay us a visit. But let me tell you one thing—we don't have any pomp and show; we do nothing ostentatiously.' Suddenly, pointing to Nilima, he said, 'She is my ideal. Like her, we follow the path of simplicity. She carries no outward sign of widowhood; looked at from outside, she seems to be steeped in luxury. But I know about her austerity, her strict self-discipline.'

Kamal remained silent. Suffused with awe and reverence, Harendra continued, 'You have no respect for Indian antiquity;

the ideals of India don't attract you. But tell me, where else do you find such glory, such ideals ascribed to womanhood? Boudi is the mistress of this house; to Sejda's motherless son, she's like a mother. The entire responsibility for this household rests on her shoulders. But she has neither any personal interest nor any entanglement. Now tell me, in which country do widows give so much of themselves?'

Kamal's face lit up with a little smile. She said, 'Where's the good in it, Haren Babu? Perhaps there's no such instance in the world of being the selfless mistress of someone else's house and a selfless mother to someone else's son. Its uniqueness might make it strange or rare, but how can it make it good?'

Harendra fell silent on hearing this. Nilima opened her eyes wide with astonishment and looked fixedly at Kamal. Kamal aimed her next words at her. 'However people might glorify it with splendid words and clever epithets, nobody can respect this playacting of a housewife's part. It's better to abandon such glory.'

Harendra said with deep agony, 'What advice—to break up a well-run household and go away! Nobody expected that from you.'

Kamal said, 'But this household is not her own. Had it been, I wouldn't have offered such advice. This is how men intoxicate us with activity. When we drink in the heady wine of their applause, our eyes glaze over and we treat it like the fulfilment of our womanhood. I remember Harish Babu of our tea garden. When his sixteen-year-old sister was widowed, he brought her to his house, showed her his horde of children, cried and said, "Dear sister, from now on they are your children; why should you worry, sister? Bring them up, become their mother and the mistress of this house; make your life meaningful. This is my blessing upon you." Harish Babu was held to be a good man, the entire garden rang with his praise. Everybody said, "Lakshmi's a lucky girl." Indeed she was. Only women know that there's no greater misery, no greater fraud. But by the time this becomes clear, it's too late to correct it.'

'What happened then?' asked Harendra.

'I don't know, Haren Babu,' said Kamal. 'I couldn't see the end of Lakshmi's self-fulfilment; I had to leave before that. But my carriage has arrived. Come, I'll tell you about it on the way. Goodbye.' And she got up instantly.

Nilima stood speechless, making a namaskar. Her eyes seemed to burn like embers.

THE WORD 'ASHRAM' HAD SUDDENLY SLIPPED OUT OF
Harendra's mouth before Kamal. Abinash was not wrong in
mocking him when he heard it. A few poor boys stayed
there free of cost and went to school. In fact, Harendra had
had no intention of projecting his dwelling place in such
a glorious light. It was quite an ordinary affair with a very humble
beginning. But these matters are such that once born of the
donor's generosity, they grow at relentless speed. Like stubborn
weeds, they lose no time in extracting all sap from the soil
and transmitting it to their roots and branches. That is what
happened in this case as well. This needs to be explained in detail.

Harendra had no brother or sister. His father had amassed
a lot of money in the law. After his death, Harendra was left
only with his widowed mother. She too died soon after her son
finished his studies. Thus he had no near relation to press
him into marriage, or to take the initiative in chaining him
down. His studies once over, Harendra, for want of anything
else to do, devoted himself to the service of the people and the
nation. He befriended a lot of sadhus, withdrew the accumulated
interest from his bank account and formed a Famine Prevention
Society, helped an eminent leader in flood relief, joined a
Rehabilitation Society and brought the blind, the lame, the
dumb and the deaf home to nurse.

As his fame spread, hordes of philanthropists came and
said, 'Give us money, we shall serve others.' All his surplus
funds were exhausted; he now needed to break into his capital.

Things had come to this pass when one day he suddenly met Abinash. However distant might have been the link, Harendra learnt for the first time that there was still somebody left in the world with whom he could claim kinship. There was a post going vacant in Abinash's college. With some effort, Abinash got Harendra appointed to it and brought him to Agra. In the historic towns of that part of India, many large, old-fashioned mansions were still obtainable at low rent. Harendra rented one of these. It was now his ashram.

Harendra met Nilima during the few days he had stayed in Abinash's house on first arriving in Agra. This young woman did not lurk behind the curtains because Harendra was a stranger, or extend hospitality through the servants. She came out before him in person from the very first day. She said, 'Don't hesitate to ask me for whatever you need, Thakurpo. I'm not the mistress of the house, but the responsibility of being mistress has now fallen on me. Your Dada has said, "I'll dock your pay if this cousin of mine isn't properly looked after." Please don't cause any loss to this poor woman, brother. Tell me what you need.'

Harendra did not know what to say. His diffidence made him shrink so much that he could not look at the speaker of these sweet, simple words in the face. But it took him only two days to regain his ease. He could not but be easy, such was this woman's graceful, natural affection and her innate hospitality. From her face, her dress, her speech, one could not tell that she was a widow, that she had no real shelter in this world—that she was, moreover, a stranger in this house. Yet one could sense that these features alone did not make up her full personality.

She was not exactly young—probably nearing thirty; but her light, laughing ways belied her age. Only a close scrutiny revealed that she was continually girdled by an invisible barrier: neither the servants nor the master of the house could penetrate it.

Harendra spent two weeks in this house, in this atmosphere. Nilima was upset when she suddenly heard one day that Harendra had rented a house. 'Why did you do it so hastily, Thakurpo?' she asked. 'Aren't you comfortable here?'

Harendra said with a smile, 'I would have had to go some day, Boudi.'

'Perhaps,' replied Nilima, 'but your eyes still say that you are obsessed with the idea of serving the country. Why don't you spend a few days more in your Boudi's custody?'

Harendra said, 'I'll still be doing that. It's only a ten-minute walk. How can I stray from your sight?'

Abinash was working in his room. He called out from there: 'He'll go to perdition. I tried so hard to persuade you, Haren: "Don't go, stay here." But would you listen? What's more important—your own prestige, or your Dada's request? Very well then: go to your new shelter and serve the Lord of the Poor. It's no use pressing him, Younger-Wife. He's a sannyasin[1] at the Charak festival. His life will be in vain if he can't whirl about with his back pierced.'

In the new house, Harendra employed a servant and a cook and, like a modest and peace-loving teacher, absorbed himself in his work at college. There were many rooms in this large mansion. All but two remained vacant. Nearly a month later, the vacant rooms began to trouble him. He was paying the rent but getting no benefit from them. So a letter went out to Rajen, the secretary of his Famine Prevention Society. He had been interned for two years because of his enthusiasm for freeing the country. He had been released five or six months earlier and was hunting out old friends and acquaintances. On receiving Haren's letter and the train fare, he arrived immediately. 'Let's see if I can find you a job,' proposed Harendra. 'All right,' said Rajen.

Satish was Rajen's intimate friend. He had somehow escaped internment and was trying to start a brahmacharya ashram in an obscure village in Midnapore district. Within a week of receiving a letter from Rajen, he gave up his idea of becoming a sadhu and came down to Agra. He did not come alone: he very kindly brought along a follower from the village. With cogent arguments and evidence from the scriptures, Satish firmly established that India alone was a holy land and the saints and sages were her gods; that we had lost everything by forgetting to be celibate ascetics; and that no other country in the world was comparable to ours because we had been so long the original teachers of the world, the preceptors of men. Hence at present the only duty of Indians was to set up innumerable brahmacharya ashrams in every town and village. If it were at all possible to free the country, it would be done in this way.

Such talk cast a spell on Harendra. He knew of Satish, but had not met him; so he thanked Rajen inwardly for this piece of luck and counted himself fortunate that he had not married. Satish had a great store of noble speeches, and he continued his disquisitions for some days: 'We are the progeny of the sages and seers of this holy land; our ancestors once taught the world; hence we are sole heirs to the right of becoming such gurus another day.' Could anyone born of Aryan blood be such a monster as to disagree with this? No one could, and no one present was perverse enough to do so.

Harendra became enthusiastic. But since the matter involved contemplation and meditation, it was kept secret as far as possible. Only Rajen and Satish sometimes went to their native villages to collect recruits. Those who were young entered school; those who had passed out of school joined one of the colleges with Harendra's help. In this way the house was soon packed with boys of various ages. Outsiders did not know much about this, nor did they show any interest. People knew only that a few poor Bengali boys pursued their studies from Harendra's house. Even Abinash did not know more than this, nor did Nilima.

Under Satish's stern diktat, fish and meat were banned in the house. Rising at the holy hour of dawn, everybody had to recite hymns, meditate and carry out breathing exercises as prescribed in the scriptures. Then they did their lessons and household work. But even this did not satisfy the authorities: the path of prayer and discipline grew harder and harder. The cook ran away, the servants were sacked, so their duties fell on the boys. On some days they managed to cook one dish, on others not even that. Their education began to suffer—they were scolded at school but their regime was not relaxed, such was its rigour. The only concession was allowing attendance at feasts in other people's houses.

Harendra had forced this exception to the rules when Nilima was celebrating the completion of a vow. Apart from this, there was no mercy at all. The boys went barefoot and with dishevelled hair, and Satish's alert eyes were constantly on guard lest any unauthorized luxury enter through some minute crevice. This was how the days passed at the ashram.

Not only Satish, but Harendra too was proud of what they were attempting. They did not say much to outsiders; but often among themselves, Harendra, swollen with complacency and self-satisfaction, would say that, if he could make even one of the boys a true human being, he would think he had attained the highest success in life. Satish would not say anything, only modestly bow his head.

Both Harendra and Satish were troubled by one thing. For some time now, both had sensed that Rajen's attitude had changed. He did not show any interest in the affairs of the ashram. He often abstained from the morning prayers and rites. When asked, he would say he was not well; but he showed no symptoms of illness. He would not divulge what his grievances were, why he was behaving in this way. Sometimes he went out at dawn and did not return all day. When he came back at night, his expression would deter even Harendra from asking him anything. Yet all this was against the rules of the ashram. No one except Harendra was allowed to stay out after nightfall. Rajen knew this very well, but did not care. Satish was the secretary of the ashram and hence responsible for its discipline. He did not openly complain to Harendra about these irregularities, but sometimes he would hint that it was inadvisable to keep Rajen at the ashram—the boys might be corrupted. It was not that Harendra did not appreciate this, but nevertheless, he did not dare speak out.

Once Rajen stayed away all night. A hot debate broke out when he returned in the morning. Harendra said with amazement, 'Well now, Rajen, where were you last night?' Rajen attempted a smile and said, 'Under a tree.'

'Under a tree! Why?'

'It got very late—I didn't want to wake you up.'

'Well, what made you so late?'

'Just wandering about.' And he went into his room.

Satish was standing nearby. 'What's going on?' Haren said to him.

'How should I know?' said Satish. 'You see how he dodged even your questions.'

'You're quite right. This is getting to be too much.'

Satish gravely said, 'You know the police had put him away for two years.'

'I know,' said Haren, 'but that was on a false suspicion. He hadn't really done anything.'

Satish added, 'I too was on the point of being jailed merely because I was his friend. The police still keep an eye on him.'

'Not impossible,' observed Harendra.

Satish responded with a sad smile: 'I'm afraid that they might grow fond of our ashram because of him.'

Harendra turned silent and thoughtful at this. Satish too was silent for a while, but suddenly said, 'Perhaps you know that Rajen doesn't even believe in God.'

'No, I didn't,' said Harendra in astonishment.

'I know he doesn't,' said Satish. 'He doesn't have a jot of respect for the activities, rules and regulations of the ashram. You'd better get him a job somewhere else.'

Harendra said, 'Jobs are not fruit to be plucked off a tree. They take a lot of getting.'

'Then please make the effort,' rejoined Satish. 'You being the founder-president of the ashram and I its secretary, it's my duty to apprise you of everything. You're very fond of him, and he's my friend too. That's why I didn't want to say anything against him, but now I think it's my duty to warn you.'

Harendra was tense. He said, 'But I know he has a stainless character . . .'

Satish nodded and said, 'Yes, even his greatest enemy can't accuse him on that score. Rajen is a lifelong virgin, but he isn't a brahmachari. The real reason for his abstinence is that he hasn't the time to ponder that there are such creatures as women on this earth.' He paused and continued, 'I make no charge against his character; it's exceptionally spotless, but . . .'

'Why "but"?' asked Harendra.

Satish said, 'We used to share a room in Calcutta. He was then a student in Campbell Medical School, and he was also studying privately for the B.Sc. Everybody thought he would top the list; but just before the examination he suddenly went away somewhere . . .'

Harendra asked in astonishment, 'You mean he studied medicine? But he told me that he had been admitted to the Shibpur Engineering College, and ran away because the course was too hard for him!'

Satish said, 'If you check, you'll learn that he came first in his third year at college. All the teachers were very upset when he left for no reason. His wealthy aunt had been supporting him: she was vexed by this and stopped the money. It must have been around then that you came to know him. When he returned after wandering for two years, his aunt, at his own suggestion, got him admitted to the Medical School. He used to be first in class in every subject, but after three years he suddenly gave it up. It was the same excuse: "It's too hard, I can't cope with it." He then came and took refuge in my house. He said he would study for the B.Sc., supporting himself by tutoring, and then take up work as a village schoolmaster. "All right, do that," I said. For the next fifteen days he neither ate nor bathed, nor did he sleep—the way he studied was astounding. Everyone said, "This is the way to be first in every subject." '

Harendra knew nothing of this. Very interested now, he asked, 'And then?'

Satish said, 'What he next began to do was also astonishing. He didn't touch his books. His notebooks and pencils lay forgotten—nobody knew where he went or where he stayed. When he came back, we were frightened to look at him: he had neither bathed nor eaten all that time.'

'And then?'

'Then one day the police came and went on a rampage through the house. They threw away this, scattered that, opened that other, shouted down one, arrested another—you can't picture it if you haven't seen it with your own eyes. The people who lived in the house were all humble clerks. Two of them developed heat stroke from sheer fright. We thought there was no escape—the police would arrest us all and perhaps hang us.'

'And then?'

'Towards the evening they arrested Rajen and me—since I was Rajen's friend—and went away. They let me go after four days, but we lost all trace of Rajen. Before releasing me, the English officer took pity on me and warned me over and over, "*One step, only one step!* There's only *one step* between your house and this jail. *Go!*" I had a dip in the Ganga, paid a visit to goddess Kali at Kalighat, and returned home. Everyone said, "Satish, you've been lucky." I went to my office. My English boss sent for me, handed me two months' salary and said, "*Go.*" I heard that they'd made all kinds of searches and enquiries after me.'

Harendra remained dumbfounded for some time, then slowly asked: 'Then you're certain that Rajen . . .'

Satish said apologetically, 'Don't ask me. He's my friend.'

Harendra was not pleased. He said, 'To me, too, he's like a brother.'

Satish said, 'You should consider one point. It's true that they harassed me for no reason, but finally they did let me go.'

Harendra said, 'It's against the law even to harass the innocent. Those who can do that can do worse things.'

Saying this, he left for college, but he was inwardly disturbed: not because he was worried about Rajen's future, but because he was afraid that his plans to bring up the boys as true human beings, saving the country, might be frustrated. Whether Satish's account was true or not, Harendra was convinced that it would be unwise to draw the attention of the police to the ashram. Particularly since Rajen was openly violating the rules of the place, it was advisable to move him elsewhere by getting him a job, or on some other pretext.

A few days later, there were two days of holiday for a Muslim festival. Satish asked for permission to go to Varanasi. Harendra had an ambitious plan to establish ashrams all over India modelled on the one at Agra, and Satish was going to Varanasi for this purpose. When Rajen came to know of it he said, 'Haren-da, let me also go with him for a few days.'

Harendra said, 'He's going because he has work.'

Rajen said, 'I want to go because I have no work. I have the money to pay the train fare out.'

'And what about the fare back?' asked Harendra. Rajen kept quiet.

Harendra said, 'For some days now I've been on the point of telling you something, but haven't been able to.'

Rajen smiled and said, 'You don't need to tell me, Haren-da. I know what it is.' Then he went away.

They were to go by the night train. As they were leaving, Harendra waited by the door. He tucked something wrapped in paper into Rajen's hand and whispered, 'I'll be very sorry if you don't come back, Rajen.' Having said this, he at once hurried back to his room.

They both returned ten days later. Satish drew Harendra aside and cheerfully said, 'The little you told him that day has worked, Haren-da. All this time Rajen has put in a superhuman effort to set up the ashram at Varanasi.'

'He puts superhuman effort into everything he does!' said Harendra.

'Yes, he's done just that. If only he could put in a quarter of that labour for our own ashram!'

Harendra said hopefully, 'He'll do it, Satish, he'll do it. Perhaps he hadn't understood things correctly all this time. I'm sure you'll find him working relentlessly now.' Satish hoped the same.

Harendra said, 'I'd postponed something till your return. Do you know what I've decided? We can't keep the existence and the purpose of our ashram secret any longer. We must have the support of the country and the people. And we must spread our methods of work among the masses.'

'But won't it disrupt our own work?' asked Satish doubtfully. 'No,' said Harendra. 'I've asked a few people over this Sunday. They're coming for a visit. We must convince them about the education, dedication, abstinence and purity inculcated by the ashram. I'm putting you in charge.'

Satish asked, 'Whom are you expecting?'

Harendra said, 'Ajit Babu, Abinash-da and my Boudi. Shibnath Babu is not in town now—I heard he's gone to Jaipur on some business. But perhaps you've heard of his wife Kamal— she too will come. And if he's well enough, perhaps I can persuade Ashu Babu as well. As you know, none of them is an ordinary person. We must be able to earn their true respect that day. That's your responsibility.'

Satish humbly lowered his head and said, 'Bless me so that I can do that.'

On Sunday the guests arrived shortly before evening. Only Ashu Babu didn't come. Harendra met them at the entrance and showed them in with due respect. The boys were busy with their routine tasks. One was lighting the lamp, one sweeping, one drawing water, one kindling the oven and another getting the ingredients ready. Harendra said to Abinash with a smile, 'Sejda, these are our ashram boys—those whom you call wretches. We don't have servants and cooks—they do all the work themselves. Boudi, come into our kitchen. We're celebrating a festival today. Come and see all the preparations.'

Everybody followed Nilima to the door of the kitchen. A boy of ten or twelve was kindling the oven; another boy of the same age was slicing potatoes. Both stood up to greet them. Nilima asked affectionately, 'What will you be having today, boys?'

The boy said gleefully, 'Today's Sunday. On Sundays we have potato curry!'

'And what else?'

'Nothing else.'

In bewilderment Nilima asked, 'Only potato curry? No dal or gravy or anything else . . .'

The boy only said, 'We had dal yesterday.'

Satish was standing beside them. He explained, 'By the rules of our ashram we don't have more than one dish at a meal.'

Harendra smiled and said, 'We can't afford it, Boudi; how can we? My brother-in-mission's explanation keeps up the honour of the ashram before outsiders.'

Nilima asked, 'There are no maids or servants either, I suppose?'

Harendra said, 'No. If we called them in, we'd have to say goodbye to the potato curry. The boys wouldn't like that.'

Nilima did not ask any more questions. Her eyes grew moist as she looked at the boys' faces. She said, 'Thakurpo, let's go somewhere else.'

Everyone understood what she meant. Harendra was inwardly pleased and said, 'Come. But Boudi, I knew you wouldn't be able to tolerate this.' He looked at Kamal and continued, 'But you are habituated to this kind of life—you alone will understand its value. That's why I invited you so respectfully that day to this brahmacharya ashram.'

Seeing Harendra's profoundly serious face, Kamal smiled and said, 'My own case is different. Haren Babu, do you call this fruitless exercise in poverty, carried out with such ostentation among such small children, a way to bring up true human beings? They are brahmacharis, I suppose? If you want to bring them up, do it the easy, natural way—don't bow them down prematurely with the burden of false privations.'

The sternness of her words disconcerted Harendra.

Abinash said, 'You didn't do well to invite Kamal, Haren.'

Kamal was embarrassed and said, 'It's true. No one should invite me anywhere.'

Nilima said, 'But I'm different. You'll never be disregarded in my house. Come, let's go and sit upstairs. Let's see what other fireworks Thakurpo has in store for us at his ashram.' She smiled gently to cover Kamal's embarrassment.

The ashram parlour on the first floor was quite spacious. The antique ornaments on the ceiling and the walls were still there. There were a bench and four chairs, but as a rule no one sat on them. A carpet was laid out on the floor. Today being a special day, a white sheet had been spread over it with a few cushions borrowed from the neighbouring Lalaji's house. In the middle of the room there was a twelve-branched lamp of floral cut-glass work, and in one corner a wall lamp with a green shade. These too had been borrowed from Lalaji. Everyone was happy to enter this room after the dark, joyless atmosphere below.

Abinash leaned on a cushion and, stretching out his legs, said contentedly: 'Ah, what a relief.'

Harendra was pleased and asked, 'Do you like this room of our ashram, Sejda?'

Abinash said, 'Now you're putting me in a fix, Haren. Kamal is present, and I dare not praise anything in front of her—she might prove at once with razor-sharp logic that everything here is bad, from the designs on the roof to the carpet on the floor.' He looked at her, smiled a little, and continued: 'I may not have any other assets, but you must admit that I've built up the capital of accumulating age. On the strength of that, let me tell you one thing today. I don't deny that truth is often unpleasant. But that doesn't mean that whatever is unpleasant is true. Shibnath has taught you many things, but I find he left out this one.'

Kamal's face flushed, but it was Nilima who replied. She said, 'Shibnath is at fault; we must punish him with a fine. But when it comes to acting the guru, no male seems any the less. I beseech you, utter a few more words of wisdom from the stock of your years—let's all listen and be blessed.'

Abinash burned inwardly—not only because he was being ridiculed in company, but because the sharp edge of the irony both attacked and humiliated him. For some time now, a hot wind of disaffection from some obscure source had been blowing between him and Nilima. It was nothing as terrible as a storm, but it often drove motes of hay or dust into their faces. It was like a slightly loose tooth—you could chew with it, but it hurt to chew. He said to Harendra, 'I don't feel offended, Haren. Your Boudi isn't wrong—she knows me very well. She knows that my capital is simple and old-fashioned; it may have substance but no sap.'

Harendra asked, 'What does that mean, Sejda?'

Abinash said, 'You won't understand, you're an ascetic. But from the way my Younger-Wife has suddenly started admiring Kamal, she should earn much merit if she puts Kamal's experience to use.'

The ugliness of this jibe offended his own ears, but his arrogance was leading him to say something more. Harendra stopped him, saying in a hurt tone, 'Sejda, all of you are my guests today. I have cordially invited Kamal on behalf of the ashram. If you forget that, we shall all be very sorry.'

Nilima said, 'Then Thakurpo, remind him also that if somebody is addressed as Younger-Wife, she does not really become a wife. One must know the limits of the control one can exercise over her. Let me add this much at least to Mukherjee Mashai's store of experience. It may be of use to him one day.'

With folded hands, Harendra said, 'Spare us, Boudi! Should all this battling over experience take place in my house? Sort out the rest of your disagreement when you're back at home, else we shan't survive. I didn't invite Akshay because felt nervous about him; but I seem to be meeting the same fate anyway.'

Both Ajit and Kamal laughed at this. Harendra said, 'Ajit Babu, I hear you're going home tomorrow.'

'From whom could you have heard this?'

'I had gone to bring Ashu Babu. He said that perhaps you'll be leaving tomorrow.'

'Perhaps,' said Ajit. 'Not tomorrow, though, but the day after. And it's not certain that I'll go home. Perhaps I'll turn up at the station towards the afternoon, and set out on my next journey by the first train leaving, in whichever direction—north, south, east or west.'

Harendra said with a smile, 'It's rather like becoming a world-weary wanderer—that is, having no fixed destination.'

'Yes', said Ajit.

'But what about returning?'

'I haven't yet decided about that.'

Harendra said, 'Ajit Babu, you're a fortunate man. But if you need someone to carry your baggage, I can offer you such a person. You won't find a better friend to have with you in alien places.'

Kamal said, 'And if you need a cook I can offer you an unrivalled one. You'll have to admit this cook has the right to boast.'

Nothing seemed to interest Abinash any more. He said, 'What's the point in staying on here? Why don't we get ready to leave?'

Harendra said deferentially, 'Won't you talk to the boys? Won't you give them a few words of advice, Sejda?'

Abinash said, 'I didn't come to give advice. I came only to accompany the others. I don't think they need my company any more.'

Satish appeared with a number of boys. They were of various ages, from ten or twelve to nineteen or twenty. It was winter. They wore no warm clothes and no shoes—perhaps because shoes were not a necessity. The arrangements for meals have already been described. These were a part of the training in a brahmacharis' ashram. Harendra had prepared a beautiful speech for the day. Rehearsing it in his mind, he began with appropriate gravity. 'These boys have dedicated themselves to the country. Bless them so that they may propagate the great ideal of this ashram in every town and village.'

Everyone gave their full-throated blessings.

Harendra said, 'If time permits I'll express my views later on.' He then turned to Kamal and said, 'We invited you specially today to say a few things for everyone to hear. The boys are hoping to hear something from you which will make their life's vow shine brighter.'

Kamal flushed with diffidence and hesitation. She said, 'But I can't make a speech, Haren Babu.'

It was Satish who replied. 'Not a speech, only some advice. Just something to stand them in good stead in working for the country.'

Kamal asked him, 'First tell me what you mean by working for the country.'

Satish said, 'Anything that makes for the total welfare of the country is work for the country.'

Kamal said, 'But different people have different notions of welfare. If your idea doesn't match mine, my advice will be of no use to you.'

Satish was in a quandary. He could not find an appropriate reply. To help him out, Harendra said, 'Whatever leads to the liberation of the country constitutes the only welfare for the country. Is there anyone in the land who doesn't admit this truth?'

Kamal said, 'Haren Babu, I'm afraid to say there is, for

everyone will be furious. Or else I myself would have said that there is no better word than "liberation" to deceive and be deceived. Liberation from what, Haren Babu? From threefold misery or from worldly ties? Tell me, what did you determine to be the sole well-being of the nation when you set up this ashram? Is this your ideal of serving your motherland?'

Harendra hastily said, 'No, no, no, not this, not this. We don't want this.'

Kamal said, 'Then say this is not what you want, that your ideal is different: that your aim is not withdrawal from worldly life or indifference to it, but to live along with all the wealth, all the beauty, all the life on this earth. But what you're training the boys for is not this goal. They have no warm clothes, no shoes on their feet. They wear worn-out dhotis, their hair is dishevelled. Will the nation's Lakshmi send us the key of her storehouse through those who live on one meagre meal a day and grow up in deprivation, in whom the joy of acquiring things dies in the heart? Haren Babu, take a look at the world. Those who have got a great deal have easily given things away. There is no need for a school of austerity like this to make them *graduates* in self-denial.'

Satish asked in bewilderment, 'Do you mean that devotion to religion and initiation into sacrifice are not needed in the struggle for the nation's freedom?'

Kamal said, 'First let's be clear what we mean by a freedom struggle.'

Satish hesitated. Kamal smiled and said, 'You seem to imply that such a struggle simply means throwing off the yoke of foreign rule. If that is so, Satish Babu, I give you my word that, though I've neither taken to religion nor been initiated into sacrifice, you'll always find me in the front rank. But shall I find all of you there?'

Satish did not speak. He grew somewhat agitated, and following his restless gaze to its object, Kamal could not turn her eyes away for some time. This, then, was Rajendra. Only Satish had noticed him as he entered silently and stood near the door. He had been looking at him all this time without turning his gaze, as if in a stupor, and he looked on in the same way even now.

Once seen, Rajen's appearance was hard to forget. He might have been twenty-five or twenty-six. His complexion was so fair that at first glance it seemed unnatural. His forehead was large, balding in front even at this age; his eyes were deep-set and very small, like a mouse's eyes gleaming from its dark hole. His thick lower lip hung forward as if suppressing a strong determination within him. If one saw him without warning, one would think it better to avoid such a man.

Harendra said, 'This is my friend Rajendra—not only a friend but like a younger brother to me. I haven't seen such a wonderful worker, such a great patriot, such a fearless, honest man, Boudi. It's him I was talking about the other day. He lays things aside casually, just as he obtains them easily. He's a strange man, Ajit Babu. It's him that I had in mind when I suggested someone to carry your baggage.'

Ajit was about to say something when a boy entered to announce that Akshay Babu had come.

'Akshay Babu!' exclaimed Harendra in astonishment.

'Yes, my friend, yes,' said Akshay as he entered the room, your dearest friend Akshaykumar.' Then he suddenly gave a start and said, 'Oho! What's happening today? Everyone seems to be here. I had come out for a drive with Ashu Babu in his car. He dropped me here on the way. As I was passing, it suddenly struck me that I might drop in at Hari Ghosh's cowshed.[2] That's why I've come. Splendid!'

No one responded to this because there was nothing to say; no one believed him either. This was not Akshay's usual route, and he seldom came to this house.

Akshay looked at Kamal and said, 'I had thought of going to see you tomorrow morning, but I don't know the place—it's just as well that we've met. There's some good news.'

Kamal looked at him in silence. Harendra asked, 'What's the good news? If it's good it certainly can't be secret.'

'What's there to hide?' said Akshay. 'On the way here we came across that Parsee sewing-machine seller, that very man who had gone to borrow money on Kamal's behalf the other day. We stopped the car and heard the news.' Pointing at Kamal, he continued, 'She had bought a machine on credit and was paying her bills by sewing shirts and so on. Now Shibnath's disappeared, but of course that couldn't be an excuse for defaulting on the payment! So he had taken away the machine, but today Ashu Babu paid the full price and bought it. Kamal, send someone tomorrow morning to fetch it. Why didn't you tell us that you were in such straits?'

All of them were wounded to the core by the brutal cruelty of his tone. Even Abinash flushed as he realized why Kamal looked so pale and haggard.

Kamal said in a subdued voice, 'Give him my thanks and tell him to return it. I don't need it any more.'

'Why? Why?'

Harendra said, 'Akshay Babu, get out of this house. I didn't invite you—I didn't want you to come, yet here you are. Shouldn't there be some limit to a man's *brutality*?'

Looking up suddenly, Kamal saw Ajit's eyes brimming with tears. She said, 'Ajit Babu, have you brought your car? Could you please reach me home?'

Ajit did not speak. He only nodded his head in compliance. Kamal made a namaskar to Nilima and said, 'Perhaps we won't meet again soon. I'm leaving this place.'

No one dared to ask where she was going and why. Nilima only took her hand in her own and pressed it a little. The next moment, Kamal did a namaskar to Harendra and followed Ajit out of the room.

15

SITTING IN THE CAR, KAMAL REMAINED SOMEWHAT ABSENT-
minded, staring at the sky. As the car stopped, she looked
this way and that and said, 'Where have you brought me,
Ajit Babu? This isn't the way to my house!'

'No, it isn't,' said Ajit.

'Not the way! Then shouldn't we be going back?'

'That's up to you. If you order me, I'll go back.'

Kamal was surprised. It was not so much the strange
reply as the unnaturalness of his voice that perturbed her.
She remained silent for some time; then stiffened herself
and said with a smile, 'I didn't ask you to come the wrong
way, so I don't have to order you to set yourself right. It's
your responsibility to take me to the right place—my duty is
only to trust you.'

'But Kamal, what if my idea of responsibility is wrong?'

'Ajit Babu, one can't pass judgement on an "if". First let
me be convinced that you're mistaken, and then I'll judge.'

In a faint voice, Ajit said, 'Take your time to judge;
I'll wait.' He remained quiet for a few moments, then
suddenly said, 'Kamal, do you remember that other day? It was
as dark then as it is now.'

'So it was.' Having said this, she opened the car door, got
down and climbed into the front seat beside Ajit. It was a
dark, lonely night, absolutely still. For some time no one spoke.

'Ajit Babu!'

'Yes?'

144

A storm was raging in Ajit's heart. His response stuck in his throat.

Kamal asked again, 'Tell me what you are thinking about.'

Ajit's voice began to quiver. He said, 'Do you remember how I behaved at Ashu Babu's house the other day? Till then I had thought that your past made up the greatest part of your life; how could I compromise with it? I had stretched forward the shadow behind you till it covered your face, forgetting that the sun moves. Well, no more of that. But can't you tell what I'm thinking now?'

Kamal said, 'Am I such a fool that, in spite of being a woman, I won't understand even after this? I understood it when you took this road.'

Ajit slowly put his left arm on her shoulder and kept silent. After some time he said, 'Kamal, I fear I won't be able to control myself any more today.'

Kamal did not draw away. There was no trace of surprise or bewilderment in her attitude. In a quiet, relaxed tone, she said, 'There's nothing to be surprised about, Ajit Babu. That's how things are. But you are not simply a man. You are an upright gentleman. How will you get me off your shoulders afterwards? You won't be able to do anything so mean.'

In a rapt voice Ajit said, 'Why should I have to?'

Kamal smiled and said, 'I'm not concerned about myself, Ajit Babu. I'm concerned only about you. I wouldn't worry if you could do such a thing, I'm worried because you can't. I'd be sorry to thrust such a heavy punishment on you for a single night's mistake. That's enough. Let's go back.'

Ajit heard her words but did not heed them. In a flash, the blood in his veins turned furious. He drew her forcibly to his breast and said passionately, 'Can't you trust me, Kamal?'

Kamal stopped breathing for a moment. 'I can,' she said.

'Then why do you want to go back? Come, Kamal, let's go away.'

'Let's.'

Ajit was about to start the car, but suddenly stopped and said, 'Isn't there anything you want to take from your house?'

'No, but what about you?'

Ajit had to think. He slid his hand into his pocket and said, 'I have no money on me. That's something we'll need.'

Kamal said, 'You can easily get money by selling the car.'

Ajit said in amazement, 'Sell the car? But it's not mine, it's Ashu Babu's.'

'So what?' said Kamal. 'Ashu Babu will never bring up the matter out of shame and embarrassment. Don't worry about it. Let's go.'

This left Ajit dumbfounded. His left arm had rested on Kamal's shoulder all this while; it slackened and dropped. He remained silent for a long time. Then he said, 'Are you joking?'

'No, I'm serious.'

'Do you seriously think I would steal something that belongs to someone else? Could you yourself do such a thing?'

Kamal said, 'I would have answered your question had you been staking on my ability to do it. You don't have the courage to steal someone else's property. Now turn the car back and take me home.'

On the way back Ajit gently asked, 'Do you think it's something great to have the courage to steal someone else's property?'

Kamal said, 'I didn't speak of it as something petty or great. I only said you didn't have the courage.'

'No, I don't have the courage and I'm not ashamed of it either.' He paused a little and added, 'Rather, I would be ashamed if I did. And I'm sure all decent men will agree with me.'

'It's easy to agree,' said Kamal. 'It fetches you praise.'

'Only praise? Nothing more? Haven't you ever come across a decent, civilized person?'

'Even if I have, I'll talk about it some other day if the time comes, not now.' She paused for a moment, then went on: 'In reply to your argument, someone else might have sneered and said, "Didn't it prick your well-bred conscience to try to steal away Kamal?" But I can't say that, because Kamal is no man's property. She belongs to herself and to no one else.'

'And I presume she can't ever become someone else's property?'

'That's a matter for the future, Ajit Babu. How can I reply now?'

'I don't think you'll ever be able to answer that. I think that's why such cruelty from Shibnath didn't hurt you. You have shaken it off very easily.' He sighed as he spoke. A few bullock carts appeared in the headlights. There seemed to be a village nearby. The villagers had left the carts scattered on the road and driven the bullocks home. Ajit drove carefully past this spot and said, 'Kamal, it's hard to understand you.'

She smiled and said, 'How is it hard? You rightly understood that if you took the wrong road, you could lead me into error.'

'Maybe I got it wrong.'

She smiled again and said, 'So you were mistaken about the road, you were mistaken in trying to deceive me, and on top of that you're mistaken about yourself! When will you set right this great load of mistakes, Ajit Babu? Learn to have a little respect for yourself. Don't demean yourself before yourself like this.'

'But can you respect yourself merely by denying your mistakes?'

'No, you can't. But there are ways and ways of denying. You alone don't make up this world—if you did, that would solve every problem. But there are others here too, and their likes and dislikes, their ways and conduct, also touch us. So if the final outcome is not to your liking, you will only demean yourself if you deplore it as a mistake. Could there be a greater lack of respect for yourself?'

Ajit was silent for a while, then said, 'But what if you really have made a mistake? Didn't you feel any remorse over your affair with Shibnath? Do you want me to believe you didn't?'

Kamal seemed unable to make a proper reply to this. She said, 'It's up to you to believe it or not. I've never complained to anyone about him.'

'You're not the person to complain. But haven't you ever reproached yourself for your own mistakes?'

'No.'

'Then I can only say that you're very strange—you're an extraordinary woman.'

Kamal did not reply to this; she held her peace. After about ten silent minutes Ajit suddenly asked, 'If I were to repeat this mistake tomorrow, could I see you again?'

'Ajit Babu, I can only reply to an "if" in terms of an "if". You shouldn't expect a definite response to an uncertain proposal.'

'That means you believe my infatuation won't last even till tomorrow?'

'I feel that isn't impossible.'

Ajit was hurt and said, 'Whatever I might be, Kamal, I'm not Shibnath.'

'I know that, Ajit Babu,' answered Kamal. 'I might even know it better than you do.'

Ajit said, 'If you did, you wouldn't think I tried to deceive you with falsehoods, that there was nothing true about it all.'

Kamal said, 'We weren't talking of falsehoods, Ajit Babu, we were talking of infatuation. They are not the same thing. And if you'd wanted to deceive anyone out of infatuation, it was yourself. I know you didn't want to defraud me.'

'But in the end you're the one who'd have been defrauded. You didn't refuse to go with me, although you were certain that my night's infatuation would fade by daylight. Come, was it all a joke?'

Kamal smiled a little. 'Why didn't you try it out? The way was open; I never once stopped you.'

Ajit sighed and said, 'If you didn't, then I can only say you're very difficult to understand. Let me tell you something, Kamal. Just as the love of a woman confounds the heart, so also her beauty benumbs the intellect. Yet the first is as great a truth as the other is a lie. You knew this was not my love but a moment's infatuation. How could you bring yourself to encourage it? However proudly the mist might cover the sun, Kamal, it's the mist that's a lie. The sun is constant.'

Kamal looked at him steadily for a moment in the dark. Then she quietly said, 'That's only a poetic metaphor, Ajit Babu; it's neither logic nor truth. The mist came into being in the very ancient past, and it exists to this day. It has covered the sun time and again and will keep on doing so. I don't know whether the sun is constant, but the mist hasn't been proved a lie. Either both are ephemeral or both are eternal. Likewise, even if desire is momentary, that moment is not unreal. It comes again and again with its momentary truth. The jasmine doesn't live as long as the sunflower, but who would reject it as unreal? You accuse me of encouraging a single night's infatuation. Is long life the greatest truth for you, Ajit Babu?'

Realizing that Ajit did not understand her words, she continued, 'The time has not yet come for you to grasp what I'm saying. That's why your anger against Shibnath knows no bounds; but I've forgiven him. I don't complain at all for not having got more than I did.'

Ajit said, 'That means you've trained your mind to be so indifferent. Tell me, don't you have any complaint against anyone in the world?'

Kamal looked at him and said, 'Yes, against one person.'

'Won't you tell me who it is, Kamal?'

'What good would it do you to know about somebody else?'

'About somebody else? Well then, I'll at least be relieved to know that you're not angry with me.'

Kamal said, 'Will you be happy if assured of that? But there's no time for all that. We've arrived. Stop the car and let me get down.'

The car stopped. Someone was standing beside the road in the darkness. Both of them were startled as he drew near.

Ajit asked nervously, 'Who are you?'

'I'm Rajen. You saw me at Haren-da's ashram today.'

'Ah yes, Rajen, what brings you here at this hour of night?'

'I've been waiting for you. Soon after you left, a man from Ashu Babu's house came to the ashram to look for you.' He turned to Kamal as he spoke.

'Why was he looking for me?' asked Kamal.

'As perhaps you know, there's a lot of influenza all around and many people are dying of it. The man said Shibnath Babu is very ill. He was brought to Ashu Babu's house in a litter. Ashu Babu thought that you were at the ashram, so he sent for you.'

'What's the time now?'

'I think it's past three.'

Kamal reached out to open the car door and said, 'Climb in, we'll drop you at the ashram on our way.'

Ajit did not speak a single word. He drove the car like a puppet and stopped in front of Harendra's house. When Rajen got down, Kamal said, 'Thank you. You've taken a lot of trouble to give me the news.'

'It was my duty. Let me know whenever there's need.' Having said this, he went away. There was no build-up, no ostentation: he simply let them know in simple words that this was part of his duty. She recalled what she had heard about this youth that evening from Harendra: on the one hand, his extraordinary ability to pass examinations, on the other the extreme indifference that let him relinquish success on the verge of achieving it. He was young, he had just entered his prime; even at this age he had kept nothing for himself, but given it all away for the sake of others.

Ajit had been silent throughout. He felt drained after hearing it was three at night. His mind, buffeted by the blows and counterblows of an incoherent catechism, grew dark at the unrelieved sordidness of their nocturnal adventure. Probably no one would ask him any questions; maybe no one would have the courage to do so; but they would all paint the unknown history from beginning to end in full colour, with brushes steeped according to their own propensity, fancy and malice. But what agitated him even more was this shameless woman's undaunted truthfulness. She seemed to have no need in the world to tell a lie, as though she was flouting and showing up everybody in the world.

Furthermore, he did not know who might have arrived in the house because of Shibnath's illness. As Ajit imagined them interrogating this woman, his blood seemed to freeze.

Suddenly he felt that he despised Kamal, and cursed himself for having lost his senses even for a moment, led like a self-oblivious lunatic by her eager assurances.

As he entered the gate, he saw Ashu Babu himself at the open window. He seemed to be waiting eagerly for him. At the sound of the car he looked out and said, 'Is it Ajit? Who's that with you? Kamal?'

'Yes.'

'Jadu, take Kamal to Shibnath's room. Perhaps you've heard that he's ill?' As he said this, he came downstairs himself. 'This change of season is unhealthy in any case; and on top of that, all kinds of diseases are breaking out and a lot of people are dying. I myself haven't been feeling well since morning. I'm rather feverish.'

Kamal anxiously said, 'Then why are you awake? There's no lack of people to look after things.'

'Who is there? The doctor came to see the patient. Mani sent me off to bed and is keeping vigil herself, but I couldn't sleep. You were late in coming. Kamal, should you remain angry with somebody if he's ill? It's not as if people don't quarrel, but you didn't even try to find out where he had been for the last three or four days, or where he might have been lying with this fever. That wasn't right of you. Now you'll have to bear the brunt.'

Kamal was surprised, but realized that this simple-hearted man knew nothing of what was going on. She kept quiet. In order to appease her supposed anger, Ashu Babu went on, 'I learnt from Harendra that you were not at home; I immediately understood that Ajit hadn't let you go. He likes to wander about, and he'd taken you along. But imagine what would have happened if you'd had an accident in the dark.'

It seemed to Ajit that the stone oppressing his being had rolled away. No evil possibility seemed to enter this man's spotless heart. It always shone with impeccable purity. Inwardly, Ajit paid homage to him in love and reverence. But Kamal had not listened to everything he said—perhaps she had not felt the need. She asked, 'Why did he come here instead of going to the hospital?'

'Hospital!' said Ashu Babu in amazement. 'That means you aren't yet reconciled?'

'I'm not saying this out of anger, Ashu Babu. What I'm saying is only reasonable and natural.'

'It's neither reasonable nor natural. But I admit that Mani should have sent him to you instead of bringing him here.'

'No, she shouldn't have,' replied Kamal. 'Mani knew that I didn't have the money for his treatment.'

Her words reminded Ashu Babu of something else. He felt deeply embarrassed. Kamal went on: 'Not only Manorama but Shibnath Babu himself knows that illness can't be cured by nursing alone. One needs medicines and proper diet. Perhaps it was better that the news reached her instead of me. He seems destined to live long.'

Ashu Babu turned pale with embarrassment and shook his head repeatedly as he said, 'Not at all, Kamal. Nursing is everything. Proper care is the best medicine; doctors are only a formality.' Remembering his dead wife, he added, 'I have suffered that way myself, Kamal. I have learnt this lesson from repeated brushes with illness. Go in. He's yours: whatever you think best will be done. While I'm here, there'll be no lack of medicines and proper food.' He led her out as he said this. Ajit did not know what to do, but nonetheless accompanied them.

They entered the patient's room on tiptoe so as not to

disturb him. Manorama was worn out, having stayed awake through the night in a chair beside the bed. She seemed to have just dropped off to sleep, resting her tired head on the patient's chest. Shibnath too lay in repose, his clasped hands resting on her neck. A dark screen suddenly seemed to descend on the father's eyes at this undreamt-of scene; but it was only for a moment, and the next moment he fled from the room. Kamal and Ajit looked at each other. Then they too went out as silently as they had entered.

16

THERE WAS A COVERED VERANDA ALONG THE CORRIDOR. AJIT and Kamal came out of the sickroom and stood there. A squat lantern of smoked glass hung above them; even by its dim light, the pallor of Ajit's face was plain to see, as though his blood had drained away at some sudden blow. There was no third person present; yet he asked with all the deference due to a lady not his kin, 'Would you like to go home now? If so, I'll arrange it.'

Kamal looked at him silently. Ajit said, 'You shouldn't stay in this house a moment longer.'

'Should you?'

'No, not I either. I'll go away somewhere tomorrow morning.'

'That's better,' said Kamal. 'I'll leave then too. For the time being, let me sit in this chair for the rest of the night. You go and get some rest.'

Ajit looked at the narrow chair and said hesitantly, 'But . . .'

Kamal said, 'It's no use saying "but", Ajit Babu. It makes for a lot of problems. I can't go home now, nor can I go to your room. So go, don't wait any longer.'

In the morning the servant came and called Ajit to Ashu Babu's bedroom. He was not yet out of bed. Kamal sat in a chair near him: she had already been summoned.

Ashu Babu said, 'I've been unwell since yesterday, and today it seems——well, Ajit, please sit down.'

When he had done so, Ashu Babu went on: 'I heard you're going away this morning. I can't ask you to stay back either.

155

Well, goodbye. Even if we don't ever meet again, rest assured that I have blessed you with all my heart—so that you can forgive us and be happy in life.'

Ajit had not yet looked up at Ashu Babu's face. As he did so now, he fell silent at the point of replying. 'Fell silent' does not express it: he seemed suddenly to have forgotten how to speak. He could not have imagined such a profound change in a person over a few hours on a single night.

Ashu Babu was himself silent for two or three minutes, then said to Kamal: 'I have called you here, but I feel like hanging my head rather than looking you in the eye. How can I tell anyone of all that took place in my heart last night?'

He paused and continued, 'Akshay once said that Shibnath doesn't stay with you. I didn't pay much heed to his words. I thought it was an exaggeration born of animosity. You were in trouble for want of money, but even then I didn't understand the reason. Now everything is clear—there's no room left for doubt.'

Both his listeners remained silent. He went on, 'I've often treated you badly, but I've loved you from the first day we met, Kamal. That's why I'm repeatedly struck by a single thought: if only we hadn't come to Agra!' As he said this, a tear rose to the corner of his eye. He wiped it away and only exclaimed, 'God!'

Kamal went and sat at the head of his bed. She laid her hand on his forehead and said, 'You're running a fever, Ashu Babu.'

Ashu Babu drew her hand between his own and said, 'Let it be, Kamal. You're very intelligent: tell me what to do. That man's presence in my house seems to make me burn all over.'

Kamal looked up and saw Ajit's troubled face. On getting no response from him, she said after a moment's silence, 'Tell me what you want me to do.' As there was no reply, she fell silent again, then continued: 'You don't want to keep Shibnath Babu here, but he's ill. That being so, either send him to the hospital or, if you know where he lives, send him there. If you think it better to send him to my place, you can do that too. I have no objection, but you know I haven't got the means for his treatment; I can nurse him with all my strength, but can do no more.'

Full of gratitude, Ashu Babu said, 'I don't know why, but I had expected just this reply from you. I knew you couldn't be stone-like in response to a stony-hearted man. He is yours, take him home. Don't worry about the expenses: that's my responsibility.'

Kamal said, 'But one point should be made clear before all else.'

Ashu Babu hastily said, 'You don't need to tell me, Kamal, I know. One day all this dirt will be cleansed away. You don't need to worry: so long as I'm alive, I won't let you be the victim of unjust persecution.'

Kamal looked at him and remained still. She did not speak.

'What are you thinking, Kamal?'

'I was wondering whether you should be told something. I think you should, otherwise nothing will be made clear and dirt will keep piling up. You are rich, you are generous, it's not difficult for you to spend money on others. But if you have the mistaken notion that you are being kind to me, that should be set right. I shan't accept your alms under any pretext.'

Ashu Babu recalled the incident of the sewing machine. He was pained, and said, 'If I've made a mistake, Kamal, can't you forgive me?'

Kamal said, 'The mistake wasn't so serious then as it could be now. You think that saving Shibnath is a way of saving me, but that's not so. Now do as you like, I have no objections.'

Ashu Babu said, 'I know how you feel; it's neither unnatural nor unjust. Well, let's have it that I'm trying to save Shibnath; I'm not showing any kindness to you. Will that do?'

Kamal showed signs of irritation. She answered, 'No, that won't do. If I can't make you understand, I'm helpless. If you can't send him to the hospital, send him to Haren Babu's ashram. They look after many people; they'll look after him too. Whatever you want to spend, you can spend there. I'm very tired. Let me go now.' She made a determined effort to get up.

Ashu Babu was annoyed by her words and conduct. He said, 'This is too much, Kamal. You are unfairly distorting what I wanted to do, with the well-being of both of you at heart. I know that in one way this is a matter of endless shame for me and that I must suffer deeply if I don't stop this immorality now. But it's not true that I'm trying to find a way out because my own daughter is involved. I can save Shibnath in many ways, but that's not all I want. I made this proposal in the hope that you might win him back by nursing him with your heart's care. I didn't do it out of mere selfishness.'

The words were true, moving and full of sincerity, but they had no impact on Kamal. She replied, 'It's precisely this that I wanted to impress on you, Ashu Babu. I'm not unwilling to nurse him. I've nursed many people at the tea garden—I'm accustomed to it. But I don't want to get him back, either by nursing him or by refusing to nurse him. I don't say this out of resentment or by way of empty boasting. Our relationship is broken and I can't put it together again.'

Her words carried neither heat nor emotion: they were utterly plain and simple. It was this that silenced Ashu Babu completely. The next moment he said, 'What's this you're saying, Kamal? You want to give up your husband for such a trifling reason? Who taught you this?'

Kamal remained silent. Ashu Babu continued, 'Whoever might have taught you so in your youth taught you wrong. This is unjust and unbefitting—whatever home you may have been born into, you are a Bengali woman. This is not your path or mine—you must learn to forget it. Don't you know, Kamal, what is virtuous in one country is impious in another? And it's better even to die in one's own faith.'

His eyes blazed as he said this, and when he finished he seemed to be gasping for breath. But the person he addressed remained unmoved.

Ashu Babu spoke on: 'This illusion was once leading us to perdition. But a few noble souls saw the error. They called to the people of the country, "Where are you going like madmen? You want nothing, you lack nothing, you don't have to beg of anyone. Only turn your eyes and look at the treasures of your own house. Your forefathers have left you everything, only reach out and gather it." I've seen everything there is to see in England with my own eyes. I wonder what would have happened to me if they hadn't uttered their warning in time. I remember my younger days—the state of the educated people at that time!' So saying, he raised his folded hands in homage to the great departed.

Kamal looked up and saw that Ajit was gazing at him, wonderstruck. His rapt imagination seemed to have robbed him of consciousness.

Ashu Babu's trance had not yet left him. He said, 'Kamal, if they hadn't done anything else, they would have been immortal among the people of our country only for this.'

'Only for this!'

'Yes, only for this. Because they told us to turn our eyes from the outer world towards our own home.'

Kamal asked, 'If there are lights shining outside, if the sun rises in the east, should we still turn our backs and look at our home in the west? Would that imply love for our country?'

Perhaps the question did not reach Ashu Babu's ears. Absorbed in his own flow, he went on, 'It's only because of their foresight that we regained faith and respect for our country, its religion, its myths and history, its customs and rituals, its traditions and laws—everything that was perishing under foreign pressure. As a people, we were on the road to ruin, Kamal; it was not an easy escape. Who do you think made us realize that unless we retrieved all of that, we would not survive?'

Ajit suddenly stood up excitedly. He said, 'I never imagined that you held such ideas. I'm only sorry that I hadn't understood you for so long, that I didn't sit at your feet and take lessons from you.'

He was about to say more in this vein, but he was interrupted. The servant entered and announced that Harendra Babu and some others had come to pay a visit. The next moment, Harendra entered with Satish and Rajen. He said, 'I was told that Shibnath Babu is asleep. I called on the doctor too on my way here. He thinks it's nothing very serious; Shibnath will be better soon.' He made a namaskar to Kamal and sat down with his companions.

Ashu Babu nodded in agreement, but his eyes were on Ajit and it was him he addressed. 'Aren't you forgetting that I spent my entire youth in England? There are many things which you can't see from close by but only at a distance. I clearly see the change in educated minds. This ashram of Harendra, the attempt to spread its branches in various cities—

isn't it all possible today only for this? Ask him if you don't believe me. The same celibacy, the same relentless continence, the same reintroduction of the old laws and customs—are all these not efforts to bring back those ancient days? If we forget this, if we lose confidence in it, have we anything left to hope for? Will you find anywhere in the world the equal of our ideal of the forest hermitage? The men who once built our society, those ancient lawgivers, were not merchants but sannyasins. Our ultimate fruition lies in our ability to absorb their gifts unquestioningly with bowed heads. That is our only road to well-being, Kamal; there's no other.'

Ajit was silent, Harendra and Satish overwhelmed: what was this Indian sahib saying today? Rajen had no idea of what had occasioned this sudden discussion. An unmixed respect could be seen growing on everyone's face.

The speaker himself was no less surprised: not only by the force of his oratory, but because he had never had an opportunity to speak in this way to anyone before. He felt a surge of inexpressible joy. For the moment, he seemed to have forgotten his own immediate grief. He said, 'Do you understand, Kamal, why I made this request to you?'

Kamal shook her head and said, 'No.'

'No? Why not?'

Kamal said, 'You were telling us exultantly that there is a growing trend among the educated to overcome the influence of foreign education and return to the old ways. You believe that this will do good to the country, but you didn't give us any reason for thinking so. Many ancient customs and practices were on the verge of extinction; now an effort is being made to resurrect them. That may be so, but where's the proof that it will do any good, Ashu Babu? You didn't explain that.'

'What! I didn't?'

'No, you didn't; you said exactly what any blind anti-reformist and eulogist of the past would say. There's no evidence that the resurrection of everything defunct is necessarily good. It also happens that evil things are re-established in this world under the spell of delusion.'

Ashu Babu found no answer to this, but Ajit said, 'No one spends energy on retrieving what is evil.'

Kamal said, 'They do, not because it is evil but because they think what is old must be self-evidently good. I had wanted to tell you one thing at the very beginning, Ashu Babu, but you didn't pay heed. Whether it's a social custom or ceremony or a spiritual rite, if you cling to it because it belongs to your country, you might be praised for patriotism but you can't please the god of the country's well-being. He is offended by it.'

Ashu Babu answered in amazement: 'What are you saying, Kamal? If you abandon the faith, the rites and customs of your country and take alms from others, what will you have left of your own? By what identity will you declare yourself a human being before the world?'

Kamal said, 'The claim will automatically come to you; you won't need any identity. The world will know you without that.'

Ashu Babu said agitatedly, 'I don't understand you, Kamal.'

'You can't be expected to, Ashu Babu. That's the way things are. In this changing world, the truth that appears in new forms at every step taken by the dynamic human mind cannot be recognized by everyone. They think, "Where did this nuisance come from?" Do you remember the Shibani you saw that day in the shadow of the Taj? You won't find her today in the person of Kamal. You might wonder, "Where has the woman I saw disappeared?" But such is the true identity of a human being: I hope this is how I shall always be known to people, Ashu Babu.'

Pausing a little, she added, 'We've lost our tack in the storm of argument and counter-argument: we've forgotten the real issue. But I'm very tired. I must go.'

Ashu Babu looked on, silent and bewildered. On some matters he understood the girl faintly, on others not at all. Only one thing repeatedly struck him: the storm she had talked about had swept away all his pleas and arguments as it would a blade of grass.

Kamal stood up. She signalled to Ajit and said, 'You brought me here; will you take me home?' But now it seemed he was too embarrassed to look up.

Kamal laughed a little to herself. Then stepping forward, she suddenly placed her hand on Rajen's shoulder and said, 'Rajen Babu, my brother, please take me home.'

Rajen was surprised to be addressed so endearingly. He looked at her once and said, 'Come.'

As they reached the door, Kamal turned and said, 'Ashu Babu, I haven't withdrawn my offer. If you agree to send him on those terms, I'll do my utmost. If he survives, so much the better; if not, it's his misfortune.' With this, she left. Everyone in the room sat dumbfounded. To the ailing master of the house, even the glow of dawn seemed pale and unwelcome.

Rajen escorted Kamal half the distance to her house. He said he would return to see her in a few hours, after finishing some work. Kamal did not refuse: perhaps because she was unmindful, perhaps for some other reason. She walked home briskly and found that the door leading upstairs was still locked. The low-caste woman who worked for her had not come. She gathered from the grocer across the street that the maid was ill and her young granddaughter had come to leave the keys of the house.

Kamal opened the door and started her household work. She had scarcely eaten since the previous day: she thought she would quickly cook and eat something and then have a little rest. She badly needed to rest, but today it seemed she just could not finish her housework. She had not noticed how much rubbish had gathered everywhere, how she had been spending her days amidst disorder. Everything that her eyes now lit on seemed to reproach her. The crumbling plaster from the ceiling had gathered in the crannies of her bedstead and had to be removed; the overflow from the sparrow's nest had landed on her bed, and she had to change the sheets; the pillowcase was very shabby and had to be removed; the table and chairs were in disarray, the doormat was stiff with mud, the mirror so filthy that it would take a whole morning to clean it; the ink had dried in the ink-pot and the pens had disappeared, and there was no sign of any blotting paper. Wherever she looked she found such a super-abundance of untidiness that it seemed the house had long been deserted. She forgot her bath and meal; she had no idea how the day passed. It was evening when, having finished all the work, she went downstairs to wash the grime off her body.

All these days Kamal had clearly known that she could not stay here alone: it was neither possible nor justifiable. How would she pay the rent month after month? She had to go; but so far she had somehow been unable to settle the day of departure. Morning followed night and night followed morning without giving her the break to step out of all this. From time to time that day, she had felt rising within her the obscure question of why, since she felt no attachment to the house, she had worked so hard today, why it had been necessary. Each time the problem struck her, she would come out on to the balcony and look vaguely at the street, as though trying to forget something, and then return to work. In this way she brought both her work and the day to an end.

Although the day ended every day, it did not end like this. After sunset she lit a lamp and began cooking her meal. To fill up the time, she turned over the pages of a book, sitting up in bed. But so tired was she today that she could not tell when her eyes and the book both fell shut.

When she woke up the lamp had burnt out and the red glow of daylight filled the room through the open window. The day rolled on, but the maid did not turn up. It became necessary to find out where she lived and ask how she was. With this in mind, Kamal changed her sari and was about to go out when she heard footsteps downstairs, and her heart began to beat faster. A voice called, 'Are you in? May I come up?'

'Yes, do.'

The man who entered was Harendra. He pulled up a chair, sat down and said, 'Were you going out?'

'Yes. I heard that the old woman who works for me is ill. I was going to see her.'

'Bad news. It must be influenza. It seems to be turning into an epidemic in Agra. They've already begun dying in the slums. If it gets to be as bad as in Mathura or Vrindavan, we'll have to run away or else die. Where does this old woman live?'

'I don't know exactly. I've heard it's somewhere nearby. I'll have to find out.'

Harendra said, 'It's very infectious. Be careful. But perhaps you've heard how things are developing here?'

'No,' said Kamal, shaking her head.

Harendra looked at her and was silent for a moment. Then he said, 'Don't worry; there's nothing to worry about. I would have come yesterday but couldn't make the time. Our Akshay Babu didn't turn up at the college. I heard he's ill, and you saw for yourself yesterday that Ashu Babu has taken to his bed. Abinash Babu too has been running a fever since last evening. Boudi's face also seemed rather pinched: I hope she doesn't catch it as well.'

Kamal looked on silently and seemed preoccupied. Harendra said, 'And of course there's Shibnath Babu. One can't tell with influenza—but he refused to go to the hospital. He was taken home yesterday afternoon. I must ask after him today.'

'Who's there with him?' asked Kamal.

'A servant. There are some Punjabi contractors lodging in the rooms upstairs. They're said to be good people.'

Kamal fell silent. After some time she said, 'Can you send Rajen Babu to me?'

'I can, but where shall I find him? He went out early in the morning today. It seems the epidemic has broken out badly in a leather workers' colony somewhere. He's gone to nurse them. If he comes to the ashram at mealtime, I'll tell him.'

'Who took him home?' asked Kamal about Shibnath. 'You?'

'No, Rajen. It's from him that I learned the Punjabis are looking after him. But whatever they might do, we needn't worry now that Rajen knows about it—he'll start nursing him himself. It's a great relief that he doesn't pick up illnesses. As long as the police don't arrest him, he's equal to a hundred men. It's only before them that our friend is helpless, else there's nothing in the world that can subdue him.'

'Is there any chance of his being arrested?'

'I wish there were. At least the ashram would be safe.'

'Why don't you tell him to go away?'

'That's difficult. He'd go away so effectively that he wouldn't return even if you offered your head as the price.'

'What's the harm if he doesn't return?'

'Harm? You don't know him. Those who don't can't calculate the loss. If the ashram ceased to exist, I could bear that loss but not his going for good.' Harendra paused for a minute and then suddenly changed the subject. He said, 'There's been an amusing incident. No one could have imagined it. Yesterday when I returned from Abinash-da's place very late at night, I found Ajit Babu in the ashram. I was afraid of what it might mean. Had the illness turned worse? No, nothing of that sort; he'd come bag and baggage to become an ashramite. He'd already sealed matters with Satish—vowed to spend his life in the service of the ashram according to its rules: he was not to be budged from his resolution. It'll be good for us to have a wealthy companion, but I was afraid something might be wrong. In the morning I went to Ashu Babu. He said, "It's a worthy resolution, but there's no want of ashrams in India. If he were to leave Agra and go to some other place, I could last out here for a while longer. Now it seems I'll have to leave."'

Kamal did not express any kind of surprise. She remained silent. Harendra said, 'I'm coming from that house. I don't know what to say to Ajit Babu when I get back.'

Kamal realized there must have been much discord over Shibnath's removal. Perhaps no one had said anything clearly and openly; everything might have happened silently, yet the harshness had obviously surpassed all earlier conflicts. Nonetheless, she made no reply but sat silently as before.

Harendra went on: 'I think Ashu Babu has heard everything. He's deeply hurt by the way Shibnath has treated you. He almost turned him out of his house. But perhaps Manorama didn't want it. Shibnath is her music guru, she may have wanted him nursed under her own eyes; but that couldn't be. Her rift with Ajit Babu might be because he took Ashu Babu's side on the question of Shibnath.'

Kamal smiled and said, 'There would be nothing strange about that. But who told you all this? Rajen?'

'He? He isn't that sort of man. Even if he knew, he wouldn't tell. It's just my guess. So I feel that, as there's bound to be a reconciliation, why rub Ajit up the wrong way? It's better to be silent. As long as he stays in the ashram, he won't lack hospitality.'

'Yes, that would be best,' said Kamal.

Harendra said, 'I must go now. I'm worried about Sejda, he grows weak very quickly. I'll come again tomorrow—if I can find the time.'

'Yes, do come.' Kamal stood up and did a namaskar, adding, 'Don't forget to send Rajen. Tell him that I've sent for him because I'm in deep trouble.'

'Deep trouble?' said Harendra, amazed. 'I'll send him as soon as I find him, but can't you tell me about it? You can consider me your true friend.'

'I know you are. But you must send him.'

Rajen turned up in the afternoon.

'Rajen, you must do something for me.'

'Of course I will. But yesterday, there was at least "Babu" affixed to my name; has even that been dropped today?'

'So much the better: your name's lighter. But if you'd prefer it, I can add the affix again.'

'No, there's no need. But how should I address you?'

'Everyone calls me Kamal and I find no disrespect in that. I would feel ashamed if my name were to be burdened with affixes. You don't need to address me formally as *apni*, either. Just call me by my name.'

Rajen avoided a direct response to this and said, 'What have I got to do?'

'You have to be my friend. People say you're a revolutionary. If that's so, our friendship will last.'

'What use will this lasting friendship be to me?'

Kamal was surprised and hurt. She heard the clear note of suspicion and indifference. 'You mustn't say such things,' she said. 'Friendship is rare, and my friendship's even rarer. Don't belittle yourself by being disrespectful to someone you don't know well.'

But this reproof did not seem to touch the man. He said easily, with a smiling face, 'It's not a question of disrespect. I only told you that I don't see the need for friendship. If you think it'll be of use to me, I won't contradict you. I only wonder what that use might be.'

Kamal's face flushed. It was as though somebody had humiliated her with the lash of a whip. She was highly educated, extremely good-looking and acutely intelligent. She had thought she was the treasured object of male desire. She firmly believed that her radiant spirit was invincible. In this world women had shown hatred for her, men had tried to burn her up with terror or even affected to ignore her; but this was something different. She felt reduced to dust by this man's contempt. Shibnath had deprived her but he had not clothed her in the rags of destitution.

A suspicion grew strong in Kamal's mind. She asked, 'You must have heard a lot of things about me?'

'Yes,' said Rajen. 'They often speak about you.'

'What do they say?'

He tried to laugh a little as he said, 'My memory's very poor in such matters. I remember almost nothing.'

'Really?'

'Really.'

Kamal did not try to cross-examine him: she believed his word. She understood that this man was not curious about women's lives. He had indeed forgotten such things as fast as he heard them. She understood something else too— why, in spite of being given the right to address her informally, he had not accepted it and was still addressing her as *apni*. No woman's shadow had yet fallen on his immaculate male heart. He did not feel the temptation to become intimate by using the informal *tumi*.

Kamal was inwardly relieved. After some time she said, 'Do you know that Shibnath Babu has separated from me?'

'I know it.'

Kamal said, 'There was a fraud in our marriage ceremony, but there was no deception in our hearts. Everyone was suspicious; they gossiped about it, they said it wasn't a permanent union. But I wasn't afraid: I said, "Even if it's weak, once we've accepted it mutually I don't care how many twists the outward knot might have." Rather, I thought it better not to tie up hand and foot the person whom I was taking for a husband. What did it matter if the barrier to his freedom remained a little slack? If the heart's bankrupt, you might call in merchants to extract due interest on the priests' chants, but the capital is lost. But it's no use telling you all this: you won't understand.'

Rajen remained silent. Kamal said, 'One thing that I didn't

know then is that he's so greedy for money. Had I known, I could at least have avoided the charge of torture.'

'What does that mean?' asked Rajen.

Kamal immediately restrained herself. 'Let it be,' she said. 'You needn't hear about it.'

The sun had set some time ago, and darkness slid into the room. Kamal lit a lamp, put it on a corner of the table and returned to her place. She said, 'However that may be, take me once to his house.'

'What will you do there?'

'I want to see it all with my own eyes. I'll stay on if necessary. If not, I'll lay all responsibility for him upon you, and feel relieved. That's why I sent for you. Nobody else can do it. There's no end to people's animosity towards him.' As she spoke, she rose to turn up the lamp.

Rajen said, 'All right, let's go. Let me fetch a tonga.' He went out.

In the tonga Rajen said, 'You want to end your worries by giving me charge of nursing Shibnath Babu. I might have done so, but I shan't be able to stay here any more. I shall have to go away soon. You must make some other arrangement.'

Kamal anxiously asked, 'The police are pestering you, I suppose?'

'Oh, I'm quite used to their attentions; it's not because of them.'

Remembering what Harendra had said, Kamal asked, 'Then perhaps the people at the ashram have asked you to quit. But those who are so terrified of the police shouldn't set about serving the nation with such fanfare. After all, why should you leave? There's someone in this very town who isn't afraid to give you shelter.'

'I suppose that person is yourself,' said Rajen. 'I'm taking note of your promise; I won't forget it easily. But few people in India are not afraid of the police. Had there been more such, this country would have had fewer problems.' He paused and said, 'But I'm not going away because of that. I can't accuse the ashram either. I don't know about the others, but Haren-da can't possibly tell me to go.'

'Then why must you go?'

'I'll go because of myself. We're all working for the country, but neither my ideas nor my methods agree with theirs. The only point in common is our love. I'm dearer and closer to Haren-da than his own brother; it can't ever be otherwise.'

Kamal's anxiety lifted. She said, 'What can be greater than that, Rajen? If hearts agree, it doesn't matter if opinions don't. It's not that people can live together only when they think alike or act alike. What kind of education is it that doesn't teach you to respect others' opinions? Opinions and actions are both external things, Rajen; it's the mind that really matters. But if you hold the other two greater and thus move apart, it would mean denying the very constancy of love that you spoke of. It would be like that bookish phrase, sacrificing the substance for the shadow.'

Rajen didn't say anything. He only laughed.

'Why are you laughing?'

'I'm laughing because I hadn't laughed earlier. In the case of your marriage, you had taken the union of hearts as the only reality and had dismissed as nothing the anomaly in the external rituals. But since that wasn't real, everything between the two of you has become unreal.'

'What do you mean?'

Rajen said, 'I don't belittle the union of hearts, but to proclaim it loudly as something unique has become high fashion these days. It expresses both open-mindedness and magnanimity, but not the truth. It's like saying that only the mind matters in this world and everything else is an illusion, a shadow-play. That's wrong.' Pausing a little, he went on, 'You have called the ability to respect differing ideas a sign of great education. But who can respect all ideas? Only he who has no idea of his own. Your education teaches you to silently ignore contrary ideas, but not to respect them.'

Kamal remained speechless in utter bewilderment. Rajen went on: 'That is not our principle, we don't bring devastation to this world by false respect even towards a friend—we crush and grind him. That is our work.'

Kamal said, 'You call this work?'

'We do,' said Rajen. 'Of what use is the union of hearts if the conflict of ideas hinders my action? We want unity of ideas and unity in action; we have no use for the luxury of emotionalism. Shibani . . .'

Kamal was surprised. 'You too have heard this name of mine?'

'I have. In the world of action, affinity of conduct is what matters, not the affinity of hearts. Let the heart keep its own place: let He who is hidden judge what is hidden, we must have practical unity. That's our touchstone—we test everything by it. Why, the union of two hearts can't create music unless there is a harmony of tone beyond them. Otherwise you only have a cacophony. The king's power lies in the external unity of the army that fights for him. He doesn't care for the unity of hearts. Our motto is regulation and discipline. If you belittle this, you are drugging yourself with the narcotic of the heart. That's another name for wantonness. Coachman, stop, stop! This is his house, Shibani.'

Before them stood an old, derelict house. They got down

silently and entered a room on the ground floor. Shibnath opened his eyes at the sound of footsteps, but perhaps he could not recognize them in the dim light. The next moment he closed his eyes and sank into a doze.

17

KAMAL LOOKED ROUND AND WAS DUMBFOUNDED. THE ROOM was in an utter mess. It hardly seemed possible that someone could live in it. On hearing their voices, a Hindustani lad of sixteen or seventeen appeared. 'This is Shibnath Babu's servant,' said Rajen. 'He does everything from preparing his food to giving him his medicines. It seems he's been sleeping since sundown and has just woken up. If you have any instructions about the patient, he's the person to tell. I think he'll be able to follow them; he's no fool. I heard his name yesterday but can't remember it. What's your name, boy?'

'Phagua.'

'Did you give him his medicines today?'

The boy raised two fingers of his left hand and replied in Hindi, 'I've given two doses.'

'Anything else?'

'Yes, some milk.'

'Well done. Did any of the Punjabi babus upstairs come to see him?'

The boy thought for a while and said, 'I think one of them came at midday.'

'You think! Why, what were you doing then? Sleeping?'

'Phagua, do you have a broom here?' asked Kamal. Phagua nodded and went to fetch it. Rajen said, 'What will you do with a broom? Thrash him with it?'

Kamal gravely said, 'Is this a time for jokes? Have you no pity or compassion?'

'I used to. But I lost that while working for flood and famine relief.'

Phagua returned with the broom. Rajen said, 'I'm dying of hunger. Let me go somewhere and get something to eat. Meanwhile do whatever you like with the broom and this boy. I'll come back to take you home. Don't worry—I'll return within a couple of hours.' He left without waiting for a reply.

The locality, at the farthest end of the town, soon fell desolate and silent. The clamour and footsteps of the tenants upstairs also stopped: they had obviously gone to bed. No one came to ask after Shibnath. The night outside grew darker. Phagua was nodding off on a blanket on the floor: it was time to lock the front door, when there was the sound of a bicycle bell. The next moment Rajen pushed the door open and came in. Looking around, he took in the complete change the room had undergone in that short while, and stood mute for some time. Then, laying the small bundle he was carrying on a side table, he said, 'You're not like other women. One can rely on you.'

Kamal silently turned and looked at him. Rajen said, 'You've even managed to make the bed. You might have found a fresh sheet somewhere, but how did you move him?'

Kamal softly replied, 'It's not difficult if you know how.'

'But how did you get to know? I wouldn't have expected you to.'

Kamal said, 'Is it your monopoly to know about things? I've nursed many patients at the tea garden in my youth.'

'I see.' Rajen again looked round and said, 'Here's some food. Wasn't there some water in the pitcher? Help yourself. I'll wait.'

Kamal looked at him, smiled and said, 'I didn't ask you to get anything for me. What made you think of it?'

'It came to me on a sudden impulse,' said Rajen. 'When I had eaten my fill it somehow struck me that you too might be hungry, so I bought some food on my way back. Do start—don't waste time.' He picked up the pitcher of water and put it by her. An enamel-plated cup was lying close at hand. 'Wait a little,' he said, 'let me wash this.' He went out with it. The previous day he had discovered where everything was kept in this house. Hunting out a piece of soap, he said, 'You've been handling a sick man. It's just as well to be careful. Wash your hands before you eat. I'll pour the water over your hands.'

Kamal remembered her father. He too spoke unemotionally but was full of sincerity. She said, 'I don't mind washing my hands, but I can't eat this food. Perhaps you don't know that I cook my own food, and I don't eat such rich and expensive things. Don't worry. I'll eat as usual when I go home.'

'Then it's no use getting late. Let's go back. I'll reach you home.'

'Will you come back here again?'

'Yes.'

'How long will you stay here?'

'At least till the morning. I've left some money with the Punjabis upstairs and I'll wait till I've worked out some arrangement. I'm a little tired, but I don't mind. I hadn't imagined that he'd be so badly neglected. Let's go. There are no carriages around here—we'll have to walk. On my way back I'll pay a visit to the leather workers' slum. I know two of them were just getting ready to die: I must find out what they've been up to.'

It again occurred to Kamal that this man had no feelings. He was almost like a machine. Some mysterious compulsion impelled him continually to work, and he went on working. He did not work for any profit to himself, nor even perhaps with any expectation. Activity was rooted in his blood; it came as easily to him as the air he breathed and the water he drank. But others were amazed by it and wondered how it was possible. Kamal said, 'Well, Rajen, you are yourself a doctor, aren't you?'

'A doctor? No. I only studied at that Medical School for some time.'

'Then who's looking after him?'

'Yama.'

'What do you do then?'

'I canvass on his behalf. I'm his admiring Chief Disciple.' He looked at Kamal's bewildered face for a moment and smiled. 'He's not only Yama but King Yama. I salute the man who first hailed him as king, for king indeed he is—as kind as wise. If there really is a creator of this universe, then I'll wager Yama is His best creation.'

Kamal asked in a subdued tone, 'Are you being facetious, Rajen?'

'Not at all. When Satish-da hears me, he turns grave; Harenda loses his temper and calls me a cynic. At their ashram they have collectively sharpened various strange weapons of austerity like rigour, self-control and sacrifice, and have declared war on Lord Yama, so they think I'm deriding them. But I'm not doing that. They don't visit the slums where the poor live. If they did I think they would grow very loyal to the King. With hearts full of reverence, they would sing the praises of the Lord of Death and would not upbraid him for being malign.'

Kamal said, 'If you really hold this view, is it wrong to call you a cynic?'

'We can judge of the wrong later. Will you come once with me to the leather workers' slum? They're ready and waiting, not only for the present spate of influenza but any other occasion——cholera, smallpox, plague. There's no medicine, no diet, no bed to lie on, nothing to cover their bodies with, no one to give them water——if one sees it suddenly one wonders if there's a solution to it all. Then I see the solution, stop worrying and say to myself, "Don't be afraid, my man—— however hard the problem might be, He who's charged with solving it will soon be here." In other countries there are other arrangements, but in this Land of the Gods the King of Kings has himself taken charge. In that way we are much more fortunate. But how did we get talking about such things? Come, it's getting late, we have a long way to walk.'

'But won't you have to walk back the same distance?'

'Yes, I will.'

'How far is your leather workers' slum?'

'Quite near. Within a mile or so.'

'Then cycle there and see them. I'll wait till you return.'

Rajen said in astonishment, 'How can that be? You haven't eaten for two days.'

'Who told you so?'

'You remember we were talking about sudden impulses. I found this out on an impulse. I peeped inside your kitchen as I came by. The rice was cooked and waiting, but the state of the rice bowl left no doubt it was last night's. That means two days of total fasting. So either come with me, or eat what I've brought. The excuse of cooking your own food won't serve today.'

'Won't serve!' repeated Kamal, smiling a little. 'But why are you so worried about me?'

'I don't know why. I'm trying to find out. I'll let you know as soon as I do.'

Kamal reflected for a while. She said, 'Do, don't be shy.' Again she fell silent, then resumed, 'Rajen, your elders at the ashram have scarcely known you for what you are; so they think of you as a nuisance. But I know you, and you should know me too. But that needs time. It won't happen by our bandying words.' She remained still for a little while and then said, 'I cook my own food, eat only once, and that too the food of the poorest—a handful of rice and dal. I have not taken any vow on the matter, so I can break the rule when I like. But I shall not break it simply because I haven't eaten anything for two days. I shan't forget your concern, Rajen, but I can't do what you say. Don't be cross.'

'I won't.'

'What are you thinking?'

'I'm thinking that our introductory session hasn't gone too badly. I don't think I'll forget it soon.'

'Why should I let you forget it soon?' said Kamal, suddenly breaking into a laugh. 'But don't wait any longer. Go, but come back as soon as possible. I'll spread a blanket over that big armchair. After a few hours' sleep, we'll go home in the morning. All right?'

Rajen nodded and said, 'All right. I thought I'd have to spend another sleepless night. But I've been granted leave: you've taken charge of nursing your husband. Very well. I don't think I'll be late returning; don't fall asleep before I come.'

'No,' said Kamal, 'but who told you that this man is my husband? Perhaps the Punjabi gentlemen? Whoever told you was joking. If you don't believe me, ask him one day.'

Rajen did not say anything. He went out silently.

Shibnath seemed to have been waiting for this. He turned on his side, opened his eyes and asked, 'Who was that man?' Kamal was taken aback at the sound. His voice was clear, without any trace of weariness. His glance was a little drowsy, but his face looked almost normal, with no more than the weariness of a man suddenly woken from sleep. Kamal could not believe that such a serious illness could have abated so soon. Hence she took a long time to reply. Shibnath again asked, 'Who was that man, Shibani? Did he bring you here?'

'Yes, he brought me, and he also brought you here yesterday.'

'What's his name?'

'Rajendra.'

'Do the two of you stay in the same house now?'

'That's what I'm trying to arrange. I'll be lucky if he agrees.'

'I see. Why did you bring him here?'

Kamal did not reply to this, nor did Shibnath ask anything more. He closed his eyes and lay still. After a long silence he asked, 'Who told you that I have nothing more to do with you? Do people say that I've said so?'

Kamal did not reply to this either, but put a question. 'Even if I didn't realize you hadn't married me, surely you knew it yourself? Why didn't you tell me so when you went away? Were you afraid that I might stop you, or weep and beat my head and create a scene? You knew very well that I'm not like that. So why didn't you tell me?'

Shibnath was silent for a few moments; then he said, 'If I rent a separate house for a few days to cope with the pressure of business, does it mean I've deserted you? I'd thought . . .'

He could not finish. Kamal stopped him, saying, 'Let it be,

I don't want to know all that.' But as she said this, she felt ashamed of her own agitation. She fell silent for a while, calmed herself and at last asked, 'Were you really ill?'

'What else?'

'Then why did you go to Ashu Babu's place instead of mine? Your earlier conduct hurt me, but this has utterly humiliated me. I know you'll gloat to yourself on hearing that I've been hurt, but this knowledge is my consolation. I can endure my sorrow only because you are base; I couldn't have otherwise.'

Shibnath stayed silent. Looking fixedly at him, Kamal continued, 'You know I've endured everything, but I couldn't endure driving you out of the house. That's why I've come here to nurse you—not to win you back.'

Shibnath said slowly, 'I'm grateful to you for your kindness, Shibani.'

Kamal said, 'Don't call me Shibani. Call me Kamal.'

'Why?'

'I feel revolted when I hear that name. That's why.'

'But this was the name you once loved best to hear!' He gently took Kamal's hand between his own. Kamal did not move. She found it distasteful even to tug her hand away.

'Why do you keep quiet and not answer?'

Kamal remained speechless as before.

'What are you thinking, Shibani? Tell me.'

'Do you know what I'm thinking? I'm thinking how wicked you must be to remind me of that fact.'

Shibnath's eyes glistened with tears. He said, 'I'm not wicked, Shibani. One day you'll see your mistake and your remorse will know no bounds. Why I rented another house . . .'

'Have I asked you even once why you rented another

house? I only wanted to know why you didn't tell me before coming away. I wouldn't have held you back even for a day.'

Tears filled Shibnath's eyes. He said, 'I didn't have the courage to tell you, Shibani.'

'Why?'

Shibnath wiped his eyes on his shirtsleeve and said, 'First of all there was so little money, and then I had to go somewhere or other every day—to buy stones, to dispatch goods. So I thought a house nearer the station . . .'

Kamal rose from the bed, sat in a chair at a distance and said, 'I don't feel sorry for myself any more, only for someone else. But today I even feel sorry for you, Shibnath Babu.'

It had been a long time since she had addressed him by his name. She said, 'Look, you can't carry on trading in the world's market with downright deception as your sole capital. Perhaps you won't meet me again, but you will remember me. Let bygones be bygones. But in future, try to see life from a different angle. If you do, you might even be happy. Don't forget this—please don't. Even now I really wish you well, and that you may be well.'

Kamal struggled to hold back her tears. Even after this conversation, she could not hit Shibnath so hard as to tell him why Ashu Babu had had him moved out of his house.

A cycle bell rang outside. Shibnath fell silent and turned over on his side.

Rajen came in and said in a low voice, 'Ah! So you're still awake. How's the patient? Did you give him any more medicines?'

Kamal shook her head and said, 'No, I didn't give him anything more.'

Rajen pointed to the patient and said, 'Let's be quiet, else he'll wake up. That won't do him any good.'

'No. But what have your leather workers been up to?'

'They're good people; they've kept their word. Before I got there, Lord Yama's buffalo had carried off the two souls; all I need do is hand over the two bodies to the municipal buffalo cart tomorrow morning. About eight others are gasping—I'll take you along tomorrow to see them. I think you'll learn a lot. But what about my rug-bed in the armchair? Have you forgotten about it?'

Kamal made up the bed. 'Ah! What comfort,' sighed Rajen as he lay down, stretching his legs along the arms of the chair. He said, 'I'm sweating with all this running about. Have you got a fan?'

Kamal picked up a fan and drew her chair close to him. 'Go to sleep; I'll fan you. There's no need to worry about the patient. He's all right.'

'Fine! So everything's all right.' And he closed his eyes.

18

INFLUENZA WAS NOT AN ENTIRELY NEW DISEASE IN THIS LAND. People used to call it 'dengue' and treat it with neglect and contempt, thinking it could do no more than cause a few days' suffering. No one ever imagined it could so rapidly assume such an epidemic, uncontrollable form. Hence people were first dumbstruck by the stern cruelty of its unlimited power. Then those who could, began to flee. Relatives counted for no more than strangers. Nursing was out of the question: many patients did not even have anyone to give them a last drop of water. Whether in town or village, the situation was the same.

The state of Agra was no different. Within a few days, the appearance of this densely populated, prosperous town changed completely. Schools and colleges were closed, the shops in the markets shut down, and the river bank was almost desolate. The main roads were silent and deserted except for the timorous footsteps of Hindu and Muslim corpse-bearers. Looking around, it seemed that not only the people but even the trees, houses and buildings had turned pale with fear.

As the town lay sunk in this state, many of the inhabitants, burning with anxiety, sorrow and bereavement, made up their differences. It did not require the effort of discussion or mediation—it just happened. Those who had still survived, those who had not yet been obliterated from the face of the earth, seemed by virtue of that to be close kin to each other. People who had not spoken to each other for a long time now met on the street with moist eyes: one's brother, another's

185

child or wife had died meanwhile. They no longer had the strength of mind to turn away their faces in hatred. Sometimes they exchanged words; sometimes not, only taking their leave silently, wishing each other well.

Not many in the leather workers' quarter survived. As many died as fled. Rajen alone was enough to look after the remaining ones: he had taken charge of their final destiny. Kamal had come to join him as assistant, confident in her youthful experience of nursing sick coolies in the tea garden. But within two or three days, she realized that the resources of her experience were useless here. The misery of the leather workers beggared description. One shuddered on stepping into their huts. There was nowhere to sit or stand: until she went there, Kamal had not known the ghastly form sheer filth could assume. She had no idea of how to protect herself in such surroundings and nurse the sick. She had accompanied Rajen with the proud boast of yielding to none in recklessness and fearing nothing in the world, not even death. She had not lied; but on arriving there, she realized that her powers were not limitless. Within a few days her blood seemed to be drying up in terror. And yet, when she returned home, Rajen reassured her that he had never seen such courage: 'You've warded off the real blast of the storm. There's no more need. Go home and rest for a few days. They can never repay what you've done for them.'

'And what about you?'

Rajen said, 'I'll quit too after I've seen them go. Do you think I want to die?'

Kamal did not know what to say. She looked at him for a while, then retreated silently.

It was not that she had not been home at all during

these days. She came once a day to cook and carry the food back with her. On the one hand she felt relieved at not having to return to that terrible place; on the other, an unuttered anguish possessed her completely. She had forgotten to ask about Rajen's meals today. But however big this omission might be, it could not compare with the situation in which she had left him.

With the closure of the schools and colleges, Harendra's brahmacharya ashram had also closed down. Satish had undertaken to escort the boy-brahmacharis to a safe place and take care of them. Harendra could not go himself because of Ashu Babu's illness. He now turned up at Kamal's house. Greeting her, he said, 'I've been here every morning for the last five or six days, but I couldn't find you. Where were you?'

When Kamal mentioned the leather workers' quarter, Harendra was amazed. 'I heard hordes of people were dying there. Who gave you this idea? Whoever it was, he is to blame.'

'Why?'

'Can you ask? Going there virtually amounts to suicide. We'd thought that after Shibnath Babu left Agra, you too had gone away somewhere else only for a few days, of course, otherwise you wouldn't have kept on these rooms. Well, do you know anything about Rajen? Is he in town or has he gone away? He has sunk so utterly without trace that it's impossible to find him.'

'Do you need him urgently?'

'No, not what people normally mean by "need". Yet there is a need, because if I too stop asking after him he'll be left with no one to do so except the police. I believe you know where he is.'

Kamal said, 'I do know. But it's no use telling you. It's culpable curiosity to ask where somebody is after driving him out of your house.'

Harendra remained silent for a while. Then he said, 'But it's not my house, it's our ashram. We couldn't go on having him there, but I shan't have any one else blaming me for it. Well, I'll be off. I've tracked him down quite a few times before this. I'm sure I'll do so this time too. You can't hide him from me.'

Kamal smiled on hearing this and said, 'If I could, do you think it would put an end to my misery?'

Harendra smiled too, but there was an emptiness in his smile. He said, 'There are many others in Agra besides me to answer this question. Do you know what they'd say? They'd say, "Kamal, human misery isn't all of one kind, but many. They have various natures and various remedies." So if you meet them, discuss the matter and decide it with them. He was silent for a while, then spoke again: 'But you're making a fundamental mistake. I'm not one of these people. I haven't come to bother you unnecessarily, because I'm one of those who really respect you.'

Kamal looked at him and asked gently, 'On what grounds do you respect me? My ideas and attitudes don't match yours in the slightest.'

Harendra promptly replied, 'No, they don't, but I still respect you greatly. And I repeatedly ask myself why.'

'Have you found any answer?'

'No, but I hope I will one day.' After a short silence, he said, 'I heard something about your past from you and something from Ajit Babu. By the way, perhaps you know that he's staying at our ashram now.

Kamal nodded and said, 'You told me so earlier.'

Harendra said, 'The strange chapters of your life have been laid before us so simply and frankly that it's hard to pass summary judgement on them. Your life seems to have been like a lawsuit in defence of every idea I have so long held to be wrong or vicious. I don't know when and where we'll find the judge, or what the verdict will be, but one can't but respect somebody who stands up so fearlessly, without any need of a veil.'

Kamal said, 'Is it so important to take a fearless stand? Haven't you heard of those utterly shameless people who always walk down the middle of the road? You haven't seen the English tea planter, but I have. Their shameless, fearless impudence not only flouts modesty, but seems to thrust it aside by the neck. Their audacity is boundless, but is it something to respect?'

Harendra had not expected such a rejoinder, at least not from this woman. Unable to find an immediate reply, he said, 'That's different.'

Kamal said, 'How do you know it's different? Seeing him from the outside, people thought my father to be one of them too. I know it wasn't so, but the truth couldn't rest on my knowledge alone. Where's the evidence before the world?'

Again Haren had nothing to say, so he kept quiet. Kamal went on: 'All of you have heard my story, probably with great relish. You are silent as to whether my actions were good or bad, whether my life is pure or tainted. You respect me only because what I do is carried out openly, defying everybody, and not in secret. Haren Babu, I haven't had so much respect from the world that I can lightly dismiss what I get; but as you've come to know so much about me, you should also know that this respect hurts me more than the disrespect shown by Akshay Babu and his like. I can tolerate that, but this is unbearable.'

Harendra remained speechless as before. He felt deeply humiliated by Kamal's words, and still more at the cold severity of her voice. After a while he asked, 'Can't you believe that one can respect a person in spite of differences in ideas and attitudes—at least, that I can do so?'

Kamal replied very calmly, 'I didn't say that I can't believe it, Haren Babu. I say such respect oppresses me.' She paused and then continued, 'There's not much difference between your ideas and principles and those of Akshay Babu and his circle. Except for their excessive and gratuitous severity, you're all much the same. So also with your respect. The defiance shown by my not hiding or suppressing myself has earned me your admiration. Of what value is it, Haren Babu? Rather, when I think about it, I feel repelled that you've been applauding me only for that.'

Harendra said, 'Was it wrong to applaud you? Does courage matter nothing in life?'

Kamal said, 'Why phrase all your questions in such extreme terms? I don't say it matters nothing. I only say that it's rare, and dazzles by its rarity; but there are greater things that, viewed from outside, look like want of courage.'

Haren shook his head and said, 'I don't get your meaning. What you say often sounds like riddles, but what you are saying today goes even beyond that. You seem to be utterly distracted today. You don't know what you're saying, or to whom.'

'That's true,' said Kamal. She remained silent for a while and then said, 'Perhaps so. Perhaps I myself hadn't known all this time what it is to be truly respected. I was startled the day I found out. Don't take offence, Haren Babu, but compared to that, everything today seems to be a mockery.' As she spoke, her stern gaze was overshadowed by a soft quietude. Harendra had never seen this image of Kamal. He was convinced that she was addressing some other, absent person; he merely provided an occasion for the address. That's why everything appeared like a riddle to him.

Kamal went on: 'Just now you were praising my reckless courage. By the way, do you know that Shibnath has left me?'

Harendra hung his head in embarrassment and said, 'Yes.'

Kamal said, 'We had agreed privately that if the occasion arose, we would part very easily in this way. Not by signing documents—just casually.'

Harendra said, '*Brute*.'

Kamal said, 'That applies to your friend Akshay Babu. Shibnath is a worthy person. I don't have many complaints against him. And what's the use of complaining? In the heart's court, ex parte justice is the only kind of justice available; there isn't any appeal bench either.'

Harendra said, 'That means you don't accept any bond other than that of love.'

Kamal said, 'At first there was no other bond between us. And had there been, what use would it have been to get it endorsed? The external tie of a paralysed limb is a huge burden. It oppresses you the more you try to make it work.' She was silent for a moment and then continued, 'You think that I say all this only because we didn't have a real marriage; that otherwise I wouldn't have. I could have even so, but that wouldn't have solved my problem so easily. The paralysed limb would have hung on to this day and, like most women, I'd have had to bear the burden of that misery all my life. I've escaped that, Haren Babu. Luckily, the door to freedom was open, and I could escape.'

Harendra said, 'You might have escaped, but if everyone wanted to keep the door of freedom open like this, the very foundation of the social system would be uprooted. No one can imagine the shape of that horror—one can't even think of the possibility.'

Kamal said, 'It can be conceived of, and you'll have to do so one day. That's because the last chapter of human history is yet to be written. If a day's ceremony were to bar one's way to freedom forever, it couldn't be accepted as a preferable system. There are precepts for mending every error in the world: no one sees anything wrong with that. So how can I admit that it's good to deliberately remove the means of correction where there's the greatest risk of error and the greatest need for remedy?'

Harendra had always felt a deep compassion for the miseries of this young woman. He never took part in the hostile discussions about her; he would protest when her opponents brought out all kinds of proof of her allegedly irrefutable baseness. When they condemned her by citing instances of her brazen ways and shameless utterances, Harendra, though defeated in argument, would do his utmost to convince them that these were not true of her life: that there was some hidden mystery which would surely be revealed one day. They would sarcastically reply that if she would only reveal it, the Bengalis of Agra would have peace. If Akshay were present he would angrily say, 'You are all alike. None of you have my strong faith. You can neither accept nor reject. Some high-sounding modern English catchwords seem to have bewitched you.'

Abinash would say, 'My dear Akshay, it's not that we've heard those catchwords from Kamal for the first time; we knew them before. They can be picked up today from two or three books translated from English. It's not the glitter of the catchwords that has taken us in.'

Akshay would sternly ask, 'The glitter of what, then? Of Kamal's beauty? Abinash, Haren is young and unmarried. He can be forgiven. But it seems she has even charmed the rest of you in the ripeness of your years.' He would look askance at Ashu Babu at this point and then continue: 'But it's only the gleam of the will-o'-the-wisp: it's born of slime. I can dearly foresee that she'll drag many people into the slime. But she can't seduce Akshay: he knows the true from the false.'

Ashu Babu would smile wryly at this, but Abinash burned with rage. Harendra would say, 'You're a true hero, Akshay Babu. I wish you victory. The day that you see us wallowing in slime, you can flap your elbows and dance on the shore. None of us will blame you.'

Akshay would reply, 'I never do anything unseemly. I'm a householder and I conform to society as my simple understanding dictates. I don't want to give a new interpretation to marriage, nor do I collect a host of rascally young men and deal in brahmacharihood. Go, brother—let the dust of more feet gather at your ashram; then you won't lack prayer and worship. Soon the ashram will turn into the sage Vishwamitra's hermitage, and you'll have set up a record for all time.'

At this, Abinash would forget his anger and burst into uproarious laughter, while Ashu Babu's face also lit up with a soft, suppressed smile. Nobody had faith in Harendra's ashram: it was thought of as his private fad.

Harendra's face would flush in anger, and he would

say, 'One can't reason with beasts. They have to be dealt with by other means. But because such arrangements haven't yet been made for you, you can butt whoever you like with your horns. You don't discriminate between the decent and the vile, between men and women.' Then turning to the other two he would say, 'But how can you do this? His ugly insinuations seem a huge joke to you.'

Abinash would say with embarrassment, 'No, no, why should we indulge him? You know Akshay has no sense.'

Harendra would retort, 'You have less sense than he does. It's just that one can't see a person's mind, Sejda. If one could, very few people would have the face to laugh and joke. Shibnath deceived Kamal with the illusion of marriage, but I firmly believe Kamal took that deception for a truth. She didn't want to slight him in others' eyes, bargaining with him over give and take, profit and loss. But even if she doesn't want to do so, why should all of you let him go free? Shibnath is the object of her love, but who is he to you? You couldn't tolerate her misplaced forgiveness of Shibnath. That's the seed capital of your hatred for her. You may bank on it as long as you can, I'm quitting.'

Having had his say, Harendra left in anger that day. In his heart he was certain that one day Kamal would confirm she had genuinely been deceived in accepting a Shaivite marriage as the real thing: that she had not knowingly and deliberately sought shelter with Shibnath like a harlot. But today the very foundation of his faith crumbled. He had an unusual and deep sympathy—not only for a Harendra, Akshay or Abinash, but for everybody, man or woman. That is why he would associate himself with all kinds of work for the good of the people and the nation. This trait lay at the root of his brahmacharya ashram, his generous philanthropy, his habit of sharing things with everyone. But he had never imagined that she would, to his face, give such a devastating reply to his question.

Harendra was immeasurably devoted to India's religious ideas and customs, her unique and distinguished civilization. He never denied its aberrations, whether caused by long bondage or through weakness of individual character; but he was deeply distressed by this audacious contempt, this denial of the basic principles of that ethos. He was repelled by the thought that Kamal's father was a European and her mother a harlot: the blood of profligacy ran in her veins. He kept silent for two or three minutes and then said, 'I'd better go now.'

Kamal could not gauge Harendra's feelings. She only noticed a certain change in him. She asked softly, 'But what about the problem that brought you here?'

Harendra raised his face and asked, 'What was that?'

Kamal said, 'You'd come to ask about Rajen, but you're going back without having learnt anything. Tell me: has there been any unpleasant comment about his staying here? Tell me the truth.'

Harendra said, 'Even if there is such comment, I don't share in it. I'm happy as long as he's out of police custody. I know him well.'

'But what about me?'

'You don't care about such things.'

'That's largely true. At least I'm not on oath to conform to these things. But it's not enough to know your friend. You must know the other party as well.'

'I think that's superfluous. I have no fears about someone whom I've come to know well over a long time. Let him stay wherever he likes. I'm not worried about him.'

Kamal looked silently at him for a few moments, then said, 'People have to pass many examinations, Haren Babu. The answers one day may not match the questions of the previous one. You shouldn't judge anyone so conclusively: you'll be deceived.'

Harendra realized that Kamal was not talking in general terms but hinting at something specific. Yet he dared not ask her for more details. He dropped the subject of Rajen and began to talk about something else. He said, 'We have decided to punish Shibnath as he deserves.'

Kamal was surprised. 'Who are "we"?' she asked.

'Whoever they are, I'm one of them,' said Harendra. 'Ashu Babu is ill; he has promised to help me when he recovers.'

'Is he ill?'

'Yes, for the last seven or eight days. Manorama has already left. Ashu Babu's uncle, who lives in Varanasi, came to take her away.'

Kamal silently heard this.

Harendra went on, 'Shibnath knows that the arm of the law can't reach him. Sure about that, he has cheated the wife of his deceased friend; he has deserted his own ailing wife, and brazenly ruined you. He knows the law very well, but he doesn't know that it's not the last word in the world. There are things beyond it.'

Kamal asked with amusement, 'But what punishment have you determined for him? Will you arrest him and hitch him to me again?' She laughed a little.

The idea suddenly seemed so ridiculous to Harendra that he too could not but laugh. He said, 'But it's intolerable that he should evade his responsibilities with such impunity, according to his whims. Of course there's no reason why he should be hitched to you.'

Kamal said, 'Then what's the use of bringing him here? Will you give me the job of keeping watch over him, or will you force him to compensate me? First of all, I won't accept his money, and secondly he hasn't got any. I know how poor Shibnath is, even if no one else does.'

'Then won't he be punished at all for such a grave offence? However that may be, at least he needs to be told that you can still buy whips in the market.'

Kamal anxiously said, 'No, no, don't do any such thing. That would be too humiliating for me. I've burned so long with anger at the thought that he absconded like a thief: would I have stopped him from leaving if he'd been frank with me? At that time, the humiliation of his hide-and-seek seemed monstrous to me. Then suddenly there was this summons from death's very quarter. Now that I've seen countless deaths with my own eyes, I've begun thinking along new lines. I now feel that his cowardice, in not telling me he was leaving, honours me. His secrecy, his deceit and all his frauds seem to add up to that. He gained me by deceiving me; but when he left, he had to repay the entire debt, both principal and interest. I have no grievances: I've got back all my dues. Give my regards to Ashu Babu and tell him that he mustn't spell disaster for me by trying to do me good.'

Harendra failed to understand a single word of all this. He stood staring in amazement.

Kamal said, 'Everything in this world isn't meant to be understood by everyone, Haren Babu. Don't be hurt. But no more about myself. Kamal and Shibnath are not the only people on earth; others too live here, they too have their joys and sorrows.' With these words, she seemed to dispel in a moment the thick cloud of pain and misery with an innocent and tranquil smile. 'Tell me how everyone is,' she said.

Harendra said, 'Tell me who you want to know about.'

'Well, first tell me about Abinash Babu. I'd heard that he was ill. Has he recovered?'

'Yes, but not fully. One of his cousins lives in Lahore. He's gone there with his son to convalesce. He may not be back for a month or two.'

'What about Nilima? Has she gone with them?'

'No, she's here.'

'Here?' asked Kamal in surprise. 'Alone in that lonely house?'

Harendra hesitated a little and then said, 'She really was put in a difficult situation, but God saved her. The opportunity arose for her to go to Ashu Babu's house and nurse him.'

The news was so bizarre that Kamal did not ask anything more. She only waited curiously for the details. Harendra got over his hesitation, and signs of deep anger appeared in his voice, for he had had a little altercation with Abinash over this matter. Harendra said, 'A person can do what he likes in his own house, but he can't go to stay with his elder cousin taking along the grown-up widowed sister of his own wife. So he said to me, "Haren, you too are my relative; perhaps your house . . ." I replied, "First, I'm your relative, and a distant one at that; I'm not related to her. Secondly, it's not my house but our ashram. Thirdly, the boys have now gone elsewhere and I'm alone." At this Sejda was extremely worried. He couldn't stay in Agra, people were dying all around; his cousin was sending letters and telegrams pressing him to come. He was in a great quandary.'

Kamal asked, 'But haven't I heard that Nilima still has her parents?'

Harendra nodded and said, 'Yes, she does. I've also heard

that she has a large household full of in-laws, but these factors weren't discussed. Suddenly one day, along came a remarkable solution. I don't know which side the proposal came from, but Boudi took charge of the ailing Ashu Babu.'

Kamal remained silent.

Harendra smiled and said, 'But there's every hope that she won't lose her job. When Dada comes back, she can take up her old post of housewife.'

Kamal did not respond to this sarcasm, but remained silent as before.

Harendra went on, 'I know that Boudi is a really virtuous woman. She couldn't desert Sejda in his time of trouble: perhaps that's what closed all those other roads for her. But it seems this road wasn't open either when she was in distress. It makes me realize how helpless women are in our country, even for no fault of their own.'

Kamal still sat silently, saying nothing.

'Perhaps you're laughing to yourself on hearing all this. Aren't you?'

Kamal shook her head and said, 'No.'

Harendra said, 'I often go to see Ashu Babu. Both of them asked about you. Boudi was extremely anxious—would you like to go there one day?'

Kamal instantly agreed and said, 'Why not today, Haren Babu? Let's go and see them.'

'Today? Well, let me go and get a tonga if I can find one.' He was about to leave the room when Kamal called him back and said, 'If the two of us travel together in the same tonga, your friends at the ashram may be angry. Let's walk.'

Harendra turned and said, 'What does that mean?'

'Nothing. It's just something I said. Let's go.'

19

WHEN HARENDRA AND KAMAL REACHED ASHU BABU'S HOUSE, it was almost afternoon. The master of the house was half-reclining on his bed, reading that day's *Pioneer*. His temperature had been normal for the past few days; his other symptoms were also abating, but he was still weak. As they entered the room, Ashu Babu put aside his paper and sat up. His face showed how glad he was. He had been afraid that Kamal might not visit him again. So he held out his hands to her and said, 'Come and sit near me.' Sitting her down on a stool near his bed, he asked, 'How are you, Kamal?'

She answered with a smile, 'I'm very well.'

Ashu Babu said, 'It's so only by the grace of God. Times are so bad that it's hard to imagine anybody being well. Where were you for so long? I've asked Harendra every day, and he's come back and said that your house is locked and there is no trace of you. Nilima thought you might have gone away somewhere for a few days.'

It was Harendra who replied to this. 'Nowhere else,' he said. 'She was right here in Agra. She was out nursing in the leather workers' quarter. I found her today and brought her here.'

Profoundly alarmed, Ashu Babu said, 'In the leather workers' quarter? But the newspapers say that place has been emptied out by the epidemic! You were among them all these days? Alone?'

Kamal shook her head and said, 'No, not alone. Rajen was there with me.'

On hearing this, Harendra looked at her but did not say anything. His glance implied: 'You didn't tell me so, but I had guessed it. Who but I should know that once providence set off such massive havoc, Rajen wouldn't move a step away from those poor devils?'

Ashu Babu said, 'That boy's a strange person. I haven't seen him more than two or three times, but to me he seems made of some unearthly metal. Why didn't you bring him along with you? I would have asked him about the situation. The newspapers don't give the full picture.'

'No, they don't,' said Kamal. 'But it'll be quite some time before he returns.'

'Why?'

'The locality has yet to be emptied completely. He has vowed not to leave before he has seen off the last of them.'

Ashu Babu said, 'Then how did you get leave? Do you have to return there? I can't prevent you, but I feel deeply concerned, Kamal.'

Kamal shook her head and said, 'It's not a question of concern, Ashu Babu. There's cause for concern everywhere. But I've spent all the wound-up energy of my watch. I don't have the strength to go back there. Only Rajen has stayed back. Nature sends some people to earth with so much life in their body's machine that they neither tire nor break down. This man is one of them. At first I used to wonder how he would survive in that dreadful place. How long would he live? When I came away, I couldn't stop worrying. But now I'm not afraid any more. I've realized that nature keeps such people alive in her own interest: who else would bear witness to the devastation when death rushes into poor men's houses like a flood? I was talking to Haren Babu about this today. When

I came out of Shibnath Babu's room at night's end, my head bowed in shame . . .'

Ashu Babu had heard of this incident. He said, 'What's there to be ashamed of, Kamal? I heard that you went to his house of your own accord to nurse him.'

Kamal said, 'I'm not ashamed of that, Ashu Babu. But when I found that he was not ill—that the whole thing was a sham, that he had simply tried to earn your compassion by a hoax—even though it failed and you turned him out—I can't tell you what I felt like. I couldn't even tell my companion— only I left the place somehow, silently, in the darkness of night. One thing that repeatedly struck me on the way back was that there's neither virtue nor honour in punishing that petty, resourceless person in one's anger.'

Ashu Babu said in amazement, 'What did you say, Kamal? Is Shibnath's illness a hoax? Isn't it genuine?' Before she could reply, everyone turned at the sound of footsteps near the door and saw Nilima enter with a bowl of milk. Kamal raised her hands in a namaskar. Nilima placed the bowl on a small table beside the bed, returned the greeting and sat down quietly, fearing that she had interrupted the others' conversation.

Ashu Babu continued, 'But this shows weakness on your part, Kamal. It is out of keeping with your nature. I always thought you never forgave anything unjust, anything false.'

Harendra said, 'I don't know about her nature. But she has told me herself that her views have changed after seeing death in the leather workers' slum: whatever she might have wished earlier, she no longer wants to complain against anyone.'

Ashu Babu said, 'But what about the enormous cruelty he has shown you?'

As Kamal looked up, she saw Nilima staring at her as if avidly awaiting a reply, otherwise she might have kept silent and not gone beyond what Harendra had said. But now she answered, 'These questions now appear pointless to me. Today I'm ashamed to cry for what is not and why it is not. In the same way, I would hang my head in shame to be angry that he did so little for me. My only request to you is not to harass him over my misfortune.' She suddenly seemed to have exhausted herself. She threw her head back on the chair and closed her eyes.

Nilima broke the silence. Indicating the bowl of milk, she softly said, 'It's getting cold. See if you can drink it, or else I'll tell them to warm it again.'

Ashu Babu took the bowl, drank some of the milk and laid it down. Nilima leaned forward, examined it and said, 'You must drink it all. I won't let you break the doctor's orders.' Ashu Babu leaned back wearily against his bolster and said, 'The body itself is the best prescriber. You should remember that.'

'I don't forget it. You do.'

'That's a failing of old age. It's not my fault.'

Nilima said with a smile, 'Isn't it just! You have a long way to go before you can blame old age for your lapses. Well, let us take Kamal to the next room and chat with her for a while. Meanwhile, why don't you close your eyes and rest a little? May we go?'

Perhaps this was not what Ashu Babu had in mind, yet he could not but consent. He only added, 'Don't go too far. Make sure you can hear me if I call.'

'All right. Come, Thakurpo, let's go and sit in the next room. 'She led them away.

Nilima was naturally sweet-spoken, and her manner of speech had a special distinction. But the few words she spoke today sounded even sweeter than usual. Harendra did not mark it, but Kamal did. What escaped the man's eyes caught the woman's attention. It might be enough for the ordinary person to think that, as Nilima had come to nurse a sick man, it was not surprising that she cared about his health; but Kamal was not an ordinary person. In Nilima's extreme alertness, her exquisite softness, she seemed to find matter for deep wonder, not on one score but several. Kamal could not think for a moment that the lure of property had overwhelmed this young widow. She had gauged her to that extent at least. To cite Ashu Babu's youth and charm would be not merely inept but ludicrous. Kamal went searching in her mind for the cause of Nilima's amazing behaviour.

There was another side to the matter as well: it concerned Ashu Babu himself. Everybody had assumed implicitly that no temptation could tarnish the ideal marital love that this simple, serene man held holy in his heart with firm, exemplary devotion. He was not very old when Manorama's mother died— not yet past his youth. Ever since, hordes of relatives and non-relatives had zealously tried to uproot the memory of his deceased wife and plant a new image in its place. But no one had found a way to storm the gates of that impenetrable fortress. Kamal had heard all this from many people. She sat silently in the room, seemingly unmindful but actually wondering whether this man had the slightest idea of Nilima's state of mind: and if he had, whether that had affected the stern principles of conjugal life that he had upheld like an inviolable religion.

The servant brought in tea, bread, fruit and other things.

Handing these to her guests, Nilima went on talking about various matters—Ashu Babu's illness and general health, little anecdotes of his natural courtesy and childlike simplicity that had struck her over these few days, and so on. Women generally coveted Harendra as a listener. In response to his encouraging enquiries, Nilima grew more and more voluble. Impressed by the sincerity of her speech, Harendra did not mark whether it was the same boudi he had seen at Abinash Babu's, the same woman who now renounced the sweet solemnity of her blooming youth, her measured witty jests, her sober conversation befitting the norms of widowhood—everything familiar about her—for a sudden garrulity like a talkative girl's.

Nilima suddenly noticed that Kamal had had nothing except a few sips of tea. As Nilima protested in a hurt tone, Kamal said, smiling, 'Have you forgotten my ways so soon?'

'Forgotten? What do you mean?'

'It means you don't remember my eating habits. I don't eat anything at odd times.'

'And in spite of a thousand requests, she won't do otherwise,' added Harendra.

Kamal said with the same smiling expression: 'That means I haven't given up my obstinacy. I wouldn't put it so vaingloriously, Haren Babu. It's just that I've got accustomed to this habit.'

As they came out on the road, she asked, 'Where are you going now?'

Harendra said, 'Don't worry, I shan't enter your house. But it would be wrong of me not to escort you back to where I brought you from.'

It was already dark. There were few people about. Suddenly,

in a very intimate way, Kamal drew his hand between hers and said, 'Come with me. Let's test how finely you have come to judge of right and wrong.'

Harendra was deeply alarmed and embarrassed. He saw clearly that there was danger in walking down the road like this, and that it would bring deep disgrace if they suddenly met someone they knew. But he could not think of being so harsh and unseemly as to draw his hand away without warning. The business seemed shocking to him; but he had to put up with that perilous condition until they reached her door. As he began to take his leave, Kamal said, 'Where's the hurry? There's only Ajit Babu at the ashram.'

Harendra said, 'No, today he isn't there either. He's taken the morning train to Delhi. Perhaps he'll return tomorrow.'

Kamal said, 'What will you eat when you return to the ashram? You haven't got a cook.'

Harendra said, 'We do our own cooking.'

'That is to say, you and Ajit Babu?'

'Yes. But what makes you laugh? We're not bad cooks.'

'I know that.' But she continued with true gravity, 'Ajit Babu is away, so you'll have to cook for yourself when you return. If you aren't repelled by the prospect, I would very much like to invite you to a meal. Will you eat what I cook?'

Harendra was deeply hurt and said, 'This is very unfair of you. Do you really think I'd refuse your cooking out of some revulsion?' He fell silent for a few moments and then said, 'I haven't hesitated to tell you how I'm one of those who respect you. My only objection is that I don't want to trouble you at this unseemly hour.'

Kamal said, 'You'll see for yourself that it won't be much trouble for me. Come.'

As she sat down to cook she said, 'My arrangements are frugal, but what I've seen at your ashram can scarcely be called ample either. So at least I'm assured that, even if you don't enjoy my food, you won't find it as inedible as others might.'

Harendra said happily, 'Our arrangements at the ashram are indeed as you saw. We really do live very frugally.'

'But why do you? Ajit Babu is rich, and you're not exactly poor. There's no reason for you to suffer such hardship.'

'There may not be any reason,' answered Harendra, 'but there is a need. I believe it's because you too understand the need that you've laid down similar rules for yourself. But if an outsider is surprised and asks you, could you give him your reasons?'

Kamal said, 'If I can't give it to outsiders, I can to insiders at least. I really am very poor. I can't manage better than this with the means I have. My father left me nothing, but he taught me the secret of being free of the kindness of others.'

Harendra gazed at her in silence. He knew how helpless Kamal was in this strange place. It was not only a matter of money: she could expect nothing from any quarter as regards company, respect or sympathy. Yet he could not but note that such utter helplessness had not unnerved this woman in the least. Even now she did not beg for alms—rather, she gave alms. Even now she had resources to bestow on Shibnath, the source of so much distress to her. Perhaps in order to encourage and console her, he said, 'I don't want to argue with you, Kamal, but I cannot but think that your poverty too is unreal, like ours. If you so wished, your misery would vanish like a mirage. But you don't wish that, because you too know that, if willingly embraced, misery can be enjoyed just as much as wealth.'

Kamal said, 'It can indeed; but do you know why? Because it's an unnecessary misery—a show of misery. All playacting involves some fun—there's nothing wrong with enjoying it.' She gave him an amused smile.

This suddenly struck a discordant note. Harendra remained speechless for a while at the jibe, then replied, 'But you'll admit that life grows trivial in the midst of plenty, while human character grows true and noble in poverty and suffering.'

Kamal lowered the pan from the stove and put something else on it. She said, 'To develop as a true being, one needs some truth in other ways too, Haren Babu. You're rich, you have no real want, but you're busy setting up a make-believe poverty, and Ajit Babu is keeping you company. I don't understand the *philosophy* of your ashram, but I do understand that nothing great can be achieved by the travails of poverty—only a little pride and arrogance. You can easily see this if you look around a little without being blinded by prejudice: you won't have to travel across India to find instances. But let's drop the argument. I've almost finished cooking. Sit down to eat.'

Harendra said disappointedly, 'The problem is that you can't understand Indian *philosophy*. There's infidel blood in your veins, so the ideals of Hinduism appear ridiculous in your eyes. Come, let's see what you've cooked.'

'Just a moment,' said Kamal, laying out a mat for him to sit on. She was not at all offended.

Looking at her, Harendra suddenly said, 'Well, suppose a person really were to give away everything he had and descend into real poverty and privation, then it couldn't be ridiculed as playacting. In that case . . .'

Kamal interrupted him and said, 'No, then it wouldn't be ridiculous. It would be time to beat one's head and bewail his madness. Haren Babu, I too used to think like you once. I too would be overcome by the intoxication of fasting; but now I'm beyond such delusions. Whether suffered willingly or unwillingly, poverty and misery are nothing to boast about. They have nothing at their core except emptiness, weakness and evil. During the epidemic in the leather workers' slum, I saw to what depths poverty can degrade man. Another person has also seen it—your friend Rajen. But you can't learn anything from him—nobody knows what's hidden in him, as in the dense Assam forests. I'm often amazed that you chose to drive him away—as the proverb goes, "Throwing away a jewel to cherish a piece of glass." Haven't you done precisely that? Didn't you hear any protests from within you? Strange!'

Harendra did not reply, and remained silent.

Kamal's provisions were meagre, but she fed her guest with scrupulous care. As he sat down to eat, Harendra repeatedly recalled Nilima: he knew no greater exemplar of the ideal of serene grace and womanly purity. He said to himself, 'However different they may be in education, training, taste and inclination, in service and tenderness they are equal. Because those others are external matters, they can be endlessly different and one can argue about them endlessly. But one's heart finds rest when one perceives the essence of womanhood, far from all conflict of opinion—a beauty hidden in the depths of the heart.'

Harendra had no appetite that day, for various reasons; but he ate more than he wanted to, only to please one person. He took a fancy to some vegetable dish and finished it off. He said, 'I've often turned up at odd hours and troubled Boudi in just this way.'

'Who? Nilima?'

'Yes.'

'Did it trouble her?'

'No doubt. But she never admitted it.'

Kamal said with a smile, 'It's not only you: all men are equally stupid.'

'But I've seen it with my own eyes,' protested Harendra.

'I know that,' said Kamal. 'That pride in ocular evidence will be the death of you.'

Harendra said, 'You people have no less conceit. On those occasions Boudi would have to go without food; but although she'd fast she wouldn't give in.'

Kamal looked at him in silence.

Harendra said, 'Bless us that our stupidity might be immortal: ours is the better bargain. We refuse to die of starvation through pride in our subtle intelligence!'

Kamal did not respond to this either.

Harendra went on, 'From now on I shall test the subtlety of your intelligence from time to time.'

Kamal said, 'You won't be able to. You'll pity me because I'm poor.'

Harendra was initially taken aback on hearing this. Then he said, 'It's awkward replying to this. Do you know why? Because mendicancy doesn't suit a person who's meant to be a queen. Your poverty seems to ridicule all the rich men's daughters in the world.'

The words pierced Kamal's heart like an arrow.

Harendra was about to say something else. Kamal interrupted him and said, 'You've finished eating. Get up. I'll hear you all night in the next room; let's finish what's to be done here.'

Taking him into her bedroom presently, Kamal said to him, 'Today I won't let you go before I've heard the history of your Boudi, however late it might get. Tell me.'

Harendra was in a quandary. He said, 'But I don't know everything about her. I first met her in Agra at Sejda's place. In fact, I know nothing about her—only what most people here know. But one thing I do know better than others do, and that is her spotless purity. She was only nineteen or twenty when her husband died. She had opened all her heart to him. That memory has never been wiped out and never will be; it will remain intact till her last day. The men only talk about Ashu Babu; I don't deny that his devotion is extraordinary too, but . . .'

'Haren Babu, it's very late. You can't go home. Shall I make up a bed for you in this room?'

'In this room?' asked Harendra in astonishment. 'But what about you?'

'I'll sleep here too,' said Kamal. 'It's the only room.'

Harendra grew pale with embarrassment. Kamal smiled and said, 'But you're a brahmachari. Surely you have nothing to fear?'

Harendra only stared at her dumbly. He couldn't imagine such a proposal. How could she, a woman, bring herself to utter it?

His unbounded confusion shook Kamal as well. She stood still for a few moments and then said, 'My mistake, Haren Babu. Go home. This is why Nilima, the object of your infinite reverence, couldn't find shelter in your ashram but only at Ashu Babu's place. You know of only one kind of encounter between an unrelated man and woman in a lonely house: you have yet to learn that to a man, a woman can be anything but

a woman. And you a brahmachari! Don't wait any longer—go
back to the ashram.' Having said this, she disappeared into the
dark balcony outside.

Harendra stood like an idiot for two or three minutes
and then slowly climbed down the stairs.

20

NEARLY A MONTH PASSED. THE INFLUENCE OF THE EPIDEMIC ABATED.
A few stray cases were heard of here and there, but not
fatal ones. Kamal was in her room, intent on some sewing,
when Harendra entered. He carried a bundle which he put
down on the floor near her and said, 'I'm sorry to push you
when I see how hard you're working. But these people are
so insistent that, whenever they meet me, they ask, "Is the
work done?" I tell them bluntly, "It'll take a long time. If you're
in a hurry, tell me and I'll return you the cloth." But it's funny
how someone who's once tried out your handiwork won't
go anywhere else. Just see. The Lalas have sent along this bolt
of handspun silk and this specimen kurta.'

Kamal looked up from her sewing and said, 'Why did
you accept it?'

'Do you think I did so easily? I told them it couldn't be
done before six months, and they agreed. See, they even thrust
the money into my hand.' He slapped down a few coins wrapped
up in a banknote.

Kamal said, 'If I keep getting so many orders, I'll have to
hire somebody to help me.' She unwrapped the bundle, took
a close look at the old sample kurta and remarked, 'It was
stitched by the master tailor of some big shop—I can't make
anything like this. I'll simply spoil the expensive cloth. You'd
better return it to the man.'

Harendra said in surprise, 'Is there a better tailor than you?'

'There are in Calcutta if not here. Tell him to send it
to Calcutta.'

213

'No, no, that can't be. Do what you can—it'll be good enough.'

'No, Haren Babu, I can't do it. If I could, I would have.'

She suddenly smiled and said, 'Ajit Babu is a rich, fashionable person. Why should he agree to wear any worthless old thing I might make him? There's no point in spoiling the cloth unnecessarily. Take it back.'

Harendra was totally astonished. He asked, 'How do you know it's Ajit Babu's?'

Kamal said, 'I can read fortunes. Such expensive cloth, advance payment and yet six months' grace—Hindustani Lalajis are not so stupid, Haren Babu. Tell him that I'm not worthy of stitching his clothes. I can sew cheap garments for the poor, but I can't do this.'

Harendra was in a quandary. At last he said, 'He wants it very much. I didn't let on for a long time for fear you might come to know, and think we were somehow trying to give you something. I'd told him to buy some cheap ordinary cloth, but he didn't agree. He said, "This is not a dress for daily use. This will be a garment made by Kamal herself. I want to wear it on special occasions, at festivals. I'll preserve it carefully." I think there's no one on earth who respects you more than he does.'

Kamal said, 'But didn't many people hear just the opposite from him sometime ago? Perhaps you'll remember that too if you try. Just think.'

It had happened only a few days ago: Harendra remembered perfectly. He was a little embarrassed and said, 'It's not untrue; but many people had such notions at one time. Perhaps Ashu Babu alone did not, but I even saw him looking perturbed one day. Take my own case. Today I don't have to prove my words; but where would I stand if you were to test my present respect and devotion for you on yesterday's touchstone?'

'Have you tracked down Rajen?' asked Kamal.

Harendra understood that all sentimental discussions were suspended for the day, as once before. He said, 'No, not yet. But I hope I will——once he turns up of his own accord.'

Kamal said, 'I wasn't asking about that . . . I'd only asked you to find out whether the police have arrested him.'

Harendra said, 'I've enquired. He's not in their shelter right now.'

The news did not put Kamal at peace, but she felt somewhat relieved. She asked, 'Can't you try to find out in the leather workers' quarter where he's gone, and when? Haren Babu, I know how fond you are of him. These questions may seem superfluous; but for a few days now I've been in such a state that I can't think of anything else.' She looked so perturbed that Harendra was deeply struck. But the next moment she lowered her face and returned to her sewing.

Harendra stood there silently. Question after question arose in his mind: his curiosity knew no bounds, the questions almost escaped his lips; but he controlled himself, because he could not now determine the outcome of these questions. After some minutes, Kamal herself spoke. Having finished her sewing, she laid it down with a sigh of relief and said, 'That's enough for today.' Then she looked up and exclaimed in surprise, 'What's this? Why are you standing? Couldn't you pull up a chair and sit down?'

'You didn't tell me to sit down.'

'What a thing to say! Won't you sit down if I don't ask you to?'

'No, one shouldn't sit down unless one's asked to.'

'But I didn't tell you to stand either—so why do you keep standing?'

'By that logic I shouldn't be standing either. I admit my wrong.'

Kamal laughed. She said, 'Then I also admit mine. It was wrong on my part to have been unmindful for so long. Please sit now.'

As Harendra drew up a chair and sat down, Kamal suddenly turned grave. She pondered something and then said, 'Look, Haren Babu, both you and I know that there's nothing in all this, yet it hurts. That I forgot to tell you to sit down, that I didn't give you the treatment due to a guest—these lapses have not escaped your notice, although we're such good friends. No, no, I'm not saying you're angry, but somewhere inside you you're a little hurt. People can't fully do away with these conventions—there's always some trace left somewhere. Isn't that so?'

Harendra did not understand her meaning and looked at her in some bewilderment. Kamal went on: 'So much confusion arises in life from such things, yet this is what people most often forget. Isn't that so?'

Harendra asked, 'Are you saying all this to me or to yourself? If it's meant for me, speak a little more dearly. I can't understand these riddles.'

Kamal said smiling, 'These really are riddles. The road seems straight and clear: one doesn't see any peril frowning ahead. It's only when you stumble and bleed that you realize you should have been more careful: isn't that so?'

Harendra said, 'That may be true of roads; at least, one must be careful on the streets of Agra. The ashram boys often meet with such accidents. But the riddle remains a riddle. I still don't understand what it means.'

Kamal said, 'There's nothing to be done about it then, Haren Babu. Everything can't be fully understood as soon as told. Just see, nobody taught me such things, but I've had no difficulty in understanding them.'

Harendra said, 'That only means you're fortunate and I'm not. Either speak in a language simple people can understand, or else stop. The more I try to draw out your meaning, the more complicated it seems, like one of those Chinese fireworks. I can't make head or tail of your argument: it starts from an unknown or unknowable premise and ends God knows where. Are you saying all this with Rajen in mind? I know him too. If you speak plainly, perhaps I'd understand something of your meaning. Otherwise, if I go on listening in this way to a sleeptalker, I'll lose faith in my own wits.'

'In your wits, or in mine?' asked Kamal with a smile.

'In both.'

Kamal said, 'I don't know why, but since the morning I've been thinking not only about Rajen but about everyone—Ashu Babu, Manorama, Akshay, Abinash, Nilima, Shibnath—even my father . . .'

Harendra objected, You mustn't go on like this: you'll turn sombre again. Your parents have passed away: I can't bear to have them dragged back to earth. Rather, speak about those who're alive. You wanted to talk about Rajen—why don't you do so? I'll listen. He's my friend, I know him and love him. Trust me: I might run an ashram and do all kinds of other things, but I won't deceive you. Like everybody else, I too like listening to love stories.'

Kamal's gravity at once turned to mirth. She asked, 'Do you only like hearing about others' love? You have no temptations of your own?'

'No,' replied Harendra. 'I'm the gang leader of the brahmacharis. If Akshay's party came to know any such thing about me, they'd eat me alive.'

Kamal smiled again and said, 'No, they wouldn't. I'd tell you how to escape.'

Harendra shook his head. 'You won't be able to do that. Even if I close down the ashram and flee, I shan't escape them. Now that Akshay has come to know me, he'll keep me on the path of virtue wherever I go. Why don't you speak about yourself instead? Start from the point where you said you can't ever forget Rajen. I want to hear how you've come to love that young rascal so much.'

Kamal said, 'I ask myself that very question time and again.'

'Don't you have any clue?'

'No.'

'I don't think you ever will, and I don't believe you're truly fond of him.'

'Why can't you believe it?'

'Never mind. I think I've already told you once. In any case, there are better *candidates* for your love. Do consider their *cases* before you reach a conclusion. That's my only request.'

'But *cases* can't be judged on conjecture, Haren Babu. You have to put up evidence. Who'll do that?'

'They'll do it themselves. They're ready with the evidence: they'll appear as soon as you call them.'

Kamal did not reply; she only looked up and smiled a little. Then she neatly folded the pieces of sewing, finished and unfinished, put them in a cane basket, and stood up. She said, 'It must be time for your tea, Haren Babu. I'll go and make some tea while you sit here.'

Harendra said, 'I've been sitting all this while. But I have no fixed time for tea. I drink it when I get some, and don't if there's none going. You needn't trouble yourself about it. May I ask you a question?'

'Of course.'

'You haven't visited anybody for a long time. Have you stopped doing so on purpose?'

Kamal was surprised and said, 'No. I never thought of it that way.'

'Then why not pay a visit to Ashu Babu today? He'll really be glad. You went there only once during his illness. Now he's well. The doctor has ordered him not to go out, otherwise he'd have come here himself one day.'

Kamal said, 'That wouldn't be unexpected of him. I ought to have gone, but couldn't because I was tied down with work. It was remiss of me.'

'Then why not go today?'

'Let's—but in the evening. Just sit down while I make some tea.' So saying, she left the room.

As they came out on the road in the half-dusk, Harendra said, 'It would have been better to have gone while it was light.'

'It wouldn't have been,' said Kamal. 'Somebody who knows us might have seen us.'

'So what? I don't care about such things any longer.'

'But I care about them now.'

Harendra thought she was being sarcastic. He said, 'But what will those acquaintances think if they hear that nowadays you hesitate to come out with me alone?'

'Perhaps they'll think I'm joking.'

'But can someone who knows you think otherwise? Tell me.' This time Kamal kept quiet. Getting no response, Harendra said, 'I don't know what's wrong with you today. Everything seems mysterious.'

Kamal said, 'It's better not to understand what's not meant

to be understood. I can't forget Rajen—I remember him most whenever you come. He couldn't find a place in the ashram. He could easily have stayed under a tree, but I didn't let him do so. I fondly brought him home. He came to this room, but that didn't confine his mind. It remained free in every way, like light and air. I seemed to find a new aspect of the male in him. I haven't yet considered whether it's good or bad—it might take me a long time to judge.'

Harendra said, 'That's a great consolation.'

'Consolation? Why?'

'I don't know.'

Neither spoke after this. They both seemed somewhat abstracted. Harendra might have taken a roundabout route on purpose. By the time they reached Ashu Babu's house, the evening was well advanced. There was no need to announce their arrival, but since Harendra had not come for five or six days, he asked the servant who let them in whether his master was well. The servant touched their feet and said, 'Yes, he's quite well.'

'Is he in his room?'

'No, they're all chatting together in the front room upstairs.'

'Who are "they"?' asked Kamal as they went upstairs.

'Boudi—perhaps others as well,' said Harendra. 'I don't know.'

As they pushed aside the curtain, both of them were a little surprised. The air inside the room was heavy with the mingled smell of cigar and perfume. Nilima was not there. Ashu Babu was puffing a cigar, his legs sprawled along the arms of his chair. Near him, an unknown woman was sitting very straight on a sofa.

Her appearance was as pungent as the atmosphere of the

room. She was a Bengali woman, but seemed to have no taste for speaking Bengali. Perhaps she was not used to it either. From the instant they stepped into the room, Kamal and Harendra heard her speaking continuously in English.

Ashu Babu turned and looked at them. His face lit up with joy as his eyes fell on Kamal. He attempted to sit up, but could not do so quickly. 'Come, Kamal, come,' he said, throwing away his cigar; then, pointing to the unknown lady, 'This is a relative of mine. She arrived the day before yesterday. I hope I can persuade her to stay here for some time.' He stopped for a while and said, 'Bela, this is Kamal. She's like a daughter to me.'

The two women made namaskars to each other.

'And what about me?' asked Harendra.

'Ah yes, of course. This is Harendra—a very close friend of Professor Akshay. You'll get to know each other better, Harendra—don't worry.' He beckoned to Kamal and said, 'Come near me, Kamal. Let me hold your hand and sit quietly for some time. I've been longing to do this for some days.'

Kamal went across smilingly and sat beside him. Stretching out her hands, she drew his heavy arm on to her lap. Ashu Babu affectionately asked, 'Did you have dinner before coming?'

Kamal shook her head and said, 'No.'

Ashu Babu sighed gently and said, 'But what's the point of asking? I won't be able to make you eat anything in this house.' Kamal remained silent.

21

ASHU BABU LOOKED AT BELA, SMILED A LITTLE AND SAID, 'Does my description fit the original? Do you admit that you shouldn't have ridiculed it as an old man's *extravagance*?'

The lady remained silent. Ashu Babu caressed Kamal's hand a little and said, 'People are surprised at the exterior of this girl, but it's just as amazing to see her inward appearance too. Isn't that so, Harendra?'

Harendra too remained silent. Kamal replied smiling, 'It's doubtful whether that's true. But there's no doubt that if anyone has mocked you for being *extravagant*, she's perfectly correct. You have no sense of proportion.'

'Nonsense!' exclaimed Ashu Babu, and continued in a tone of deep affection: 'I know I can't possibly make you eat in this house, but tell me what you ate at home today.'

'What I do every day.'

'Still, tell me. Bela thinks I'm exaggerating.'

Kamal said, 'That means you've been talking a lot about me in my absence.'

'I won't deny that we have.'

The servant entered with a small card on a silver tray. The writing caught everyone's attention and surprised them all. Ajit had once been like a son of the house; but though he was still in Agra, he did not come there any more. Perhaps this was to be expected. But the embarrassment and hesitation implicit in the avoidance had created such a distance between the two parties that not only Ashu Babu but everyone present was startled at his unexpected appearance.

A shadow of deep anxiety fell on Ashu Babu's face. He said, 'Bring him here.'

Ajit presently entered the room. He had not expected to find so many people, known and unknown.

'Sit down, Ajit,' said Ashu Babu. 'Are you well?'

Ajit nodded and said, 'Yes. How are you? Do you feel better now?'

'I'm hoping the illness has left me,' answered Ashu Babu.

The enquiries about each other's well-being ended here. There might have been some more exchanges had Kamal not been present; but Ajit did not dare look in her direction for fear of meeting her eye. After everyone had sat silent for two or three minutes, Harendra began. He said, 'Are you coming straight from home?'

Ajit was relieved to have to say something. He said, 'No, not quite. I had to make a little detour in search of you.'

'In search of me? What did you want?'

'It's not I but someone else. He has called for Rajen maybe four times since midday. I asked him to wait but he wouldn't. Perhaps it's not in his nature to wait patiently.'

Harendra said in alarm, 'Who's this man? What does he look like? Why didn't you tell him that Rajen isn't here?'

Ajit said, 'I did. I don't think he believed me.'

Harendra rose in agitation and left, entrusting Ashu Babu with the charge of reaching Kamal home. After he left, Ashu Babu said, 'Kamal, I haven't seen this boy Rajen more than two or three times. You don't see him unless you're in danger. But I think I can say I love him dearly. He seems to carry something precious with him. Yet Harendra tells me he's very *wild*—the police have their eye on him, and there's every risk that he might suddenly get into trouble and I'll never come to know of it. Just see how he's suddenly vanished, and nobody can trace him.'

'If you suddenly hear he's in danger, what will you do?' asked Kamal.

Ashu Babu said, 'I can only tell you when the time comes, not now. During my illness, Nilima and I heard many accounts of him from Harendra. As I listened, I seemed to see before me the true image of self-sacrifice for others' sake. I pray to God he isn't in danger.'

No one said anything, but in their hearts all must have joined in the prayer.

'I don't see Nilima today,' remarked Kamal. 'I suppose she's busy with her work.'

Ashu Babu said, 'Indeed, she's an active person and keeps herself busy day and night; but today I heard she's taken to bed with a headache. She must be feeling quite ill, for it's not in her nature to do so. Unless you saw it with your own eyes you wouldn't believe that a person could nurse the sick so well and so untiringly.'

He paused for a moment and then continued, 'I first met Abinash in Agra. We visit each other occasionally—we don't really know each other very well. But now I feel how absurd the distinction is between one's own folk and strangers. There's no one who's your own in this world, Kamal, and no one who's a stranger. No one knows whom the stream will draw near you and whom it will bear away.'

Kamal and Ajit understood, though Bela did not, whom these words alluded to and the grief that prompted them. Ashu Babu went on, as though talking to himself: 'Since I recovered from my illness, many things in this world have appeared differently to me. Why all these drags and bonds, I ask, why these wranglings over good and evil? Man willingly blinds himself by piling up errors and deceptions. He still has to learn many unknown truths through many ages— only then, perhaps, can he truly grow human. The great aim of all his refinement and civilization seems to be to give pain rather than pleasure.'

Kamal looked on in amazement. She did not fully grasp what he was saying. It was like seeing an approaching figure through a mist; yet the gait seemed familiar.

Ashu Babu stopped of his own accord. Perhaps Kamal's amazed look had made him self-conscious. He said, 'I have more things to tell you. Come another day.'

'I will. I must go now.'

'Goodbye. The car's waiting below. I've kept Basdeo on call so that he can drive you home. Ajit, why don't you go with her? He'll drop you at the ashram on the way back.'

They both made namaskars and left the room. Bela came with them to the car and said, 'There was no time today to get to know you. But the next time we meet, I won't let you get away so easily!'

Kamal nodded, smiled and said, 'That'll be my good fortune. But I'm afraid you might change your opinion of me once we're better acquainted.'

The two sat side by side in the car. After they had turned a bend, Kamal said, 'It was as dark that night as it is now. Do you remember?'

'Yes, I do.'

'The madness of that day?'

'I remember that too.'

'Do you remember that I'd consented?'

Ajit smiled and said, 'No, but I remember that you made fun of me.'

Kamal said in surprise, 'I made fun of you? No, never.'

'Of course you did.'

'Then you were mistaken,' said Kamal. 'Anyway, I'm not doing so today. Come on, let's go away today.'

'Nonsense! You're very naughty.'

Kamal smiled and said, 'Why should I be naughty? No one's so quiet and good-natured as I am. Just think: you suddenly commanded. "Kamal, let's go away!" and I agreed instantly and said, "Yes, let's!"'

'But that was only a joke.'

'All right, let it be a joke,' said Kamal, 'but what wrong did I do? You used to call me by the familiar tumi, but you've suddenly grown formal and begun saying apni. Just think how miserably I spend my days, how I barely manage to feed myself by stitching your clothes. There is no limit to your wealth—but have you asked after me even once? Would you have let Manorama be in such straits? See how thin I've grown working day and night.' As she laid her left hand on Ajit's, his whole body suddenly seemed to tremble. He tried to say something faintly; but Kamal drew back her hand and called out, 'Driver, stop! Stop! We've come all the way to the lunatic asylum. Turn the car back! I hadn't realized where we were going in the dark.'

'Now you blame the dark,' said Ajit. 'The only consolation is that the poor darkness can't protest against even a thousand unjust charges. It doesn't have the right.' And he laughed a little.

Kamal also laughed and said, 'Yes, that's so. But justice isn't everything in life. It's only because injustice too has its place that the world goes on; otherwise it would have come to a halt long ago. Stop, driver!'

Ajit opened the door. Kamal got down and said, 'The

dark is guilty of other offences too, Ajit Babu. One's afraid of going through it alone.'

Taking the hint, Ajit silently stepped out and joined her at once.

Kamal said to the driver, 'Now go home. He'll be late in returning.'

'What's that you say? Where shall I find transport in these parts to take me home so late?'

'I'll arrange something.'

The car went away. 'I know you won't arrange anything,' said Ajit. 'I'll have to walk three or four miles in the dark. But I could easily have gone back in the car after dropping you here.'

'You couldn't, because I couldn't have left you to the uncertain mercies of that ashram without giving you something to eat. Come in.'

In the house the maid had lit the lamp and was waiting. She opened the door as soon as called. Going upstairs, Kamal laid out the pretty mat in the kitchen for Ajit to sit on. Everything was ready: she lit the stove and started cooking. Then sitting down near him, she asked, 'Do you remember that other day like this?'

'Of course I do.'

'Well, can you tell me the difference between that day and this?'

Ajit looked hesitantly round the room, trying to recollect where the things had been placed then and now. Kamal said with a smile, 'You won't find it in that way even if you look all night. You must look elsewhere.'

'Can you tell me where?'

'Towards me.'

Ajit suddenly shrank within himself in a kind of bashfulness. He gently said, 'I could never look properly at your face. Others can, but I don't know why I've never been able to.'

Kamal said, 'There lies the difference between you and others. They could do so because their looks lacked all respect for me.'

Ajit was silent. Kamal went on, 'I had determined to find you somehow or other. I hadn't hoped to meet you at Ashu Babu's place today. But when that happened, I knew I had to bring you here. The meal is only a pretext: I won't let you go after you finish it. I won't let you go anywhere tonight. I'll keep you shut up in this house.'

'What good will that do you?'

'I'll explain that later on,' said Kamal. 'But if you still go on addressing me as apni, I really shall be hurt. Once you used to call me tumi, though I hadn't asked you to do so; you chose to on your own. I have done no wrong since then that you should change. Now, if I'm offended and don't reply you'll be hurt.'

Ajit nodded and said, 'I suppose I will be.'

Kamal said, 'There's no "suppose" about it; you certainly will feel hurt. You came to Agra for Manorama's sake. When she went away as she did, everyone thought you wouldn't stay here a moment longer. Only I knew you wouldn't be able to go. Now tell me: do you believe that I too love you?'

'No, I don't.'

'Of course you do. That's why I have so many complaints against you.'

Ajit eagerly asked, 'So many complaints? Let me hear one.'

Kamal said, 'That's precisely why I didn't let you go home. First let me tell you about my own woes. Having no other means, I have to make my way by stitching clothes for poor people. This I can bear. But how can I agree to charge money for sewing your clothes simply because I'm poor?'

'But you don't accept charity.'

'No, I don't—not even from you. But is there no way in this world to get things done except through charity? Why didn't you come and insist, "Kamal, I won't allow you to do such work"? What could I have said in reply? If today by some mishap I were to lose my power to earn a living, should I have to go begging on the streets although you are here?'

The pain implicit in her words caused him anguish. He said, 'That could never be, Kamal—not while I'm alive. I'd never thought about you in this way. I still can't believe that you're the same Kamal we all know.'

Kamal said, 'Let them know whatever they wish. Are you only one of them? Nothing more?'

Ajit did not reply to this question, perhaps because it was very difficult. Both of them fell silent. Perhaps both felt the need to question their own selves rather than each other.

There was little to cook: it didn't take long. As he sat down to eat, Ajit gravely said, 'It's strange that however wealthy a person may be, he can't but enjoy the fruits of your earning. Yet you won't take anything from anyone, won't let anyone support you—not even if he dashes his brains out for you.'

Kamal smiled and said, 'Why do all of you accept what I give? Moreover, when did you try to dash out your brains?'

Ajit said, 'I've wanted to do so many times over. And I eat your food because I succumb to your insistence. If today I say, "Kamal, I'm taking charge of you from now; give up this beggarhood"—you will, very likely, break out so harshly that I'll be left speechless.'

Kamal asked, 'Did you ever say such a thing to me?'

'I think I did once.'

'And I didn't pay heed to it?'

'No.'

'Then you hadn't said it so as to make me heed you. Perhaps it remained in your mind and was never put into words.'

'Well, suppose I say it now?'

'Then suppose I too say "No"?'

Putting down the food he held in his hand, Ajit said, 'That's it. We have never understood you even for a single day. Just as I didn't grasp your words when I first saw you at the Taj, so are you a mystery to us even today. You've just asked me to take charge of you, and then at once you say "No".'

Kamal smiled and said, 'Let me hear you say "No" in this way. Say that you won't eat again as you've eaten today. I'll see how you keep your word.'

'How can I keep my word?' retorted Ajit. 'You won't let me go until I've eaten.'

But this time Kamal did not smile; she calmly said, 'It's not yet time for you to take charge of me. When the time comes I shan't be able to say "No". It's getting late. You'd better finish eating.'

'I shall. Can you tell me whether such a day will ever come?'

Kamal shook her head and said, 'I can't. You'll have to find the answer for yourself one day.'

'I don't have the power. I searched very hard once but couldn't find it. From now on I'll only live with hand outstretched in the hope that you'll give the answer.'

Ajit began to eat in silence. After a while, Kamal asked, 'What made you suddenly go to Harendra's ashram instead of coming here?'

'I had to stay somewhere,' said Ajit. 'As you know very well, I couldn't leave Agra.'

'You think I know that?'

'Yes, of course you do.'

'If that's so, why didn't you come straight to me?'

'Had I come, would you really have taken me in?'

'But you didn't really come. Never mind. But life in Harendra's ashram is very hard. It's part of their discipline. How could you put up with so much hardship?'

'I don't know how I did, but now I don't even think about such things. I'm now one of them. Perhaps this will be my life for all time to come. I haven't been idle all this time either. I've sent out people to set up ashrams at different places; I have hopes of three or four. I would like to go out once myself.'

'Who gave you this idea? Harendra, I suppose?'

Ajit said, 'If he has, he's done so innocently. Those who have seen the ruin of this country with their own eyes—the cruel suffering of the poor, the deep disgrace of our irreligion, the cowardice born of our weakness . . .'

Kamal interrupted him: 'I don't deny that Harendra has seen all this, but you've only heard of it. You've not yet had the chance to see it with your own eyes.'

'But surely all this is true?'

'I haven't said it isn't, but is setting up ashrams a remedy?'

'Why not? India doesn't simply mean a tract of land with the Himalayas on the north and the ocean on three sides. Its ancient civilization, its distinctive religion, the sanctity of its ethics, the majesty of its morals and its devotion—that is India. That's why it's called the land of the gods. Is there any course other than spiritual endeavour to save it from utter debasement—to make the life of pure-hearted boys, vowed to brahmacharism, meaningful and glorious?'

Kamal cut him short. 'You've finished your meal. Wash your hands and come to the other room—no more of all this.'

'Won't you eat?'

'Do I ever eat two meals a day that I should do so now? Please get up.'

'But I must go back to the ashram.'

'No, you can't. Come into the next room. I have many things to hear from you.'

'All right, let's go. But it's forbidden for us to stay away from the ashram at night. However late it may be, I have to go back.'

Kamal said, 'That rule is for the ashramites who have been initiated, not for you.'

'But what will people say?'

Kamal could never keep her patience at the mention of 'people'. She said, 'People can only slander you; they can't protect you. You needn't be afraid of the person who can——I'm much more truly yours than "they" are. The other day you'd asked me to go with you but I couldn't; today I can't but go. Come into the other room. There's nothing to be afraid of about me. I'm not the sort of woman to be an object of men's lust. Please get up.'

Leading him to the other room, Kamal made up the bed with a new set of bedclothes. For herself she casually, carelessly laid out another bed on the floor and said, 'I'm coming. I shan't be more than ten minutes, but don't fall asleep.'

'I won't.'

'If you do, I'll prod you out of sleep.'

'You won't need to, Kamal. All sleep has fled my eyes.'

'Well, we'll test that later on,' said Kamal as she left the room. The maid had left long ago. Kamal had to put away the utensils, carry the dirty dishes out into the balcony, bolt the door downstairs, carry out many such small household chores. Only then would she be free.

Sitting alone in the room, on the neat bed made by Kamal with the utmost care, Ajit sighed deeply—not for any grave reason, only from a contentment born of deep satisfaction. Perhaps he felt a tinge of excitement, but no heat of desire: only the honeyed touch of a mellow joy seemed to wrap him silently.

Ajit was a rich man's son, brought up in luxury. But since entering Harendra's brahmachari ashram, he had turned his eyes elsewhere in the relentless pursuit of the essential Indian spirit along the arduous path of poverty and self-mortification. Suddenly his eyes fell on a few small chrysanthemums embroidered in yellow around the pillowcase. In a corner of the sheet, a little creeper of unknown breed was embroidered in silk. That was all the decoration— a very modest matter. Many people have such things in their homes. Kamal had done it in her leisure hours. Ajit was charmed. He was turning it over in his hand when Kamal, having finished her work, came into the room. He looked up at her and exclaimed, 'It's very nice!'

Kamal was a little surprised. 'What's nice? That little creeper?'

'Yes, and those yellow flowers. You've done this yourself, haven't you?'

'An excellent question,' said Kamal with a smile. 'Do you think I hired a craftsman to do it? Do you need anything of this kind?'

'No, no, no, I don't. What should I do with it?'

Kamal smiled at his vehement, bashful refusal and said, 'Take it to the ashram and put it on your bed. If anyone asks, tell him that Kamal sat up at night to make it.'

'What nonsense!'

'Why should it be nonsense? No one makes things of this

kind for oneself; only for others. Do you think I embroidered these flowers for myself to sleep on? I knew someone would come one day—I had set this apart for him. When you go away in the morning, I'll give you all these.'

Now Ajit himself smiled and said, 'Kamal, am I so stupid?'

'Why?'

'Should I believe that you embroidered these with me in mind?'

'Why not?'

'Because it isn't true.'

'But will you believe me if I tell you the truth?'

'Of course I will. There's no limit to your jesting—I still blush when I remember what happened that day in the car. But that's different. I know that when you're not joking you never tell a lie.'

'Then if I say that I'm not really joking but telling the truth, will you believe me?'

'Of course I will.'

'In that case I'll tell you the truth today. It happened before Rajen arrived—that is to say, when he'd been driven out of the ashram but had not sought shelter with me. I was in a similar state. When all of you turned me away in contempt, when I had no one to ask for help in this alien place—it was during those days of utter misery that I worked that little embroidery. Perhaps I'd never have known whom I had in mind when I did it. I'd almost forgotten about it. But today, as I came to make the bed, I suddenly thought, "No, not anything else. I can't let you sleep on something that someone else has used earlier."'

'Why not?'

'I don't know. It was as though someone had nudged me

and spoken those words.' She was quiet for a moment, then went on: 'Suddenly I remembered that I had these things in my box. You were washing after your meal. Knowing that you'd soon be back, I opened the box and hurriedly laid them out. Only then did I realize that you were the person I had in mind when I embroidered these flowers, leaves and creepers, sitting up through the night.'

Ajit was silent. A sudden blush appeared on his face, to vanish in the wink of an eye.

Kamal herself remained quiet for some time and then asked, 'Tell me, what are you thinking of so silently?'

Ajit said, 'I'm silent because I'm unable to think.'

'Why?'

'Why? Your words have set a storm raging in my heart. Only turmoil—neither joy nor hope.'

Kamal looked at him silently. Ajit slowly went on: 'Kamal, let me tell you a story. Our household god Radhaballavji once appeared before my mother in visible form in the puja room in our house. He took food from her hand and ate it sitting before her—she saw it with her own eyes. None of us believed her; everyone took it to be a dream. But till her dying day she could not overcome her sorrow at our disbelief. Today your words remind me of that incident. I know you're not joking, but I think that, like my mother, you too are under some immense misconception. There are many phases in a man's life when he remains in the dark about himself. Then, suddenly perhaps, his eyes open. It's like that with me. I've travelled so long to so many places around the world; yet it's only after coming to Agra that I've been able to see myself. All I have is money, and that was left me by my father. I have nothing of my own that can make you love me without my knowing it.'

'Don't worry about the money,' said Kamal. 'Now that the ashramites have come to know of it, they'll take care of it for you.' She laughed and resumed: 'But if only I'd known earlier that you were so destitute in every way, would I ever have fallen in love with you? Moreover, when did I have the time to judge your goodness or badness? I only had a kind of inkling in my mind: I didn't know how to track it down. It was only ten minutes ago, as I stood in front of the bed, that someone suddenly whispered the message in my ears.'

Ajit asked, in utter amazement, 'Only ten minutes ago! Do you really mean it? If that's so, this is madness.'

'Of course it's madness,' answered Kamal. 'That's why I asked you to take me somewhere else. I didn't beg you to marry me and settle down to family life.'

Ajit was deeply abashed. He said, 'Why do you call it begging? It isn't begging, it's the rightful claim born of your love. But you didn't claim your right: what you asked for is as short-lived as a bubble, and just as unreal.'

Kamal said, 'Its lifespan may be short, but why should it be unreal? I'm not one of those who want to cling to a long life as the only reality.'

'But this joy has no permanence, Kamal.'

'It may not. But I don't agree with those who, because real flowers wither, adorn their vases with everlasting flowers made of pith. I told you once before that no joy is lasting: it has its allotted span of transient days. That's the highest treasure of human life. If you tie it down, you kill it. That's why marriage has permanence but no joy. It hangs itself with the thick rope of unbearable permanence.'

Ajit remembered that he had heard exactly the same sentiments from her earlier. It was not just something she said;

it was her innermost conviction. Shibnath had not married her; he had deceived her, but she never complained about it. Why hadn't she? Today, for the first time, Ajit understood clearly that she had consented to this deception. His mind was filled with revulsion at such monstrous contempt for this ancient and holy ceremony of the human race.

After a moment's silence, he said, 'It would be improper of me to boast to you, but I don't want to hide anything from you any more. People say the highest expression of manliness is to sacrifice women and wealth. I accept this as a concept, and I don't doubt that there's nothing nobler than fulfilling oneself through such sacrifice. I have wealth enough, and no great fascination for it; but my heart dries up when I think that nowhere in my life has there been someone to love, and never will be. I'm afraid I shan't be able to conquer this weakness till I die. If that's my fate, I'll leave the ashram and go away. But your summons is a still greater sham. I can't respond to it.'

'Why do you call it a sham?'

'Of course it's a sham. Manorama never really loved me. I can understand her conduct, but I've seen Shibani's love for Shibnath with my own eyes. At that time it appeared limitless; but now every trace of it has vanished.'

Kamal said, 'It may have vanished today, but was it only a dissimulation on my part that struck you then?'

'Only you can answer that,' said Ajit. 'But it now seems to me there can be no greater hypocrisy in a woman's life.'

Kamal's eyes grew stern. She said, 'Let women judge what is true or false in a woman's life. Men needn't assume that task—neither towards Manorama nor towards Kamal. This is how justice has been violated, women dishonoured and men's hearts defiled and constricted down the ages. And that's why this mock trial has never been resolved. Injustice doesn't only harm one party, Ajit Babu; it devastates both. Few men are so fortunate as to receive what Shibnath then enjoyed; but it's no longer so. One can demand to know why it isn't, asserting one's authority with a thick stick held in a thick male fist; but one can't win it back that way. It's true that things were then such, and just as true that they no longer are. If I don't want to cover it over with the rags of subterfuge, will your male judgement declare it the greatest falsehood of my woman's life? Is this the wise verdict that we look for from you?'

'But how else can we judge it?' asked Ajit. 'Why should people honour something that is so ephemeral, so brittle?'

Kamal said, 'I know they won't. The life of a flower that blooms in a corner of my courtyard is only half a day. That stone with which I grind my spices is much more durable. Where will you find a better yardstick to measure truth?'

'Kamal, this is no argument. These are only angry words.'

'Why should I be angry, Ajit Babu? Those who deal only in permanence set a price on things in this way. It's the same doubt that kept you from responding to my call: how could you trust someone who wouldn't sign herself into lifelong bondage? To someone who doesn't appreciate flowers that stone is the greater reality by far. There's no risk of it withering away: it'll last forever, not for half a day. It will always crush and grind as needed for the kitchen, it'll prepare the ingredients you need to swallow your rice with: you can depend on it. Life becomes tasteless if it isn't there.'

Ajit looked at her and said, 'Why such sarcasm, Kamal?'

Perhaps the question did not reach Kamal's ears. She went on talking as if to herself: 'People don't understand that the object called the heart isn't made of iron; one can't rely on it.

It's not that the heart doesn't feel sad about all this; but that is its nature, its reality. Yet this is neither stated nor admitted. What greater debasement can there be in life? That's why no one understood how I could forgive Shibnath so totally. They would have understood if I'd cried my heart out and then turned she-hermit in my youth, but this they could not accept: they grew embittered with distaste and indifference. Leaves wither and fall off the tree; new leaves heal the wound. That's considered false, but if a dry tendril clings fast to the tree in spite of being dead, that constitutes a truth.'

Ajit was listening intently. As soon as she ended, he said, 'We often forget one thing, that you don't actually belong to our kind. Your blood, your beliefs, all your education are foreign. You can never overcome their violent impact on you. It's on this point that you constantly clash with us. It's getting late, Kamal. Let's stop this useless wrangling—our ideal is not for you.'

'Which ideal? The ideal of your brahmacharya ashram?'

Ajit was vexed by this provocation. 'All right,' he said. 'That, if you like. These abstruse matters are not meant for foreigners. You won't understand them.'

'Not even if I become your disciple?'

'No.'

Now Kamal laughed as though she were a different person. 'Well, tell me,' she said, 'what should I do to get your name struck off the rolls in that den of sadhus? That ashram has really become an eyesore to me.'

Ajit said as he lay down, 'You readily called Rajen in and gave him shelter. I suppose you didn't feel any awkwardness in doing so?'

'What was there to feel?'

'Perhaps you don't think about such things.'

'What don't I think about? The opinions you people hold?'

'I suppose you've never been afraid for yourself either?'

'I can't say never; but why should I be afraid of a brahmachari?'

'I see,' said Ajit, and fell silent. Then suddenly he burst out: 'A worm lives in the darkness underground. It knows it'll die if it comes out into the light——there are many creatures ready with open mouths to devour it. Its only means of self-defence is to hide. But you know that humans are not worms, not even if they're women. It's laid down in the Shastras that one's ultimate strength lies in realizing one's own self. This knowledge is your real strength: isn't it, Kamal?'

Kamal did not say anything; she only kept looking at him.

Ajit said, 'You have such a natural indifference to what women hold as their sole possession in life that, however we may carp, it seems to protect you every moment of your life like a ring of fire. Our attacks turn to ashes before they can touch you. You were just telling me that you don't belong to the class of women who are objects of men's lust. This is becoming clear to me tonight as I sit face to face with you. I also understand where you find the courage to ignore both our criticism and our praise.'

Raising her face in feigned surprise, Kamal said, 'What's the matter, Ajit Babu? Your words seem enlightened.'

'Tell me frankly, Kamal,' said Ajit, 'are my opinions as worthless to you as others' are?'

'What good would it do to you to know the answer?'

'Kamal, I've never boasted to you of my strength. In fact I am inwardly as weak as I am lonely. I can't do anything by force.'

'I know that far better than you,' she said, smiling.

'Do you know what I feel?' said Ajit. 'I feel it would be as easy for me to win you as to lose you.'

'I know that too,' said Kamal.

Ajit nodded to himself and said, 'That's it. It's not only a question of winning you today; what would happen if I were to lose you one day in the same way?'

'Nothing would happen,' Kamal said quietly. 'Losing me would seem equally easy then. As long as I were with you, I'd teach you that wisdom.'

Ajit was profoundly shocked. He said, 'When I was in England, I saw how easily they separated forever, and on what trivial grounds. I would wonder if anything left an impact on them. And if this is the nature of their love, how can they pride themselves on being civilized?'

Kamal said, 'Ajit Babu, it may not be as easy as it seems from outside by reading the newspapers. But how I wish that one day this propensity of men and women becomes as free and natural as light and air.'

Ajit stared at her silently. He said nothing; but as he turned over to sleep, tears came to his eyes, somehow from somewhere.

Perhaps Kamal saw this. She came up to the corner of the bed and began stroking his hair. But she did not utter a single word of consolation.

Through an open window, the eastern sky could be seen growing lighter.

'Ajit Babu, I think there's no time left for sleep.'

'Yes, I must get up now.' And he wiped his tears and sat up.

22

ASHU BABU HAD PERHAPS NEVER CLAIMED BEFORE HIS CREATOR to be anything more than an ordinary man among ordinary men. Just as he had accepted his vast ancestral property with unruffled pleasure, he had accepted his vast bulk and its accompanying ailments as a natural affliction. He did not have to meditate to realize, with his heart no less than his head, that God did not create the world's joys and sorrows with him in view, that they operated by their own laws: he had grasped this by natural instinct. Just as he did not heap curses on providence after the calamity of his wife's death, he did not cry and beat his head when Manorama, the utmost treasure of his love, left him, turning his hopes to ashes. Through his resentment and despair, a familiar voice in his heart would repeatedly tell him that that is how things are. Such sorrows have befallen many people many times; that was how the world went. There was nothing novel about it, it was as ancient as existence itself. It was neither manly nor useful to keep this grief alive and send its waves surging through the world. Hence all sorrows quietened within him of their own accord, and set up such a ring of serenity that everyone entering it felt his burden made light.

Ashu Babu's life had always been like this. Even after coming to Agra, there had been no change despite many adversities; but the single exception now began to attract general notice. Suddenly from time to time his impatience could not be concealed; his speech seemed to infringe on gratuitous harshness; the uncalled-for sharpness of his remarks sounded strange even to the servants. Yet it was hard to tell why this should be so. Such aberrations had seemed inconceivable even at the height of his illness; and now he was on the mend. Whatever the reasons, a little observation would show that a fire was burning in the depths of his heart: the sparks would sometimes break out.

Although he had not yet said anything explicitly, there were hints that his days in Agra were numbered. Perhaps he was waiting to get a little better: then, just as he had arrived without warning, he would depart in the same way.

Many of the leading Bengalis of the town came these days in the evening to enquire after him. The magistrate and his wife, the district sub-judge (a Rai Bahadur), the college teachers—all those who had not been able to go elsewhere—together with Harendra, Ajit and all the Bengalis who had devoured much mutton and pilau here in happier times. Only Akshay never came, because he was away. When the epidemic broke out, he had left for his village home with his wife. Perhaps he was waiting for things to get a little cooler. Kamal never came either after that one visit.

Ashu Babu loved gatherings, but now he couldn't attend them so wholeheartedly. Even when present, he mostly remained silent. People gladly forgave him, as they knew of his failing health. All the duties that Manorama used to perform earlier were now carried out by Bela, she being a relative. There were no lapses of hospitality. Outsiders would savour the entertainment and leave with hearts replete, silently thanking their unassuming host and wondering how this ailing man could regularly arrange such perfect gatherings.

How it was made possible remained a secret. Nilima did not come out before everybody: she had neither the habit nor the inclination. But her hidden vigilance reached every corner of the house. It was as penetrating as it was silent. Perhaps no one except Ashu Babu felt its flow, as quiet as the flow of blood in one's veins.

The late autumn was nearly half over; but somehow it had not yet turned very cold. One morning, however, there was a light drizzle which turned into a shower towards the afternoon. There was no prospect of visitors. The windows were shut ahead of time. Ashu Babu sat in his armchair, reading a book with his legs stretched out and his body covered with a shawl, when Bela said with some irritation, 'Everything in this wretched place is topsy-turvy. I came here sometime ago, in June or July. I'd never imagined there could be such a shortage of water anywhere. I wonder what made anybody build the Taj Mahal in such a barren place.'

Nilima sat sewing nearby. She said without raising her eyes, 'Not everybody can understand that.'

'Why?' asked Bela unsuspectingly.

Nilima replied, 'How can people sunk in worldly pleasures understand that all great things in this world are born out of human suffering?' The retort was so inconceivably cruel that not only Bela but Ashu Babu too was startled. Looking up from his book, he saw Nilima carry on with her sewing as if no such words had passed her lips.

Bela was not a quarrelsome woman; moreover, she was fairly well educated. She must have been over thirty-five, and had seen and experienced much. But through careful grooming, her youthful charm had not waned. At a casual glance, she still seemed to be as in her youth. She was fair, her face had a special grace; but on closer observation it seemed coarse from a certain lack of tenderness. Her eyes sparkled with a lively expression, constantly wandering as though they lacked the stability to rest on anything, as though they had no depth or root. She was fit for delights and pleasures; if suddenly cast amidst sorrow, she would embarrass the master of the house.

As Bela emerged from her confusion, her face flushed with anger for a moment. But it offended her courtesy and upbringing to quarrel angrily; she controlled herself and said, 'It's no use making insinuations against me: not only because it's a trespass on my privacy, but because, however high-minded it may be to go around grieving and wailing, I can neither do it nor draw any good from it. I only want to retain my self-respect; I have no greater wish.'

Nilima went on working. She made no reply.

Ashu Babu was inwardly displeased; but lest the argument grow fiercer, he hastily said, 'No, no, Bela, surely there was no insinuation against you. She must have meant it in a general way. I know Nilima's nature. She could never behave in that way—never.'

Bela curtly said, 'So much the better. We have been together so long, I wouldn't have thought it possible.' Nilima said neither yes nor no; she went on sewing as if there was no one in the room.

Bela had a little history of her own which it is necessary to mention here. Her father was a lawyer, but he could acquire neither fame nor wealth in his profession. No one knew about his religious beliefs; he followed neither Hindu, Brahmo nor Christian practices. He used to love his daughter dearly and educated her beyond his means. We have already noted that the attempt had not entirely failed. It was he who had lovingly named her Bela. Even if he did not follow any particular sect, he had his own circle. Within it, Bela's name soon spread as a charming and educated young woman; hence it did not take long to acquire a wealthy groom for her. He had recently qualified from England as a barrister. After a spell of time to get acquainted and understand each other's inclinations, they had a civil marriage according to statute. Thus ended the first phase of their intense devotion to the law.

The second phase consisted of indulgence and entertainment: travelling together, holidaying separately and so on. Rumours circulated about both. They are irrelevant; but the relevant part was soon exposed. The groom was caught red-handed, and the bride's party threatened to file a divorce suit. Friends tried for a reconciliation, but the educated Bela was a champion of gender equality. She did not pay heed to this humiliating proposal. The poor husband, however flawed his character, was not altogether a bad man. He loved his wife as much as it lay in him. He humbly confessed his offence and prayed with joined hands to be relieved of the trials of the law, but the wife would not forgive him. After much tribulation, a solution was finally reached. By agreeing to pay a large sum in cash as well as a monthly alimony, he was spared the ignominy of a lawsuit.

Having won the conjugal battle, Bela proudly proceeded to various hill stations such as Simla, Mussoorie and Naini Tal to repair her shattered health. All this had happened six or seven years earlier. Her father died soon after. He had in no way supported her conduct; rather, he was deeply distressed by it. He had some remote relationship with Ashu Babu's deceased wife; hence Bela counted as Ashu Babu's relative. He had been invited to their marriage, and made the acquaintance of her husband. Drawing on these links, Bela had come to Agra as Ashu Babu's kinswoman: not as a complete stranger, nor a helpless seeker for shelter. Her situation was very different from Nilima's.

But the reality took a different form. No one in the house had a jot of doubt about the respective positions of the two women. The cause was unknown, but the line of authority was undisputed.

It was Bela who first spoke after a long silence. She said, 'I admit it wasn't made explicit, but I've no doubt that Nilima said that to denigrate me.'

Perhaps there was no doubt in Ashu Babu's mind either; but he asked in a surprised tone, 'Denigrate you? For what, Bela?'

'You know everything,' said Bela. 'There was no lack of people to criticize me earlier and there won't be now. But I ignored them all in order to uphold my dignity and the dignity of all womankind; I won't care about them today either. When I refused to live with my husband at the cost of my dignity, it was women who slandered me the most. And even now, it's their clutches that I find hardest to evade. But I wasn't afraid of them since I had done no wrong, and I'm not afraid today for the same reason. I'm entirely pure in my own conscience.'

Nilima did not look up from her sewing, but said slowly, 'Kamal once said that conscience isn't such a great thing in life. All questions of right and wrong can't be decided by an appeal to conscience.'

Ashu Babu was surprised and said, 'Did she say so?'

'Yes,' said Nilima. 'She said conscience was a fool's weapon. It cuts both ways—you can't rely on it.'

'Let others say so, but you mustn't utter such things, Nilima,' said Ashu Babu.

Bela said, 'I've never heard anything so audacious.'

Ashu Babu was silent for a moment and then said slowly,

'Audacious indeed. Kamal's boldness knows no limits. She lives by her own laws. Her words can't always be either understood or accepted.'

'I also live by my own laws,' said Bela. 'That's why I couldn't even accept my father's bidding. I abandoned my husband but could not humble myself.'

Ashu Babu said, 'That was a very sad business; but even if your father could not assent to it, I did.'

Bela said, '*Thanks*. I haven't forgotten it, Ashu Babu.'

Ashu Babu said, 'That's because I fully believe in equal rights and equal duties for men and women. A great flaw in our Hindu society is that the husband need fear no judgement even if he commits hundreds of offences; but there are a thousand ways for him to punish his wife for a trifling fault. I have never been able to accept this as a just dispensation. That's why when Bela's father wrote to me asking for my opinion, I replied that though it was neither pleasing nor decorous, if she wanted to abandon her profligate husband, I could not forbid her by saying it would be wrong.'

Nilima raised her eyes in undissembled surprise and asked, 'Did you really reply like that?'

'Of course I did.'

Nilima fell silent. Faced with that silence, Ashu Babu began to feel a kind of unease. He said, 'There's nothing to be surprised about, Nilima. Rather, it would have been wrong on my part not to have written so.'

Pausing a little, he said, 'You're a great admirer of Kamal; tell me, what would she have done in this case? What reply would she have given? That's why the other day, when I introduced her to Bela, I emphatically said, "Kamal, I've seen only one woman who thinks like you, who's proved herself as brave as you are, and that's Bela."'

Nilima's eyes suddenly filled with anguish. She said, 'That poor girl has been put outside the pale of orthodox society; why drag her in?'

Ashu Babu grew concerned. 'No, no, Nilima, I'm not dragging her in. I'm only citing her as an example.'

'That amounts to dragging her in,' retorted Nilima. 'You said just now that everything she says can't be understood or accepted. In that case how can she serve as an example?'

Ashu Babu did not understand where he had gone wrong. He replied in a hurt tone, 'I think something's the matter with you today, for whatever reason. Let's not carry on the discussion right now.'

Nilima ignored his words. Instead she said, 'You had consented to their separation at that time, and today you have unhesitatingly cited Kamal's example. Had Kamal been in Bela's place, she alone knows what she would have done. But if Bela were to follow Kamal's example, she should be living by stitching clothes for poor workmen. Perhaps she wouldn't even get their custom every day. Whatever Kamal might have done, she wouldn't have consented to eat the food and wear the clothes provided by the very husband she had spurned and attacked. She would have killed herself rather than demean herself so.'

Ashu Babu was so overwhelmed that he could not reply. Bela sat as though thunderstruck. Nilima used to spend her days in fun and laughter, as if it were her duty to humour everybody. Neither of them had reckoned that she could turn ruthless so swiftly.

Nilima fell quiet for some time and then resumed: 'It's true I don't sit at your gatherings, but the things that are discussed there about some people reach my ears; otherwise perhaps I wouldn't have said anything. Kamal has never spoken ill of Shibnath; she has never spoken of her distress to anyone. Do you know why?'

Ashu Babu could only ask in bewilderment, 'Why?'

'It's useless explaining why,' answered Nilima. 'You people won't understand.' She paused and continued, 'Ashu Babu, it's a very crude maxim that husband and wife have equal rights. Don't think that I'm objecting to the rights demanded by women in spite of being one. I'm not protesting; I know them to be true, but a group of witless truth-delighting men and women have made this truth so confused by their words and actions that I'm tempted to call it false. I beg you with folded hands that henceforth you avoid teaming up with others in talking about Kamal.'

Ashu Babu was about to reply; but before he could do so, Nilima picked up her sewing things and left the room.

Amazed and distressed, he said, 'I don't know what she has heard and when, but she's blaming me quite without cause.'

It had stopped raining, but the gloomy sky brought an untimely darkness into the room. As the servant carried in the lamp, Ashu Babu again took up his book. He could not concentrate on the printed words, but it seemed even more impossible to face Bela and talk to her.

Providence was merciful. Ajit and Harendra, the two self-mortifying penitents, stormed into the room, having travelled all the way jostling under a single umbrella. As a result, both were drenched on one side each.

'Where's our Boudi?' they demanded.

Ashu Babu was ecstatic: he had not expected anyone to come on a day like this. He got up elatedly to greet them. 'Come, Ajit. Come and sit down, Harendra.'

'Yes, but where is she?'

'What's this! You're both soaked.'

'Yes indeed, but where's she gone?'

'I'll send for her.' As Ashu Babu prepared to call out, Nilima herself entered through the curtains of the inner quarters. She was carrying dry clothes. 'Wonderful,' said Ajit. 'Can you tell the future?'

'I didn't need to,' replied Nilima. 'I saw you from the window. The way you were walking down the road under one broken umbrella, each sacrificing himself for the other—not only I but everyone in the land must have seen you.'

'Two of them under one umbrella!' exclaimed Ashu Babu. That's why you're both drenched.' He burst out laughing.

Nilima said, 'Perhaps they believe in egalitarianism. They wouldn't do either party an injustice, so they made a hair-splitting division of the umbrella. Come on, Thakurpo, change your clothes.' She handed the garments to Harendra. Ashu Babu kept silent.

Harendra said, 'There are two dhotis but only one kurta.'

'It's a very big one, Thakurpo; it'll do for both.' She gravely sat down on a nearby chair.

Harendra said, 'It's Ashu Babu's kurta. No doubt it could accommodate not only two but four people; but you'd have to hang it up like a mosquito net, not wear it.'

Bela had sat so far with a pale, downcast face. Now she could not control her laughter, so she got up and went out. Nilima silently looked out of the window.

Ashu Babu said with affected seriousness, 'My dear Harendra, I've been reduced to half by my illness. Don't mock me any more. Can't you see how it upsets the women? One has gone out, unable to stand it, and the other has turned her face away in a sulk.'

'I wasn't mocking you, Ashu Babu,' said Harendra. 'I was praising the glory of immensity. Jokes and mockery might threaten mere mortals like us; they can't touch beings like you. So let your body be immortal like the eternal Himalayas; let the ladies be silent; and let not the rain be an excuse for depriving the meaner sort of men from their usual quota of sweets.'

Nilima looked up and smiled. She said, 'It's been customary since old times to praise one's elders, Thakurpo. It's a settled tradition and you're adept at it. But today you'll have to vary the routine. Today, if the younger ones are not flattered, the share of sweets for the meaner sort will fall to zero.'

Bela came back from the veranda and sat down.

'Why, Boudi?' asked Harendra.

Nilima's eyes glistened with deep affection. She said, 'I haven't heard any sweet words for a long time. I'm greedy for some more.'

'Then shall I start?'

'Well, let it be for the time being. Go and change in the next room. I'll send you another kurta.'

'But after we've changed?'

Nilima said with a smile, 'After that—let me go and see what I can arrange for the meaner sort.'

Harendra said, 'You needn't bother to arrange anything. Just open your eyes and look round. Your glance, like the goddess Annapurna's,[1] will bring overflowing bounty wherever it falls. Come, Ajit, there's nothing to worry about.' He dragged Ajit by the arm into the next room.

23

'THERE'S NO SIGN OF THE RAIN STOPPING,' SAID AJIT.

'No,' said Harendra. 'So we'll have to walk once again in the dark all the way to the ashram, sharing the same broken umbrella to prove our egalitarian theories. Of course we don't have to think about the next part of the operation—that's been concluded here. We'll only have to change our wet clothes again and go to bed.'

Ashu Babu anxiously said, 'Then why didn't you have a full meal here?'

'No, no, let it be,' said Harendra. 'What does it matter? Don't worry about it, Ashu Babu.'

Nilima broke out in giggles and then, in a complaining tone, said, 'Thakurpo, why are you unnecessarily worrying a sick man?' To Ashu Babu she said, 'He is a sannyasi grown ripe in his ascetic ways. No one can fault him for eating too little. It's Ajit Babu that I'm worried about. From the way he ate today, it's obvious that he isn't maturing fast enough even in such virtuous company.'

Harendra said, 'Perhaps there's still some evil in his heart. He'll be found out one day.'

Nilima looked at him for a moment and said, 'May your words prove blessed, Thakurpo: let it be so. Let him harbour a little vice, let him be found out. I'll offer sacrifices to Kali of Kalighat that day.'

'Then get ready to do so.'

Ajit said in deep vexation, 'What nonsense is this, Haren Babu? You're disgusting.'

Harendra did not say anything more. Looking at Ajit's face, Nilima grew acutely curious, but she too kept silent.

After the talk about Ajit had died down, Harendra said to Nilima, 'Kamal is very annoyed with our ashram. Perhaps you remember, Boudi.'

Nilima nodded and said, 'Yes, I do. Does she feel the same way even now?'

'Not exactly the same,' said Harendra. 'Her hatred has grown more intense. That's the only difference.' He went on, 'It's not only us; she's equally enamoured of all religious institutions. Whether you talk of brahmacharihood or asceticism or God Himself—as soon as she hears it, she bursts into flame with such devotion and love! If she's in good humour, she can even condescend to be amused to see these foolish grown-up boys at play. It's quite wonderful!'

Bela was listening quietly. She said, 'Is God too a matter of sport to her? And you were comparing me with her, Ashu Babu!' She looked at their faces one by one, but didn't find encouragement anywhere. Her harsh voice did not seem to reach anybody's ears.

Harendra went on speaking: 'Yet there's such unwavering restraint, such a silent moderation and serene resignation in her that it leaves you amazed. Do you remember the business of Shibnath, Ashu Babu? He was nothing to us, yet we couldn't tolerate his wrongdoing; our hearts burned to punish him. But Kamal said "No." I still remember how she looked that day. There was no hatred, no anguish in that "No", no expectation of applause for her generosity, no arrogance of forgiveness: her benevolence seemed full of unmixed compassion. However grave Shibnath's offence might have been, she was startled at my proposal and said, "Shame on you! No, no, it can't be." In other words, she could not think of demeaning herself by being cruel to the man she had once loved: she silently swept away all his faults from public view. And she seemed to do it without effort or agitation, or any weeping and lamenting. It was like a stream flowing effortlessly down a mountain.'

Ashu Babu only remarked, 'That's true.'

Harendra continued: 'I feel very angry when she wants to laugh away not only my own ideal but our collective religion, heritage, customs, moral obligations—everything. I know that gross alien blood is flowing in her veins and, likewise, an aggressive alien religion in her heart; yet I can't answer her boldly to her face. Some confident power seems to shine through her speech, as though she has found out the true meaning of life. She seems to recognize it not through any teaching, not through feelings and perceptions, but directly with her eyes.'

Ashu Babu was pleased. He said, 'The same thing has also struck me a number of times. That's why she acts exactly as she speaks. Even if her judgement is mistaken, there's a glory in that mistake.' He paused and went on: 'Look, Haren, it's good in a way that that scoundrel has left her. Virtue would have been dishonoured if he had cast a shadow over her forever. It would have been as offensive as casting pearls before swine.'

'On the other hand,' said Harendra, 'she's so full of compassion that I haven't seen any woman like her except Boudi. In the way she cares for others, she's like the goddess Lakshmi. It's perhaps because she's superior to men in so many ways that she presents herself so humbly before them. It's really wonderful: her heart seems to melt down to her feet.'

Nilima smiled and said, 'Thakurpo, in your previous birth you were probably some queen's panegyrist: the training hasn't left you yet. It would be better for you to give up teaching young boys and take up that profession instead.'

Harendra smiled. He said, 'What to do, Boudi? I'm a simple man and I speak out what I feel. But just ask Ajit Babu: he'll roll up his sleeves and get ready to attack me. Never mind: if he lives, he'll come to see how things are.'

Ajit cried out angrily, 'What's all this, Haren Babu? It seems I'll have to leave your ashram one of these days.'

Harendra said, 'I know you'll have to one day. But keep your patience meanwhile.'

'Then say whatever you like. I'll leave.'

Nilima said, 'Thakurpo, why don't you wind up your brahmacharis' ashram? Then you'll be free, and so will the boys.'

Harendra said, 'Boudi, the boys may be free, but there's no such hope for me—at least not while that man Akshay's there. He'll see me off to the house of death.'

Ashu Babu said, 'It seems you're all afraid of Akshay.'

'Yes, we are. It's easier to swallow poison than to digest his jibes. So many people died of the influenza, but not he. He neatly escaped.'

Everybody began laughing. Nilima said, 'Although I don't speak to Akshay Babu, I'll go to him just once and ask him to forgive you. You seem to be burning away inside you.'

Harendra said, 'It's only we that burn, Boudi: people like you are above such torment. God has created this fire for us; you are beyond its reach.'

Nilima blushed and only said, 'What else?'

'Yes, that's indeed so,' remarked Bela.

There was silence for a while. Then Ajit spoke. 'The other day I read a beautiful story on exactly this subject. Didn't you read it?' he asked Ashu Babu.

'No, I don't remember having done so.'

'It's in one of the monthly magazines you get from England. It's a translation of a French story and it's written by a woman. I think she's a doctor. In a little introduction about herself, she says that she's just crossed her youth and stepped into middle age. There it is—on that shelf.' He pulled out the magazine and sat down again.

'What's the title of the story?' asked Ashu Babu.

Ajit said, 'It's somewhat strange: "Once When I Was a Woman".'

Bela said, 'What does that mean? Has she since joined the ranks of men?'

Ajit said, 'The author seems to be speaking about herself; and maybe because she's a doctor, her account of the changes in the female body sometimes seems tasteless. For example . . .'

Nilima hastily said, 'Please, Ajit Babu, spare us the examples. Let them be.'

Ajit agreed. He said, 'But the inward picture she has drawn—that is, of the female heart—is striking even if not pleasing.'

Ashu Babu grew curious and said, 'Ajit, why don't you read it aloud, skipping over the awkward bits? Let's hear it. The rain hasn't yet stopped, nor is it very late.'

Ajit said, 'I can read it out only if I skip some parts: it's a long story. You can read it in full later if you like.'

'Please read it aloud,' said Bela. 'At least it'll help to pass the time.'

Nilima wanted to go away; but as she had no pretext for doing so, she stayed on, somewhat embarrassed. Placing himself before the lamp, Ajit opened the book and said, 'There's an introduction which is worth summarizing. The person whose lifestory it is, is cultured, charming and well born. The story does not say whether she is chaste, but it implies that if she ever transgressed, it was in her early youth, a long time ago.

'Many people had fallen in love with her at that time. One of them solved the problem by suicide, another crossed the seas and went to Canada. But though he went away he did not give up hope. From that far-off place, he wrote so many letters asking her to relent that had they all been preserved, they would have made up a whole ship's load. He did not expect any reply, nor did he get any. Then they met after fifteen years.

'The man was astonished. He does not seem to have realized that fifteen years had passed, and that the person he had known as a young woman of twenty-five was now forty. There were many enquiries after each other's well-being, many complaints and imprecations. But there was no trace of the fire that had earlier sparkled in her eyes, the tempest of frenzied desire that would burst open the gates of his senses. It was all like a far-off dream. Women can be deceived about everything except this. Here the story starts.' Ajit bent over the pages of the book in order to begin reading.

Ashu Babu interrupted him. 'No, no, Ajit, not the English text. Your Bengali account brought out the simple theme of the story very well. Go on in the same way.'

'How can I?'

'Of course you can. Just go on as you've been doing.'

'My command of language is not as good as Haren Babu's,' said Ajit. 'If the story's not to your taste, put it down to my want of art.' He continued with the story, sometimes glancing at the book and sometimes ignoring it.

'The girl returned home. She had never loved or desired that man. Rather, in her heart of hearts, she had always prayed that God might end his infatuation, that he might be freed from the torment of fruitless love, the longing for an impossible goal. It appeared that God, by that time, had granted her prayer. They did not exchange a single word on the subject. It was clear that, whether he returned to Canada or not, he would no longer make them both miserable by pitiful entreaties for her love. The insoluble problem had been solved. The woman had always denied him; she still did so. But the final "no" came from the other side. The woman had never dreamt there could be such a difference between the two situations. Men's lustful looks had always vexed and embarrassed her. Why should she complain if she was no longer subject to them, if the passing of her youth had stilled the desire and infatuation of men? Yet when she returned home, the whole world appeared strange to her eyes. It was not a question of love or the passionate union of souls. Those were something else—grand matters. But had she ever known that in the unconscious depths of her heart, she had set up a throne for what was not grand—what was carnal, ill-omened, ugly and momentary? Had she known that the cruel humiliation of a man's indifference could wound her so deeply?'

'Ajit's a fine narrator,' remarked Harendra. 'He's read the story with great attention.'

The women looked on silently without comment.

'Yes,' said Ashu Babu. 'How does it go on, Ajit?'

Ajit continued: 'It suddenly occurred to her that not only this man but many others had loved her for a long time, prayed to her, been eager for a single word from her smiling lips. She had not kept count of the many who had once crossed her path every day at every step. They hadn't gone away: she still came across them from time to time. But they no longer sought her. Was it her voice that had cracked? Her smile that had changed? It was only the other day that things seemed so different—only ten or fifteen years ago: had she lost everything in that span of time?'

Ashu Babu suddenly exclaimed, 'She had lost nothing, Ajit—except perhaps her youth, her capacity for motherhood.'

Ajit looked at him and said, 'Exactly. Have you read the story?'

'No.'

'Then how did you know this so well?'

In reply Ashu Babu only smiled and said, 'Go on.'

Ajit went on, 'On returning home, she lit a lamp and stood before the big mirror in her bedroom. As she changed into her nightclothes she looked at her reflection in the mirror and, for the first time, her vision seemed transformed. Had she not been rejected by her once-ardent admirer, she would not have realized that her most precious treasure as a woman—what you have termed her capacity for motherhood—had grown dim and feeble: it was moving towards inevitable death, not to be recovered in this life. This treasure had worn away fruitlessly, as from an endless flow of water over her inert body. But the message that such a treasure was so short-lived reached her only now, at the end of the day.'

Ashu Babu sighed and said, 'That's how things are, Ajit, that's how they are. Many important things in life are prized only when they're lost. What happens next?'

Ajit said, 'There's a meticulous survey of the body once youth has waned, as she saw it in the mirror: what it was and what it had come to be. But I can neither report nor read out that description.'

Nilima quickly interposed: 'Yes, yes: leave it out, Ajit Babu. Skip that part and go on.

Ajit said, 'Towards the end of the analysis, the woman says that just as there is nothing so beautiful on earth as the physical beauty of a woman, there is nothing so ugly as its deformity.'

'But that's going too far, Ajit,' said Ashu Babu.

Nilima shook her head in protest and said, 'No, not at all. It's true.'

Ashu Babu countered, 'But this woman hadn't reached the age of deformity, Nilima.'

'She can be said to have,' replied Nilima. 'It isn't a matter of a woman's longevity as measured in years. It's something much more ephemeral: whoever else might forget it, no woman can.'

Ajit was pleased. He nodded and said, 'The heroine herself makes the same reply. She says, "The only reality of the remaining years of my life will be the wait for the end. There is no consolation, no joy, no hope in this, but it will spare me the ignominy of derision. The relics of my decayed treasure might yet steal the heart of some wretched male; but that fascination will be as much an agony to him as a sham to me. I cannot deck up a beauty which has outlived its purpose and pass it off as current: I cannot deceive myself in that way, nor can I deceive someone else."'

No one said anything. Only Nilima exclaimed, 'Beautifully put! I like those words enormously, Ajit Babu.'

Like the others, Harendra too had been listening attentively. He was not pleased by this remark. He said, 'Boudi, your enthusiasm is excessive; you're saying this without sufficient thought. The silk-cotton flower on a high branch seems beautiful at first sight, but it holds a low place among flowers. Is a woman's body so worthless that it has no other purpose than this?'

Nilima replied, 'The writer doesn't say it has no other purpose. She sensed that these wretched men might have other needs.' She smiled a little and continued, 'You were talking of excessive enthusiasm, Thakurpo. Akshay Babu isn't here today. Had he been here, you'd have learnt from him what form that excess is taking these days.'

Harendra answered, 'I shan't perish just because you're abusing me, Boudi.'

Ashu Babu also smiled at this and said, 'In fact, Haren, I too feel that the author has hinted at the real purpose served by a woman's physical beauty.'

'But can that be right?'

'It's difficult to think it isn't if we look at the world.'

Harendra grew excited. He said, 'Whatever you may think by looking at the world, I find it hard to accept when I look at humankind. Human needs far exceed those of animals: that's why human problems are so various and so complex. Their glory lies in that: you can't sort them out by passing them through a sieve, Ashu Babu.'

'That's also true. Let's hear the rest of the story, Ajit.'

Harendra was offended. He interrupted to say, 'You can't do that, Ashu Babu. I shan't let you avoid answering by making a trifle of the matter. Either agree that what I'm saying is true, or else point out my mistake. You've read a lot and experienced a lot: you're a very learned man. I can't let Boudi win the day by slipping through the gaps in your loose argument. You must say something.'

Ashu Babu smilingly said, 'You're a brahmachari. If you fail to judge beauty, you have nothing to be ashamed of.'

'No, I won't accept such a reply.'

Ashu Babu remained silent for a while and then said

gently, 'It embarrasses me to argue more fiercely and prove you wrong. In fact, Haren, it's better that the deep significance of women's beauty should remain undefined.' Pausing a little, he continued, 'As I was listening to Ajit's story, I remembered a sad tale from a long time back. In my youth I had an English friend who loved a Polish woman. She was truly beautiful; she earned her living by giving piano lessons to girls. Besides being beautiful, she had many gifts: we all wished them well. We were sure there would be no obstacle to their marriage.'

'So what was the problem?' asked Ajit.

Ashu Babu said, 'Only over the matter of age. One day her mother arrived from their country. In the course of conversation it came out that the bride was over forty-five.'

Everybody was startled by this. Ajit asked, 'Did the girl hide her age from all of you?'

Ashu Babu said, 'No, I'm sure she wouldn't have concealed it had she been asked. She wasn't that kind of person. But it never occurred to anyone to ask her. Such was her physique, the beauty of her face and the sweetness of her voice, that no one had ever thought she could even be thirty.'

Bela exclaimed, 'Strange! Did none of you have eyes in your head?'

'Of course we did. It simply goes to show that all wonders of the world can't be made out by the eye.'

'And how old was the groom?'

'Of my age—at that time, I suppose, twenty-eight or twenty-nine.'

'So what happened?'

'It's quickly told,' said Ashu Babu. 'In a moment, the young man's heart seemed to harden against that middle-aged woman. It all happened long ago; yet it pains me whenever I think of it. There was much weeping, much grief; much to-ing and fro-ing, much imploring; but he couldn't overcome his revulsion. He simply couldn't think of marrying her any more.'

Everyone remained silent for a while. Nilima asked, 'But if the situation were reversed, I suppose it wouldn't be thought an impossibility?'

'Probably not.'

'But isn't there a single surviving marriage of that kind in their country? Aren't there any such men there?'

Ashu Babu smiled and said, 'There are indeed. The writer of Ajit's story perhaps had such men in mind when she used the adjective "wretched". But it's getting quite late, Ajit. How does the story end?'

Ajit looked up with a start. He said, 'I was thinking more about your story. In spite of their deep love, why couldn't the boy accept her? How could such a great truth turn false in an instant? The woman must have pondered over that one point all her life: "Once when I was a woman"! The woman past her prime could never have pondered till then how womanhood ends effectively without the woman being aware of it.'

'But how does your story end?'

Ajit said calmly, 'No more of it today. The end of youth had not yet quite ended: the story concludes with this pitiful delusion of the heroine about herself and others. I'd rather tell it some other day.'

Nilima shook her head and said, 'No, no, let it remain unfinished.'

Ashu Babu agreed with her. He said with pain, 'In fact, this is the most miserable time in the lonely life of women. Perhaps that's why men everywhere grow sly, intolerant, carping, even cruel towards such women—elderly, unmarried—and try to avoid them, Nilima.'

Nilima smiled and said, 'Don't say this of all women, Ashu Babu; you should say "unfortunate women like you, with neither husband nor son".'

Ashu Babu did not reply, but he took the hint. He said, 'Yet women blessed with a husband and children grow so fulfilled in affection, love, grace and sweetness that they never even notice when and how such a great crisis in their lives has passed by.'

Nilima said, 'I don't envy such fortunate women, Ashu Babu; I've never felt any urge to do so. But can you tell me the way out for women like myself, whose misfortunes have made them give up all hope for the future?'

Ashu Babu remained speechless for a while. Then he said, 'I can only echo the words of the great: I can do nothing more. They advise you to sacrifice yourself for others. There's no want of misery in the world, nor of instances of self-dedication. I too know all this; but I don't know whether women can find true, untrammelled, sustaining happiness in this way, Nilima.'

Harendra asked, 'Did you always have this doubt?'

Ashu Babu seemed to shrink a little inwardly. Pausing a while, he said, 'Haren, I don't really remember. It was only two or three days after Manorama had left: my heart was heavy, my body inert. I was lying in this chair when suddenly Kamal arrived. I affectionately made her sit near me. She tried not to touch my wound, but she could not avoid doing so. The subject came up, and she lost control of herself. You know what disdain she has for everything ancient. It seems to be her *passion* to demolish all such things. I can't sincerely agree with her: my lifelong predilections grow rigid with alarm, yet I can't find words to express myself and end up admitting defeat. That day, too, I remember talking about women's dedication to others; but Kamal didn't agree. She said, "I know more about women than you do. That tendency doesn't arise from their fulfilment but from their sense of void: it comes about by emptying the heart. It isn't a habit, it's a lack. I don't have the slightest faith in the self-dedication that comes from deficiency."

'I didn't know what to answer; yet I said, "Kamal, if you knew about the inner spirit of Hindu civilization, I could perhaps have made you understand that our greatest achievement lies in attaining salvation through the doctrine of sacrifice and renunciation. It's by following this path that so many widows have realized the highest purpose of their lives."

'Kamal smiled and said, "Did you see anyone realizing it so? Name one such person." I hadn't imagined she would ask such a question. I'd rather thought she'd accept what I said. I felt everything getting confused . . .'

Nilima said, 'Well, why didn't you name me? Perhaps you didn't think of me?'

This was a cruel jest. Harendra and Ajit both hung their heads, and Bela turned away her face.

Ashu Babu was nonplussed, but he did not show it. He said, 'No, I really didn't think of you—just as things near you escape your eyes. It would really have been a fitting reply to have mentioned your name; but since it didn't occur to me, Kamal said, "You mocked me about my education, but doesn't the same apply equally to you in full measure? You stuff women's heads from infancy with an *idea* about what constitutes their fulfilment; they proudly recite what they've learnt by rote and think it to be the truth. You deceive yourselves, and they too perish in the futile conceit of self-complacency."

'She continued in the same breath: "You ought to remember the women who burnt themselves on their husband's funeral pyres. The vanity of both parties, those who burnt themselves and those who incited them, mounted to the skies at the thought that nowhere on earth was there such an example of ideal widowhood."

'I couldn't think of a reply, but she didn't wait for one. She went on: "There's no reply to this. What can you say?" She paused and then, looking at my face, said, "In almost every country, there's an ancient and widespread spiritual fascination with the word 'self-sacrifice'. It intoxicates us. The wonderful immateriality of the next world totally eclipses the narrow, trivial materiality of this one. It leaves no room for man or woman to consider whether life affords anything better. The conditioned mind seems to take you by the ear and make you accept it as a self-evident truth—much like that business of sati. But no more of all this today. I must go."

'As she really seemed about to leave, I anxiously said, "Kamal, it appears that your mission is to crush all popular customs, all established truths with your contempt. Whoever taught you this didn't do the world any good." Kamal replied, "My father taught me all this." I said, "I've heard from you that he was a wise and learned man. Didn't he teach you that man truly realizes himself by total sacrifice? That the soul truly assumes its own being by freely consenting to suffer?"

'Kamal said, "He would say that only those who conspire to suck others wholly dry teach others the misguided doctrine of total self-sacrifice. Those who don't understand what suffering means rhapsodize about the glory of suffering. Such suffering doesn't emanate from the immutable laws of the world; it's something you willingly call into the home. It's a child's toy, a pointless luxury—nothing more."

'I was stupefied with amazement. I said, "Kamal, did your

father teach you only the doctrine of hedonism, only to denigrate what's noble in this world?"

'Perhaps Kamal hadn't expected this reproof. She was aggrieved, and said, "You're talking intolerantly, Ashu Babu. You certainly know that no father can teach his daughter such things. You're being unjust to my father. He was a virtuous man."

'I said, "If he really taught you all that you're saying, it's difficult to judge him charitably. When you learnt that after Manorama's mother's death I couldn't love any other woman, you said that showed my weakness of spirit, that it had nothing glorious about it. You had belittled this devotion to the memory of a dead wife as futile self-persecution. You found no meaning in self-restraint."

'Kamal replied, "I don't even today, Ashu Babu. Such self-restraint clouds the joy of life with its arrogant assertiveness. It's nothing substantial, only an illusion of the mind; it needs to be held in check. Restraint implies abiding by certain limits. In the audacity of power, you can overstep the limits of restraint itself: then it can't be held estimable any more. Haven't you ever felt that overrestraint is a kind of unrestraint, Ashu Babu?"

'Indeed, I had never thought about it. So, what I always had thought sprang to my mind. I said, "You're simply juggling with words. Your arguments are full of pleas for sensual pleasure. The more man tries to cling to things and indulge in them and devour them, the more he loses out. His hunger for pleasure is not satisfied—rather, his inordinate desire keeps growing forever. That's why our lawgivers said, 'Nor is desire ever satisfied by gratifying desires, just as fire burns more fiercely as more and more ghee is poured on it.' The intensity of desire grows the more it is indulged."'

Harendra agitatedly said, 'Why did you quote the Shastras to her at all? What happened then?'

Ashu Babu said, 'She laughed and asked, "Are there such things in the Shastras? But of course there must be. They knew that the desire for knowledge grows as you cultivate knowledge; the thirst for religion intensifies as you practise religion, the desire for piety grows strong with the practice of pious acts—you feel there's more and more left to be done. This is also like that. They did not regret that there was no satisfaction. They were men of judgement."'

Harendra, Ajit, Bela and Nilima all four broke into laughter. Ashu Babu said, 'This is not something to be laughed at. I was amazed at the girl's jibes and sneers. I controlled myself and said, "No, that wasn't their intention. They pointed out that there's no satisfaction in sensual pleasure, no end to desire."

'Kamal paused a while and then said, "I don't know why they pointed out such an unnecessary moral. It's not like watching a folk theatre in the marketplace, or listening to the neighbour's gramophone. You can't suddenly tell yourself in the middle of it, 'That's it—I've enjoyed myself quite enough: I don't want any more.' The essence of pleasure doesn't lie in external gratification. It starts from the root of life—from there it provides our lives with hope, joy and spirit for all time. Scriptural condemnation lies baffled at its doorstep but can't ever touch it."

'"That may be so," I answered, "but it's an enemy to man, and man must conquer it."

'Kamal said, "It won't grow less powerful if you abuse it as an enemy. It has its rightful place by firm contract with nature. Who's ever been able to dismiss those rights simply by revolting against them? To take one's life because of one's misery doesn't mean conquering misery. But it's through this kind of logic that people grope for peace at the gates of evil. They don't find peace, and they lose their comfort as well."

'It appeared that she was only taunting me.' Ashu Babu fell silent for a while, then said, 'I don't know what happened to me, but the words slipped out of my mouth: "Kamal, think just once about your own life." The words sounded harsh to my own ears as I uttered them: there was really nothing about her life to make insinuations about. Perhaps Kamal herself was surprised, but she was neither angry nor piqued. She said quite placidly, "I think about it every day, Ashu Babu. It's not that I haven't suffered misery, but I haven't accepted it as the ultimate truth of my life. Shibnath gave me whatever he had to give, I took whatever was mine to receive. Those little moments of joy are treasured like jewels in my heart. I have neither turned them to ashes in my soul's fire nor stood with hands outstretched for alms before a dried-up fountain. When his love for me exhausted itself, I said goodbye to him without grief; I felt no need to darken the sky with smoky lamentation and complaint. That's why my attitude towards him at the time appeared surprising to you: you wondered how Kamal could forgive such a heinous offence. But more than the offence, what I was conscious of that day was my own impoverishment."

'There seemed to be tears at the corners of her eyes. Perhaps I was mistaken, but my heart was wrung with pain: how little was the difference between her and me! I said, "Kamal, I too have a store of this wealth—the treasure of seven kings. Why should we be greedy for more?"

'Kamal looked on in silence. I asked, "Can you love anyone else in this life either, Kamal? Will you be able to accept him body and soul?"

'She said in a firm voice, "I have to live in that hope, Ashu Babu. If today the sun sets prematurely behind clouds, should I say that darkness is the only truth? If tomorrow the sky is resplendent with light, should I cover my eyes and say it's not light but a lie? Shall I keep up this child's sport to the end of my days?"

'"The night doesn't come just once, Kamal. Won't it return when daylight is gone?"

'"Let it come," she said. "When it comes I shall live through the night with faith in the dawn."

'I sat still in amazement. Kamal went away.

'A child's sport! It had seemed to me that the streams of our thought had converged through grief. But now I found it wasn't so: they were as far apart as heaven and hell. Life means something different to her—it has nothing in common with our view. She doesn't believe in destiny; past memories don't block her path. To her the unknown is only what is yet to arrive. That's why her hopes are as unrestrained as her joys are unconquerable. She isn't willing to cheat herself because someone else has cheated her.'

Everyone remained silent.

Ashu Babu suppressed a sigh and went on, 'She's a strange girl. I felt boundless distress and indignation that day; yet I couldn't but admit to myself that her words weren't simply a speech learnt from her father. Whatever she has learnt, she has learnt intensely and confidently. How young she is! Yet she seems already to have understood the true nature of her mind.'

He added, 'It's quite true. Life really isn't child's play. This great gift of God was not meant to be that. How could I tell her that if one person disappoints another, the emptiness triumphs permanently?'

Bela slowly said, 'That's a lovely thought.'

Harendra stood up silently and said, 'It's quite late, and the rain's about to stop. I'd better leave.'

Ajit also stood up but did not say anything. They made their namaskars and went out.

Bela went to bed. Nilima had a few small chores left, but today they remained undone. She too withdrew silently, but was preoccupied. Ashu Babu lay waiting for his servant, his eyes covered with his hands.

It was a huge house. Nilima's and Bela's bedrooms were at opposite ends of it. Lamps had been lit in them. As soon as they entered the remote, lonely rooms, all the talk and debate seemed to blur. But extraordinarily enough, as they stood before their mirrors before undressing, both women had the same thought at exactly the same time: 'Once when I was a woman!'

24

KAMAL HAD LEFT AGRA TEN OR TWELVE DAYS EARLIER FOR AN unknown destination, but Ashu Babu needed to see her urgently. Everyone was worried, but the black cloud of disquiet hung most thickly over Harendra's brahmacharya ashram. The celibates Harendra and Ajit were shrivelling up faster in competitive anxiety for her than they would have done had they lost their very Brahma.[1]

It was they who finally located her. It was a simple enough matter. An Anglo-Indian whom Kamal had known at the tea garden had recently come down to Tundla on a new job with the railways. He was a widower with a two-year-old daughter. Unable to cope domestically, he had called Kamal over, and she had spent the time helping him settle down. She had returned home that morning. In the afternoon, Ashu Babu sent his car across and waited for her eagerly.

Bela had been invited to the magistrate's house. She too was waiting for the car.

Nilima was at her sewing when she suddenly remarked, 'The man has no family; there's no woman in the house other than a little girl. Yet Kamal could spend ten to twelve days in his house so easily!'

Ashu Babu turned his head with great difficulty and looked at her. He could not understand the import of these words.

Nilima went on speaking as if to herself: 'She's like a fish in a river: you don't ask whether she's getting wet. She doesn't worry about her living, she has no guardian to control her, and no community of her own to frown on her. She's utterly free.'

273

Ashu Babu nodded and said softly, 'It really is rather like that.'

'She's brimming with youth and beauty, and her intelligence also seems boundless. Look at that boy Rajen! How little they knew each other, but when no one would shelter him for fear of trouble, she readily brought him to her house. Her sense of duty didn't wait upon anyone's opinion. What no one could do, she did effortlessly. When I heard about it, I felt everyone had been dwarfed beside her. And yet women must be careful about so many things!'

'They ought to be careful, Nilima,' said Ashu Babu.

Bela said, 'We too could become so recklessly independent if we chose.'

'No, we couldn't,' retorted Nilima. 'Neither you nor I, because we don't have the power to wash away the black mark that the world would put on us.' She paused and said, 'I too once had such wishes, so I've thought about it from many angles. I'm burning from the injustice inflicted by a male-built society—I can't explain how I've been burnt. All that burning got me nowhere, but I hadn't recognized its true nature before I saw Kamal. "Women's liberty", "women's independence" are words on everybody's lips these days; but they stay on the lips and don't go any further. Do you know why? I've now found out that liberty can be obtained neither by theoretical arguments, nor by pleading justice and morality, nor by staging a concerted quarrel with men at a meeting. It's something that no one can give to another—not something to be owed or paid as a due. Looking at Kamal, you can easily understand that it comes of its own accord—through one's own fulfilment, by the enlargement of one's own soul. If you break the shell and release the creature inside the egg, it doesn't win freedom: it dies. There lies our difference from her.'

She went on to say to Bela, 'See how she went off somewhere for ten or twelve days. Everyone was deeply worried about her, but nobody dreamt that she might do something to disgrace herself. Tell me, would people have been so confident about us? Who would have granted us such glory? No one, either man or woman.'

Ashu Babu looked at her for a moment in surprise and said, 'You know, Nilima, that's quite true.'

'But if she had had a husband,' asked Bela, 'what would she have done?'

Nilima said, 'She would have served his wants, cooked his food, kept the house clean and tidy; if she had children she would have looked after them. In fact, if she had no help and was short of money, she wouldn't have had the time to come and see us.'

'So then?' said Bela.

'What then?' returned Nilima. She broke into a laugh and said, 'Not to work, not to know grief or sorrow or want or complaint, only to wander aimlessly about everywhere—can this be the measure of a woman's freedom? God Himself has endless things to do, but who thinks He is in bondage? Don't I myself work hard in this household?'

Ashu Babu looked at her raptly in utter surprise. He had never heard anything like this from her.

Nilima continued, 'Kamal doesn't know how to sit idle. In such an event she would have immersed herself in household chores, attending to her husband and children. She wouldn't have felt the strain as long as her family life flowed over her like a stream of joy. But the day she felt that her work for her husband had become burdensome, I warrant no one in her family would be able to hold her back.'

'That's perhaps true,' Ashu Babu responded softly. A

familiar car horn could be heard nearby. Bela looked out of the window and said, 'Yes, it's our car.' A servant soon came in with a lamp and announced Kamal's arrival.

Ashu Babu had been waiting for this moment these last few days, but now his face turned pale and grave at the news. He had sat up straight in his armchair; he now fell back.

Kamal entered and made her namaskars. She sat down on a chair next to Ashu Babu and said, 'I heard you were worried about me. Who could have known that all of you love me so much? In that case I'd have told you before going off.' She drew his plump, slack hand tenderly between her own.

Ashu Babu's face was averted. It remained so: he made no reply.

At first Kamal thought he was offended because she had gone away before he had fully recovered and not enquired after him for so long. Taking his plump fingers between her own, slender as champak buds, and drawing close to his ear, she whispered, 'I confess I've done wrong. I'm sorry.' But when he said nothing in reply even to this, she was very surprised, and afraid as well.

Bela was ready to start. She stood up and said deferentially, 'If I'd known you were coming I wouldn't have accepted Malini's invitation. But now if I don't go they'll be very disappointed.'

'Who's Malini?' asked Kamal.

'She's the wife of the local magistrate,' explained Nilima. 'Perhaps you don't remember her name.' She said to Bela, 'You must go, otherwise their musical evening will be spoilt.'

'No, no, it won't be spoilt, but they'll be very hurt. I hear they've invited a few others as well. So let me say good-bye for now. We'll sit and talk some other day. Namaskar.' She left rather too briskly.

Nilima said, 'It's better that she's been invited out today; otherwise it would have been awkward to talk frankly. Well, Kamal, how did I address you earlier—formally or informally, as apni or tumi?'

'Tumi,' said Kamal. 'But I haven't been so long in exile that you should forget that.'

'No, I hadn't forgotten, but I felt a little uncertain. It's natural. We've been looking for you for the last seven or eight days. For me it wasn't simply a search. It was like a vigil or meditation.'

But the arid solemnity of a religious vigil was not apparent on her face. Kamal took her words lightly, as stemming from natural affection, and said, 'What have I done to deserve such good fortune? I've been abandoned by everyone, Didi. No respectable person wants to have anything to do with me.' The use of 'Didi' was new. Nilima's eyes moistened, but she kept silent.

Ashu Babu could not hold his peace any more. He turned his face and said, 'Respectable society can answer this charge if it feels the need; but I know that if anyone ever truly wanted contact with you in this life, it's Nilima. Perhaps you've never drawn so much love from anyone else.'

'I know,' said Kamal.

Nilima hastily stood up—not because she had to go anywhere, but because she was always uncomfortable at discussions of this type, with personal implications. Even people close to her had often misunderstood this reaction, yet it came naturally to her. She quickly changed the subject and said, 'I have two pieces of news for you, Kamal.'

Kamal understood her state of mind. She smiled and said, 'Very well, let's have them.'

Nilima pointed to Ashu Babu and said, 'He's hiding his face from you out of shame. So I've taken on the task of telling you: Manorama and Shibnath are going to marry. They've both written asking for the consent and blessings of her father and his future father-in-law.'

Kamal's face turned pale at the news, but she immediately checked herself and said, 'Why should he be ashamed of this?'

'Because she's his daughter,' answered Nilima. 'Ever since he received her letter, he's been repeating just one thing: so many people died in Agra, why wasn't God kind to him? As far as he can tell, he's never done anything wrong; he'd sincerely believed that God felt kindly towards him. This sense of injury has become his greatest misery. He couldn't discuss the matter with anyone except me; he called you day and night in his thoughts. Maybe he thinks you alone can suggest a way out.'

From the corner of her eye, Kamal saw that a few tears had trickled out from Ashu Babu's closed eyes. She reached out her hand and wiped them away. Then she too sat silently.

After a long time she asked, 'That was one piece of news; what's the other?'

Nilima wanted to convey it with a touch of humour but could not quite manage that. She said, 'Nothing very serious really—it's just that it's so unexpected. Everyone was anxious about our Mukherjee Mashai's health. He's recovered, and his Dada and Boudi have forcibly married him off again, despite his great reluctance. He has bashfully conveyed the news to Ashu Babu in a letter. That's all.' Again she started to laugh.

There was neither happiness nor amusement in that laughter. Kamal looked at her face and said, 'So both bits of news are about marriages. One has already taken place and the other been agreed on. Why were you looking for me? I couldn't have stopped either of them.'

'Perhaps he was looking to you to stop them all the same,' answered Nilima. 'But I wasn't looking for you, my dear; I was only calling God with body and soul that I might see you and make my peace with you. If I were to begin cursing my fate at having been born a woman in Bengal, I wouldn't know where to stop. In my stupidity, I've lost both my father's shelter and my in-laws'—never mind all the other losses I've suffered—and now I've even lost my brother-in-law's shelter.' She pointed to Ashu Babu and went on, 'There's no limit to his generosity. Maybe I can stay with him for the short while that he's here; after that I see nothing but darkness before me. So I thought I'd ask you for shelter; if I don't get it, I'll kill myself. I can't drag on till the last day of my life begging mercy from males, like garbage drifting downstream and getting stuck now at one landing place and now at another.' Her voice grew heavy as she said this, but she held back her tears.

Kamal looked at her and only smiled a little.

'Why did you smile?'

'Because it's easier to smile than to reply.'

'I know,' said Nilima. 'But these days you keep vanishing suddenly, no one knows where. That's what makes me afraid.'

'What if I do?' said Kamal. 'If you need me, you won't have to go looking for me, Didi. I myself will search you out across the world. You can be sure of that.'

'Give me the same assurance, Kamal,' said Ashu Babu, 'so that I too can feel as secure.'

'Order me to do what you want.'

'You won't have to do anything, Kamal; I'll do whatever needs to be done. Just guide me so that I don't fail in my duty as a father. It's not only that I can't consent to this marriage; I can't allow it to take place.'

Kamal said, 'The consent is your affair; you may choose not to give it. But how can you stop the marriage? Your daughter is an adult.'

Ashu Babu could not control himself. This hard fact had been tossing in his mind day and night, precisely because it could not be denied. 'I know that,' he said, 'but a daughter should also remember that she cannot outgrow her father. After all, it's not just the consent that's mine to give: so is the property. People have grown accustomed to Ashu Vaidya's weakness, but they forget that he has another side to his nature.'

Kamal looked him in the face and said gently, 'Let them remain unaware of it, Ashu Babu. But even if you remind them, must you begin with your daughter?'

'Yes, a defiant daughter.' After a moment's silence he continued, 'She's my only child; she has no mother. Only God who created a father's heart knows how I brought her up. If I were to express that paternal anguish, my faltering words would mock not only me but the Father of all fathers. Besides, how can you understand this? A father doesn't only have affection, he has his duties as well, Kamal. I've come to know Shibnath in his true colours. I see no other way to save my daughter from his ruinous clutches. I'll write to them tomorrow that Mani shouldn't expect a single paisa from me hereafter.'

'But what if they don't believe that letter? Supposing they think that a father's anger won't last long, that he'll amend his own unjust ways—what then?'

'In that case they'll suffer for it. My duty is to write, theirs to believe me or not.'

'Are you really determined on this?'

'Yes.'

Kamal sat silently. Ashu Babu himself remained quiet for some time in anxious expectation, but inwardly he felt restless. He said, 'You're very quiet, Kamal: why don't you answer?'

'Why, you didn't ask me anything. Whenever there's a difference of opinion in this world, the strong punish the weak. This has been the order since ancient times. What's there to say about it?'

Ashu Babu grew very indignant. He protested and said, 'What are you saying, Kamal? The relationship of father and child isn't a trial of strength, that I should be bent on punishing her because she is weak. A father alone knows how hard it is to be hard; but isn't my harsh resolution meant to save her from error? Don't you really understand this?'

Kamal nodded and said, 'I do. But if she disobeys you and does anything wrong, she will be punished for it. Why should you, out of anger and simply because you couldn't prevent your own grief, increase the burden of her misery a thousandfold?'

Pausing a little, she said, 'You are the closest of all her relatives. Will you give away your daughter as a helpless destitute to a person whom you know to be so degenerate? Won't you leave her any road anywhere by which to return?'

Ashu Babu looked on bewildered. He could not utter a word; only his eyes filled with tears, and large drops rolled down.

After some time he wiped his eyes on his sleeve, cleared his throat and slowly shook his head. 'The path of return is open now and now only; it won't remain so afterwards. I pray to God that I don't have to see her return after leaving her husband.'

'That's wrong of you,' said Kamal. 'I would rather hope that if she ever recognizes her error, the path of correction remains open. Humanity has grown human only by rectifying itself in this way over a long time. Mistakes are nothing to be afraid of, Ashu Babu, as long as another path remains open. You're so apprehensive today because to you that other path appears to be closed.'

Had Manorama not been his own daughter but someone else's, Ashu Babu would easily have grasped these simple words. But a sense of the inevitable misery of his only child's future rendered all Kamal's appeals futile. He could only say in a tone of vague entreaty, 'No, Kamal, I see no way other than stopping this marriage. Can't you suggest anything?'

'Me?' Kamal now understood his intent. Her gentle voice turned grave for a moment as she prepared to spell it out, but it was for a moment only. As her eyes fell on Nilima, she restrained herself and said, 'No, I can't help you at all in this matter. I don't know whether you can frighten her by threatening her with disinheritance; but if she is frightened, I'd say that you've fed her, put her through her lessons at school and college and thus brought her up, but that you haven't made a human being of her. If she now has a chance to make good that lack, why should you stand in her way?'

Ashu Babu did not like what she said. He asked, 'Do you mean that it's not my duty to stop it?'

'At least not with threats,' rejoined Kamal. 'Had I been your daughter, I might have been stopped by you, but I wouldn't ever have respected you after that. That's how my father brought me up.'

'No doubt, Kamal,' said Ashu Babu. 'He saw your well-being to lie in this direction. But I don't: I see clearly that no one can truly love Shibnath. It's just her infatuation, something false. Once the moment's addictive trance is over, Mani's suffering will be boundless. Who'll save her then?'

Kamal said, 'The problem lies in the addiction. There'll be nothing to fear when she recovers from the trance. Her sound health will protect her.'

Ashu Babu demurred. 'This is simply juggling with words, Kamal; it's not good reasoning. The truth is very different. She'll have to suffer heavily for her wrongs: no casuistry can exempt her from that.'

'I said nothing about exemption, Ashu Babu,' replied Kamal. 'I know that one is punished for one's mistakes. That involves suffering but no shame. Mani hasn't tried to cheat anybody. If she acknowledges her mistake and returns, she shouldn't have to return in humiliation. That's all I wanted to convince you of.'

'But I don't feel reassured. I know she'll see her mistake, but she'll have to live on long after that. What will keep her alive then? Where will she find support?'

'Don't talk in that way. If the end of suffering were only to suffer, it would truly be useless. But it replenishes on one side what it loses on the other; otherwise how would I survive today? So rather bless her that, once she sees her mistake, she is able to free herself: no temptation, no apprehension should eclipse her spirit at that moment.'

Ashu Babu kept silent. He shied away from replying, but still more from accepting her words. After a long while he said, 'Through the eyes of a father, I see Mani's future to be dark. Do you still insist that I shouldn't stop her, that my only duty is silent acquiescence?'

'If I were her mother, I would have acquiesced. Perhaps,

like you, I too would have suffered when I thought about her future, but I wouldn't have obstructed it in this way. I would have said to myself, "The problem that she faces today in her life is greater than all my anxieties. It cannot but be accepted."'

Ashu Babu kept silent for some time and then said, 'I still don't understand, Kamal. Mani knows all about Shibnath's character, all about his misdeeds. Once she objected to letting him enter this house. The enchantment that now overshadows her good sense and morality is not true love; it's a spell, an infatuation. A father's duty is to resist this cheat by every means.'

Now Kamal fell completely silent. She saw at last the basic difference in their thinking. Their premises were so categorically different and so impossible to prove, that their argument had to be in vain. Kamal understood that if she looked for a thousand years in the direction of his gaze, she would not come across his truth: the familiar test of judgement, the moral discrimination, the fastidious calculations of good and evil, happiness and misery—the same use of engineers to build a firm foundation. Such people wanted to work out their love by mathematical calculation. In his own life, Ashu Babu had loved his wife wholeheartedly. She was long dead, yet perhaps even today that love had not lost its grip on his heart. It was an incomparable affection. All this was true, yet it was equally true that he and Kamal belonged to different categories of being.

There was nothing so fruitless as to argue whether this was good or bad. Not once in their married life did Ashu Babu have any difference with his wife, nor had any ill-feeling touched their hearts. Who can deprecate the pride and virtue of a man who has led a long married life in undisturbed peace and comfort? The world has sung hymns to this; poets have made themselves immortal by writing of such rare tales; men have hankered ceaselessly to obtain such love in their own lives. How could Kamal be so audacious as to belittle something of unchallenged, eternal glory?

But what about Mani? Despite knowing all about the dissolute wretch to whom she was bent on sacrificing herself, she was not afraid to step beyond the circuit of her knowledge. The father was heartbroken at the prospect, her friends were depressed: she alone wasn't anxious. Ashu Babu knew there was no honour, no goodness in this marriage, that it was based on deception; once the infatuation was over, there would be no place to hide a lifetime's disgrace and misery. All this might be true, but how could she make Ashu Babu understand that, after she had lost everything, what remained for the supposedly deluded girl would still be greater than her father's happy, peaceful, long-lasting married life? How could one argue with a person to whom the final outcome was the only measure of value? For a moment, Kamal felt like saying, 'Ashu Babu, infatuation isn't always false. The flash of lightning that illumines your daughter's heart for an instant might be brighter than her father's unquenched flame.' But she held her peace.

Having spoken so clearly about a father's duty, Ashu Babu was waiting impatiently for a response; but Kamal sat silently as before with lowered face. Clearly she did not want to talk about it any more—not because she had nothing to say, but because she felt no need. But if someone stays silent in this way, the respondent's mind cannot be at peace. In fact, at the core of this elderly man there was a real devotion to truth. He was shamed and confounded by fears about the hard days ahead for his only child. Whatever his tongue might say, he recoiled from exercising arrogant force simply because he had the power to do so. The more he saw of Kamal, the more his wonder and respect for her increased. In the eyes of the world she stood condemned, rejected by respectable society, left out from gatherings; yet it was the silent contempt of this young woman that he feared most, it was she who made him diffident.

He said, 'Kamal, your father was European, but you've never been to those countries. I on the other hand have spent a long time there and seen much of them at close quarters. Whenever I was invited to a party to celebrate a love marriage, I gladly attended; and I also wiped my tears when I saw the marriage break up after indifference, neglect, promiscuity and torture. If you'd been there, you too would have seen these things.'

Kamal looked up and said, 'I can see that even though I haven't been there. Instances of such break-ups are mounting in those countries every day. That's only natural. But while it's quite true, it's wrong to form a conclusion about their real nature on that basis. That's no way to judge, Ashu Babu.'

Ashu Babu felt somewhat embarrassed as he saw his error. One could not argue with Kamal in this way. He said, 'Well, let that be, but look at our own country. Think of the foresight of the founders of customs that have continued down the ages! Here the responsibility is not on the bride and groom but on the parents and elders. Hence the judgement isn't befuddled by unrestrained passion; the partners are attended through life by a sober, unwavering good.'

'But Mani isn't out to calculate the good, Ashu Babu,' said Kamal. 'She wants love. The one can be ensured by the wise advice of elders, but no one except the heart's god can reckon the other. But I'm annoying you to no purpose with my arguments. A person whose house is only open on the west can't see the sun rise at dawn; it's only seen when the sun sets at dusk. If one tries to compare the colour and appearance of the two, one will go on arguing forever. It's getting late: I'd better be going.'

Nilima had been silent all through, without contributing a word to the debate. Now she said, 'I too didn't understand all that you said, Kamal, but at least I've understood that the other windows of the house should also be open. The fault lies not with the vision but with the closed windows. If you look out of only one opening till the day you die, you'll never see anything new.'

As Kamal got up to go, Ashu Babu said in a tone of desperation, 'Don't go away, Kamal: stay a little longer. I can't eat anything, I can't sleep—I can't tell you what's going on continually in my heart. But let me try once more to understand what you said. Do you really suggest that I should sit idle while this ugly business takes place?'

'If Mani loves him, I can't call it ugly,' observed Kamal.

'But that's just what I'm trying to tell you, Kamal. This is infatuation, it isn't love. One day the illusion will be shattered.'

'It's not only illusions that are shattered, Ashu Babu,' said Kamal. 'So is true love. That's why most love marriages are short-lived. That's why those countries are so infamous, and why there are so many divorce suits there.'

Ashu Babu seemed to see new light on hearing this. He said with buoyant eagerness, 'Say that again, Kamál, say that again. I've seen such cases with my own eyes.'

Nilima looked on in wonder.

'But what about the practice of marriage in this country?' asked Ashu Babu. 'What do you think of that? The bond never breaks all through life.'

'It should not, Ashu Babu,' said Kamal. 'Here it's not the *frenzy* of inexperienced youth, it's a calculated transaction worked out by sagacious elders. The capital in that business doesn't consist of dreams—it's pure solid stuff, tested by seasoned experts with open eyes. If there's no fatal mistake in the calculations, it won't crack easily. Wherever this is done, it's a strong bond—it lasts through life like a fast knot.'

Ashu Babu sighed and remained silent.

Nilima was looking on silently. She slowly asked, 'If what you say is true, if true love breaks as easily as a delusion, on what can we rely? What will people pin their hopes on?'

Kamal said, 'They'll have the sweet, intimate memories of a lost paradise, and beside it a sea of sorrow. There seemed no end to Ashu Babu's peace and happiness, but he had no more treasure than that. Didi, what can we do but pardon someone whom fate has fobbed off with so little?'

She paused and continued, 'People looking on from outside think all is lost. Friends grow alarmed, they reach out to bar one's way; they're convinced that there's nothing outside their calculations but a big zero. But it's not so, Didi. What remains when everything is lost can be held in the palm, like a jewel. It can't be flaunted in a pageant, so the lookers-on are disappointed and jeer as they return home. They say there's been a disaster.'

Nilima said, 'There are reasons for saying so, Kamal. Jewels are not meant for everybody, certainly not for the rabble. People who're only happy when decked out with gold and silver from top to toe won't understand the value of your tiny diamonds and gems. Those who want a lot feel secure only after tying knot upon knot. They put a price on something only by its weight and show and bulk. But it's useless to try and show the sunrise from a western window, Kamal. Let's end the discussion.'

Ashu Babu slowly said, 'Why should it be useless, Nilima? It isn't useless at all. But never mind, I'll keep quiet.'

'No, you won't,' said Nilima. 'Is there truth only in Kamal's thoughts and not in a father's wise judgement? That can't be so. What's true for her may not be true for Mani. Whatever truth there may be in a wife's separating from a wayward husband, I'm sure there isn't a lot of truth in Bela's separating from her husband. Truth lies neither in deserting the husband nor in serving him like a slave. These are simply two roads leading left and right: you have to work out your own destination. You can't do that by argument.'

Kamal looked on silently.

Nilima said, 'The sun doesn't only rise; its setting is just as important. If love lay only in youth and beauty, the father wouldn't need to worry about his daughter; but it isn't so. I haven't read books, I have little knowledge or intelligence. I can't convince you with arguments, but I think you haven't really hit the truth yet. Respect, devotion, affection, trust— all these can't be won by scrambling for them: they show up after long suffering, long delay. And when they do, all talk of youth and beauty hides its face, no one knows where.'

The quick-witted Kamal understood in a moment that this was irrelevant to the present discussion. It was neither attack nor support, merely Nilima's own opinion. She looked and saw that in the bright glow of the lamp, under the dark shadow of her disarrayed black hair, an ineffable beauty had lit up Nilima's face; her soft placid eyes were brimming with tears.

It was pointless to ask, thought Kamal, whether it was a new sunrise or the setting of a weary sun. Without giving thought to east or west, she saluted that radiant corner of the sky.

After two or three minutes, Ashu Babu suddenly gave a start and said, 'Kamal, I'll think again over what you've said; but don't entirely neglect what we've said to you. Many people have accepted it as true; one can't fool so many people with something false.'

Kamal smiled and nodded in a preoccupied way, but addressed her reply to Nilima. She said, 'If you can fool one child with a lie, you can fool a hundred thousand. The bigger number doesn't guarantee greater intelligence, Didi. Those who once said that the history of the love between man and woman was the most authentic history of human civilization came nearest to the truth; but those who proclaimed that the wife was required only to bear sons, not only humiliated womankind but blocked the path to their own greatness. Because they built their foundation on this untruth, the resultant misery hasn't yet found an end.'

'But why are you saying this to me, Kamal?'

'Because it's you I need to tell most urgently that they who swathed our body with ornaments of flattery, to spread the message that motherhood was woman's ultimate fulfilment, defrauded the entire race of women. Whatever situation you may have to face in life, Didi, don't ever accept this false notion. That's my last request. But no more argument. I must go.'

'Very well,' said Ashu Babu wearily. 'The car is waiting to take you home.'

Kamal said to him in a pained voice, 'You love me so much, but there's nothing in common between us.'

'There is, Kamal,' said Nilima. 'But it's not a similarity tailored to a master's orders, it's a similarity born of God's creation. People appear different, but the same blood is flowing through their veins, beyond sight. Hence, whatever outer discord there may be among them, the strong inner attraction never fails.'

Kamal came up to Ashu Babu, put a hand on his shoulder and said softly, 'But remember, you mustn't be angry with me instead of with your daughter.'

Ashu Babu said nothing but remained silent.

'There's an English word, *emancipation*,' said Kamal. You know that in ancient times, one great significance it carried was the freedom obtained by a child from the father's stern control. But the children didn't conjoin to create this word; it was done by mighty paterfamiliases like you, men who wanted to loosen the bonds and free their daughters. Even today, regardless of the quarrels women may pick in the cause of *emancipation*, the reality is that, in the present world order, it's the men who eventually grant emancipation, not we women. My father used to say that it's the masters who freed the slaves of the world, people belonging to the master-class who fought for the cause. The slaves didn't earn their freedom by wrangling and arguing. That's the way things are. It's the law of the world: the strong emancipate the weak from the bondage of the strong. So also, men alone can liberate women. The responsibility lies with them. The responsibility of liberating Manorama lies with you. Mani can rebel, but there's no freedom for a child in a father's curse—only in his unstinted blessing.'

Even now Ashu Babu could not speak out. This undisciplined girl had been born amidst insult and indignity, but she had wiped out the shameful constraints of her birth from her mind. Her reverence and love for her deceased father knew no bounds. He had not seen her father; his own beliefs and attitudes made it difficult for him to respect that man, yet his eyes filled with tears for him. Ashu Babu's break with his daughter had pierced him like a spear, yet looking at the face of another man's daughter, he seemed to guess how people could be bound for ever even after severing all ties. He drew down her hand from his shoulder and remained silent for a while.

'May I go now?' asked Kamal.

Ashu Babu let go her hand and said, 'Yes.' He could say nothing more.

THE WINTER SUN HAD SET. THE EVENING SHADOWS WERE darkening the room. Before lighting the lamp, Kamal wanted to finish an urgent piece of needlework. Ajit was sitting on a chair nearby. It seemed he had stopped in the middle of saying something and was waiting eagerly for an answer.

News of the Manorama–Shibnath affair had reached their circle of friends. The day's conversation had started with that. Ajit's point of departure was that, when he arrived in Agra, he had had a firm premonition that matters would end like this.

But Kamal expressed no curiosity about the reasons for his suspicion.

Ajit had gone on talking incessantly, finally reaching a point where he could proceed no further without a response.

Kamal was sewing so intently that it seemed she could not spare the time to look up. Two or three minutes passed in silence. It seemed they might continue indefinitely in this way, so Ajit had to try again. He said, 'It's surprising that you couldn't even guess what was in Shibnath's mind.'

Kamal did not look up, but shook her head and said, 'No, I couldn't.'

'Can anyone believe that you were so simple as never to have a moment's doubt?' Ajit asked.

'I don't know whether anyone else can believe it or not, but can't you?' Kamal answered.

Ajit said, 'Perhaps I can, but only when I look at your face; not otherwise.'

Now Kamal looked up, smiled and said, 'Then look at me and say whether you can.'

Ajit's eyes flashed. He said, 'I'm sure what you're saying is true. You didn't distrust him, and the result is as you see.'

'I admit it; but tell me, what did you gain by your suspicions?' She smiled a little again and resumed her work.

But Ajit went on rambling for another ten or fifteen minutes; then, tiring of this, he said in exasperation, 'Sometimes it's yes and sometimes it's no. Can't you talk except in riddles?'

Kamal replied as she straightened out her stitching, 'Women love riddles. It's their nature.'

'Then I'm sorry I can't praise their nature. You must learn to speak plainly, otherwise you won't get any work done in this world.'

'You too must learn to make out riddles, otherwise we have problems on our side.' With this she folded up her work, put it in a basket and said, 'Those who're too eager to be explicit publish their speeches in newspapers if they're orators; write prefaces to their own works if they're writers; and play the heroes in their own plays if they're playwrights. They think they should express through gestures what they can't express in words. The only thing I don't know is what they do when they fall in love. But please wait a little while I light the lamp and bring it.' She quickly rose and went to the next room. She came back in a few minutes, put the lamp on the table, and sat on the floor.

Ajit said, 'I'm neither an orator nor a writer nor a playwright, so I can't make any excuses on their behalf. But I know what they do when they fall in love. They don't conspire to marry after the Shaivite custom——they step along the straight familiar path. They take care that when they are no more, their spouses have the means to live, that they aren't left to the landlord's mercy or put to humiliation.'

'Enough, enough!' Kamal cut him short. She continued with a smile, 'If they build such a solid structure that it can only serve for a tomb, with no space for a living man to breathe, they are saintly men.'

'May we come in?' someone suddenly called from the door. It was Harendra's voice, but who were the 'we'?

'Come in, come in,' Kamal went to the door to welcome them. Harendra was there with another young man. 'You've met Satish,' said Harendra, 'but only once, at our ashram. I hope you haven't forgotten him.'

'No,' said Kamal with a smile. 'The only difference is that he wore white that day; today he's in yellow.'[1]

'That's just an external manifestation of his ascent to a higher plane,' said Harendra. 'He's just come back from Varanasi, scarcely two hours ago. He's exhausted; moreover, he isn't well disposed towards you; yet hearing that I was coming here, he couldn't restrain himself. Such is the magnanimity of brahmacharis like us.' He peeped into the room and continued, 'Here you are! Another confirmed brahmachari already here! So it seems I needn't worry: my ashram is disintegrating, but another one seems about to spring up.' As he said this he entered the room, invited Satish to take the only vacant chair, and made himself comfortable on the bedstead.

Satish was a little hesitant to sit down, as it was the only vacant seat in the room and Kamal was standing. Harendra had not overlooked this, yet he smilingly said to Satish, 'Sit down, my dear fellow, you won't lose caste. However high you might have risen by going to Varanasi, don't forget that there are higher places in this world.'

'No, that's not the reason,' said Satish with embarrassment as he sat down.

Kamal smiled at him and said, 'You have no right to mock others, Haren Babu. You are the founder of your ashram and also its head and provost. Your followers are young and have little experience: their only duty is to obey your orders and enjoinments. So . . .'

'That "so" was quite uncalled for,' said Harendra. 'It may be that I'm the founder of the ashram, but the head and the provost are my two friends Satish and Rajen. One's charge was to advise me, and the other's to disobey me as far as possible. There's no trace of one, and the other has returned with a replenished store of wisdom. I'm afraid I won't be able to keep pace with him any more. What troubles me now is what to do with our half-starved flock of boys. He took them around Varanasi and Kanchi and has now brought them back. I could tell just by looking at them that there hadn't been any lapse in following the rituals. My only regret is that, had they been made to do a little more austere meditation, I wouldn't have had to pay their return fares.'

'Have the boys grown very thin?' asked Kamal in a pained voice.

'Thin?' said Harendra. 'Maybe there's a word for it in ashram language—Satish should be able to tell you—but have you seen a modern painting[2] of Kacha in the hermitage of Shukracharya?[3] You haven't? Then you can't understand what I mean. As I looked down from the balcony, they seemed just like a group of Kachas marching down in file from heaven to the ashram. Still, I consoled myself that when our ashram disintegrates, they won't starve, they can work as models in any art studio in the country.'

'They say you're winding up the ashram,' said Kamal. 'Is it true?'

'Quite true. I can't bear your sharp tongue any longer. That's also a reason why Satish has come here. He thinks that you're not really an Indian woman, so you can't recognize the truth that lies at the heart of India. He wants to explain it to you. It's up to you to understand, but I've assured him that whatever I do, they've nothing to fear. I don't know which of the four ashrams of life[4] our Ajitkumar will adopt, but the news is going round that he'll spend generously to set up ten or twenty ashrams like ours in various places. He has the money as well as the heart. And Satish will no doubt head one of them.'

Kamal smiled bemusedly and said, 'There's no better cover for wrongdoing than philanthropy. But what will Satish Babu gain by imparting the truth about India to me? I haven't asked Haren Babu to close down his ashram, nor would I prevent Ajit Babu from opening ashrams all over India with his money. My objection is only to accepting it as truth. How can that harm anybody?'

Satish said in a humble tone, 'You can't gauge the harm from outside. But if I ask a few questions, not to argue but simply to learn, will you please answer me?'

'Satish Babu, I'm really exhausted today.'

Satish did not heed this protest. He said, 'Haren-da said jokingly just now that however much I might have risen by going to Varanasi, there are higher places in this world. He meant this house. I know he has endless regard for you. There's no great loss if the ashram breaks up; but if he's demoralized by what you say, that loss can't be made good.'

Kamal remained silent. Satish went on: 'You know

Rajen very well. He's a friend of mine. We couldn't have been friends if we hadn't agreed on fundamental issues. Like him, I too want India to attain the highest prosperity through total emancipation. With this in mind, we wish to gather young men together and bring them up. We're not at all allured by an imaginary life in heaven after death. But a spiritual order can't be formed without austere discipline. And not only the boys, we too have accepted that ascetic rigour. There is suffering in it and there always will be. An ashram is a place where one attains a great good through immense hardship. There's nothing to laugh at in this.'

Since there was no response, Satish continued, 'Whatever may have been the condition of Haren-da's ashram, I won't discuss it because it might turn personal. But one can't deny that the Indian ashram at its core feels a deep respect and commitment towards the heritage of India. Renunciation, celibacy and self-abnegation are not virtues of the weak and powerless. In these, in the past, the materials for nation-building were inherent. It's only by this path that the dying spirit of India can be revived. Through the rituals and observances of the ashram, we are trying to keep alive this faith and reverence. Through echoing hymns and the flames of holy fires, the ashram of an austere, spiritual India had once taken up the mission of working for the genuine welfare of the nation. Is there anyone so foolish as to deny that the need for it is not lost?'

Satish's speech had the force of sincerity. The words were noble and traditional, so that he almost knew them by heart. Towards the end, his soft voice changed to lively excitement and his dark face grew flushed. Watching him silently with unblinking eyes, Ajit was thrilled from top to toe; and Harendra, however he might have inveighed against his own ashram, was tossed between faith and doubt by this recital of the ancient glories of the institution. Looking him piercingly in the face, Satish said, 'Haren-da, we are dead; but how can you forget that the science of our rebirth is inherent in this ideal of the ashram? You want to break it up, but is breaking something so very important? Isn't it more important to build something up? What do you say?'

Then, turning to Kamal, he asked, 'How many ashrams have you seen with your own eyes? With how many of them are you closely familiar?'

It was an awkward question. 'I haven't really seen a single one,' said Kamal, 'and barring yours, I have no acquaintance with any other.'

'Then?'

Kamal smilingly answered, 'Can the eyes see everything? I saw the hardships of your ashram with my eyes; but the business of gaining some great good remained invisible.'

Satish said, 'You're mocking us again.'

Seeing his indignant face, Harendra softly remarked, 'No, no, Satish, it isn't mockery; she's just speaking in riddles. It's her nature.'

'Nature! Pleading one's nature can't excuse such conduct, Haren-da,' exclaimed Satish. 'It insults and denigrates what has always been seen as sacred and venerable in the Indian tradition. One can't simply overlook it.'

Haren replied, pointing to Kamal: 'We've often had this argument with her. She says we have no obligation to the past. The passage of time makes a thing ancient, but it acquires virtue by its own qualities. It doesn't grow venerable because of its antiquity. If a savage nation that once buried parents alive wanted to dictate our duty in the name of ancient ritual, how would we stop them?'

'You can't compare the ancient Indians to savages, Haren-da!' exclaimed Satish angrily.

'I know that, Satish,' replied Haren, 'but what you're saying isn't based on reason. It's just bluster.'

Satish grew still more excited. 'We never thought you'd be trapped by atheism one day, Haren-da!'

'You know perfectly well that I'm not an atheist. But to abuse somebody can be nothing more than insult; you can't establish your views that way. Hard words are the weakest thing in life.'

Satish felt ashamed. He bent down to touch Harendra's feet, then raised his hand to his forehead. He said, 'I didn't mean to insult you, Haren-da. You know how much we respect you. But I'm distressed to hear you say you don't believe in the eternal Indian practice of meditation. The materials and the labour with which people once built up this vast nation, this great civilization, constitute a truth that has never disappeared. I see it written in golden letters that this is our inherent religious being—our very own. We can revive this great but moribund nation through those very elements, Haren-da. There's no other way.'

'That may not be possible, Satish,' replied Harendra. 'This is only your own belief, and only you value it. It was in reply to some such argument that Kamal once pointed out how in the primeval world a huge creature evolved with colossal bones, vast bulk and an enormous appetite. It set out to dominate the world with those assets: they were authentic to the time. But another day, that very bulk and appetite brought death to it. What was valued one day became false on another and razed it ruthlessly from the world. Those bones have simply turned to stone, objects of archaeological study.'

Satish could not immediately think of a reply. He said, 'Do you then mean that the ideal of our ancestors was wrong? Was there no truth in their doctrine?'

'Maybe there was at the time, but perhaps not any longer,' answered Harendra. 'I don't see why it should depress us, Satish, if the path that led to heaven that day now leads us to the gates of hell.'

Satish fought to control his suppressed anger. He said, 'All this is simply the result of your modern education: nothing else.'

'Quite possibly,' said Harendra. 'But if modern education can light the way to welfare in this age, I don't see anything shameful about it.'

Satish sat speechless and still for a long time, then slowly uttered, 'But I see reason for a thousand kinds of shame, Haren-da. The wisdom and ancient doctrines of India make her unique: they are her life. If our country has to attain freedom by sacrificing those thoughts and doctrines, such freedom won't be a victory for India. It would be a victory of the Western ethos and Western culture. That would be another name for defeat. Death would be better than that.'

His agony was sincere. Realizing this, Harendra kept silent. But the answer now came from Kamal. There was no trace of the familiar banter in her expression. In a quiet, low, restrained voice, she said, 'If you could sacrifice your prejudices as you have sacrificed yourself, Satish Babu, it wouldn't have been hard for you to understand that humankind was not created for concepts and distinctions; rather, those were created for humankind and are valued for its sake. If humankind degenerates, what's the use of glorifying its doctrines? India's thought may not triumph, but her people will. So many men and women would then be blessed with deliverance. Look at Young Turkey. As long as Turkey clung to her age-old customs, rituals and traditions handed down through generations, thinking them to be true, she was defeated again and again. Today she has achieved the truth by a revolution—all her dirt and filth has been flushed away; who dares laugh at her today? Yet once upon a time, those old ideals had brought her victory, bestowed wealth and prosperity upon her and endowed her with the spirit of humanity. She took them as eternal truths and thought she could win back her lost glory by clinging to them. She couldn't dream that they must evolve. Today her delusion is dead but her people have come alive. There are other examples of this kind, and there will be more. Satish Babu, self-confidence and self-conceit are not the same thing.'

'I know that,' said Satish. 'But the West may not have found the final answer to humanity's questions either. Might not their civilization also be destroyed one day?'

Kamal nodded in assent. 'Yes, that's possible. I believe it will be so.'

'Then?'

'There's nothing surprising in that,' said Kamal. 'Satish Babu, evil is not the enemy of the good. The real enemy of the good is the better. That's what India has to recognize. The day when the better comes forward and demands an answer to its question, the good will have to stand aside and hand over the sceptre. The hordes of Scythians, Huns and Tartars once conquered India by brute force, but they couldn't bind its culture; instead they were bound by it. Do you know why?

The real reason is that they themselves were petty men. But the Mughals and Pathans could not be tested thus because the French and the English arrived. Their lease has not yet run out. One day they'll have to render an answer to India; but let that be. If India lets herself be bound by Western knowledge, science and civilization, it might be a jolt to her pride, but not to her well-being. I'm sure of that.'

Satish shook his head violently and said, 'No, no, no. It would be disastrous if one said such things to those who have neither faith nor reverence, whose beliefs are built on sand.' He looked askance at Harendra and went on, 'It was just in this way that, not so long ago in Bengal, a few individuals, straying from the true and ideal, with the outlandish audacity of half-baked knowledge, took up Western science, Western philosophy and Western culture as something great. They distracted and vitiated the mind of the nation. But providence could not tolerate such mischief: our conscience revived by way of reaction. We recognized our error. The wise men who in those dark days brought back home the bewildered, centrifugal mind of the nation, are to be revered not only in Bengal but all over India.' He joined his hands and raised them to his forehead as he concluded.

Everyone felt the truth of what he said. It was not surprising that both Ajit and Harendra followed suit, offering namaskars in homage to those great men. Ajit added quietly, 'If they had not done so, a great many people would have converted to Christianity.'

He looked at Kamal's face as he said this, and saw reproach, not assent, in her eyes; yet she kept silent. Perhaps she didn't wish to reply: she understood Ajit well. But when Harendra also mumbled in inarticulate agreement, the contradiction between his earlier words and this faltering uncertainty moved her to speak. 'Haren Babu, there is a type of person who doesn't believe in ghosts but is frightened of them. You're like that. This is simply self-deception, and nothing could be more wrong. This country will never lack money to found monasteries; nor will there be any dearth of disciples. Satish Babu will get along without you, but your hypocrisy in forsaking him will cause you lifelong remorse.'

She paused for a while, then said: 'My father was a Christian. He never wanted to know what I was, nor did I myself. He didn't need to know, and I didn't care. I hope I remain indifferent to religion till the day I die. But one day, people will ask who weighed more in the balance of the nation's destruction: those you just reviled as wanton, or those you hailed as venerable.'

Satish felt as though someone had lashed him with a whip. He sprang up in acute distress and said, 'Do you know their names? Have you ever heard of them?'

Kamal shook her head. 'No.'

'Then you must first know about them.'

'All right,' smiled Kamal, 'but I have no fascination for names. I don't believe that learning names is the end of our knowledge.'

Satish's eyes flashed with scorn and revulsion by way of reply, and he darted out of the room.

There was no doubt that he had left in anger. In order to ease the situation, Harendra feigned a smile and said, 'Kamal is Eastern to look at, but her nature is Western. The one can be seen, but the other remains completely hidden. That's why people are mistaken about her. One can swallow the food she serves, but it's hard to digest: it turns the stomach. She has neither belief nor sympathy for anything in our tradition.

She feels no pain in rejecting anything as outdated. She doesn't understand that a fine pair of scales don't by themselves ensure accurate measurements.'

'I do understand,' said Kamal. 'What I can't accept is to be paid for one thing and supply another. That's what I object to.'

'I've decided that I'll wind up the ashram,' said Harendra. 'I've begun to doubt whether this kind of training will really teach boys to recover our lost freedom, the true well-being of our country. But I don't know what to do with these boys whom Satish has coaxed away from their impoverished homes. I can't even hand over their charge to Satish.'

'It's better that you don't,' remarked Kamal. 'But please don't try to mould them into something extraordinary or unearthly. There are boys from poor, deprived families in every country. Try to bring yours up the way they do everywhere else.'

'I'm not yet convinced on that score, Kamal,' said Harendra. 'Maybe I can find teachers to teach them their books; but I doubt whether they can be brought up as true men if they're cut off from their initial training in self-restraint and renunciation.'

'Haren Babu,' said Kamal, 'you think so deeply about a problem that you can't find a simple solution. I'm afraid you'll make them either rise to be gods or turn into unruly animals. The easy, simple and natural graces of the world are hidden from your sight. You obscure your mind with an imaginary, second-hand sense of guilt and make it sordid and fear laden. Is what I saw at the ashram the other day the result of self-restraint and renunciation? What have they got out of it? Only a burden of woes foisted on them by other people, a deprivation of rights and the hunger of the deceived. In

China they bind women's feet to keep them small. Many say that makes them beautiful. I can even tolerate that, but when the women themselves are charmed by the beauty of their crippled, disfigured feet, there remains no ground for hope. While you were wallowing in self-congratulation, I asked them, "How are you, boys?" They glibly answered, "We're very happy." They didn't even give a thought to the matter. The very faculty of thought was dead in them—so ruthless is your regime. Nilima Didi looked at me and perhaps sought an answer; but I had no answer except to beat my breast and weep. Inwardly I thought, can such boys restore my country's freedom in the days to come?'

'Forget about the boys,' said Harendra. 'Rajen, Satish—they're grown-up youths. They too have renounced everything, haven't they?'

'You don't really know Rajen, so you'd better forget about him too. But it's young people that are most attracted by renunciation. Youth is a force; what but an opposite force can tame it?'

'Please don't be angry, Kamal,' said Harendra, 'but after all there's not a drop of renunciation in your blood. Your father was European. You were brought up by him as a child. Your mother belonged to this country, but it's better not to talk about her. Apart from your beauty, you've inherited nothing from her. So your Western education has taught you these materialistic ways.'

'I'm not angry, Haren Babu,' said Kamal. 'But you shouldn't say such things. A nation can't become great simply by indulging in pleasures and luxuries. When the Muslims made this mistake, they lost the virtues of both indulgence and renunciation. The same mistake could cause the downfall of the Europeans too. The West doesn't lie outside this world; it can't survive by ignoring this universal law.'

She was silent for a moment and then resumed, 'Then you'll have the chance to snigger and say, "Well, didn't we say so? We knew it was only a few days' romp and would soon end. But look at us. We have survived!"' As she spoke, a bright smile spread across her face.

'I wish such a day were really to come,' said Harendra.

'One shouldn't say such things, Haren Babu,' returned Kamal. 'If such a great people were to stoop and fall, the dust would darken many lights. That would be a sad day for humanity.'

Harendra stood up and said, 'That day is yet to come, but I'm sensing bad days ahead for myself. Many lights are turning dim. Kamal, your father has taught you only to put out lights, not to set them up. Well, I'll be going. Are you staying back for some time, Ajit Babu?'

Ajit made a move to get up but did not.

'Haren Babu,' said Kamal, 'if the light shines on your eyes and not on the road, you'll stumble and fall into the ditch. Whoever puts out that light is your friend.'

Harendra sighed and said, 'I sometimes think I came to know you in an unlucky moment. I don't have much confidence in myself any more. Yet I can say that whatever glow of erudition, intelligence and virility the West may show, it's nothing compared to what India has to offer.'

Kamal replied, 'You're like the boy who fails in class and starts railing at a Master of Arts. There's something called self-respect, Haren Babu, but there's also something called self-conceit.'

Harendra was angry. He said, 'There may be many such words. But you can't deny that India was once the world's teacher in all respects, when the ancestors of many other peoples were scrambling among the trees. India will once again be restored to the teacher's seat. I'm sure of it.'

Kamal was not at all annoyed. She laughed and said, 'Those others have now come down from their trees to the ground. But if you want to please yourself by rehearsing how in the remote past one's ancestors were the world's preceptors, or how in the remote future one's descendants will again take up the parental profession, you'd better turn to Ajit Babu. I have a lot of work to do.'

'Well, goodbye,' said Harendra. His face was grave and melancholy as he went away.

26

SOME EIGHT OR TEN DAYS LATER, KAMAL WENT TO VISIT ASHU Babu. Those few days had seen upheavals in the lives of those who make up this story. They were, however, neither sudden nor unexpected. The wisps of clouds heralding the storm, carried by erratic bursts of wind, had been gathering over many days. The outburst seemed inevitable, as indeed it was.

The doorman was absent from his post. Although nobody ever used the veranda on the ground floor, a table and some chairs were usually placed there, and a few portraits of famous men adorned the walls. Even these were missing now. Only a lantern, black with soot, remained hanging from the ceiling. Rubbish had gathered in the corners—no one had thought it necessary to remove it. There was an air of carelessness everywhere: the master of the house was clearly about to leave. Kamal climbed upstairs to Ashu Babu's room. It was late afternoon, and he lay reclining in his chair as usual. There was no one else in the room. At the sound of the curtain being drawn aside, he opened his eyes and sat up. His effusive greeting revealed that he had not expected her.

'Why, it's Kamal! Come, my dear, come.'

Kamal seemed struck by his appearance. 'Kakababu, you look old today!' she exclaimed.

Ashu Babu smiled. 'Old? Isn't old age God's blessing, Kamal? When the soul inside has grown old, there's nothing so sad as a young exterior. It's as pathetic as turning bald in one's youth.'

'But you don't look too well either.'

'No.' And without giving her a chance to press further, he asked, 'How are you, Kamal?'

'Well. I'm never ill, Kakababu.'

'I know: neither physically nor mentally. That's because you have no greed. You make no demands; that's why God gives to you so freely.'

'Gives me? Just what have you seen Him give me?'

'This is not the magistrate's court, Kamal, that you can browbeat me and win the case. I admit that in the eyes of the world I have myself got all kinds of things. The thought prompted me to turn out my coffers this morning and check their contents. But I found them empty, Kamal, except for the countless zeroes that have meaninglessly puffed up my account. People have been deceived by the bulkiness of the bag: there's nothing inside. The mathematician mistakenly attributes a value to zero, my child. I find none. When they line up beside the number one, it's that one that turns into a crore. A crowd can never make up a quantity. Where the substance is missing, the zeroes are an illusion. And so is my supposed good fortune.'

Kamal did not argue. Instead she drew up a chair and sat near him. Ashu Babu placed his hand on hers and said, 'My child, the time has finally come for me to go: tomorrow, or perhaps the day after. I'm old and I can't hope to meet you again. But this I do believe, that you'll never forget me.'

'I won't,' said Kamal. 'And we shall meet again. But Kakababu, though your coffers are empty, mine aren't. They actually hold substance, not illusion.'

Ashu Babu made no answer, but he saw the truth of her words.

'We shan't be able to hold you here much longer, Kakababu. I knew that the moment I entered the house. Now you're here only in body; your heart has already said farewell to the place. Where will you be going? To Calcutta?'

'No,' replied Ashu Babu, shaking his head slowly. 'A little further away. I'd promised my old friends that I'd go to see them once more if I remained alive. You too have nothing to hold you here, Kamal. Will you come with me to England? Then if I don't return, the others back home might get the news from you.'

The significance of the unspecific 'others' was not lost on Kamal. But to spell them out would have been needlessly cruel.

'I won't demand any nursing, my child. Have no fears on that score,' continued Ashu Babu. 'I've no wish to increase my obligations to others in order to drag this useless body around. But who could have guessed, Kamal, that even this lump of flesh could create complications? It makes me die of shame to think of it. Yet who could have imagined it? It amazes me.'

Struck by a sudden suspicion, Kamal asked: 'I don't see Nilima Didi. Isn't she at home?'

'I haven't see her since yesterday morning. She's probably in her room. Harendra will be coming to take her away today.'

'To his ashram?'

'The ashram doesn't exist any more. Haven't you heard? Satish has left with some of the boys. Only a handful of homeless orphans have stayed back. Haren dreams of moulding them according to his own idea. Haven't you heard about it? But then how could you have done?'

He paused and then continued: 'The day before yesterday, after the visitors had left, I read out to Nilima a letter I had just completed. She'd seemed rather preoccupied lately: I rarely saw her. The letter was addressed to one of my employees in Calcutta, urging him to complete the arrangements for my trip to England. I'd also sent him the draft of a new will—possibly my last—to show my lawyer and send back for my signature. There were some other matters as well. Nilima sat sewing. Her lack of response made me look up. Her head had lolled back across the arm of the chair, and her sewing lay on the floor. Her eyes were closed and her face was quite ashen. I put her on the floor and splashed some water from my glass on her face, then fanned her with the newspaper. I tried to call for the servant, but my throat was dry. It couldn't have been more than a few minutes before she opened her eyes and hastily sat up, trembling all over. She then bent forward, hid her face in my lap and burst into tears. I sat holding her; I was at a loss for words. She wept inconsolably. Small incidents and bits of conversation that had earlier gone unnoticed now appeared to me in a new light. A long time seemed to pass before I finally helped her up.'

Kamal gazed silently at Ashu Babu's face. He controlled himself with a visible effort and continued, 'It was only for a few minutes. Before I could compose myself and speak to her, Nilima stood up and rushed out of the room, like an arrow from a bow, without throwing a glance behind her. She didn't say a word; nor did I. I haven't seen her since.'

'Hadn't you guessed this?' asked Kamal quietly.

'No, not in my wildest dreams. If it had been somebody else I might have suspected deceit and selfishness. But to suspect Nilima of being mercenary is itself a sin. What a strange thing is a woman's mind! Who would have thought that a comely young woman could love this old decrepit body and this weary, impotent heart, so utterly worthless in the dying days of their life? Yet it's true—there's nothing false about it.' An anguished sigh escaped this virtuous, elderly man, full of pain, discomfiture and frank shame. After a few minutes' silence, he went on: 'But I know she wants nothing from me. All she asks for is to serve me—to try to lessen the loneliness and insecurity of my old age. It's sheer kindness and pity on her part.' As Kamal remained silent, he continued: 'A few days ago the matter of Bela's divorce came up in conversation. Nilima was furious when she heard that I'd supported Bela's demand for divorce. From then on, it seemed she just couldn't tolerate Bela. The public humiliation which Bela had inflicted on her husband was something Nilima couldn't accept. She refused to sympathize with Bela's revengeful attitude. It was her belief that a wife's achievement lay in her dedication not to abandon her husband but to win him back. She argued that the wife is actually disgraced if she tries to avenge her dishonour: that such dishonour is the touchstone on which her love is tested. And what kind of self-respect is it, she said, that allows Bela to accept money for her needs from the very man she has driven out? It would be far better to hang oneself. I'd often thought that Nilima was overreacting; today I wonder what love might not bring about. Beauty, youth, wealth, honour— all these go for nothing: the real spirit of love lies in forgiveness. The trouble begins when the spirit of forgiveness is missing. It's then that we wrangle about beauty and youth, that the *tug-of-war* starts between love and self-esteem.'

Kamal still looked at him and remained silent.

Ashu Babu continued: 'Kamal, you're her ideal; but for once her moonbeams seemed to outshine your sun's rays. She's mellowed what she took from you in the liquid sweetness of her heart and spread it everywhere. Over the past two days I've traversed two centuries of thought, Kamal. I've known a wife's love: I can tell its true form and savour. But now I'm overwhelmed by the thought that conjugal affection is only one facet of a woman's love. It comprises an intense desire to give oneself away despite all hurdles, all sufferings. I couldn't accept her love with open arms; but words can't describe my gratitude and respect for her proffered gift.'

Kamal realized that everything around him which had so long been obscured by the shadow of his marital love was now coming to light.

'And yes,' said Ashu Babu, breaking into her thoughts, 'I've forgiven Mani. I shan't let her be harassed any longer by her father's sulks. I know she's going to suffer: the world won't let her escape. But for myself, though I can't consent to what she's done, let me bless her so that she finds herself again through her suffering. I pray to God that He may judge her weakness and follies kindly.' His voice grew heavy with emotion.

They remained sitting silently for a long time. Then Kamal gently asked, stroking his plump arm, 'Kakababu, what have you decided about Nilima Didi?'

An unseen power suddenly seemed to draw Ashu Babu upright. 'My dear, I tried to explain this to you before, though I never could; and today I may have lost the power to do so. But I've never doubted the ideal of single-minded, devoted love. I don't question Nilima's love; but just as that is true, so is my refusal. This is not a futile self-delusion. I can never convince you with arguments, but I firmly believe that it's through such apparent frustrations that humankind progresses. I can't imagine where, but progress it must. Else the world is a lie: all creation is a lie.'

He continued, 'Take Nilima, for instance. She could have been anybody's cherished treasure, but today she doesn't have a home to call her own. The futility of her life will impale me all my remaining days. If only she'd loved someone else, I keep thinking! What a mistake she's made!'

'She may yet correct the mistake, Kakababu,' said Kamal.

'How can that be? Do you believe it's possible for her to love anyone else?'

'It isn't impossible. Did you imagine it was possible in your case?'

'But Nilima! A girl like her?'

'I don't know,' said Kamal. 'But do you want her to lead a hopeless life in remembrance of a man she couldn't have as her own, whom she never could have?'

Ashu Babu's bright face darkened somewhat. 'No,' he said, 'I don't wish that, but you won't understand my meaning either. What I can do, you cannot. The basic sense of life's truth is different in you and me—utterly different. Those who believe that this life is the soul's ultimate gain can't wait: they must drink up even the last drop here and now. But we believe in the idea of rebirth. We can wait indefinitely— we don't have to gorge.'

In a quiet tone Kamal said, 'I admit what you say, Kakababu. But I can't accept your prejudice as reason. I won't have the patience to wait at the Almighty's doorstep hoping for the impossible. I hold that life true and good which I find with my natural senses amidst everybody and everything. I want this life to overflow with fruit and blossom, beauty and riches. I don't want to insult this life by neglecting it in the hope of greater gain in the life to come. Kakababu, people like you have willingly deprived yourselves in this way. Since you've made light of this earthly life of joy and good fortune, that life has made light of you before the world. I don't know whether I'll ever meet Nilima Didi again, but if I do I'll tell her this.'

Kamal stood up. Ashu Babu abruptly gripped her hand. 'Are you leaving, my dear? The thought of your going away always fills me with emptiness.'

Kamal sat down again and said, 'But I can hardly give you any comfort, Kakababu. At this time when you are so sick in body and mind, when what you most need is consolation, I seem only to be hurting you in every way. Yet I don't love you less than anyone else, Kakababu.'

Accepting this in silence, Ashu Babu said, 'And think of Nilima! Isn't that amazing too? But do you know the reason for it, Kamal?'

Kamal said smilingly, 'Perhaps it's because there are no quicksands in your heart, Kakababu. The quicksand can't even bear its own weight, it slips away from beneath itself and makes itself sink. But the solid earth bears the weight of stones and iron: you can build castles upon it. All women won't understand Nilima Didi. But those who are tired with the games that life plays, those who want to lay down their burden and breathe freely, will understand her.'

'Yes,' said Ashu Babu and sighed. 'And what about Shibnath?' Kamal replied, 'Ever since I came to understand him properly, all my anger and complaints have been wiped away, my frenzy has cooled. Shibnath is talented, he's an artist and a poet. Continual love impedes the creativity of such people, it hinders their natural bent. That's what I'd tried to say that day at the Taj. Women only provide the pretext for such people—they actually love nobody but themselves. They split their minds into two halves and play a game of love for a while; but it's because the game ends that their voices give out such wonderful melody, otherwise they'd choke and dry up. I know Shibnath hasn't deceived Mani; she has beguiled herself. The golden glow that lights up the clouds at sunset lasts only a moment; but who dares call its existence a lie?'

'I know,' said Ashu Babu. 'But colour alone isn't enough in life, and no metaphor can wipe away this pain. What about that?'

A weariness came over her face. She said, 'Kakababu, that's why the same question keeps cropping up again and again. When you go, leave Mani the blessing that she might discover her true self through her suffering. May everything meant to wither and die fall away from her, letting her know herself clearly. And you too must realize that marriage is one event in life out of many—no more. The day people took it as the ultimate end for a woman—that's the day the biggest *tragedy* of women's lives began. Before you leave this country, set your daughter free from these shackles of falsehood. That's my last plea to you.'

The unexpected sound of footsteps at the door made them look up. Harendra came in.

'I've come to take Boudi away, Ashu Babu. She's ready to leave. I've sent for a carriage.' Ashu Babu's face grew pale.

'Right now? But soon it'll be dark.'

'It's not a great distance, only a few minutes' ride,' replied Harendra. His face was as grave as his speech was firm.

'That's true,' said Ashu Babu softly. 'But it's almost evening. Couldn't you wait till tomorrow?'

Harendra took a piece of paper from his pocket and handed it to Ashu Babu. 'You decide,' he said.

The letter read, 'Thakurpo, if you can't take me away

from here, please let me know. But don't accuse me later of having kept you in the dark.——Nilima.'

Ashu Babu was dumbfounded. Harendra said, 'I'm not a close relative of hers, but you know her nature. I didn't dare wait after such a letter.'

'Will she be staying in your house?'

'Yes, till we can make better arrangements. I thought that as she'd stayed in this house so long, there could be no great objection to my house either.'

Ashu Babu remained silent. He refrained from asking why such excellent logic had not been exercised all these days. The servant entered to announce that the magistrate sahib had sent his servant to collect the memsahib's luggage.

'Show it to him,' said Ashu Babu. As his eyes met Kamal's, he said, 'Bela left this house yesterday. The magistrate's wife is a friend of hers. I'd forgotten to give you the good news, Kamal. Bela's husband has arrived——I think there's been a *reconciliation*.'

Kamal expressed no surprise. She only said, 'Why didn't he come here?'

'Perhaps it hurt his pride,' answered Ashu Babu. 'When she sued for divorce, I'd supported the idea in my reply to Bela's father's letter. Her husband could not forgive that.'

'You supported the idea?'

'Why should that surprise you, Kamal? I see nothing wrong in deserting a dissolute husband. Surely it would be wrong to deny the wife this right?'

Kamal stared at him. She realized yet again that there was no deceit in this man. His actions and his thoughts were exact reflections of each other.

Nilima took her leave from the threshold of the room. She neither entered it nor looked at anyone.

For a long time Kamal went on stroking Ashu Babu's hand. No words were exchanged between them. Before leaving she said, 'There'll be nobody from the old times left in this house except Jadu.'

'Jadu?'

'Yes, your old servant.'

'But he isn't here, my dear. His son is ill. He took leave and went home five days ago.'

Again there was no exchange for a long time. Then Ashu Babu suddenly asked, 'Have you any news of that boy Rajen?'

'No, Kakababu.'

'I wish I could see him once before I leave. You two are like brother and sister, two flowers off the same tree.' Having said this, he was about to relapse into silence when a thought suddenly seemed to strike him. 'Both of you are poor; but your poverty is like that of Lord Shiva. You seem to have infinite wealth and fortune which you carelessly scatter here and there, so contemptuously that you won't even hunt for it.'

Kamal laughed and said, 'What are you saying, Kakababu! I don't know about Rajen, but I slave away day and night for a few rupees.'

'That's what I hear,' said Ashu Babu. 'And it makes me think.'

Kamal was late in returning home that evening. As she finally left, Ashu Babu said, 'Don't worry about me. She who has never left me won't desert me today either.' He pointed to the portrait of his deceased wife on the opposite wall.

On reaching home, Kamal discovered that entry into her house would not be easy. The doorway was jammed with at least a dozen boxes and suitcases. Her heart trembled. She made her way upstairs with difficulty. There were loud voices in the kitchen. She peeped in. She found Ajit, helped by the Hindustani maid, boiling a kettle on the stove and looking for tea and sugar.

'What's all this?'

Ajit started and looked round. 'You seem to keep your tea and sugar locked up in an iron safe. The kettle's almost boiled dry.'

'But how do you expect to find out where I've put my things? Come away, let me make the tea.'

Ajit moved aside.

'But what's all this? Whose boxes and cases are these?'

'Mine. Haren Babu has given me notice.'

'But that could only have been notice to leave his premises. Who gave you the idea of coming here?'

'Oh, that was my own idea. I've lived all this while on others' ideas. Now I've come up with my own.'

'Well done,' said Kamal. 'But are those things going to remain downstairs? They'll be stolen.'

This alarmed Ajit. 'I hope they haven't already been stolen. There's a leather case with a lot of money in it.'

Kamal shook her head and said, 'Wonderful! There's a species of human beings who don't come of age till they're eighty. They always need a guardian. God in His mercy arranges one for them. Forget the tea and come downstairs. We'll try to carry up your things between us.'

27

THE LANDLORD HAD JUST COME AND COLLECTED THE FULL month's rent. Among the bundles and boxes scattered around the room, Ajit lay reclined on a deckchair with his eyes shut. His face was shrunken: one could tell by looking at him that there was no joy in his heart. Kamal was checking the luggage and listing the items on a piece of paper. There was no sign of tension in her preparations for leaving: she made it seem like a routine job. She was only a little more silent than usual.

An invitation to dinner had arrived from Harendra— delivered not by hand but by post. Ajit read the letter. A dinner party was being thrown on the occasion of Ashu Babu's departure. Many people they knew had been invited. In a corner of the letter was a brief message: 'Kamal, my friend, do come. Nilima.'

Ajit showed her that portion and asked, 'Will you go?'

'Of course. I'm not such an important person that I can turn down invitations. But what about you?'

Ajit's voice betrayed his hesitation. 'I don't know. I don't feel well today.'

'Then don't go.'

Ajit's eyes were on the letter before him, otherwise he would surely have noticed Kamal's amused smile. It had somehow become common knowledge to the Bengali community that the two were leaving Agra; but the details were not yet known, and speculation hovered in the air like unseasonal clouds. It would not have been difficult to obtain definite information: a simple question to Kamal would have told them that they were heading for Amritsar. But no one could muster the courage to ask.

Ajit's father, a disciple of Guru Gobind Singh, had built a bungalow in the great Sikh pilgrim-town, near Khalsa College. He used to spend a few days there whenever possible. The house had been rented out after his death but had recently fallen vacant. It was in this house that they had decided to put up for some time. The luggage would go by truck. They themselves would start by car early the next morning. This was Kamal's wish——to revive memories of their first day together.

'Will you go alone to Haren's?' asked Ajit.

'Why not? The door of the ashram will always be open for you; you can go whenever you like. But I can't hope for that, so I might as well take the opportunity to visit them for the last time. What do you say?'

Ajit remained silent. He could clearly see that under various pretexts, many sharp and bitter barbs, stated and unstated insinuations would fly there in one direction only. It would be cowardly to desert a lonely woman faced with such an attack. But he did not have the courage to accompany her, nor could he very well forbid her to go.

A new car had been bought. Shortly after dark, the chauffeur drove Kamal to the ashram. A new, expensive carpet had been laid out for the guests in the large room upstairs. There were many lights and a lot of noise. Ashu Babu sat in the middle with a few gentlemen around him. Bela was there with another lady——Malini, the magistrate's wife. A man sat talking to them with his back to the door. Nilima was not to be seen; perhaps she was busy elsewhere.

Harendra entered the room and immediately noticed

Kamal standing by the door. 'Kamal! When did you come? Where's Ajit?' he cried in surprised welcome.

All eyes immediately turned to her. Kamal could now see the face of the man talking to the ladies. It was none other than Akshay. He had grown a little thinner: although he had escaped the influenza, he had not been so lucky with the malaria in his native village. It was fortunate that he had returned, otherwise he would never have met Kamal again. He would have had to live with the loss.

'Ajit Babu hasn't come. He isn't well,' she said. 'As for me, I arrived quite some time ago.'

'A long time ago! But where were you?'

'Downstairs, having a look at the boys' rooms. You've cheated religion of its due; I was finding out whether you'd betrayed the work ethic as well.' She entered the room laughing as she said this. She was like a slender monsoon creeper lifting its head high with all the resources for its own survival rather than for others' needs. It had no fear or anxiety about hostile surroundings—as though there was no question of guarding it by a barbed-wire fence.

She entered and sat down. It was nothing to speak of—yet she appeared to spread a glow of distinction with her beauty, presence and natural dignity.

Harendra's words echoed this very feeling. It might have been a lapse of courtesy in front of two other women, but he said with great emotion, 'At last our meeting is complete.'

Akshay said, 'Why? Which subtle doctrine of philosophy did her arrival bear out?'

'There!' said Kamal, laughing. 'Now answer his question.'

Quite a few people, including Harendra, looked the other way, perhaps to hide their laughter.

Subdued, Akshay said, 'Do you remember me, Kamal?'

Ashu Babu was vexed. He said, 'It's enough if you recognize her. Can you, Akshay?'

'Now, that's an unfair question to ask, Ashu Babu,' complained Kamal. 'It's his business to know people. If you doubt that, you strike at the root of his profession.'

She said this in such a way that no one could help laughing; but they were afraid that this irrepressible man might say something unpleasant in reply. In fact Harendra had not wanted to invite Akshay; but as he had recently returned to Agra, it would have been awkward not to ask him.

Humbly and nervously, Harendra said, 'Ashu Babu is leaving the town and perhaps this country. It's a matter of good fortune for anyone to have known a man like him. We are lucky to have done so. Today, when his body is sick and his mind weary, let us say goodbye to him as pleasantly as we can.'

His words were few and simple, but everybody was touched as they looked at the serene, honest face of this elderly man. Ashu Babu was ill at ease. To avoid becoming the focus of conversation, he broached another subject. He said, 'Akshay, I believe you've heard that Harendra's ashram has closed down. Rajen had left earlier and Satish also went the other day. Harendra wishes to bring up the few remaining boys in a straightforward, practical way. All of you have been telling him many things for a long time, but to no effect. It's your duty to thank Kamal.'

Akshay smarted inwardly, but he replied with a dry laugh: 'Was it her words that bore fruit? Well, whatever you may say, I'm not surprised, Ashu Babu. I'd guessed so long ago.'

Harendra remarked, 'That's only natural. It's your business to know people for what they are.'

Ashu Babu said, 'I still think there was no need to wind the place up. All religions are fundamentally the same, a matter of following some ancient rituals to attain salvation. Those who don't believe in rituals or can't observe them shouldn't be forced to do so, but why discourage those who have the perseverance? What do you say, Akshay?'

Akshay said, 'Of course.'

But as soon as Ashu Babu looked at Kamal, she shook her head and said, 'You're not saying this from firm conviction, Ashu Babu; rather out of dismissiveness and disbelief. If I thought as you did, I'd never have spoken a word against the ashram. But it's not so: rituals and observances come to outgrow men's faith, just as the king's men become more important than the king.'

Ashu Babu laughed and said, 'It may be so, but does that mean that we must accept your simile as logic?'

Kamal's face showed that she was not joking. She said, 'Is it only a simile, Ashu Babu? I admit that all religions are really one. In all countries in all ages, it has meant the unattainable pursuit of an unknowable object: you can't bring it within your grasp. Men don't quarrel over sunshine or air; they fight over their share of food—what one can possess as one's own and leave to one's progeny. That's what counts as real in the business of life. Everyone knows that the fundamental aim of all marriages is the same; but how many of us truly accept it? What do you say, Akshay Babu, isn't that so?' She laughed and turned away.

Everybody understood the allusion. The angry Akshay wanted to say something harsh but could not find the words.

'Yet you yourself have such disdain for rituals, Kamal,' said Ashu Babu. 'That's why it's so difficult to understand you.'

'It isn't difficult,' said Kamal. 'Just draw away the curtain before your eyes. Others might not, but you'll understand it at once: otherwise how could I have won your affection? There's a bank of mist between us, yet I have won it. I know I hurt you by what I say, but I really don't want to dismiss rituals as false; all I want is to reform them. I want to strike life into what has become dead with time. I disdain them as they are because I know their true worth. If I knew them to be false, I'd have gone along with everybody else in false devotion, attuning myself to the lie. I wouldn't have revolted at all.'

She paused before continuing: 'Think of the days of the European Renaissance. They wanted to create something new, but didn't touch their rituals and ceremonies. They daubed some fresh paint on the old forms and secretly worshipped them. They didn't go to the root of the matter, and the *fashion* disappeared in a short while. I was afraid that Haren Babu's high ambition would vanish in the same way. But there's nothing to fear, he's managed all right.' She laughed.

Harendra could not join in the laughter; he remained grave. He had indeed done as she said, but his heart had not yet really consented to his action: it grew heavy from time to time. He said, 'The problem is that you believe neither in God nor in salvation, Kamal. But those who are intent upon knowing those unknown objects, who are eager to determine their essence, must proceed through stern discipline and strict adherence to ritual. I don't feel proud about winding up the ashram. The day Satish left with the boys, I felt how weak I was.'

'Then you didn't feel rightly, Haren Babu. My father used to say that the more subtle and complex one's God is, the more one ties oneself in knots. The grosser you make Him, the simpler he will become for you. It's like business: the higher your turnover, the greater your losses. If you scale it down, you might not make a profit, but you'll reduce your losses. I've talked to Satish, Haren Babu. He'd introduced many traditional rules in the ashram, with the intention of returning to the ancient days. He used to think that if you could wipe out two thousand years from the world's age, that would make for the highest profit. The Puritans of England had looked for such profit too. They thought that by fleeing to America and eliminating seventeen centuries, they'd recreate the pristine Biblical age. Today many people know the outcome of their calculations; only the monastics don't know that the real moment of ruin comes when you try to uphold modern practices by the philosophy of a bygone age. I might have harmed your ashram, Haren Babu, but I know I haven't harmed its surviving inmates.'

Akshay, a professor of history, knew about the Puritans. Everyone remained silent; but he nodded slowly in agreement.

Ashu Babu started saying, 'But the bright image of the history of that age . . .'

Kamal interrupted him. 'No matter how bright it might be, Ashu Babu, it's only a picture. That book is yet to be written through which one can imbibe the true life of society. However proudly you may talk, you can't build a society by the book. You can't bring back either the age of Rama or the age of Yudhisthira. Whatever might be written in either the Ramayana or the Mahabharata, you can't reach the common man by riffling through their verses, just as you can't get back to your mother's womb, however safe it may be. Humanity is an ensemble of all the human races.

They are all around you. Is it possible to escape the pressure of the atmosphere by tucking yourself into a blanket?'

Bela and Malini had been listening quietly. They had heard much about this young woman; but today, encountering her like this, they were amazed by the confident speech of this deserted, resourceless girl.

Ashu Babu immediately expressed just this reaction. He said, 'Whatever I might say by way of argument, Kamal, I accept many of your premises, and I don't despise even what I can't accept. This very house had its door closed to women only a few days ago. I'm told Satish had even felt that the place had been defiled by inviting you here. But today we've all been invited. Anyone can come in.'

A young boy came and stood at the door. He was wearing clean, decent clothes, and there was joy and satisfaction on his face. He said, 'Didi asked me to tell you that dinner's ready: shall we serve it?'

'Of course,' said Akshay. 'It's getting late.'

As the boy left the room, Harendra said, 'Boudi's entry into this house has freed us from having to bother about meals. She didn't have any place to stay—yet Satish left in a huff.'

Ashu Babu's face flushed for a moment. 'I suppose Satish had no alternative,' continued Harendra. 'He's an ascetic and a brahmachari. This might have disturbed his concentration. But I'm not always sure which of my actions was for the best.'

Kamal said unhesitatingly: 'This one, Haren Babu, this one. When self-control doesn't come spontaneously, it hurts others and becomes unbearable.' Having said this, she looked for an instant at Ashu Babu. Perhaps there was some hidden suggestion in her glance. But it was Harendra that she addressed again: 'Such people extend themselves in the image of their god. That's why the worship of their god descends to the worship of their own self: there's nothing else they can do. Humankind is not simply male or female, it's a union of the two. If you ignore one half and seek to aggrandize yourself with the other, you lose your god without gaining your own self. Don't worry about people like Satish, Haren Babu. Their salvation lies in God's own hands.'

Almost everyone disliked Satish, so everyone laughed at the last remark. Ashu Babu laughed too, but added: 'There's a lofty concept in our Hindu Shastras, Kamal: self-knowledge, that is, to know one's own self deeply. The sages say that here lies all the knowledge of the world and all wisdom. This is also the way to attain God. It needs meditation. You're not a believer; but those who are, those who want to attain Him, can't succeed in their meditative concentration if they don't deprive themselves of many worldly things. I don't take Satish into account, but this is the heritage we have derived from an unbroken tradition, Kamal. This is yoga.[1] The whole of India, from the ocean to the Himalayas, believes in this idea with unswerving reverence.'

His eyes grew moist with piety, faith and emotion. In a flash, Kamal saw a pious, resolute Hindu heart burning like an unquenchable lamp in some secluded depth beneath the veneer of Western habits and manners. She wanted to say something but felt inhibited. The inhibition was only for fear of hurting this old man, worshipper of truth and sensual discipline. But on getting no reply from her, Ashu Babu himself asked, 'Isn't this the truth?'

She shook her head and said, 'No, Ashu Babu, it's not. This belief exists in all religions, not only Hinduism. However, nothing becomes true simply by strength of faith—not even by strength of renunciation or self-sacrifice. Many lives have been bartered for trivial differences of opinion. It has demonstrated the power of human obstinacy but not the truth of the idea. I don't know what you call yoga, but if it means self-analysis and self-contemplation in a secluded place, I would insist that all errors and illusions enter our life through those two gateways and no other: they are the companions of ignorance.'

Not only Ashu Babu but Harendra too kept silent at this, in wonder and pain.

The boy came again and announced that dinner had been served. Everyone went downstairs.

28

WHEN DINNER WAS OVER, AKSHAY FOUND KAMAL ALONE FOR A moment and said to her confidingly, 'I heard you're going away. You've visited almost everybody you know sometime or other, except for my place . . .'

Kamal was utterly astonished: not only by the change in his tone, but by his addressing her as apni. Everyone addressed her informally as tumi: she never complained nor took offence. But in Akshay's case there was another factor. He used to think that affording this woman the courtesy of apni was excessive, even an abuse of respectable norms. Kamal knew it, but she had felt it beneath herself to take note of this pettiness: she was afraid of provoking an altercation. She smiled and said, 'You've never asked me over to your house.'

'No. It was wrong of me. Won't you find time to come once, before you leave?'

'How can we, Akshay Babu? We're starting early tomorrow morning.'

'Early in the morning?' He paused and said, 'If ever you return to this place, I invite you to visit my house.'

Kamal smiled and said, 'Can I ask you something, Akshay Babu? How did your views about me change so suddenly? They should have grown more rigid instead.'

Akshay said, 'In the ordinary way they would have done. But I returned from my village with some new experiences. Your example of the Puritans has stirred me deeply. I don't know whether the others understood it or not—it wouldn't be surprising if they didn't—but I know a lot about them. There's something else too. Most of the people in our village are Muslims. They still hold firmly to their fifteen hundred-year-old truths. The same dispensations and prohibitions, rules and laws, rites and customs—nothing has changed.'

Kamal said, 'I know almost nothing about them; I've never had the opportunity. If what you're saying is true, I can only say that it's time for them as well to think afresh. They'll have to admit one day that the bounds of truth were not fixed in some ancient past. But come upstairs.'

'No, I'll take your leave from here. My wife's ill. You've met so many people; won't you see her once?'

'What does she look like?' asked Kamal curiously.

'I don't really know,' replied Akshay. 'No one in our family has ever asked such a question. My father brought home a nine-year-old girl as his son's bride. She had neither the time nor the need for education. She cooks and serves meals, she keeps her rites and makes her vows, offers puja and says her prayers. She regards me as the lord of this world and the next. When she's ill she doesn't want to take medicines. She says that the water touched by her husband's feet will cure all diseases. If it doesn't, it means the wife's reached the end of her span.'

Kamal had got some hint of all this from Harendra. She said, 'You're a lucky man—at least in respect of your wife. Such implicit faith is rare these days.'

'Perhaps so,' answered Akshay. 'I don't know exactly. Perhaps this is what's called one's luck in wiving. But sometimes I feel there's no one I can call my own, that I'm totally alone in this world. Well, goodbye.'

Kamal raised her hands in a namaskar.

Akshay started walking away, then turned back. He said, 'May I make a request?'

'Please do.'

'If ever you find time and happen to remember me, please write and let me know how you are, how Ajit Babu is, all that sort of thing. I'll think of you often. Well, goodbye!'

Akshay walked away hurriedly, while Kamal stood in silence. She was not judging right or wrong; she only wondered if this could be the same Akshay. And this was how, beyond all human knowledge, the conjugal life of this fortunate man had flown in untroubled peace! How eager he was for a letter, how piteously and sincerely he prayed for it!

Returning upstairs, she found everyone seated except Nilima. That was true to Nilima's nature—no one took notice of it. Ashu Babu said, 'Harendra has said something wonderful. At first it sounds like a riddle, but it's absolutely true. He says people don't understand that the pain of transgressing social norms can be borne only by strength of character, conscience and wisdom. People only look at the external offence, they don't know about the inward inspiration. That's what leads to all conflict, all hostilities.'

Kamal understood that this was aimed at Ajit and herself; hence she kept quiet. She did not say that social norms can be violated through sheer indiscipline. Perversion of the will and the promptings of conscience were not the same thing.

Bela and Malini rose. It was time for them to leave. Totally ignoring Kamal, they said goodbye to Harendra and Ashu Babu with namaskars. They had always felt themselves to be insignificant before this girl; now they finally had their revenge by ignoring her. After they had left, Ashu Babu affectionately said, 'Don't mind them, my dear. That was the only thing they could do. I too belong with them. I understand everything.'

This was the first time that Ashu Babu had addressed her so affectionately before Harendra. He said, 'They happen to be the wives of well-placed men. They belong to high society. They are *up to date* in their English, their ways and gestures, their dress and grooming. If you ignore that, you touch upon their capital, Kamal. It would be taking them too seriously even to lose your temper with them.'

'I'm not offended,' said Kamal with a smile.

'I knew you wouldn't be,' said Ashu Babu. 'Even we didn't feel offended: instead we felt like laughing. But how will you go home, my dear? Should I drop you there on my way?'

'By all means—how would I go otherwise?' She had sent back their own car in case it attracted people's attention.

'All right. But we shouldn't delay any more. What do you say?'

Everyone remembered that he had not recovered fully from his illness.

The tread of shoes could be heard on the stairs, and the next moment everyone, to their great surprise, saw Ajit standing outside the door.

Harendra gave him a resounding welcome: '*Hello! Better late than never! What an honour for the brahmacharya ashram!*'

Ajit said in embarrassment, 'I've come to fetch her.' An unexpected bravado forced the words out of him on an impulse. He went on, 'Otherwise I wouldn't have met you any more. We're leaving tomorrow morning, even before sunrise.'

'Tomorrow morning? Before sunrise?'

'Yes. Everything's ready. That's how our journey will begin.'

The affair was not unknown, but everyone seemed to turn dull with embarrassment. Nilima entered silently and stood to one side of the room. Ashu Babu overcame his diffidence and looked up. His words seemed to stick in his throat; then he slowly said, 'Perhaps we won't ever meet again. I love both of you. If you were to marry, I would have liked to see it happen before I left.'

Ajit suddenly felt like a sailor in sight of the shore. He eagerly exclaimed, 'Is that what you wish, Ashu Babu? I never dreamt of it. I've repeatedly talked of marriage, and Kamal has repeatedly shaken her head and said no. I've offered to make over to her all my property, whatever I have—to surrender decisively to her; but she hasn't agreed. Kamal, today I appeal to you again before all these people, please give me your consent. Let me give you all I have and feel free. It'll save me from the stigma of deceitfulness.'

Nilima looked on in surprise. Ajit was shy by nature: everyone was astonished at his unbounded eagerness in front of so many people. Today he wanted to give up all title to himself. He felt no need to hold anything back.

Kamal looked him in the face and said, 'Why, what are you so afraid of?'

'Maybe I'm not afraid, but . . .'

'Let the day of "buts" first come.'

'When it comes, I know you won't take anything from me.'

Kamal laughed and said, 'So you do know! Then that'll be the tightest bond with which to hold you.'

She paused and continued, 'You may not remember how I once told you not to build your house so solidly as to leave no opening anywhere. That would only make for a tomb, not a room for a living man to lie in.'

'I know you said so', replied Ajit. 'I know you don't want to hold me in bondage, yet I want it. But how shall I bind you? I don't have the strength.'

'Strength is of no use,' said Kamal. 'Rather bind me by your weakness. I'm not so cruel as to cast a helpless creature like you adrift in the world.' She glanced at Ashu Babu and went on to Ajit: 'I don't believe in god, or else I would pray that I might die only after having shielded you from all the blows of the world.'

Nilima's eyes filled with tears. Ashu Babu also wiped his moist eyes and said solemnly, 'You needn't believe in God, Kamal. It's all the same, my dear. Your self-surrender will take you up to God in glory one day.'

Kamal laughed and said, 'That would be a bonus for me worth more than the usual reward.'

'Very true, my dear. But take it from me, my blessing will never be in vain.'

Harendra said, 'Ajit, you haven't had any dinner. Come downstairs.'

Ashu Babu said with a smile, 'Is this all that your learning has taught you? Can it be that Ajit hasn't had his dinner while Kamal has eaten her fill here? She never lets that happen.'

Ajit shyly admitted that he was right. He had had dinner at home.

Remembering that it was their last evening together, no one wanted to break up the party; but it had to end in view of Ashu Babu's health. Harendra came up to Kamal and said in a low voice, 'At last you've got the genuine article, Kamal. I congratulate you.'

Kamal whispered back in the same way: 'Have I? At least bless me that it may be so.'

Harendra did not say anything more, but it struck him that Kamal's tone seemed less confident than he expected. But that was how things were. That was the law of the world.

Beckoning to Kamal from behind the door, Nilima wiped her tears and said, 'Kamal, don't forget me.' She could not say anything more.

Kamal bent down and made her namaskar. She said, 'Didi, I'll come back. But before I leave, I'll make a request of you. Don't ever reject the good in life. Its real shape is the shape of happiness: it appears only in that form and in no other. Whatever you do, Didi, don't agree once again to slave without reward in Abinash Babu's house.'

'It'll be as you say, Kamal,' promised Nilima.

When Ashu Babu got into the car, Kamal touched his feet in the Hindu manner. He laid his hand on her head and blessed her once again. He said, 'I've got the clue to a new truth from you, Kamal. Liberation doesn't come from imitation, only from knowledge. This makes me afraid that what has brought liberation to you may plunge Ajit in dishonour. Save him from such a fate. That charge is yours from now on.'

Kamal understood the hint.

He went on, 'Let me remind you of what you yourself once said. Since that day I have often thought that the history of pure love is the history of civilization, its life. At this moment of parting, I won't pick an argument over the definition of purity. I won't sully your departure with the breath of my complaint. But remember this old man's words, Kamal: an ideal is for a few people only. That's why it has value. It would be mad to drag it into the crowd: its goodness would vanish, its burden grow unbearable. From the Buddhist to the Vaishnava period, there have been many sad instances of such misery all over the world. Are you about to bring that sorrowful revolution into this world, my dear?'

In a soft voice, Kamal replied: 'That's my nature and my duty, Kakababu.'

'Your nature and your duty?'

'Yes,' said Kamal. 'Kakababu, a higher ideal will be born out of the sorrow you're so afraid of; and when it's served its purpose, a still nobler ideal will rise from the essential substance of the corpse. The good always repays its debt by sacrificing itself in this way at the feet of the better. That is the path of human liberation. Can't you see, Kakababu, that the external practice of sati changed during the Raj but its inner fire is still blazing, turning everything to ashes in just the same way? How will it be extinguished?'

Ashu Babu could not speak immediately. He only sighed, and the next moment he suddenly burst out: 'Kamal, I've not yet been able to break the fetters put upon me by Mani's mother. Call it blind attachment, call it weakness—I don't know what it is, but when I lose this fascination I'll have lost much of my humanity along with it. It's a treasure that a man wins through long devotion. Well, goodbye. Come, Basdeo.'

A telegraph-man stopped his bicycle and alighted before them. There was an urgent message. Harendra opened the envelope and read it by the car's headlights. It was a long message from the doctor at a small government hospital in Mathura district. He gave the following account.

One of the shrines in the village had caught fire; the idol, worshipped so long by so many people, was about to be destroyed in the blaze. Seeing no other way to save it, Rajen entered the flaming shrine and rescued the idol. The deity was saved, but the rescuer was not. After suffering silently for two days, he proceeded to 'the heavenly abode' of Govindji.[1]

Ten thousand people chanting hymns took out a procession with his mortal remains and cremated them on the bank of the Yamuna. At the time of his death, he had asked for this news to be sent to Agra.

This was a bolt from the blue. Tears choked Harendra's voice, and the clear moonlit night turned utterly dark before their eyes.

'Two days!' cried Ashu Babu. 'Forty-eight hours! And so near us. Yet he didn't send a message!'

Harendra wiped his tears and said, 'He didn't think it necessary. We wouldn't have been able to do anything, so he didn't want to put us to trouble.'

Ashu Babu raised his folded hands to his forehead and said, 'This means he didn't accept any human being as his own, only this country—this India. Yet God! Grant him a place at your feet! Whatever you do, don't obliterate the breed of Rajens from your world!—Basdeo, start the car.'

The loss perhaps hurt no one more than Kamal, but she did not allow the vapours of grief to subdue her voice. Her eyes seemed to spout fire. She exclaimed, 'What's there to mourn? He's gone to heaven.' To Harendra she said, 'Don't cry, Haren Babu, ignorance always extorts sacrifice in this way.' Her clear hard tone pierced everyone like a knife blade.

Ashu Babu went away. In the grief-stricken stillness, Kamal led Ajit to the car and climbed in. 'Let's go, Ramdeen,' she said.

Notes

Preface (pp. ix–xvi)

1. *Awara Maseeha*: the title of Vishnu Prabhakar's Hindi biography of Saratchandra (1973).
2. In the journal *Parichay*, Phalgun 1344 (February–March 1938).
3. In the journal *Bharatbarsha*, Chaitra 1344 (March–April 1938).
4. In *Sahitye Art o Durniti* ('Art and Corruption in Literature'): presidential address at a literary conference at Munshiganj, 1925.
5. In *Taruner Bidroha* ('The Revolt of Youth'): presidential address at the Bengali Youth Meet in Rangpur, 1929.
6. From 'Art and Corruption in Literature' (see above).
7. Ibid.
8. Saratchandra reports this in a letter to Radharani Debi, 30 Vaishakh 1338 (May 1931).
9. Letter to Dilipkumar Ray, 30 Vaishakh 1338 (May 1931).
10. In his essay 'Saratchandra' in *Sahityer Satya* (*The Truth of Literature*) (Calcutta: Lipika, 1960).

Introduction (pp. xvii–xliv)

1. Published in *Bijali*, 6th Year, No. 13; as in *Sharatsahityasamagra*, ed. Sukumar Sen (Calcutta: Ananda Publishers, 1985), p. 1996.
2. For the social history of this period, see Meredith Borthwick, *The Changing Role of Women in Bengal 1849–1905* (Princeton: Princeton University Press, 1984); Sambuddha Chakrabarti, *Andare Antare: Unish Shatake Bangali Bhadramahila* (Calcutta: Stree, 1995); Ghulam Murshid, *Reluctant Debutante: Response of Bengali Women to Modernization, 1849–1905* (Rajshahi: Sahitya Samsad, Rajshahi University, 2nd impression

1983); J. Krishnamurti, ed., *Women in Colonial India: Essays on Survival, Work, and the State* (Delhi: Oxford University Press, 1989); Bharati Ray, ed., *From the Seams of History: Essays on Indian Women* (Delhi: Oxford University Press, 1995).

3. 'Narir Lekha', published under Saratchandra's pseudonym, 'Shrimati Anila Debi', in the journal *Yamuna*, 1913; see *Sharatsahityasamagra*, pp. 2076–81.

4. See Rassundari Debi, *Amar Jiban*; Kailashbasini Debi, *Atmakatha*; Debi Saradasundari, *Atmakatha*; Nistarini Debi, *Sekele Katha*, in N. Jana et al. eds, *Atmakatha*, vols 1 and 2 (Calcutta: Ananya Prakashan, 1981). Many other personal narratives of women have been recovered and printed over the past two decades. On the work of Rassundari (possibly the first autobiography in Bengali as well as the life record of an exceptional woman), see Tanika Sarkar, *Words to Win: The Making of Amar Jiban, A Modern Autobiography* (New Delhi: Kali for Women, 1999). On the genre, see Malavika Karlekar, *Voices from Within: Early Personal Narratives of Bengali Women* (Delhi: Oxford University Press, 1991).

5. *Rup o Ranga*, January 1924–May 1925. Binodini's autobiography, *Amar Katha o Anyanya Rachana (My Story and Other Writings)* was first published in 1912 (Revised edition, Calcutta, 1987). For an English translation, see Binodini Dasi, *My Story* and *My Life as an Actress*, trans. and ed. Rimli Bhattacharya (New Delhi: Kali for Women, 1998).

6. In a different context, Tapan Raychaudhuri points out that Raja Rammohan Roy invoked the Shaiva tradition to justify the practice of taking a Muslim mistress: 'Transformation of Religious Sensibilities', Surendra Paul Memorial Lecture, reprinted in *Perceptions, Emotions, Sensibilities: Essays on India's Colonial and Post-colonial Experiences* (Delhi: Oxford University Press, 1999), p. 101. On the complex of emotions and experiences involved in intimate relations between men and women during the late nineteenth century, see another essay in the same volume, 'Love in a Colonial Climate', pp 65–95.

7. See Rajat Kanta Ray, *Social Conflict and Political Unrest in Bengal, 1875–1927* (Delhi: Oxford University Press, 1984), pp 277–84, citing the C.F. Andrews Papers, Andrews to Tagore, 15 June 1921.

8. Quoted in *Narir Mulya*: see *Sharatsahityasamagra*, p. 1951.

9. Ibid.

10. *Rabindra-rachanabali*, vol. 12 (Calcutta: Visvabharati, 1942), p. 490. My translation.

11. *Nationalism in India*, 1917, in *The English Writings of Rabindranath Tagore*, ed. Sisir Kumar Das, vol. 2 (New Delhi: Sahitya Akademi, 1996), p. 462.

12. Swadeshi ideals were spread all over Bengal in 1906–07 through the proliferation of samitis and the impressive growth of a national volunteer corps. Some of these samitis promoted markedly extremist ideas; an example being the Dacca Anushilan Samiti, set up in 1906 by Pulin Behari Das and initiating young boys of nine to twelve into a culture combining Hindu spirituality with rigorous physical exercise. Pulin Das was deported in 1908 and the samiti banned the following year, when it became a secret terrorist organization.

13. In *The Eighteenth Brumaire of Louis Bonaparte*, Marx speaks of the human engagement with history 'under circumstances directly encountered, given and transmitted from the past', when 'the tradition of all the dead generations weighs like a nightmare on the brains of the living'. It is in periods of revolutionary crisis, Marx continues, that human beings 'anxiously conjure up the spirits of the past to their service, and from them names, battle-cries and costumes'. This passage is relevant to some of the concerns of the book, but I suggest a different need: the need to consult the past in order to understand the present. See Karl Marx and Frederick Engels, *Collected Works*, vol. 11 (New York: International Publishers, 1979), pp 103–4.

Chapter 1 (pp. 1–6)

1. Cooks in orthodox upper-caste Hindu households were traditionally Brahmans.

2. A sect of 'reformed Hindus', sometimes seen as a separate religious group, who brought about significant social and spiritual reform in early modern Bengal.

3. The fact that Ashu Babu employed a Muslim chef (probably to

cook in the Mughlai style) shows his liberal, even unorthodox, views and lifestyle.

4. That is, go to the women's quarters.

5. That is, one without, the other with, items of food forbidden to orthodox upper-caste Hindus—no doubt cooked respectively by the aforesaid Brahman cook and Muslim chef.

6. Thought to be carnally stimulating items of food, and thus eschewed by orthodox Brahmans and other spiritual-minded persons.

7. A word of various meanings. As emerges later, used here as a customary appellation for one's son-in-law. But the word is also used of gurus and holy men; hence the puzzlement on the part of the company.

8. Such as an iron bangle, shell bangles or vermilion in the parting of the hair.

Chapter 2 (pp. 7–16)

1. A low caste.

2. A term for a legally void compact to live together, traditionally undertaken in the name of the god Shiva, whose own marriage to Durga or Parvati was of a wilful and unorthodox nature. Here carries a pun on the name Shibnath (Sanskrit: *Shiva-nath*, i.e. 'Lord Shiva').

Chapter 4 (pp. 25–32)

1. As his surname 'Gupta' indicates, Ashu Babu belonged to the caste of Vaidyas or physicians.

2. Following an episode in the Ramayana, a common Bengali proverb talks of putting a necklace or garland of pearls on a monkey, which cannot appreciate it. Here, of course, Ashu Babu self-deprecatingly refers to the wedding garland that Mani's mother put on her undeserving husband.

3. An old measure of weight, about 35 kilograms.

Chapter 5 (pp. 33–43)

1. A preliminary of the Hindu marriage, when turmeric paste from the groom's house is sent to the bride to be used in a ritual bath.

2. A female *brahmachari*, an ascetic who eschews consorting with the opposite sex.

Chapter 6 (pp. 44–52)

1. Asceticism as defined particularly by sexual abstinence. (Cf. note on brahmachari[ni], note 2, chapter 5.)
2. Sanskrit Shivani, feminine of Shiva, a name for the god Shiva's consort Parvati or Durga. Shibnath no doubt chose this name to match his own. (See note on Shaivite marriage, note 2, chapter 2)

Chapter 7 (pp. 53–61)

1. The god Shiva. According to legend, Shiva drank up the poison that formed in the sea and threatened to destroy the gods and the earth.

Chapter 10 (pp. 82–9)

1. A physician practising the traditional Indian style of medicine: hence a member of the Vaidya or physician caste, to which Ashu Babu and Ajit belong. (See note 1, chapter 4.)

Chapter 11 (pp. 90–101)

1. A contemptuous distortion of the servant's name 'Jadu'.
2. Uncle. A 'kaka' is one's father's younger brother, but the term is widely used as an affectionate address for men of the appropriate age.
3. A sea voyage was traditionally held to be a spiritual offence. Brahmans, and sometimes other high-caste men like the Vaidyas, would carry out rites of penance after a voyage, if they undertook one at all.

Chapter 13 (pp. 110–22)

1. A woman's term of address for her husband's younger brother or cousin. Nilima's use of this term for Harendra bears implications for her sense of her relationship with Abinash as well as with Harendra.
2. The third eldest brother (or, as here, cousin).
3. A newspaper published from Allahabad and widely read in northern India.

4. 'Bride-elder-sister', the term of address for the wife of one's elder brother or cousin. (Cf. implications of 'Thakurpo' in note 1.)

5. The goddess of bounty. Here said complimentarily of Nilima, especially as their visit would ensure a good meal for the boys.

6. Chaitanya, the spiritual leader and social reformer of medieval Bengal, renowned for his genial and forgiving spirit, among other virtues.

Chapter 14 (pp. 123–43)

1. Ascetic, holy man. At the Charak festival, on the last day of the Bengali year, sannyasins would undergo various kinds of public mortification, such as being hoisted from a pole by a hook piercing their backs.

2. A haunt of idle people, like the erstwhile house of a wealthy Calcuttan of that name.

Chapter 22 (pp. 242–52)

1. A mother goddess representing the universal nourishing and sustaining principle, but commonly taken as a goddess of food and bounty, identified with Durga.

Chapter 24 (pp. 273–92)

1. The English transliteration is ambiguous. The reference, ironic of course, is to Brahma the ultimate godhead, whose three manifestations are Brahma the creator, Vishnu the preserver and Shiva the destroyer. But the word is extended to mean the Vedas and their study, and asceticism generally—that is, the pursuit of a brahmachari.

Chapter 25 (pp. 293–308)

1. That is, saffron, the colour of asceticism and renunciation. Kamal deliberately says *halde* (yellow) rather than *gerua* (saffron) with its spiritual associations.

2. No doubt referring to the mythological and devotional paintings which, adopting the techniques of Western art, have been popular in India since the late nineteenth century.

3. Kacha, the son of the sage Vrihaspati, served his father's rival sage Shukracharya for a thousand years to learn the art of reviving the dead. In the process he also won the love of Shukracharya's daughter Devyani.

4. The four chief stages of a man's life according to traditional Hindu doctrine: celibacy (*brahmacharya*), domesticity (*garhasthya*), life in a hermitage (*vanaprastha*) and asceticism (*sannyasa*). A pun on the other meaning of 'ashram' as used throughout the book, that is, a hermitage or spiritual retreat.

Chapter 27 (pp. 321–30)

1. Used here in the true and full sense of the term, namely, total well-being and control of the human entity.

Chapter 28 (pp. 331–9)

1. Vishnu, the second member of the divine trinity. Under this name he is conceived as the deity through whom one attains heaven.